A HOPE BEYOND

Books by Judith Pella

*with Michael Phillips   †by Michael Phillips   ‡with Tracie Peterson

9704

JUDITH PELLA
AND
TRACIE PETERSON

A HOPE
BEYOND

BETHANY HOUSE PUBLISHERS
MINNEAPOLIS, MINNESOTA 55438

A Hope Beyond
Copyright © 1997
Judith Pella and Tracie Peterson

Cover by Dan Thornberg,
Bethany House Publishers staff artist.

Published by Bethany House Publishers
A Ministry of Bethany Fellowship, Inc.
11300 Hampshire Avenue South
Minneapolis, Minnesota 55438

Printed in the United States of America.

Library of Congress Cataloging-in-Publication Data

Pella, Judith.
    A hope beyond / by Judith Pella and Tracie Peterson
    p. cm. — (Ribbons of steel ; #2)
    ISBN 1-55661-863-8 (pbk.)
    I. Peterson, Tracie. II. Title. III. Series: Pella, Judith. Ribbons of steel;
#2.
PS3566.E415H66   1997
813'.54—dc21   97-21036
                                                                          CIP

To
Laura Sutter

"I have been
and always shall be
your friend."

Thanks for being my friend.

Love, Judy

JUDITH PELLA began her writing career in collaboration with Michael Phillips, a partnership that led to five major fiction series. She has also written the Lone Star Legacy series and *Blind Faith*, a contemporary romance story in the Portraits series with Bethany House publishers. These extraordinary novels showcase her creativity and skill as a historian as well as a fiction writer. With a bachelor's degree in social sciences and a nursing degree, her storytelling abilities provide readers with memorable novels in a variety of genres. She and her family make their home in northern California.

TRACIE PETERSON is a full-time writer who has authored over twenty-three books, both historical and contemporary fiction. She authored *Entangled*, a contemporary love story in the Portraits series. She spent three years as columnist for *The Kansas Christian* newspaper and is also a speaker/teacher for writer's conferences. She and her family make their home in Kansas.

With special thanks to:

Herbert Harwood, Jr.
Author of books on American railroading,
including *Impossible Challenge II*.

Anne Calhoun
Assistant Archivist,
Baltimore and Ohio Railroad Museum.

Contents

PART THREE
June—November 1842

My restless spirit never could endure
To brood so long upon one luxury,
Unless it did, though fearfully, espy
A hope beyond the shadow of a dream.

John Keats

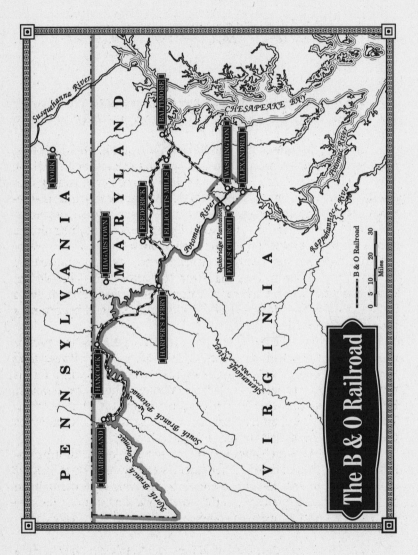

The B & O Railroad

PENNSYLVANIA

MARYLAND

VIRGINIA

Susquehanna River

CHESAPEAKE BAY

Potomac River

Potomac River

Rappahannock River

Shenandoah River

South Branch Potomac

North Branch Potomac

YORK

BALTIMORE

HAGARSTOWN

FREDERICK

ELLICOTTS MILLS

WASHINGTON

ALEXANDRIA

FALLS CHURCH

Oakbridge Plantation

HARPER'S FERRY

HANCOCK

CUMBERLAND

B & O Railroad

Miles

0 5 10   20   30

What Has Gone Before

Carolina Adams, a young woman of spirit and determination, enjoyed a pampered life in Oakbridge, her family's plantation, outside of Falls Church, Virginia.

Growing up as one of the middle siblings in a household of seven brothers and sisters, Carolina had always been eager to understand the world around her. Young ladies of the 1830s were not encouraged to educate themselves in the ways of masculine studies such as mathematics and science, but Carolina, ever the unconventional, desired to cross those boundaries. She was especially enthralled with the railroad, which she fell in love with the first time she saw a train roar into Washington City. When her indulgent father, Joseph Adams, permitted her a tutor, James Baldwin, Carolina began to realize part of her dream. Carolina's older sister, Virginia, also hoped her dreams to be fulfilled by James Baldwin—her more conventional dreams of becoming a proper southern wife.

Carolina was thrilled to have a tutor; however, James, who was once employed by the Baltimore and Ohio Railroad, put her off regarding the subject of railroads, causing Carolina to seek out the reason for his reticence. James had been involved in a railroad accident that seriously injured him and took the life of his friend and mentor, Phineas Davis. Thus, his delight and enthusiasm about railroad work was dimmed to the point that he actually feared riding a train again.

During his recovery James was thrust into the job of tutoring Carolina Adams, and of courting her older sister Virginia. James had not been eager to marry, desiring to establish his career with the railroad first, but his father finally pressured James toward matrimony because the failing family finances desperately needed him to make a good marriage.

What no one expected, least of all they, was that James and Carolina should fall in love with each other. James found healing in Carolina's friendship, and as she helped him come to terms with the past, James began to visualize his future with the railroad once more. In turn, Carolina found in James a man who was not threatened by her intelligence and regard for learning. She also found a soul mate with whom she desired to spend the rest of her life. Unfortunately, he had all but committed himself to Virginia, and Carolina was too insecure in her love to dare come between them, much less reveal her feelings to James. Likewise, James refused to confront his growing affection for Carolina.

Torn by his conflicting feelings toward the two sisters, and pressured by family expectations, James allowed himself to be carried along by events, soon finding himself engaged to Virginia. But eventually realizing he could not marry a woman he didn't love, James broke off the engagement with Virginia. However, in order to save her from too much social embarrassment, he allowed Virginia to publicly break the engagement herself. Then, unable to face Carolina and the social ostracism his ungentlemanly behavior would cause, James left Oakbridge and Washington for a position with the Baltimore and Ohio Railroad, a job that would take him far away to unsettled lands. Carolina, steeped in sorrow over the recent death of her baby sister Maryland, found the loss of James to be just as devastating.

To help Carolina through her desolation, her father, a man of deep faith, led her to a rekindled hope that is found in Jesus, and Carolina gained a deeper, more personal faith in Christ. Her desires for the future, an education, a working involvement with the railroad, and James Baldwin were all a part of her distant dreams, but with her newfound faith, Carolina learned there is a hope beyond. . . .

PART I

December 1836—
January 1837

*These railroads—could but the whistle be made musical,
and the rumble and the jar got rid of—are positively the
greatest blessing that the ages have wrought out for us.
They give us wings; they annihilate the toil and dust of
pilgrimage; they spiritualize travel!*

—Nathaniel Hawthorne
The House of the Seven Gables

One

Picking Up the Pieces

*C*arolina Adams gave a halfhearted glance at the list of Christmas gift advertisements in her current issue of the *American Railroad Journal*. She was far more interested in the articles about advancements in locomotive design. The railroad magazine, a gift from her tutor and friend James Baldwin, was not only her window into the world of railroads but also a pleasant source of news from around the country, sometimes even the world.

She was well aware of the fact that the *Journal* was not the most acceptable reading material for young ladies of sixteen, but upon its weekly arrival to Oakbridge Plantation, Carolina avidly read it from cover to cover. It was her link to the railroad, and the railroad had become her link to the future.

Very few people understood her love of this smoke-spewing beast. Railroads and locomotives were subjects best left to men. And, in a society where many people believed that such knowledge could very well cause a woman to go insane, Carolina had to fight hard to be allowed even a glimpse into such subjects. Only her father and James truly understood. But James was gone and her father was terribly preoccupied these days.

So, it seemed at times the technical pages of the magazine offered her far more than information. In a way, her moments alone with it were a kind of comfort, a link to when times had been carefree and happy.

"Ladies' hats by Willington and Tombs," she muttered to herself, glancing back at the open page. "For the best specimens of ladies' and misses' satin and beaver hats." She noted this advertisement, thinking again of Christmas. Her sister Virginia had a far greater appreciation of such finery than Carolina. Perhaps a hat would make a nice gift for her.

Thinking of Virginia caused Carolina to put down the magazine with a morose sigh. For weeks now, Virginia had barely spoken a civilized word to her. The death of their baby sister Maryland had naturally put a great damper on the holiday spirit, but for Virginia it was magnified by the fact that her betrothal to James Baldwin had been dissolved. Carolina had the distinct impression that Virginia blamed her for the entire matter. And just maybe Carolina did deserve some of her sister's ire. James had been Carolina's tutor for a few short but glorious months, and during that time Carolina and James had become friends. Unfortunately, Carolina had also fallen in love with her teacher.

Sighing again, Carolina left her mahogany writing desk and ambled to the window. It was here, in her favorite spot, that Carolina felt most at home. The window seat had always offered her much comfort and tranquility. She pulled up her knees and placed her dainty pink slippers on the brocade seat cover. At sixteen, she had been properly presented to society, and instructed and trained in the ways of running a plantation household.

Living just west of the country's capital, near Falls Church, Virginia, Carolina had also enjoyed a strong political background. This pleasured her in ways that she could never share publicly, for what young woman of such genteel upbringing would dare to boast an interest in the government?

On the surface of things, she appeared to have all life could offer, yet she felt trapped like a bird in a cage—like the slaves who worked on her father's plantation. She knew her life was better by far than that of the poor souls whose only future was to work their master's land, but she felt as helpless in deciding her own future as they must have felt in deciding theirs. Society looked upon women as the bearers of children. It was a woman's responsibility to esteem her husband, bring glory to his name, and ease his burdens. Those few men who actually admired intelligence in a woman were greatly outnumbered by the general population, who deemed it totally unnecessary to educate and enlighten the female gender. Let women be placed on a pedestal in honor of their beauty and gentle nature—but whatever you do, don't allow them to think for themselves.

Margaret Adams had fully supported this ideal. She wanted her daughters to marry and raise a fine family of properly behaved children. She had instilled a firm belief that a woman's place was to first do her husband's bidding, and then see to her family. But it was not a view shared by Carolina. There was nothing wrong with those things, but there was so much more. . . .

"My baby!"

A moaning scream tore through the strained silence of the house and brought Carolina instantly to her feet. It was her mother. Again. Carolina hurried out of her room and down the hall to see what assistance she might offer this time.

Peering into the nursery doorway, Carolina grimaced at the scene. Margaret Adams, unable to deal with the death of her youngest child Maryland, had taken up residence in the nursery. Eleven-year-old Pennsylvania Adams, affectionately called Penny, sat quivering, quite frightened, at one end of the room while several slaves tried to calm Margaret.

"Where is Mary? Where is my baby?" Margaret looked accusingly at each of the slaves. "You have taken my baby!"

Margaret didn't seem to even notice Carolina's arrival, so Carolina went to her sister first. Penny looked so frail and ghastly white that Carolina feared she, too, would succumb to the aftermath of the yellow fever that had stricken her and killed their sister little more than three months earlier.

"Mother?" Carolina called softly. "Mother, you should sit down and rest." Carolina gave Penny's shoulder a reassuring pat, then crossed the room slowly to where Margaret stood over an empty cradle. "Mother?"

Margaret Adams, a handsome woman of thirty-nine, turned and stared at her daughter as though seeing a ghost.

"I can't find her," Margaret sobbed hysterically. "They have taken her away and I can't find her."

"Mama . . ."

"Where is my Mary?" Margaret turned plaintive eyes toward Carolina.

The negresses backed away, their dark eyes hopeful that Carolina could ease the tension of the moment. Carolina reached out to touch her mother's arm.

"Mother, don't you remember?" Carolina led her to the rocking chair. "Mary died of yellow fever this August last. She and Penny were so very sick. Remember?"

Margaret stared in disbelief for a moment, and then, as if reliving the painful past once again, she finally nodded, her eyes stark with grief. "Yes . . . I remember now." She calmed a bit and allowed Carolina to help her sit. Glancing around the room, Margaret seemed to come out of her daze and realize her surroundings. "Sometimes my mind plays tricks on me. It's just so hard to imagine she's really gone."

"I know, Mama. It's hard for all of us, but especially hard for you."

Carolina glanced over to Penny, who was now being helped back into bed by one of the slaves.

Carolina knelt beside her mother and waited for her senses to fully return. These days were so troubling to Carolina. Her mother's mind had weakened in the loss of yet another child. Many years ago, she'd given over two infant sons to the fever. Carolina had never known these brothers, as they were born in the years between her older brother York and sister Virginia, but the effect on her mother had been the same. At least that was how it was told to Carolina. Apparently, Margaret had suffered tremendous melancholy after the death of her sons, and it wasn't until the birth of Virginia that Margaret was restored to her original strength. It was little wonder that Virginia had become her favorite child. She had given Margaret a reason to live.

As if thinking of her could conjure her presence, Carolina glanced up to find Virginia standing in the doorway. "Look, Mother, Virginia has come. Why don't we go into the music room? Virginia could play for you, and I'll arrange for tea."

Virginia swept into the room in a lovely forest green muslin. The gown was trimmed heavily in black, but the green and the youthful styling made it clear that the nineteen-year-old refused to give in entirely to the black bombazine of mourning.

"Come along, Mother," said Virginia. "I can take care of everything. You and I will take a short walk out to where they are butchering the hogs. We can't let that process go unsupervised, now can we?" She didn't wait for an answer but quickly added, "After that, we will return to the house and I will tuck you into bed for a rest." Virginia threw Carolina a glance, but no word of acknowledgment.

There was clear hostility in Virginia's icy blue eyes. Where Carolina had dark brown eyes and rich chocolate brown hair, Virginia's eyes were like their father's, and her hair was a shade lighter. Virginia's beauty and grace were lauded by all around her and especially captivated the young men. At one time she had been one of the most notable belles in the county, although as the years edged up to push her toward spinsterhood, Virginia was less and less regarded as such a prize. Her own stubbornness and desire to find just the right man to marry had created this circumstance. But she refused to see it that way and thus, as far as Carolina could tell, had blithely broken her most recent engagement to James Baldwin, announcing to the world that she needed to remain close to her mother in order to offer her proper care in the wake of Mary's death.

People, of course, thought Virginia the epitome of southern womanhood. The supreme sacrifice of giving up one's own interests to care for an ailing parent was highly regarded in the social circles so very important to Virginia. But Carolina had an idea that it was not for these people that Virginia had made her choice. Carolina couldn't guess what her true reasons might be, but Virginia always seemed to have ulterior motives.

Watching as her sister led their mother from the room, Carolina felt an emptiness that refused to be filled. Her entire life had been spent in the security of family and material comforts, and now it seemed that her family was falling apart.

Her two older brothers, York and Maine, were both away from Oakbridge, the plantation of their birth. Maine, having felt God's calling, attended seminary in England, while York, destined to be in the public eye, found politics and the Washington scene to be his forte. Assistant to the ailing President Andrew Jackson, York had only recently learned that he would be held over as an aide to the newly elected Martin Van Buren. The only other sibling, besides the ailing Penny, was Georgia Adams.

Poor Georgia, Carolina thought to herself. The child had been positively overlooked on numerous occasions, much to her detriment. It seemed even worse now with the other members of the family wrapped up in their own problems. Often completely unsupervised, she managed to move in adult circles and engage herself in adult activities, even though she was scarcely fourteen. She flirted outrageously with grown men and often opened her mouth to share most inappropriate conversation. It was after Georgia had relayed the intimate details of her friend Mercy Pritchard's love life that Carolina had first spoken to their father. But, steeped in his own grief because of the collapse of his wife's sanity and daughter's death, not to mention growing national economic struggles, Joseph Adams was unable to offer much help.

"Mama scared me," Penny said weakly from her bed, drawing Carolina from her brooding thoughts.

"I know, and I'm so sorry. Mama doesn't understand how frightening her cries can sound. But you don't have to worry now, Penny dear. Lydia is going to sit with you until you fall asleep." Carolina nodded to a young female slave. The wide-eyed girl took a seat beside Penny's bed.

"Would you tell me a story, Carolina?" Penny asked as Carolina turned to leave. "Just a little story?"

Carolina took pity on her sister and came to sit on the edge of the bed. "What would you like to hear about?"

"Tell me about the railroad again. Tell me about how they are going to build the railroad to go clear to the other side of America."

Carolina smiled. "Well, they are certainly going to try. First they have to be able to handle all of the mountains in between. Mountains make a very big obstacle for the locomotive engines. You see, the engines must not only go up the mountain themselves, they must pull a load of cars behind them. Sometimes the engines aren't powerful enough, and sometimes the wheels slip and slide on the rail."

"What do they do to make it work?" Penny asked, and Lydia also leaned forward as if awaiting the answer herself.

Carolina smiled. "They do all kinds of things. One thing is to use incline planes. These are places on the rail line where the road gets too steep. They put the rails into place, sometimes going straight up the mountainside for a short ways, but only if it isn't too steep. Then they lay track that goes on a flat space to kind of even things out. This makes it look like they are going to go around part of the mountain rather than straight up. They use as many sections as they need to finally reach the top of the mountain, weaving the railroad back and forth until they reach the summit. Then they do the same thing coming down the other side. Sometimes locomotive engines pull the cars up the incline planes, but some lines use horses."

Penny yawned, and Carolina knew it would only be a matter of minutes before she would fall fast asleep.

"Does our railroad use horses?" she asked.

Carolina almost laughed at her sister's choice of words. Ever since the Baltimore and Ohio had built their southern branch to the capital city, Penny had called it *their* railroad. Carolina felt the same way.

"They do on the western line," Carolina replied, patting Penny's hand. "But incline planes aren't necessary on the Washington Branch."

"Aren't the engines too heavy for the horses to pull?" Penny asked sleepily.

"They don't pull the engines. There are engine terminals on both sides of the mountain. They unhook the engine there and simply take the cars up and over and hook them up to another engine on the other side. Understand?"

Penny fought to open her eyes and finally gave in to sleep. Carolina smiled, but then a serious thought about Penny's weakness crossed her mind. The doctor hadn't thought Penny would survive the fever, and now that she had, he didn't believe she would live much longer. The fever and its aftermath had left Penny's heart weak, and because Margaret had refused to allow her children to be bled—or so the doctor said—there was little he could do.

Carolina couldn't imagine the house without Penny's sweet, gentle spirit. But then, she couldn't have imagined the house without the rambunctious Maryland. Mary, who used to so love running up and down the main staircase that, whenever she was missing from the nursery, one had only to look to the stairs in order to find her.

Rising, Carolina reached out and brushed back a sandy brown curl from her sister's face. She's so little, God, Carolina silently prayed. Please give her strength to fight this illness. Don't take Penny away as You did Mary.

Two

A Master Design

James Baldwin stood atop Jefferson's Rock, high above Harper's Ferry, and watched in anticipation the opening of the new bridge across the Potomac. Harper's Ferry was the door through which the B&O would eventually reach the Ohio, and today, with his companions, James was witnessing the dramatic opening of that door.

Harper's Ferry, nestled at the base of a low hill, was the joining place of the Potomac and Shenandoah rivers. The scenery was both treacherous and breathtaking, and even set against the harsh briskness of the winter day, James thought it a lovely place with tremendous potential. It was, in fact, the prospective trade west that drove the B&O Railroad to seek passage through the small community.

James watched as the small grasshopper engine pulled closer to the Potomac Viaduct. Behind it trailed a string of cars, some carrying supplies, others carrying passengers—all sharing this monumental moment in history. Instead of riding in the train, James had opted to view it all from his present spectacular vantage point.

He had the utmost confidence in the small but powerful engine. The design had been that of his friend Phineas Davis. Davis had died just over a year ago in the rail accident that had left James injured and confused. He had wanted to give up the railroad, and would have, but for Carolina Adams.

He smiled at the mere thought of the feisty woman-child. How she would love to be a part of this day, he thought. He could imagine her thrilling to the sight of the smoke-belching engine as it crept closer and closer to the bridge. He would have loved to share the moment with her, and had they still been on speaking terms, he would have done just that.

He frowned and walked a few steps away from the companions accompanying him for the celebration. Ben Latrobe, head surveyor and superintendent of the bridge, and Jonathan Knight, chief engineer, hardly noticed his introspective mood. They were caught up in the moment, just as James had been. The bridge represented real progress for the main stem, which had been fraught with delays lately.

James watched the smoke streaming from the engine and felt the importance of the moment. He wanted to impress every image on his mind so that perhaps one day he might relay the images to Carolina.

And he would see her again.

This he promised himself. It would probably be very far into the future, when his appearance wouldn't cause her so much grief and embarrassment, but he would return to Oakbridge Plantation one day. He smiled, remembering his days at Oakbridge. The estate was vast and beautiful, with thousands of acres of rich Virginia soil to sustain the growth of most any crop. James could almost envision Carolina walking out amid the orchards—flower blossoms snowing down on her hair and carpeting the ground where she stepped. He would see her again.

"We're still going to fix this line," James heard Latrobe assure Jonathan Knight, and the words brought his thoughts back again to the railroad.

"Do you think Louis McLane will make a good run of things?" Knight questioned. Elections had not yet been held to choose a new president for the Baltimore and Ohio Railroad, but everyone was certain the process was only a formality. Louis McLane, once a very important man in Andrew Jackson's cabinet, was expected not only to take up the position of president but to pump new blood and energy into the line as well.

Latrobe smiled. "He's the devil to work with, but the man can move mountains with the simple snap of his fingers. People respect McLane, and he isn't afraid to take a chance now and then."

James smiled, and though he wasn't a direct part of their conversation, he felt the same as Latrobe. He'd met the anticipated president of the B&O, and he liked him. McLane was a man of vision, and his vision was to see the B&O reach the Ohio as it should have years before now.

James continued watching, memorizing each detail of the day. It was cold and brisk and the air smelled like snow. All around him the dead dry vegetation of summer sparsely covered the rich brown ground, while hardwood trees stood devoid of leaves among the windswept pines. The earth rested, but not so her inhabitants.

"The area west of Harper's is going to be the death of us," Latrobe told Knight. "It's possible to continue with the basic plan, but some changes are going to be needed."

James strolled back a few feet to join his friends in their conversation. "What kind of changes?" he asked with great interest.

"Big ones. Expensive ones," answered Latrobe. "It's a good thing the Washington Branch is so profitable. We're going to need all the ready cash we can get our hands on."

Knight nodded. "The Washington line made a net revenue of over eighty thousand dollars between last October and September of this year. That's *net*, my good fellows—and it included over seventy-five thousand passengers and more than five thousand tons of freight."

"But the westward line is the main one," Latrobe said, "and that is the line that ought to be producing the best benefit to the company. Freight aplenty awaits us at the Ohio, but there are so many problems." He shook his head as though the idea of it all was too overwhelming to consider.

"What must be addressed first?" James asked, the wind stirring his dark brown hair.

"Well, we should rid ourselves of the strap iron," Latrobe replied, rubbing his bearded face. Both James and Knight nodded knowingly. Strap iron—thin iron strips attached to wooden stringers and laid upon wooden or granite sleepers—was an abomination from which the B&O could not seem to shake itself. The thin railing could scarcely handle the lightweight grasshopper engines without pulling away and bending upward from their fasteners. These created the dreaded snakeheads that caused derailments and serious injury.

"Yes, the strap has to go," James agreed. Most of the Washington Branch had been laid with the much more useful and safe T-rails. Even so, a coupler on one of these had come loose, causing the derailment that had killed his friend. Railroading was far from a perfect science.

"That, of course," Latrobe said, pulling off his tiny wire-rimmed glasses and rubbing them gently with his scarf, "is going to cost a fortune and take a tremendous amount of time. However, until we straighten out some of the more crooked areas of track and re-lay the line with T-rail, we can never develop this railroad into what it hopes to become. The new heavier, more powerful engines will never be allowed on the lines for fear of tearing up the track and being totally destroyed in the process."

"I understand you are working to straighten sections east of here," James offered.

"Talk, all talk. We're surveying, of course." Latrobe put his glasses back on and squinted. "Something about that bridge gives me great concern," he muttered offhandedly, but no one paid him much attention.

"Actually," Knight said, pulling his top hat down tight against the steadily growing breeze, "McLane desires to see the incline planes at Parrs Ridge dealt with early on."

"True enough," Latrobe answered. "We're surveying how to bypass the incline planes altogether."

"But why?" James asked. "Since it's recently been proven that locomotives are capable of hoisting the loads up and over, why not worry about that later?"

"The incline planes are impractical for speed and safety. I'm afraid they were a terrible miscalculation and will be a very expensive wrong to make right." Latrobe spoke while his eyes continued to seek the progress of the locomotive below them.

"Have you already laid out your plans—?" Suddenly James stopped. His eyes also had been focused on the train as they talked. "What's that?" He turned to Knight. "Don't you have a spyglass?"

"Yes, in my saddlebag."

James strode to where the horses were tethered, retrieved Knight's spyglass, and returned to the others. He lifted the glass to his eyes.

"What is it, James?" asked Latrobe.

"The train is slowing."

"Yes . . . it is at that."

James peered intently through the glass. He could see no reason for the slowing, though he supposed there could be some mechanical problem. Then he saw it. Only with the glass was he able to make out the bits of crumbling masonry falling into the ravine below. At first he thought it only loose rocks being kicked aside by the progress of the train. But a closer inspection revealed a cracked section of piling near the top of the bridge.

"Have a look for yourself, Mr. Latrobe," he said, handing the glass to his companion.

Latrobe focused the glass, then shook his head. "It is as I feared. This is just the kind of thing that has kept us for so long from reaching our goal. If only they would do things right from the beginning." He sighed. "So, you can see, James, there's a great deal to be done before we can begin to address the problems we just spoke of."

"I'd like to help, Mr. Latrobe," James said eagerly. "I know McLane would approve, and if you'll have me . . ."

Latrobe smiled. "I thought you'd never ask. I didn't want to impose and take you away from the engine shops in Mt. Clare. I know how you enjoy the design work, and Jonathan might not have liked to see you get so far away."

"He'll not be that far," Knight laughed.

Far enough, James thought, to feel a true sense of adventure, not to mention to be even more distanced from his problems. James felt a tremendous sense of anticipation, even more so than the excitement of seeing the new railroad bridge. All else aside, here was a chance to dig in to the actual rail line of the B&O and to be a part of the changes that would forever restructure the traffic flow between Baltimore and the Ohio River. He enjoyed his work at the yards building locomotives, but what he found he was desiring more was the actual engineering of the rail lines.

"If this is what you'd really like to do, I can use you immediately," said Latrobe.

"It was one of my original desires for railroad work. I have a passion for this railroad, and I want to immerse myself in its creation." James paused and looked up rather sheepishly. "Does that sound a bit melodramatic?"

"Not in my mind," chuckled Latrobe. "I feel the same. You know, James, I worked a short time for the Baltimore and Port Deposit Railroad, but it just wasn't the same. I was happy to return to the B&O. Here is my true calling." He waved an arm against the backdrop of the valley below. "Here is my future."

And mine, James thought. If he could not be with the woman he loved, then let him at least be with the railroad he loved.

"I see the hand of God clearly upon my choice," said Latrobe.

James looked at Benjamin Latrobe with surprise. "The hand of God?"

"Indeed. I am a strong believer in placing faith in God's guidance for our lives."

At this, Knight walked away as though ill-at-ease with the deeply personal turn the conversation had taken. James felt uncomfortable, too, but for some reason he couldn't explain, he stayed where he was.

"I've had very little to do with church and religion, Mr. Latrobe," James answered with a shrug.

"Church and religion are only a minor part of God's plan, my boy. I'm speaking of a more intimate knowledge of the good Lord."

"Well then," James began slowly, "I would have to say that my experience is limited to childhood prayers and adult questions of purpose."

Latrobe smiled. "You aren't alone in questioning the purpose and actions of God. I don't believe a day passes but that I wonder what God originally had in mind."

James took a closer appraisal of Latrobe. The Baldwin family had been acquainted with the Latrobe clan for years, but because James had always been so much younger than the Latrobe boys, he had never been close to them. That was ironic, too, since their interests were so similar. Ben Latrobe, in his mid-thirties, was of average build but with a striking appearance. His small, dark eyes gave him a stern countenance, especially accompanied by his dark, full beard. But there was a good-natured glint in those eyes. He looked almost like an Old Testament prophet who had just heard a good joke.

Latrobe had a way of putting James at ease, and the younger man spoke almost without thinking. "God seems cruel at times," James said. "I can't imagine what He must be about when He allows good people to die and evil folks to succeed."

Latrobe rubbed his beard and slightly pursed his lips. The thoughtful expression made James regret his openness. Religion and God were subjects he'd rather leave unmentioned these days.

Just when he figured the conversation was over, James was surprised when Latrobe spoke again.

"I see God as the Master Designer," said Latrobe. "He surveyed and set onto paper, if you will, His own design for mankind—much as I put together the design for the bridge below us. God laid out His plan, marking each and every item with careful consideration as to how it would fall into place with the next item in line.

"He saw the rivers, the ravines, the mountains, and He planned for each of these well in advance. Then with His plan established, He created mankind and shared His way with them. Much as I shared my designs for the Potomac Viaduct with the railroad's board of directors. What they chose to do with it from that point was up to them. What I choose to do with God's plan is up to me. Just as it's up to you."

James grew strangely disturbed at this analogy. "So you're saying it's our own fault that things happen, that people die, and that evil prospers."

"I'm saying that we take God's design and make changes to suit ourselves and then wonder why the master plan is so flawed." Latrobe looked at him with stern yet compassionate eyes. "For instance, I can tell even at this distance that the contractor did not heed my bridge design in total. He made certain changes, no doubt to save money, but for whatever reason, those changes were made without ever consulting me or seeking the truth on why things were laid out a certain way. If what we witnessed today worsens, how can I be held accountable for the problems that ensue? They refused to follow my plan."

"I suppose that makes sense. If God truly has a master plan, and we are toying with His design, I can reason in my mind why that would create problems. But how does it account for the death of good people before their time?"

"You're talking about Phineas, aren't you?"

James nodded. "Phineas and others. There are many good people who have died in the prime of their lives." Remembering Maryland Adams, he added, "Even children."

"But we cannot know the entire master plan, James. We can seek to understand the plan for our own lives, not for everyone else's. The Bible clearly shows us the right and wrong way to do things, but it cannot keep us from the free choice our will makes when God's plan seems to collide with our own."

The locomotive's whistle blasted out against the roar of the competing rivers and the factory town below them. Latrobe smiled hopefully. "Well, perhaps that obstacle is behind us now."

James studied the expression on Latrobe's face. Pure pride and delight etched the weathered skin. James thought he seemed older than his years. Latrobe went forward to speak to Knight while James stood back and watched. Deeply troubled by Latrobe's words, James wondered if the emptiness in his life had more to do with a spiritual need than an emotional longing.

Three

Plotting Revenge

*C*arolina was deeply immersed in the study of tractive power when she heard the sound of voices in the hall outside the library. She glanced up from her book but made no move when the door opened to admit Hampton Cabot, her father's New York City based commission merchant.

The elderly Adams butler announced, "Mister Cabot, ma'am."

"Miss Adams, you would put the very sun to shame," he said, stepping forward and offering her a sweeping bow as the butler quietly exited. "I must say, you make the long trip from New York a very worthwhile one, indeed."

"Mr. Cabot," Carolina said in acknowledgment of his presence.

"I see you are reading once again," Hampton said, noting the book in her hands. "What is it this time that has captured your attention?" He drew closer to her.

"Nothing that would appeal to your interest, I assure you."

Carolina wished fervently that he would leave her alone, but since setting his cap for her some months earlier, Carolina found that Hampton Cabot was a most ardent suitor.

"Carolina," he said in a voice that told her formalities were concluded, "you mustn't be this way with me. I desire to know about every interest of your life."

She gave him a quick appraisal. Hampton Cabot was a big man, standing at least six feet three and weighing some two hundred pounds. He was well muscled, fashionably dressed, and not all that bad to look at, but Carolina found him a bore. Nevertheless, he was a guest in her home and did not deserve her rudeness.

"I'm reading about the tractive power of locomotives to start the cars forward," she said, making a concerted attempt to be polite. His

31

blue eyes widened ever so slightly as he raised a single brow. Enjoying his surprise, she continued. "You see, tractive power is how you measure the ability of the engine to start the locomotive forward, while horsepower is a measurement of the locomotive's ability to maintain the cars moving forward—"

"Why would you want to waste your time in such matters?" Hampton interrupted.

Carolina smiled tolerantly. "Because I am the co-owner of my father's new railroad venture, the Potomac and Great Falls Railroad. Therefore, I feel it is important for me to understand the workings of locomotives and the railroad if I'm to be a successful part of it."

"And knowledge of tractive power will make you successful?" Hampton pushed aside his coattails and took a seat on the settee opposite Carolina.

"It's only one part. I must be educated in the workings of the railroad, or otherwise I won't be able to suggest ways to make it better." She ignored the open look of disbelief on Hampton's face. No doubt he assumed she would be of little help in any situation.

"This particular book is a new locomotive manual by DePambour. It says here that locomotive tractive power can be figured by using the formula T equals C squared, times S, times P, divided by D. That is to say, tractive force in pounds equals the diameter—"

"Enough!" Hampton said, raising his hands in protest. "Don't you know, dear Carolina, that young women should not burden their minds with such things?"

"You must understand, Mr. Cabot," Carolina said, snapping the book closed, "these are the things that my mind ponders. These are the things that interest me."

"But you are a woman of refinement. You are beautiful and talented, graceful and charming. Why waste your abilities on such masculine interests? Have your little railroad, but let the men worry about how it runs."

Carolina tightened her grip on the book and tried to remain calm. To her relief, her father chose that moment to enter the room.

"Carolina, my dear, I had no idea you were in here when I sent Hampton up. Do forgive me."

Carolina jumped up and crossed the room to kiss her father's cheek. His muttonchop whiskers tickled her lips and made her smile. "There is nothing to forgive, Papa. I was just explaining tractive power to Mr. Cabot."

"My little willow of a daughter with her powerful mind." Joseph laughed heartily and put an arm around her. "She's something else, is she not?" he asked Hampton.

"Indeed," Hampton said, then, drawing a brown paper parcel from his coat pocket, he added, "I nearly forgot in our discussion of railroad formulas, I brought this for you, Carolina."

Carolina moved away from her father, her navy woolen dress swinging silently from side to side as she crossed to take the package. "I would rather you not bring me gifts, Mr. Cabot."

"Please call me Hampton. You know how I feel about you, as does your father. Formalities are certainly unwarranted between us; after all, we aren't stuffy English nobility."

Joseph came to sit in his favorite leather chair while Carolina unwrapped the package. She had guessed it would be a book of poetry, and she was not disappointed. The book was a small collection of works by Percy Shelley with beautiful hand-engraved miniature paintings.

"I cannot accept so valuable a gift," Carolina said, extending the book back to Hampton. "It is quite lovely, but I must decline."

"Nonsense!" Hampton frowned and turned to Joseph. "Have I not told you of my serious regard for your daughter?"

"You have indeed, sir."

"Then I appeal to your sensibility. I have neither family nor wife whom I might bestow such tokens upon. I am of the most respectable intentions toward your daughter, and I deem it my pleasure to give her this small token of my affection."

"But, sir," Carolina interrupted before her father could speak, "your affection is not returned, and therefore to keep such a beautiful work under the circumstances would be a false pretense—one in which you might presume upon feelings that do not exist."

"I know very well that you've not yet come to feel for me what I have grown to feel for you," Hampton protested. "But I am asking that you would but give the idea some further consideration. Put me to the test and see if I am not sincere."

Carolina sighed, unable to put to words the feelings in her heart. She had given her love to one man, albeit a man who never knew of it. James Baldwin had belonged to her sister, and, therefore, Carolina would never have been so heartless as to try to steal him away. Nevertheless, her heart was his, and she had little interest in putting one love aside in hopes that she could extend her affections to another. Not yet at least.

Joseph interceded and reached a compromise to the satisfaction of both. "Hampton, I would suggest you allow my daughter a little more time to know you before you bestow such finery upon her. And,

Carolina, I would suggest you allow the man to pay you court, that you might know him better before making up your mind against the possibilities."

Carolina nodded, and Hampton took back the book. "If this is to be the case," Hampton began, looking first to Carolina and then to her father, "I would like to ask for permission to escort your daughter to the Washington Christmas charity ball next week."

Carolina wanted to scream a rejection, but already she could see the approval in her father's expression.

"Well, it certainly seems a good idea. This house has been too long in grief and sorrow. I think it completely appropriate that Carolina should attend the ball with you. That is, if Carolina is in agreement."

She knew that her father expected her to make an acceptance of the invitation, and so she feigned a smile and a tiny curtsy. "I would be happy to accompany Mr. Cabot to the ball."

Hampton beamed a broad smile, which displayed slightly yellowed but extremely straight teeth. Carolina picked up her science book and excused herself from their company.

"One moment," Hampton called from behind her.

Opening the door and stepping into the hall as though she hadn't heard him, Carolina had nearly reached the stairs when Hampton called to her again and strode toward her.

"Thank you for agreeing to go with me." He was trying hard to be all charm, but his face held an arrogant expression of victory. "I shall be the envy of all men."

Carolina could no longer stand his smugness. "I am only going with you because of my father. You must realize that here and now. I am not interested in courtship and marriage at this point in my life—aside from the fact that we have so little in common. Therefore, Mr. Cabot," she said, emphasizing his formal name, "you must see the futility in your interest."

"Nevertheless . . ." Cabot leaned back with an even more self-satisfied expression. His blue eyes seemed to darken. "I'm getting what I want."

Carolina lifted her chin with a defiant smile. The gauntlet had clearly been thrown down. "You are getting only an unwilling participant, Mr. Cabot. Nothing more."

Hampton reached out a hand to cup her chin and bent low to meet her petite five-foot-three frame. "I will soon make you feel otherwise, my dear Carolina." Then before she could stop him, Hampton placed a lightning-quick kiss on her forehead before he turned and rejoined her father in the library.

Carolina reached a hand to where his lips had touched her skin. Stunned by his actions, she moved away from the library in a daze. He would never make her feel otherwise. Of this she was certain.

———

From her covert vantage point, Virginia observed the exchange between Hampton and her sister. She could not hear their words, but their actions spoke loudly enough. Carolina looked for all purposes to be quite enchanted with the dashingly handsome Hampton Cabot.

Seething in rage from a sense of betrayal and envy, Virginia slammed her bedroom door, went to her wardrobe, and pulled open the doors. She sent each side crashing back with such violence that the noise echoed in the silent room like the bursting of cannon shells upon a battlefield.

Carolina had ruined her life, although Virginia would never give her the satisfaction of knowing it. James Baldwin had been content to forget the railroad after his accident. Having seen his best friend die, while suffering painful scarring injuries himself, James had buried his dreams of working for the railroad. He was finished with locomotive nonsense and had been quite content to look toward the business of banking with his father. That was until Carolina had insisted on knowing more about the railroad.

Finding her bottle of sherry hidden inside a hatbox, Virginia picked up a glass and poured herself a drink. It seemed that when matters became too overwhelming, the burning liquid could calm and clear her mind. Soothing herself in the only way that seemed available, Virginia tossed back the sherry as though it were water and waited for the welcome warmth to spread throughout her body.

She had seen a future for herself as the prosperous wife of a bank president, for surely James' father, Leland Baldwin, would not have remained at the helm forever. She had seen herself as the queen of Washington society with servants and finery to rival all others. She had seen all of this, and so much more, until Carolina had helped James to rekindle his dead dreams.

Carolina had helped James remember his first love, which unfortunately wasn't Virginia. And that was the reason James had penned a letter breaking their engagement. Virginia grimaced. He was too much the proper gentleman to dishonor her by publicly ending their plans for marriage. Instead, he had left it in Virginia's capable hands. And what could she do but comply? She had ranted and raved at her father, begging him to make James marry her, but all for naught. James had packed his belongings and left Washington City, and Virginia was left alone to face the aftermath of his departure, her sister's death, and her mother's melancholy. Now everyone thought Virginia to be self-sacrificing in her giving James up to remain at home with her mother. Even the family, with the exception of her father, believed that it had been Virginia's choice to end the engagement. She had managed to save face, but her dreams lay in tattered shreds.

Remembering the tender scene she'd just witnessed in the hallway, Virginia's scowl deepened. There had to be a way to put an end to Carolina's happiness. Her little sister seemed quite chummy with Hampton Cabot, and perhaps this was the manner in which Virginia could attack. Their mother had always held to a family tradition of the eldest daughter marrying first; maybe Virginia could bring a halt to any romantic dreams Carolina might have toward Hampton by remaining single a while longer—not that Virginia had much choice in the matter. Perhaps Carolina could burn in the same misery of lost desires and passion that haunted Virginia's every waking moment. Pouring another half-portion of sherry, Virginia replaced the glass stopper and contemplated what should be done.

Their mother might not be much help in the matter, she reasoned. Margaret had her good moments along with her bad, but Virginia knew she could not depend upon anyone but herself for accomplishing her plans.

"I'll make you pay, little sister," she whispered bitterly. "I'll show you what it means to see an end to your dreams."

Hampton's Pursuit

*C*arolina secluded herself in the library and warmed her hands periodically over the blazing hearth fire. It was a cold December morning, and the wind outside seemed to howl relentlessly. Insulated by layers of woolen petticoats and a long-sleeved gown of dark rust-colored wool, Carolina still found it difficult to get warm.

Her father and Hampton were taking a tour of the plantation slave quarters and workshops, which in turn freed her to read and be left to her own devices for a time. She'd met the opportunity with a sigh of relief and giddy anticipation. Avoiding Hampton's attention was something she'd not quite yet perfected, and with her father seeming to promote their courting, Carolina felt herself backed into a corner. She would never willfully hurt her father by being disobedient, but neither could she give serious consideration to a man she didn't love. And she most certainly didn't love Hampton Cabot.

She took up a seat at her father's expansive desk and began to study the proposed charter for the Potomac and Great Falls Railroad. Her heart skipped a beat at the sight of her name as one of the proprietors of the proposed line. The charter itself, however, drafted in the terminology of legal proposals and bureaucratic nonsense, left her restless and bored. She wanted to see iron rails and puffing steam engines, not words such as "wherefore witnesseth" and "interdependent escrow." Putting it aside, she picked up her newest copy of the *American Railroad Journal* and began to peruse the articles. Sometimes it was frustrating that her only link to the railroad was words on paper. But if that was all she had, then she intended to make the most of it.

"Of particular difficulty," she read, "is the problem of properly venting the excess boiler steam. Without allowing the steam a means by which to escape, the container in which the steam is held will eventually burst. The current safety valves are inefficient, for, in allowing steam to escape, they often do not close in a timely manner with a proper fit. Thus boiler pressure is lost."

Carolina read with some fascination about this problem. It seemed that safety valves were absolutely necessary, and that when engineers and firemen sought to circumvent their use, explosions and deaths occurred. Among the most impressive examples cited was an account of the 1831 demise of the engine *Best Friend*. It seemed that the fireman, having dismounted to attend to hitching up additional cars, grew annoyed by this constant hiss of steam and tied down the safety valve. The pressure built inside the boiler, and inevitably, an explosion took place that resulted in the boiler being thrown twenty-five feet into the air. The fireman died from his injuries, and the engineer was badly burned by the scalding water.

Carolina toyed with her father's quill pen while reading about the desperate need to improve the basic design. How she would love to go to the B&O shops in Mt. Clare and see for herself the mechanism in question. A picture was a poor substitute.

"I thought I might find you in here," Hampton Cabot said from where he stood at the now open door.

Carolina inwardly groaned but outwardly smiled as politely as she could manage. "I presumed my father's business would keep you amply occupied."

"We've finished for now," Hampton said. "It seems he has other matters to attend to, and that in turn freed me. Would you care for some company?"

Carolina knew that it wouldn't matter whether she desired his companionship or not. Hampton had clearly made up his mind to join her, and it would be unthinkably rude to reject him at this point.

"By all means. There are many wonderful volumes on the shelf," she said, glancing around the room. "You have but to pick one and find a comfortable chair."

Hampton laughed and closed the door. He was dressed smartly in a navy blue suit with a plumb-colored satin waistcoat and heavily starched white shirt. His blond hair had been carefully styled away from his broad face, and his blue eyes seemed delighted with what they observed in Carolina.

"I thought perhaps we could talk," he said. "Unless, of course, you would like for me to read to you. Perhaps romantic poetry?"

Carolina could not refrain from grimacing. The very idea of Hampton Cabot offering up words of love in this manner was something she could not tolerate.

"No, thank you. I haven't much interest in poetry at this moment. I've been reading about safety valves in steam engines. Perhaps you are familiar with them?" Carolina asked, leaning her face against her hand as though completely enraptured.

"I assure you, I am not," Hampton said, flashing her a smile. "But I am familiar with the words of Shakespeare. 'See! how she leans her cheek upon her hand: O! that I were a glove upon that hand, that I might touch that cheek.' "

Carolina instantly regained her previous composure and returned her attention to the journal in front of her. "Safety valves . . . are . . . uh . . . necessary to keep the boiler from building up too much steam." She tried to infuse her next words with detached calm. "If boilers build up too much pressure they will explode."

Hampton grinned in a wickedly leering manner. "People are like that, too. Steam is quite like passion, don't you think?"

Carolina ignored the question. "The safety valves open when the pressure builds too high, and they close again when the steam is released. This way a steady pressure can be maintained. Of course, the ideal way to maintain it is neither to feed the fire with too much nor too little fuel. This way you don't waste the steam."

"And love, too, must be steadily fed," Hampton said, refusing to give in to her railroad talk. " 'Chameleons feed on light and air: Poets' food is love and fame.' That's in the Shelley book I brought you."

Carolina closed the journal and looked at him squarely. "Quote all the poetry you like, Mr. Cabot. It will not change my love of the railroad, nor my disinterest in you."

"I think you like me more than you want to admit," Hampton said, seemingly unmoved by her harsh statement. "I think you're a little bit spoiled, and because your father has given you much too much freedom, you don't realize what you were intended for. I suggest if you want to occupy yourself you could make a better time of it over here with me." He patted the sofa invitingly.

"I'm not merely seeking to occupy myself, as you put it. I enjoy learning about the railroad and the development of our country. I enjoy expanding my mind to include new subjects, and how dare you call me spoiled? You don't even know me." Carolina felt her face grow hot as her anger mounted.

Hampton only laughed, which furthered her fury and caused her to get to her feet. Hampton, too, stood and lazily wandered over to the front of the desk. Feeling that the desk afforded her marginal security, Carolina refused to make peace between them.

"You declare yourself interested in me, Mr. Cabot, yet I find you have no real interest in the things on which I feel strongly about. You belittle me and cause me grief, all the while spouting poetry and talk of love. If you cared about how I feel . . ."

"Oh, but I do care," he said in a seductive drawl. "I'd very much like to know how you feel. But I'd rather it come in the form of how you feel in my arms rather than how you feel about locomotives."

Carolina's mouth dropped open in surprise. From the expression on his face, Hampton appeared to enjoy her discomfort, and this only fed Carolina's anger.

"Good morning, sir! I've had quite enough of this conversation." She moved quickly to the door, but not fast enough. Hampton reached out and pulled her into his arms. She could feel the hard buttons of his coat press into her body.

"I did not mean to insult you, Carolina. I rather thought you might like to know what an attractive woman I find you to be. Most women enjoy hearing their praises sung, but you appear quite different on the matter. Could it be that I am your first love?"

Carolina pushed him away. "You are not my love at all!"

"Only time will tell that for certain," Hampton said, his voice low and husky. "But I can see by the way you tremble that I am your first. Not to worry, I've experience enough for both of us, and I assure you I can make you quite content to be my wife."

Carolina could bear his leering grin no longer. She pulled open the heavy oak door with such rage that it crashed against the wall. She could hear Hampton's laughter as she hurried from the room, but it no longer mattered. Her heart was racing and her breath came in labored gasps as she found refuge in her own bedroom. Locking the door, something she was not often given to doing, Carolina hugged her arms to her body and shuddered.

The idea of finding herself in Hampton's arms had been alarming. On one hand, he infuriated her and repulsed her because he was typically male in his attitude toward women. On the other hand, his words of passion and love fascinated her and gave her cause to wonder at her own feelings. He made her feel so strange. He confused her mind and then only made it worse by throwing out statements about being her first love.

"But you aren't my first . . ." she whispered in the solitude of her room. "My heart has already been given . . . and . . ." she sighed, feeling the empty ache inside, "already broken."

Five

Divine Intervention

James felt honored to be in attendance at the B&O board meeting. Sitting at the far end of the room, he had no say on the choice for the new president, but he clearly agreed with the retired president, Philip Thomas. Though Thomas had resigned last summer, he still had a strong voice in the workings of the railroad.

"McLane is favorably received by this body," began Thomas, "to become the next president of our esteemed railroad." Thomas had agreed to continue serving on the board of directors, and everyone in the room had great respect for his opinion. Thomas was only one of two men, the other being William Steuart, who had been on the original board selected in 1827.

"I feel confident in his ability to lead us forward," Thomas concluded.

From everything James had read or heard, McLane was a mover and a doer. He would see the Baltimore and Ohio push west past Harper's Ferry, or die trying.

McLane was an energetic man, well known as a statesman and politician. He had served a dozen years in Congress and acted as ambassador to England, secretary of the treasury, and secretary of state under Andrew Jackson. He moved with complete competence and ease amid the social circles of New York, London, Washington, and Baltimore, clearly opinionated and highly respected. He was exactly the dynamic infusion of new blood that the Baltimore and Ohio so desperately needed.

"The board will meet officially after Christmas, December twenty-seventh, and a vote will be cast at that time," Joseph Patterson, the acting president, confirmed. Murmurs of approval went up in the

41

room. "I therefore propose the motion that we adjourn until such time."

"I second the motion," Thomas declared and the ayes held the vote.

As the meeting broke up, James watched the commotion in the room for several moments before getting to his feet. The atmosphere was surprisingly light considering the weighty decision that would soon be made. The Christmas spirit was probably upon them, he reasoned, and he imagined everyone hurrying home to their families. It was, after all, a season for celebration and for being with the ones you loved.

But that wouldn't be a luxury afforded to James Baldwin.

Standing away from the crowd, James mused that the future of the B&O looked far brighter than his own personal future. It thus meant more to him than ever before that the railroad include him. The railroad represented his dreams for America, as well as for himself. He longed to see the untamed West brought under control, and he envisioned the tie that would bind it all together to be a railroad tie.

"James Baldwin," a voice called out from behind him. "I hoped I might get a word with you before you hurried home."

James turned to find the brother of his old friend Ben Latrobe approaching him. John Latrobe was a family friend in his own right. He was also the general counsel for the B&O Railroad and had served faithfully with Philip Thomas, ironing out many of the legal problems that had plagued the railroad. Ben and John's father, Benjamin Latrobe senior, had been instrumental in creating the architectural styling of Washington City.

"Mr. Latrobe, a pleasure to see you again." James gave a slight bow and met Latrobe's searching eyes.

"My brother, Ben, tells me that you'll be joining him for some survey work."

James smiled. "Yes, you are quite right. The weather is holding us back now, but once the worst of winter is past us, I intend to find myself deep in the Virginia wilderness."

John nodded. "Ben has had his eye on you for a while. He likes the way you tend to keep yourself turned to the matter at hand. Not many young men would be willing to journey so far from home and family." John paused long enough to check his watch. "Speaking of which, how are your father and mother?"

James dreaded the question. He'd had no contact with his parents since his departure from Washington last October. Should he lie to John and tell them that they were fine? No doubt John knew more of the elder Baldwins than he did. Perhaps it would be better to avoid the subject altogether.

"They're well," he finally said, then catching sight of Philip Thomas, he changed the subject. "Mr. Thomas seems to be bearing a heavy load these days. I have heard it said that his illnesses are getting the better of him."

Latrobe glanced across the room to where his old friend stood in conversation with several of the new board members. "I tried to talk him out of resigning the presidency. He's convinced, however, that the railroad will not move profitably forward under his leadership." Latrobe grimaced. "You know what they'll say, don't you?"

James shook his head. "I'm not sure I follow you. Say about what?"

"They'll say the railroad positively burst into prosperity because Philip Thomas gave the job of president over to someone who knew what to do with it." Latrobe seemed quite troubled by this. "I told him that the B&O was due to swing upward and that while the public could get testy over the low return of dividends, if he left now before the improvements began, people would always assume that he was the reason for all of the problems."

"But whether he stays or goes, the B&O still has a fair number of obstacles to overcome," James offered.

Latrobe nodded. "And well I know it. McLane will have his hands full when he comes on board. Unfortunately, I'm not convinced that McLane is the man for the job."

"I've heard nothing but good of the man. I've had the pleasure to meet him on several different occasions, and he is well spoken and deep thinking."

"True enough, but is he competent in the running of a railroad?"

James chuckled. "There aren't many with enough experience to prove that point. The business is in its infancy, so you can hardly fault a man for a lack of experience."

"I suppose only time will tell as to his devotion and dedication to the B&O. And, in all honesty, I must say that I've never yet known anyone, including Mr. Daniel Webster, who possessed in the same degree the faculty of stating a case more clearly than McLane."

"Then we must give him a chance," James replied. "Just as he must give us a chance, eh?"

"Yes, I quite agree."

"Mr. Latrobe, might we impose upon you?" a gray-haired gentleman questioned from behind James.

"I will speak with you later, Mr. Baldwin," Latrobe said with a bow. "Merry Christmas to you, and my best wishes to your family."

James was relieved to find several board members drawing Latrobe away for a discussion on some matter of great importance. The reminder of Christmas only made him feel more discouraged than he was before. Family seemed so very far away. His uncle Samuel Baldwin lived not six blocks away, and yet James couldn't bring himself to even venture that far. No doubt his father would have written his only brother to say that James had turned out to be a terrible failure and disappointment as a son.

Slipping away from the board meeting, James walked out into the chilled Baltimore afternoon. A light dusting of snow covered the ground, and the heavy smell of the sea assaulted his nose. During the two and a half months he'd spent in Baltimore, James had found little to attach himself to. The small boardinghouse in which he'd secured modest accommodations was run by an elderly man who had nothing good to say about anyone. The man's only daughter had run off the year before with one of the boarders, leaving her father to fend for himself. In turn, the man had a very low opinion of his renters but tolerated them for the sake of the coin it put into his hand each week.

Shoving his hands deeper into his coat pockets, James could not abide the longing in his soul. He continued down Pratt Street, making his way deeper into the city. Several hacks slowed as they approached him, but he waved them off, thinking to save as much of his money as possible. Money was not a commodity he had in abundance. And it was money that stood as the foundation to all of his miseries.

Had it truly only been last year that he'd returned from college a happy man? His father had insisted James join him in banking, but the railroad was already in his blood, and for once in this life, James had made a firm stand to pursue his interest. But it had come at a price. His father insisted he marry, and marry wealthy. It seemed the family coffers had run dry, and James was the last hope for replenishing what had been lost on improper investments and unchecked spending.

He thought of Virginia Adams, young, beautiful, and well accomplished. She had been the chosen one. The one his mother saw as fitting perfectly into Washington's social circles. And to his father she depicted a fleshly representation of financial redemption. The only thing wrong was that James didn't love her and knew he never would. Not only had he grown weary of her contentious nature, but he saw clearly that she would never abide his work on the railroad, work which would take him away from her precious social circle. These things would have been reason enough, even if he hadn't fallen in love with her sister.

He could well imagine his father's rage upon learning that his son

44

had ducked out of the imposed engagement. James had carefully given the task of breaking the engagement to Virginia in order to keep her from shame. But to his parents, he'd honestly put to paper the deepest, most inner longings and turmoil of his heart—well, at least most of them. He'd spoken frankly of believing marriage to be a sacred institution, and as such, he could not go into it feeling as he did toward the woman who was to become his wife. Of course, he'd said nothing to them about Carolina. Why bother, when nothing would come of it anyway?

He turned on Greene Street and headed north, away from the harbor. His father would never understand. Leland Baldwin had taken James into the utmost confidence regarding the family's shaky financial circumstance, and James' actions would be perceived as a betrayal of such a trust.

He heard the slowing of yet another hack and turned to wave the carriage on when he heard his name being called from inside.

"Mr. Baldwin! Come join me." It was Benjamin Latrobe.

The carriage door swung open and Latrobe peered out. "You'll freeze walking all the way home. Come, let me give you a ride."

James rubbed his frozen cheeks with his gloved hand. "I believe I will." He climbed up and took the bench opposite Latrobe.

"Glad to see you're the sensible kind, Baldwin."

"Well, it is a bit colder than I'd thought. So where have you come from? I didn't see you at the board meeting."

"That's because I wasn't there," Latrobe said with a sly smile. "I've been Christmas shopping."

James felt a pang of regret at having joined up with his friend. No doubt Ben would be full of stories about Christmas and his family's plans for the holidays. Trying hard not to appear the slightest bit concerned with the matter, James only nodded in acknowledgment.

"Are you headed home to Washington City for Christmas?" Latrobe asked.

James shook his head. "No. My parents . . . well, that is to say . . ." he stammered and felt his face flush. His relationship with Ben Latrobe was such that a glib lie did not sit well. "My parents are out of the city for the holidays. They've gone south to be with family," he lied anyway.

"And will you join them?"

"No, I'm afraid I couldn't possibly be away from Baltimore that long. I want to keep my hand in on the railroad business, and I want very much to be present when McLane makes his appearance."

"But Christmas is in less than a week and a half. Have you no plans?"

"No, none," James admitted, then lest Latrobe feel pity for him he added, "I'll probably busy myself by catching up on my sleep and reading. A very pleasant way to spend some time, if I do say so."

"I'll not hear of it!" Benjamin Latrobe declared. "My Ellen would be positively beside herself to learn that her husband had been so inhospitable as to allow a friend to dine alone on Christmas."

"Honestly," James said, raising his hand, "I'll be in good spirits and quite content."

"I won't hear of it. You will share Christmas Day with us, and I will not take no for an answer."

James realized the futility of arguing and nodded consent. "I would be honored."

"Good. Now, tell me about the meeting. Did they vote McLane in?"

"The vote will take place two days after Christmas."

"Good. I'm certain of the outcome and anxious for the thing to be done. There's a great deal of work ahead of us, and now that the Point of Rocks fencing nonsense has been set aside, we can better focus our attention on the incline planes and the surveys west of Harper's."

"What exactly happened at Point of Rocks?" James asked. He was familiar with the reference point, which lay several miles east of Harper's Ferry along the Potomac. He knew of some trouble out there but had not heard details.

"The Chesapeake and Ohio Canal Company had an agreement that the B&O would fence portions along the Point of Rocks area for the purpose of separating the canal and the railroad. They were concerned that the canal horses would become spooked and possibly even jump into the canal at the noisy passing of a steam locomotive."

"That makes sense," James said.

"It makes sense, but we had no other recourse. The passage is barely wide enough to accommodate both the canal and railroad. And you know full well it has sparked more than one altercation between the canal workers and those of the B&O."

"Yes, I have heard."

"But there was no other logical place to build, and when the agreements were finally ironed out and the B&O allowed to build along the Potomac and beside the canal, the arrangement said that we were to build a high board fence along the entire passage between Point of Rocks and Harper's Ferry."

"I suppose the expense would be a hardship—"

"The expense was only a minor consideration," Latrobe interjected.

"To close the passageway off in that manner would make the railroad into a great ditch, and the snow and soil would wash into it from the surrounding hillsides. The tracks would never survive, and the trains would forever be halted and unable to proceed forward without some repair or adjustment being made."

"I hadn't imagined."

"Well, it is resolved now. The canal officials agreed to a compromise. We will only be required to build a few miles of post and rail fencing where the banks are particularly steep. These are areas where a sudden appearance of a locomotive might well turn disastrous for both parties. We're paying the canal two thousand seven hundred dollars to put the thing into place, and now everyone is happy. It was an answer to prayer."

"Truly?" James couldn't believe that he'd asked the question aloud.

Latrobe smiled. "Truly. I firmly believe God is in every detail of the B&O's development."

"I suppose that is quite possible," James answered honestly. "There have been numerous obstacles that have slowed down the progress, but always it seems some minor detail is overlooked. Then when found, the problems seem to work themselves out in one form or another."

"Exactly. I believe in divine intervention, my dear James. God's hand is upon the B&O as surely as is ours. Many folks might doubt His interest in mankind's meager attempts to tame the land, but not I. I know He is with us, and I know He will see it through."

James wished he could believe as enthusiastically as Ben. He wished that sometime in his life God might have revealed himself to be a guiding force. Now, with so many problems in his life, problems of his own making, James wasn't sure God would even care to deal with him.

I've made a real mess of things, he thought. Without a doubt, I've strayed from the master plan.

Six

First Kiss

The grand ballroom of Gadsby's Hotel was full to overflowing with swirling, colorful dancers. Overhead, crystal chandeliers lighted the room, and beneath the many pairs of slippered and booted feet the polished wood floors gleamed with mirrorlike reflections. The annual Christmas charity ball was held on behalf of the hospital, and from the look of it, Carolina guessed it to be a tremendous success. For years, her mother had been on the committee with Edith Baldwin in the planning of this grand occasion. It was the party that began the Washington Christmas social season, and it always set the tone for the months to come.

Carolina wished that her mother could have been a part of this year's celebration. It might have done her some good to busy herself with something other than tending Penny and mourning over the loss of Mary.

"Are you having a good time?" Hampton asked her and pulled her closer to keep in step with the waltz they were dancing.

Carolina found to her surprise that she truly was having fun. "Yes. This is a very pleasant party."

Hampton smiled, breaking the stern expression he'd worn for most of the evening. Carolina hadn't made it easy on him at all. From the moment he had first helped to hand her into the carriage, she'd shared hardly more than a noncommittal nod to his conversation. In fact, she'd conversed more with her slave Miriam, who acted as chaperone, than with Hampton.

"You truly are the most beautiful woman here," he commented against her ear. "That gown is positively stunning."

"Thank you," she replied in what she hoped was a pleasant tone. Carolina was rather fond of the gown herself. It was a fashionable creation of ivory satin and burgundy trim. The neckline was modestly high, to her relief, and the sleeves were puffed from shoulder to wrist.

"Did you purchase it here in the city?"

The strains of the music seemed to linger on the air even as the dance came to an end. Carolina quickly stepped away from Hampton, although he refused to release her gloved hand.

She glanced up and, meeting his serious blue eyes, found him quite intent on maintaining contact with her. "You were going to tell me about your lovely dress," he said, leading her away from the dance floor to one of the refreshment rooms.

"The seamstresses at Oakbridge made the dress," she answered and tried again to pull away without making a scene.

"Stop it!" he demanded suddenly, tightening his grip. "You've put me off all evening, even though I know your father told you to be nice to me."

Carolina's head snapped up. "How would you know that unless you were eavesdropping, sir?"

"I make it my business to stay informed. If that means I have to eavesdrop on occasion, then so be it. I think if you will just follow your father's advice and relax, you'll enjoy this evening."

"I am only here," she said with a nervous glance to see who else might be listening, "because it pleased my father for me to accompany you." Pausing, she considered her circumstance for a moment, then added, "Mr. Cabot, I still fail to see why you pursue me when I've made it clear that we are incompatible."

He paused at a table laden with food and smiled. "Would you care for refreshments?"

Just then Carolina spied Edith and Leland Baldwin. James' parents! She couldn't bear the thought of facing them just now. No doubt there would be many questions about her family, maybe even comments on Carolina's appearance at the party while still in a state of mourning. And even if Edith deemed not to bring those things up, no doubt there would be conversation about James. Her heart ached within her. She longed to know where James had taken himself off to and how he was faring. She wanted more than anything to hear news of him, but she couldn't bear the idea of facing Edith Baldwin. "Please, I need some air," she whispered, not considering how alluring her plea might sound.

"I believe there's a summer porch available for just such purposes," Hampton said, taking a quick glance around the room. "Although it surprises me that you should suggest such a thing."

Carolina felt her cheeks grow hot. "Oh, it has nothing to do with you. Stay here and eat for all I care. I'll find Miriam." She finally succeeded at pushing away from him and had started to make her way through the crowded room when he caught up to her.

"Come with me," he said and easily maneuvered her through the throng of people.

Carolina's mind raced with excuses for why Hampton should take her home, but none of them seemed feasible or believable. The idea of having to stand in her Christmas finery and make small talk with James' parents was something Carolina had little desire for. She probably shouldn't even be in public, since it had scarcely been three months since her sister's death. And not only was she here, but dressed in ivory instead of black! Her father had reasoned that she was young and deserved to break rules in order to have fun. Even more so, he'd never agreed with decking the house and its occupants in black to honor the memory of those who'd died. Were it not for her mother, Carolina reasoned, they'd probably never wear black at all.

"Here we are," Hampton said in a low, seductive voice. "And I see that we're very nearly alone."

Carolina glanced around the summer porch. There were huge potted trees and greenery, along with wicker settees and lounging couches. Carolina could see that the porch had been enclosed for winter, but it was still chilly, and the cold air rushed against her heated cheeks in a welcomed wave.

Hampton led her to a small settee, and Carolina gratefully took a seat. She knew Hampton would press her for conversation, but that was better than having to deal with Edith Baldwin. What would she say to the mother of the man who'd broken not only Virginia's heart, but her own heart as well?

Hampton pushed out the long tails of his black frock coat and took a seat in a wicker chair opposite the settee. His tall, solid frame seemed too big for such a chair, but the wicker held and Hampton smiled lazily.

Carolina felt rather like the fly caught in the spider's web. She tried to rationalize how she might convince Hampton to forget his romantic intentions, but when she looked at him, she thought of James. How wonderful the evening might have been if James Baldwin sat beside her instead of Hampton Cabot.

"I like it when you look at me like that," Hampton said.

Carolina, feeling horribly embarrassed by the suggestion that such a look was for Hampton, shook her head. "Hampton, you must put such thoughts from your mind."

His broad smile caused her to glance around. "What is it?" she asked hesitantly.

"You called me Hampton. No more Mr. Cabot for me. If I'd known that such an intimate setting would bloom the shy bud into a flower, I would have sought out such a place weeks ago."

"Mr. Cabot—"

"Don't," he said firmly. "Don't take on a pretense with me. I know you're attracted to me, and I know that your father approves. I don't want to play your society belle games—"

"How dare you!" It was Carolina's turn to interrupt. "I've not given you any reason to believe me less than sincere in my regard for you. I very adamantly do not wish to be courted by you, Mr. Cabot. I cannot state it much clearer than that. I agreed to accompany you here tonight because my father desired it. He has had so very little pleasure in his life of late that even such a sacrifice as this seemed worthwhile."

Hampton's laugh made Carolina's skin crawl.

"Your sacrifice, as you put it, seems not to have done you much harm," Hampton insisted. "I think you are simply protesting out of ignorance."

"I beg your pardon?"

"Ignorance." He stated the word with emphasis and leaned forward with a knowing look in his eye. "You are ignorant of the joys of love and the pleasures of romance and married life. You've no doubt heard all of those matronly horror stories whispered behind closed doors—"

"Stop it this minute!" Carolina exclaimed, jumping to her feet. "I will not hear such talk. My father should throttle you for such inexcusable behavior! I'm going to find Miriam and go home."

She moved past him, but Hampton lurched to his feet also and pulled her, struggling, into his arms. "You may protest all you like, but I see something in your expression that tells me what your lips will not admit."

"You see nothing that is real or intended for you, Mr. Cabot." She put her hands against the rock-hard wall of his chest and tried to force some space between them.

"If you don't want to make a scene, I'd suggest you settle down. I'm hardly going to force myself upon you in the middle of Gadsby's Christmas party."

Carolina calmed a little at this. Her father and mother would be mortified to find her in this compromising position. Maybe it was better not to struggle and attract attention to her predicament. She took a breath and tried to relax.

"That's better," he said, bending her slightly backward to accommodate his towering frame. Carolina had little choice but to look directly into his eyes. "You've had your head too long in your books,"

51

Hampton continued. "Men and women have much better things with which to occupy themselves, and I intend to show you one of them right now." Then before she could so much as utter a single word of protest, he crushed her lips with his own.

At first Carolina was desperately appalled and angry, but the longer the kiss lasted the more she had to make herself maintain her anger. Hampton's kiss was not all that terrible. She didn't actually respond by kissing him back, but neither did she fight. And when Hampton pulled away, she simply stared at him with an expression that surely must have registered the confusion she felt inside.

"Wasn't as bad as you thought it would be, now was it?" Hampton asked, dropping his hold on her.

For Carolina it was the first time a man had kissed her lips, and much to her surprise, it truly wasn't as bad as she'd presumed it would be. Hampton Cabot was quite accomplished in the art of kissing, or so she decided for herself. Having nothing else on which to base her assumption, Carolina nevertheless found her mind overflowing with thoughts and emotions.

"Well, say something. Surely I've not managed to tame that sharp tongue with one simple kiss." Hampton stared at her oddly, as though trying to decide what to do next.

Carolina's pounding heart seemed to slow a bit as her breathing came in less ragged gasps. Was Hampton right? Had she simply focused too long on her studies and missed out on the magic of coming of age? She thought of her girl friends and their giggled conversations of stolen kisses and moonlight walks. Always before, Carolina had found these things boring at best, but now she wasn't so sure. Perhaps her viewpoint had been totally wrong.

"Carolina?" Hampton's face seemed more apologetic now. "Are you ill?"

She managed to shake her head. How could she explain any of this to Hampton? To admit that she actually found his kiss tolerable would only encourage him to do it again, and *that*, she decided, would be absolutely intolerable. Struggling to clear the webs of doubt from her mind, Carolina reminded herself of the importance of remaining true to her dream. Her independent nature worked its way back to the surface of her mind, although now it was slightly tempered with questioning thoughts. Perhaps it wouldn't be so bad to marry and raise a family. It was, after all, something she'd always figured on doing. And if she was fortunate enough to find a man who believed in her dream of participating in the development of the railroad, then she would truly have it all.

James.

She wasn't at all surprised that his name came to her now. He believed in her dream. Again, when she glanced upward to Hampton, it was James' face she thought of. "James," she whispered faintly.

"What?" Hampton asked, leaning down. "What did you say?"

Carolina shook her head. "Nothing. I . . . I'd like to go home now. Please." To her surprise, Hampton's expression showed sudden sympathy.

"I'll find our chaperone and call for the carriage," he said, sounding genuinely concerned with her reaction. "Wait here and I'll return in a moment."

Carolina nodded and watched him walk away. Several other couples moved about the porch. Some secluded themselves behind trees for moments of pleasurable interlude. Carolina was fascinated by this. For all appearances, should anyone have seen her with Hampton, they would have presumed them to be very much in love.

But of course, she reminded herself, that was quite impossible. Hampton might kiss very well, but he wasn't James, and he didn't know her heart. With a heavy sigh, Carolina was surprised to find herself very close to tears.

Seven

Laying the Trap

*B*ut surely you see the benefit of rail service," Joseph Adams stated firmly, eyeing Hampton from across a coffee table in the Oakbridge drawing room.

Hampton lifted a cup of coffee to his lips and shook his head. "Too risky. The economy is in grave danger of falling apart. Should just the right elements come together, we will be in for a tremendous financial depression."

"But how can this be?" Joseph asked, motioning to a slave to refill his own cup. "The country has actually been out of debt and running with a surplus."

Hampton smiled tolerantly. "Joseph, you pay me well to keep you advised on such things, and that is what I am trying to do even now. The railroad is an interesting investment to say the least. I see the potential and the probability that this venture will develop into something of mass proportions, but I also see more. The railroad has an extremely slow record of turning a dividend back into the hands of the investor. You might well give over hundreds of thousands of dollars and never see a single cent of return for years."

"That's true," Joseph replied, stirring cream into his coffee. "However, I feel confident that whether I reap the benefits or not, my children and grandchildren will one day be greatly benefited by my risk."

Hampton could only think of the large amounts of capital being wasted. He was desperate to convince Joseph that heavy investments in the railroad were foolish, but none of his arguments seemed to register even moderate interest or concern in his employer's mind.

"I suppose my real worry comes in the fact that so many other elements come into play in the financial world. You have built for yourself a strong empire. Besides Oakbridge Plantation, you have vast holdings of land in the West, with a great many interested parties who would very much like to help you develop your property. I've been approached by four very respectable Englishmen who are intrigued by the idea of building factories on your Chicago properties."

"Factories? What kind of factories?"

Hampton shrugged. "They've not given me the details of their interest, as I was uncertain that you would want to sell. Chicago has doubled in size in the last couple of years, and there are many rumors to suggest that great improvements and extensions to the National Road will be funded and built to connect the eastern cities to that booming town."

"I see," Joseph said, considering Hampton's words. "The railroad would no doubt be of benefit to such a project as well."

Hampton frowned. The railroad was once again his nemesis to battle. "I'm certain the railroad will one day be a consideration, but the average citizen cannot afford such luxury. What they can afford is to use their own wagons, horses, and oxen to move them where they desire to go. If the National Road is extended and built to include a number of adjoining roadways, the people of America will not only find travel more available, but also more affordable."

"I suppose both are really necessary." Joseph looked thoughtfully into his cup. "Eventually, the railroad would provide speed and be able to haul a great deal more in a shorter time than teams of oxen upon the trail."

"Yes, but if I correctly understand the lay of the land, you own some of the very property that will be affected by the National Road expansion. Think of the hotels you could build and the services you could offer to the weary traveler. As far as sound investments go, this would turn you a solid profit as soon as the road and establishment went into place."

"I don't know. I suppose it is something to think on."

"Well, for now, as your commission merchant, I am advising you to be cautious with your investments. I didn't want to share bad news right away, especially given the holiday spirit and all, but things could be better."

"Better? In what way?"

"There are problems with this country's economic foundation that might well erupt over time to encompass the financial affairs of the average man. And while you are a man of means and prosperity, that could all change tomorrow."

"It is truly as bad as all that?"

"I'm afraid so," Hampton admitted. "As you know, last year's cotton crop was destroyed by New York's business district fire. Add to that, this year's crops were bought at only marginally acceptable prices, and if it weren't for the high percentage of English investors, we might not have seen a profit at all."

Joseph shook his head. "Sometimes I'd like to walk away from everything." He put his cup down and stared at the ceiling for a moment. "There are tremendous responsibilities with a family this size. Not to mention the obligations of the plantation system and the people here who are dependent upon us for their every need. Our northern brethren may curse slavery, but I ask you, where would these people go? How could they possibly care for themselves? Would northerners so generously take in and patiently support an uneducated man who only knows the skills of the field? No one stops to think on those things. Now with Mary gone and Margaret devastated by the loss, I want only to pull the rest of my family closer, and yet they all seem to be slipping away."

Hampton realized the opportunity Joseph's frank discussion had lent him, and he seized upon it. "What of your sons? Do they not plan to return to help with the plantation?"

Joseph's expression was one of bittersweet reflection. "I don't imagine they will. I was forced at an early age to assume the responsibilities of Oakbridge. I met the challenge and did as I knew I should, but in the course of events I lost a great deal that was important to me."

"Such as?" Hampton questioned, unable to look at the wealth around him and imagine what was lacking.

"I lost my dreams. I'd always desired to go west and explore the country, but a man of responsibility cannot very well leave his wife and family to fend for themselves." Joseph paused and smiled rather apologetically. "That's behind me now, but the reason I brought it up has more to do with your question than you might imagine. I won't force my sons to take on the duties of plantation owner when their hearts clearly lie elsewhere."

The conversation was taking on new and exciting possibilities for Hampton. Always before, he'd presumed that his advance to fortune and fame would end when Joseph died. He had believed it necessary to lay in store for himself a great treasure of wealth and the security of a socially acceptable bride. Marrying one of the Adams girls would not only assure his place in proper company, but might offer him a means of expanding his meager holdings as well.

Finally he asked Joseph, "Who will follow then after you are gone?"

"That's a good question. With Maine completely devoted to the work of God, and York ensconced quite happily in the political arena, it will most likely fall into the hands of one of my daughters and her spouse."

Hampton smiled. "I know this may sound quite bold, but given my interest in Carolina and my knowledge of your financial affairs, I wonder if you might not consider me as a possible solution. I feel confident that it will only be a matter of time until I propose marriage to Carolina."

"What!" Joseph exclaimed. "Has it grown as serious as all that?"

Hampton tried to appear humble and boyish. "I don't know how else to say this but to come right out with it. I've fallen in love with your daughter, and I hope very much for her to become my wife."

Joseph was stunned and his expression changed from one of surprise to disbelief. "But Carolina seems anything but interested."

"Yes, I know," Hampton replied. "I have to tell you something, and perhaps you will have nothing further to do with me after this, but confession is good for the soul."

Joseph eyed him suspiciously. "Then, by all means, confess."

Hampton smiled. "When I escorted Carolina to the Christmas ball, she and I, well that is to say, we shared a moment of intimacy." Hampton fought hard to keep from showing even a portion of arrogance. "I kissed her, sir, and I do apologize for my boldness."

A slight smile crept over Joseph's face. "I see. And what might I ask was my daughter's response?"

Hampton took Joseph's smile as an indication of acceptance and grinned. "She didn't refuse it, if that's what you're wondering. In fact, she was the one to suggest the seclusion of the summer porch. She's very determined when she sets her mind to something."

Joseph laughed out loud at this. "That she is. But I have to say that I'm surprised. She has adamantly refused to consider my suggestions that she accept your courtship. I don't tell you this to cause you grief, but only to offer you my insight on the matter."

Hampton nodded. "I, too, must share an insight that might well clarify the entire situation for you. Carolina admitted her interest in me. We talked all the way home from the party, and she said that her family was most important to her, but that you held her heart above all others." In fact, that ride home had passed in all but total silence. Nevertheless, Hampton continued. "You see, Carolina knows that it would grieve you to lose another family member just yet. She told me that with Maryland's death and her mother's sorrow over the loss, she couldn't possibly consider marriage."

"She said that?" Joseph seemed genuinely puzzled.

"That and so much more. I would like to say that she declared her love for me," Hampton said in a tone of false humility, "but she would not speak on the matter, especially with her slave occupying the same coach. Her eyes suggested to me, however, that she would do so in a minute, were her family obligations not so strong."

"I had no idea." Joseph got up and paced the Persian carpet in front of the fireplace.

"That is why I made the suggestion I did. Perhaps if Carolina knew that her husband would assume responsibility of Oakbridge and that she wouldn't be taken away from those she loved, she would open her heart to me and agree to marriage."

Joseph stopped pacing and looked Hampton in the eye. "The idea is not without appeal to me, Hampton. You've served my family well and have been a worthy adviser. I will take this matter under consideration, on that you may be certain."

Hampton got to his feet and reached out to shake Joseph's hand. "You won't be sorry, sir. Carolina is a wonderful young woman, and I know that your decision might well make all the difference in the world." Pulling out his watch fob, Hampton grimaced. "I must hurry now, or I'll never make the train to Baltimore."

"I'll look forward to your return," Joseph said in a thoughtful tone that suggested his mind was already considering Hampton's suggestion.

Smiling to himself, Hampton bid Joseph good-bye. Too bad Carolina was conspicuously absent. It was of no matter, he reasoned. Soon, if things went his way, she'd be answering to him for every detail of her life. Even the gray, snow-laden skies couldn't discourage him as he bounded into the Adams' carriage. The trap was laid. Now it was only a matter of time until the bait was taken.

Eight

Deciding the Future

*C*arolina sat beside Penny, faithfully rereading her favorite Bible story. Joseph and the coat of many colors fascinated Penny, and Carolina didn't mind one bit the fact that she'd already read the story three times that week.

"Miz Carolina?" Miriam peeked her head through the open door. "Yo papa says to come quicklike to the li'bry."

Carolina nodded and handed Penny the Bible. "You can read on for yourself. I'll be back as soon as I can." She tousled the sandy brown curls on Penny's head, then planted a kiss on her little sister's forehead. The frail girl beamed up a smile and yawned.

"I wanna rest just a little," she said in tones that seemed so old for a child. Not mature, but rather aged and brittle.

Carolina nodded, sadly realizing her sister's condition might never improve. Penny's heart was not even strong enough to allow limited moments of play, and Carolina noted that she slept more and more often of late.

Straightening her back and stretching, Carolina put the gloomy thoughts to the back of her mind. There were so many sad things in her home these days. It seemed better to take them out to examine one at a time. To deal with everything at once was simply too much to expect of any one person.

Sweeping away the wrinkles in her green calico gown, Carolina made her way to the library, wondering all the while what might be wrong.

"Papa?" she called out and knocked lightly upon the open door.

"Come in, Carolina," Joseph said, getting to his feet.

Carolina noted that Leland Baldwin occupied the chair nearest her father's desk, and that he, too, was struggling to stand. She held her breath, not quite sure what Leland's presence in the house might mean. Had James come, too?

She curtsied lightly and felt her chest tighten. "Mr. Baldwin." She glanced around the room nervously, assuring herself that James had not come.

Joseph kissed her lightly on the forehead, then offered her his cheek. Carolina readily kissed her father and took the chair beside Leland's. The last person she'd expected to see today was James' father. But here he was, and there was no escaping the conversation that would ensue.

"Mr. Baldwin and I have been discussing the Potomac and Great Falls Railroad," Joseph began. "There was some concern that we might wish to put an end to our venture, given the fact that James is no longer available to assist us."

Carolina fought to steady her nerves. This was her opportunity to find out where James had gone. "Where has he gone off to?" she asked, trying to sound casual.

Leland grew red in the face. "I'm not entirely certain. I believe the railroad has led him west."

Carolina looked at her father. "Does this keep us from advancing our cause?"

"Not necessarily. Leland was just showing me the new railroad stock certificates he had printed prior to Mary's death." Joseph handed her one of the certificates and smiled. "As you can see, they are most impressive."

"Yes," Carolina remarked, looking over the details of the intricately etched border. The words *Potomac and Great Falls Railroad* graced the top. "It's wonderful." She was amazed at the feeling of satisfaction it gave her to actually hold a visible part of their dreams.

"You can see for yourself that your name is listed as a board member and officer," Joseph pointed out.

Carolina found the words *Carolina Adams, Secretary, Board of Directors* situated directly under the name *James Baldwin, Vice-President, Board of Directors*. She felt her breath catch in her throat. To see them joined there on paper made her feel flushed and almost giddy. It was a sensation she'd not expected.

"How marvelous," she murmured and handed the certificate back to her father.

"Mr. Baldwin assures me the certificates will promote the sales of stock. People will see the quality, as well as the Baldwin and Adams names, and realize that this is a trustworthy investment."

"I was uncertain . . . well, that is to say . . ." Leland paused uncomfortably. Joseph and Carolina both looked at him in anticipation of his words. "Given the recent events between my son and your daughter Virginia, I was uncertain if you wished to continue with James as a partner. After all, I cannot vouch for when he will return to Washington."

Joseph nodded solemnly, but it was Carolina who spoke. "It is hardly James' fault that Virginia broke the engagement. Why should he be punished for something out of his control?"

She saw her father exchange a wary glance with Leland. It was almost as though the two men were sizing up what the other thought of her statement. She continued, only mildly confused by their reaction. "I say let James stay on, and when he returns to Washington, he can resume an active role. No doubt he's working hard with the B&O and learning much that will benefit us in the long run."

"I'm sure you are right," Joseph replied and nodded to Leland. "We shall keep him as a partner, but I suggest we move him from the active role of vice-president and allow his father to fill that position."

"I have no objections to that," she replied. "Just so long as James knows he is welcome to continue with us on this project."

"But of course," Joseph replied.

Carolina smiled at her father and noted that Leland seemed to relax a great deal. She tried to imagine what James' reaction would be to such a discussion, but she found her mind blurred with images of James' face and Hampton's kiss.

"Mr. Baldwin has also had some encouraging news from the Virginia legislature," Joseph continued. "They are considering a positive response to our request for a charter, but there are conditions that Leland and I find quite unacceptable."

"Such as?" Carolina asked seriously. She forced herself to put aside her childish memories and concentrate on the business at hand. At sixteen, she knew full well it was a privilege to be included in such a matter.

Leland pulled a letter from his satchel and handed it over to Joseph. "They want twenty-five percent of the profits, with unlimited right-of-ways, and in fifty years the railroad would become state property."

"That's robbery!" Carolina declared indignantly. "Maryland and the city of Baltimore combined receive far less than twenty-five percent of the profits from the B&O Railroad. And they certainly never demanded ownership. You can't let them get away with this, Father."

Joseph smiled at her. "I knew you'd feel quite passionately about it. Especially given the fact that while in fifty years I will be dead and gone, you'll be a feisty old woman of sixty-six."

"It isn't only that," she declared. "This railroad should be something that generations of Adamses"—she paused and looked at Leland's perspiring face—"*and* Baldwins can participate in with pride."

"I quite agree with my daughter, Baldwin."

"I must say, Carolina, your grasp of the working railroad is quite amazing to me. I thought it less than wise to allow you on as an active partner," Leland admitted, "but you are proving yourself to be well-read on the matter and highly opinionated."

Joseph laughed at this. "Of that you may be assured, my good man."

Carolina smiled but still felt an odd sense of rejection by James' father. Perhaps he was just preoccupied with his own interests, or maybe he was still unable to feel comfortable discussing such lofty matters with a mere girl. Either way, she didn't care. It didn't have to concern her; unless, of course, it altered her own plans and dreams.

———

Leland rested uncomfortably in the carriage. His gout was bothering him fiercely, but so, too, was his conscience. He could deal with swindling a world of strangers, but Joseph Adams had been a good friend for a great many years. When he showed him the railroad certificates, Leland had known the response would be one of extreme enthusiasm. What he hadn't expected was Carolina's educated participation in their discussion.

For Leland, the matter was simple. So simple, in fact, he had worried that James' departure from Washington would forever alter his own plans. He could tell from Carolina's words that she didn't know the truth of James and Virginia's broken engagement. But Joseph did. Leland could see it in his expression and read the unspoken questions in his old friend's eyes.

Apparently Virginia must have quietly shared James' unforgivably bad manners with her father. Leland cursed and threw his satchel to the opposite side of the carriage. James had ruined his plans for financial security. If only James had married Virginia, Joseph would never think twice at offering any monetary assistance needed. Plus, there would have been a hefty dowry offered, one that Leland had instructed his son to take in cash rather than land.

The twinge of pain in his chest seemed to match the one in his foot. His doctor would no doubt offer him little remedy except to advise him to take to his bed and wait out the worst of it. Most likely it was nothing more than indigestion from thinking about James. Breathing deeply he tried to steady his nerves and dismiss all thoughts of his son. The boy had no idea what trouble he'd really caused in following his heart instead of his father's direction. However, despite the congenial reception he had received at Oakbridge, Leland still worried consequences might be forthcoming in the future. Leland would have to work hard to promote healing between the two families.

There was simply too much at stake to find himself on the bad side of Joseph Adams. He was weaning himself rather rapidly away from the banking industry, knowing without a doubt that his days in that field were numbered. His bank was failing miserably, and it was only a matter of time until someone started a run on coins versus paper bank notes and the bank would fold altogether. And why? Because there simply wasn't enough capital to back the bank drafts.

He'd given it a good go, however. He'd managed to employ his brother Samuel to assist in locating a good counterfeiter and, with the aid of that man, had padded his losses with forged bank notes. It had been all too simple. The forgeries were of the highest quality, and because Leland owned the bank, no one questioned his operation. Of course, the forged drafts were drawn against other banks, and Leland had but to flood the marketplace with the counterfeits in order to benefit himself. As rival banks found themselves inundated with the forgeries, they had little choice but to fold up their operations, leaving more and more federal deposits to be placed with Leland. But now, even those days were numbered, and Leland knew the best thing to do was to move on.

The pain in his chest subsided, and Leland shifted his weight gingerly to prop his foot on the carriage seat. He cursed his age and weight and then cursed his own foolishness at not taking better care of himself.

Everything had gotten beyond his control. James. The bank. His life. It seemed as though everything had been tossed into the air and left to fall where it might. And that was something Leland could not afford to allow. He had to retain control. Especially of the railroad schemes.

Railroads were the new rage of the age, and while Leland thought them a terrible waste of honest efforts, he could see a possibility of profit in dishonest dealings. He could still remember Joseph approaching him at the celebration of the B&O Railroad's new Washington Branch.

Had it really been only a year ago, last August? It seemed as though an eternity had passed.

Joseph had taken an immediate liking to the railroad, but Leland had cautioned him to move slowly. Now Leland was the one pressing things forward, and that had all come about by the realization that there was a profit to be made with very little risk. Little risk, because Leland never intended for the investors' money to pass any further than his own pockets. People were fools. They were greedy and hungry for "get-rich-quick" schemes. And Leland was only too happy to oblige them. It quickly became apparent that Leland could propose plans for a great many railroads. On paper, they would appear quite legitimate. On paper, he would have the facts and figures, surveys and designs, all arranged to present a perfectly ordered picture. And thus, Leland's schemes were brought to life, and paper railroads became his new means of support.

Even the proposed P&GF Railroad was nothing more than paper. Oh, he made it appear to be more. The certificates had been a nice touch, he thought, and they were a good means to promote the proposed line. With the prestigious names of Adams and Baldwin on the intricately designed stock, investors were not hard to talk out of their money. It was also to Leland's benefit that the actual creation of a rail line was a long, drawn-out process of obtaining state charters, detailing surveys, and purchasing land. Not to mention that most of the equipment used in building such a line would have to come from England. It could literally take years until ground-breaking ceremonies were a reality. So it was just a matter of keeping the investors satisfied that plans were actually moving forward, in spite of the visual lack of evidence.

But none of this concerned him half as much as how he might encourage Joseph Adams to take less of a personal interest in the running of the P&GF Railroad. It would be impossible to keep the thing strictly a paper railroad if Joseph kept such an active hand in the project. Then, too, Carolina Adams could prove to be just as big of a problem for him. He would have to somehow figure a way to occupy her so that she wouldn't be wise to his conniving. He pondered this matter for a time before dozing off to the jostling of the carriage. His last conscious thoughts were of his wayward son and the unexpected void his absence had created.

Nine

Questions of Love

A week after Hampton Cabot had kissed her, Carolina still found it nearly impossible to eat, think, or sleep properly. Having tossed and turned most of the night, she sighed and forced herself to sit up in bed. She was exhausted in trying to dispel the strange emotions and sensations that crept upon her when she least expected it.

I'm not in love with Hampton, she reasoned. I just can't be. She fell back against the bed pillows and tried to rationalize her turmoil. It was just a kiss. One kiss. My first kiss.

"That must be it!" she said and jumped out of bed. "It lingers in my mind because Hampton was the first man to really kiss me."

She paced her room, the nightgown of white lawn flaring out behind her. For days now she'd been nearly heartsick. She'd been confident that she was in love with James Baldwin, but when Hampton kissed her it created a shadow of doubt in her mind. It was almost as if someone had placed a veil between her heart and the memories of James.

She flung open the wardrobe doors and studied her day dresses for a moment before choosing a dark plum-colored wool. Chilled to the bone, Carolina quickly dressed herself and was pulling on heavy black stockings when Miriam appeared.

"I s'pose yo didn't sleep a wink last night neither," Miriam said, throwing back Carolina's curtains. "Yo's gwanna run yo'self into a grave, Miz Carolina, iffen yo don get mo rest and food."

Carolina dismissed her worry. "These have been hard times, Miriam. Don't pretend with me that your rest comes any easier. And I've noticed that your waistline is considerably smaller than before Mary died."

Miriam nodded. "Times is hard and that's a fact."

Carolina took a chair at her dressing table and allowed Miriam to comb her dark brown hair into a simple chignon. Her mind trailed back to her earlier thoughts as Miriam worked in silence. Hampton wanted her, of that there was no question. But for what reasons, she was uncertain.

I'm from a good family, she rationalized. But then, so was he. He'd been orphaned and taken under her father's wing some years ago, and through Joseph's trust and tutelage, Hampton had matured and gained the highly respectable position of being the family's commission merchant. She knew that her father paid Hampton quite well, so she doubted money would be the sole motivation for a proposal. But Hampton also looked at her in a way that she'd seen other men look at Virginia. It was a look that many called passionate, but to others it was pure and simple lust.

Miriam finished with Carolina's hair and left to attend to Virginia and Georgia. Carolina moved across the room to look at her reflection in the cheval mirror. She had definitely blossomed into a woman. She ran her hands down the curving sides of her body and found a shapeliness there that even a year ago had been far less evident.

She smiled, remembering an overheard conversation at church when Mrs. Milford had commented to Mrs. Wilmington that Virginia Adams was quickly being overtaken by her younger sisters and would soon no longer be the belle of the county. Of course, at the time Carolina had presumed the comment to be more intended for fourteen-year-old Georgia Adams, who had made it her goal to break every heart within a fifty-mile radius.

Thinking of Georgia, Carolina frowned. She saw something distasteful in the way her little sister treated people, but especially in the way she treated men. Georgia seemed to flirt without shame and make promises with her eyes that she could never begin to keep. Carolina had tried to talk to her, but Georgia had snapped that if she was going to die young, she would do it only after having lived a full life. Carolina had tried to assure her that she wasn't going to die young, but Georgia would hear nothing of it. She pointed out that Mary was already gone and Penny lay sick in bed, so she wasn't about to take any chances.

If their mother had been given to more days of clarity and sense than to depression and forgetfulness, Carolina knew that Georgia would never have been allowed such behavior. Their father was too overworked and busy to take seriously the gossip about his children. After all, Carolina thought, the gossip about her desire to further her education and play a part in the railroad hadn't phased Joseph Adams at all. He couldn't abide gossip and gave it no credence whatsoever.

"Don't tell me you're too busy to bid your big brother good morning," a voice called from the open bedroom door.

"York!" Carolina squealed in delight and ran to embrace her favorite brother. Wrapping her arms around him she exclaimed, "I didn't know you were coming home!"

He easily lifted her and walked into the room, spinning her around several times before setting her back down. At twenty-two, York Adams cut a dashing figure. Lean and medium in height, his brown-black hair and steely blue eyes resembled that of their father's. Some said he was the spitting image of a younger Joseph Adams, and York very much liked the idea and took it as a high compliment.

"Thought I'd surprise everyone. My, but don't you look all grown up. I swear, if I weren't your brother, I'd be running after you like everyone else."

Carolina waved away his declaration. "No one is running after me."

"No one?" York asked with a mischievous twinkle in his eye. "That's not what I heard."

Carolina smiled. "So, tell me what you heard."

"Oh," he said, looking up at the ceiling, "it will cost you."

"Cost me what?" Carolina asked in a tone of disbelief. "York Adams, after years of keeping silent about your misbehaving deeds, I think you owe me plenty."

York laughed. "All right, have it your way." He sat down on the bed and leaned back on his elbows. "Talk in Washington is that you and Hampton Cabot are quite an item." Carolina blushed and York grinned. "I guess I heard right."

"No, you did not. Hampton fancies himself interested in courting me, but I have not given him any indication that I feel the same."

"Well, folks said you two were dancing up a storm at the charity ball. I was supposed to be there that night, but President Jackson needed me more at the White House. You do realize he's not been well?"

"Father told me," Carolina said solemnly. "I hope it isn't serious. I truly like that man."

"And he is quite taken with you. Told me to invite you to the White House Christmas party."

"What!"

"It's true." York glanced up with a look that suggested he'd not said anything of any consequence whatsoever. "That's why I'm here."

Carolina gasped. "I can't believe it. He really invited me?"

"He did indeed. He said that he knew I fancied the company of a particular young woman in Washington, but since she would be accompanying her father to the party, why didn't I bring my lovely sister Carolina."

"I'm so honored!" Carolina said, coming to sit beside him on the bed. "The President has invited me to the White House." The awe in her voice was evident. Then without warning, she jumped back up and confronted York. "What particular young woman have you fancied the company of?"

York threw her a lazy expression. "I wondered if you would catch on to that."

"Of course I would. Now tell me everything. Who is she?"

"Her name is Lucille, but I call her Lucy. She's the daughter of Henry Alexander, a congressman from Pennsylvania."

"I see. How did you meet?" she asked and once again sat down beside him.

"We met at a White House function. She attended with her father. She's acted as hostess and escort to him since the death of her mother several years ago. We were seated side by side at dinner and naturally fell into conversation."

"I'm sure that was a tremendous burden for you to bear," Carolina said with a laugh. "What does she look like?"

York rolled over on his side, and the look on his face was one of pure adoration. "She's beautiful, Carolina. Dark eyes and black hair and skin the color of fresh cream. And she's quite besot with love for me."

"Love?" she questioned. "Are you sure it's love?"

"Very much so," York replied without seeming to have any misgivings.

"And . . . well . . . do you love her?"

York sobered. "Quite deeply."

Carolina found an unexpected interest in this turn of their conversation. Naturally, she was very excited about her brother's love for Lucy Alexander, but more so she realized York might help her to better understand her own feelings.

"How do you know it's really love?" she probed.

York drew a deep breath and appeared to think on this question for a moment. "Because when I wake up, it's Lucy I think about first. And it's Lucy I consider throughout the day, and it's her face I see when I close my eyes at night."

"And that's how you know it's love?" Carolina questioned in a doubtful tone.

"That and other reasons. Lucy and I were meant for each other. We share many of the same interests and ideals. Lucy was brought up in a very politically active home, and politics and government are in her blood. She'd never balk at living in Washington, although it has been called an uncivilized town not fit for ladies. She's lived in the city with her father, sharing a small rented house and acting as his hostess when he entertains diplomats and other officials, and she would be a tremendous asset to my career."

"And that's why you love her?"

York chuckled. "No . . . well, maybe in part. But only because it goes hand in hand with what I said about her sharing my interests. I could never love a woman who feared public life and desired nothing more than a quiet plantation owner for a husband. But to answer your question, I love Lucy mostly because . . . well . . . because she's Lucy." He grinned at her as if his words explained all of the mysteries of the world.

Carolina bit her lip and pondered this information for a moment. She couldn't very well ask York about Hampton's kiss. York would find it totally out of line that Hampton had taken such liberties, and who knew what might follow after that? But she wanted so much for York to explain to her why she could still feel Hampton's lips upon her own, and why even the memory of that first kiss caused her heart to race as it was doing just then.

"Have you ever kissed her?" Carolina blurted out without meaning to.

York looked at her in complete astonishment. "What a thing to ask!"

Carolina frowned. "I didn't mean to be so nosy. I just wondered if you and Lucy . . . oh, just forget it."

York nearly roared with laughter and got up from the bed, pulling Carolina upward with him. "We're going to be late for breakfast, but because I like you more than almost anyone else in the world, I will tell you what you want to know." He leaned down and whispered in her ear, "Yes, I've kissed Miss Lucy."

But this didn't stop Carolina's curiosity; instead, it only fed the flames. "Did you . . . I mean did she . . ." She paused, trying to think of a way to sound discreet. "Did you like it?"

York rolled his eyes. "Of course I liked it. I liked it very much. Now stop asking so many questions and tell me what this is all about."

Carolina shrugged, realizing that she'd reached the limit of what York would share. "I guess I see all of my friends falling in love and getting married, and I just want to know what it is that makes them certain they've chosen the right person to spend their lives with."

York put his arm around her and led her into the hall. "Don't worry, little sister. You'll know when the right one comes along. Believe me."

Carolina hugged him and smiled. "I guess that makes sense," she replied, but in truth, it didn't. She was just as confused now as she had been before. Maybe even more.

Lucy Alexander

*I*n a gown of burgundy velvet and gold ruching, Carolina entered the White House on the arm of her brother. She felt a tremor of excitement that reminded her of the charity ball she'd attended with Hampton Cabot. But more than this, she relished the treatment she received by those in attendance. Stately women, dressed elegantly in their finery, actually greeted her with respectful regard. Gentlemen, who might not otherwise have spoken two words of greeting in normal circumstances, welcomed her with a chivalry that only intensified her enjoyment of the evening.

She was of age, and it was understood and accepted that she was to be treated as an adult. Not only this, but she had been invited to a White House function because of her family's connection to the President. This fact might have gone unnoticed, but Andrew Jackson appeared and made a clear recognition of Carolina's presence.

"I'm so delighted you came," he told her in a ragged voice that betrayed his failing health.

"I'm honored," Carolina said, curtsying low, "that you extended an invitation to me."

Jackson smiled benevolently and held out his hand to help her rise. "I so enjoyed our conversation last summer."

He referred to that afternoon he had spent on the Oakbridge veranda—an afternoon of positively wondrous delight for Carolina. She'd been allowed to speak with and ask questions of the President of the United States. And not only this, but she'd received considerate answers, and her own opinion had been sought more than once in return.

"Your visit is among my fondest memories," said Carolina, meaning every word. "I was nearly beside myself with joy when York extended the invitation for me to accompany him here."

Jackson patted her hand. "My dear, it is my pleasure. I might ask a favor of you, however."

Carolina couldn't imagine what he might need of her, and York only shrugged his ignorance on the matter when she cast a glance his way. "I'll do whatever I can," she finally answered.

"This party is hardly such that would allow for private conversation," he began, "and because I have enjoyed a great friendship with your family, particularly your father and brother, I'm hoping you will come and dine with me during the holidays and convince your father and mother to accompany you as well."

Carolina grimaced. "My mother is still quite devastated by the loss of our youngest sister," she said in a hushed tone, "and my father is constantly at her side. I doubt quite seriously that he would leave Oakbridge."

York nodded and added, "I'm certain they would be honored at the invitation but would extend their regrets."

"Quite understandable. I was greatly sorrowed to hear of your sister's death, Miss Adams."

"Thank you, sir."

"Perhaps you and York would still do me the honor of joining me one evening next week?"

Carolina looked to York, who answered for them both. "I'm certain Carolina and I could make ourselves available."

"Splendid!" Jackson replied and fell into a fit of coughing that caused Carolina to study him with grave regard. "Don't concern yourself with this old man," he told her. Dabbing a handkerchief to his mouth, he offered her a broad smile. "As long as I refrain from dancing, I shouldn't cause my doctor too much grief."

"I do pray that your health improves," Carolina said with a sympathetic smile.

"Knowing that you will share my table next week gives me all the incentive I need to recover my health."

Several people standing close enough to overhear the conversation exchanged comments of surprise and afterward seemed to look upon Carolina as someone special.

Jackson was led away to greet several important figures, while Carolina stood in complete fascination at York's side. The White House had been festively decorated in Christmas holly and pine boughs. Candles dressed with red and gold ribbons graced every corner of the impressive room and illuminated it cheerfully. Even the people themselves became ornamental extensions of holiday trimmings.

Carolina heard a group of people laughing from somewhere behind her and turned to find an enthusiastic couple sharing a mistletoe kiss. This only served as a reminder of Hampton's kiss, and for a moment a shadow was cast upon her revelry. She saw the tender way in which the woman looked into the eyes of the man who'd just kissed her. It must be love she feels, Carolina reasoned. Otherwise, how could she look at him like that?

"Is something wrong?" York asked her.

Carolina immediately sought to mask her feelings. "Why do you ask?"

"Your expression just now suggested some type of distress. I thought maybe you were overly worried about Jackson," York suggested.

"Of course, I am quite concerned about him."

"But that's not exactly what's troubling you just now, is it?"

She found such tenderness in her brother's eyes that she couldn't help but be honest. Placing her gloved hand upon his arm, she sighed. "I'm still trying to better understand love."

York chuckled. "Is that all? You might well spend an entire lifetime trying to understand such a subject." He walked her to a more private corner of the room and offered her a seat. "Why don't you explain to me why this subject is of such vital importance just now?" He sat down beside her and waited patiently for her explanation.

Carolina shook her head. "I never imagined that my head would be filled with such fanciful ideas. I suppose coming of age started a forward progression that I cannot turn my back on. Nevertheless, I'm not entirely certain that I'm ready for it."

"Who said you had to be ready for anything?"

Carolina watched the people passing by them and considered this for a moment. "York, something happened the other night. I haven't told anyone about it, and I hesitate to tell you because I don't want you to become angry about it."

York raised a brow. "I must say, you more than have my attention now. Pray continue."

"Hampton Cabot kissed me at the charity ball. We were on the summer porch, and very much alone, and he kissed me."

York frowned. "I can't pretend that Cabot's liberties are acceptable to me. Did you prompt such an action?"

"No, certainly not!" Carolina exclaimed, then reconsidered. "At least, I don't think I did. See, that's the problem, or at least a part of it. I didn't want to go with Hampton to the party, but Papa encouraged it, and because I thought it would please him, I agreed. Hampton was very nice, very polite and such, but . . . well"—she paused trying to consider how she might explain the matter to her brother—"I suppose I was the one who put myself into the position of being alone with him. I saw Mr. and Mrs. Baldwin, and for some reason I just didn't want to face them, especially Mrs. Baldwin. I know that you probably don't understand, but I asked Hampton to take me for some air. He escorted me to the summer porch, and once there he began to talk to me about romance and love."

"And what did Mr. Cabot say?"

"I don't really even remember, except that he said I'd had my nose in books so long that I didn't really understand what life and love were all about. Then he took me into his arms and kissed me." She could feel her face grow hot at this confession.

"Do you want me to speak with him on the matter?"

"No!" Carolina stated adamantly. "That is not why I mentioned it to you at all."

"Then why?"

York seemed genuinely concerned, and it touched Carolina's heart that he could care so much for her. Biting at her lower lip, she decided the truth was probably better than anything else. "York, I don't love Hampton Cabot. I can't even abide the man most of the time."

"But?"

"But . . . I enjoyed his kiss. It was my first time, you see," she lowered her eyes, unable to face her brother.

"And this is what has been bothering you?" There was amusement in his tone.

Carolina sighed again and nodded. "I suppose I'm just very confused about it all. Is it possible to enjoy someone's kiss and not be in love with them?"

"I believe it is." She looked up to find him smiling and he continued. "You certainly don't need to feel obligated to marry the man just because he kissed you. Nor do you need to concern yourself with the fact that you enjoyed it." He took her hand in his and gave it a squeeze. "I can scarcely believe you're old enough to even have this conversation with me. You've grown up so fast and become a very beautiful woman. And, because of that, I'd like to offer you a bit of brotherly advice."

"Please," Carolina said, anxiously hoping York could dispel her confusion.

"Many men will try to woo you with tender words and kisses. To speak to a woman in such a fashion is a long-practiced way of breaking her will. Honorable men will approach you with proper intentions and honest love, and they will desire that you feel the same for them. Other men will merely see that you are young and beautiful and innocent, and their intentions might well be to further their own purposes and advantages. Do you understand what I'm saying?"

"Yes, I think so. But what if I feel love for someone and then find that it isn't returned?"

"That's always a possibility and always very difficult to deal with. I'm not even sure I have the answer for you, but I do believe that if it's meant to be, both people will feel the same toward each other, in time. Just don't rush it and see what happens." Then without warning York got to his feet. "Lucy is here. Come. I want you to meet her first thing."

Carolina glanced across the room to find a young woman of exotic beauty on the arm of a thin, balding man. Lucille Alexander was stunning with her heart-shaped face and long dark lashes. Her ebony eyes seemed to take in everything at once, and Carolina found herself holding her breath as the introductions were made.

"How wonderful to meet you," Lucy said with a smile of genuine affection. "York has told me so much about you, and I honestly feel as though I already know you."

Carolina felt immediately at ease. "I'm afraid I'm just now learning about you. York scarcely makes it home these days, and when he does, he rarely has time to share his secrets with me."

Lucy laughed and whispered, "I'm afraid I may have something to do with the reason he's so long from home."

Carolina looked at York, who merely shrugged and looked heavenward. She then returned a smile to Lucy and replied, "I'd much rather he be at such a noble cause than to be burying himself in the argumentative processes of government."

"Mr. Adams, if I might have a few moments of your time," Henry Alexander interrupted, "there is a matter of importance on which I need your consideration."

"But, Father, this is a Christmas party," Lucy protested. "You promised me that you would not work so very hard during the holidays."

Henry smiled indulgently. "I assure you we will only be a few minutes. I know you and Miss Adams can entertain yourselves during that time."

Carolina watched on as Lucy interacted with her father and York. She was more beautiful than Carolina could have ever imagined. Her alabaster skin was sharply contrasted by her ebony hair and eyes. She reminded Carolina of a porcelain doll, so dainty and fragile, yet there was a fire in her eyes that spoke of strength and independence.

"I truly am happy for the time to know you better," Lucy said, bringing Carolina out of her thoughts.

"As am I."

"York tells me you enjoy reading and studying on new subjects."

"That is true," Carolina admitted.

Lucy gave her a conspiratorial smile. "I confess I'm guilty of the same."

"You?" Carolina asked in surprise.

"You can't sit at as many diplomatic and political tables as I have and not be fascinated by the details passing in conversation."

Carolina felt she'd met a kindred spirit in Lucy. "I've eavesdropped on more of my father's private meetings than I'd care to admit to. York has even helped me on one or two occasions. He's always respected my desire to learn."

Lucy nodded. "I can imagine he would. But, you see, the difference between York and other men is that York is not threatened by an intelligent woman. He's confident in himself and is very knowledgeable. And I would even go so far as to say that your brother is quite willing to learn from a woman, should he find her with knowledge of importance to him."

"York is very special," Carolina confessed. "When he told me that he'd met you, I must say I was rather jealous. Now, however, meeting you and speaking our hearts, I find that you are quite an acceptable choice."

Lucy reached out and linked her arm through Carolina's. "I know we shall be great friends, Miss Adams."

"Please call me Carolina."

"And you will call me Lucy."

"Happily," Carolina said, feeling as though she'd just been given an exquisite gift.

"Now you must tell me about Oakbridge. York says so very little about it, and even when I do get him to speak on it, he talks in acreages and crop profits."

Carolina laughed. "I've no doubt that is true. York is far happier with his politics. But as for Oakbridge . . ." She paused, looking thoughtful. "Oakbridge is a world unto itself. We're not far from Falls Church, and really not so very far from Washington City. Oakbridge sits alongside Dominion Creek, and because the creek is particularly broad where our road passes over, Grandfather Adams built a bridge of oak on which to cross."

"Thus Oakbridge," Lucy said with a knowing nod.

"Yes." Carolina continued, drawing from a mental picture of her home. "The house is of the Greek style with six white pillars and three floors of rooms. It makes a beautiful contrast in the spring and summer with its bold whiteness against the green hills and flowering gardens."

"I can just see it," Lucy said with genuine delight.

"Of course now," Carolina added rather sadly, "everything is rather brown and dingy. I can't profess a love for winter. It's then that I feel very isolated. Almost as though Oakbridge has slipped off the face of the earth."

Just then, York returned with refreshments for both of them, and Carolina put her thoughts aside. It was easy to talk to Lucy, and she could see now how expertly Lucy had drawn out all manner of information without once making Carolina uncomfortable.

Seeing her brother whisper into Lucy's ear, Carolina decided to bow out gracefully and give them time together. Just then Lucy made a surprising request. "I wonder, would it be acceptable for Carolina to spend the holidays here in Washington?"

York and Carolina both exchanged a look of surprise. York stroked his chin a moment. "Given the sorrow of our home, I believe it would do her good. She's lost too much weight and could stand with some fattening up. I know the food in your home well enough to know it has that effect on folk." He patted his midsection, but both women could see there wasn't an ounce of fat to be had on him.

"Would you like to stay on here in the city?" Lucy asked Carolina. "We have several spare rooms, and I would happily put you up in one of them. That would give us both a chance to get to know each other better and to further our new friendship." Lucy's eyes twinkled as she added, "Besides, you definitely won't feel as though you've dropped off the face of the earth while in Washington City."

Carolina was touched by Lucy's offer and couldn't imagine anything she wanted more than this. It would be wonderful to break away from the plantation and all its sorrow. Not to mention that Virginia was still snubbing her quite seriously, and Georgia's tirades were beginning to weary Carolina considerably.

"I'd be very honored, Miss—Lucy," Carolina said.

"It's settled then," Lucy replied, linking her free arm with York's.

"With you in charge, how could it be otherwise?" York commented, a light of love clearly visible in his expression.

Lucy looked up at him, and Carolina felt a tightening in her chest at the radiant look on Lucy's face. This must be true love, Carolina thought, and while she was happy for her brother, her own heart seemed to ache with an emptiness she couldn't ignore.

Eleven

Manipulating Fate

*V*irginia yanked at the hopelessly knotted thread of her embroidery. She was angry, hurt, and betrayed. Betrayed by the very family who should even now be considering her needs uppermost. After all, she reasoned, she was the one who'd had to give up her wedding to James Baldwin. Of course, her father had suggested she keep the details of their broken engagement a secret. James had given her a letter of dismissal; at least that's what Virginia called it. The letter spoke of honor and how deserving she was of true love, love that James felt he could never give her. And why not?

James' answers had been vague at best and otherwise nonexistent. His heart and interests lay elsewhere, he had penned. What malarkey! In order to save face, Virginia had little choice but to announce to the world that *she* had broken the engagement. She was heralded as the young woman who sacrificed her own happiness to care for her grief-stricken mother. Unfortunately, that attention was short-lived, and now no one even bothered to call upon her and see how she was faring. And it was all because James Baldwin had deserted her. Oh, but how she longed to smear his name and reputation with the blackness that enshrouded her heart. But of course that was impossible without impugning her own reputation as well.

Still, James' betrayal was nothing compared to her own family's. The attention she had hoped to receive for her "sacrifice" was swallowed up in Penny's needs and their mother's wavering sanity. And to make matters worse, York had taken Carolina to Washington City for a party at the White House, and no one had even bothered to ask her if she'd like to go. Joseph had explained that the invitation was a personal one, not merely inviting any family member York might choose, but that the President had specifically requested Carolina.

Glancing up, Virginia watched as her mother faithfully tucked the covers around Penny and felt her forehead. Penny, now weakened further by a chest cold that wouldn't seem to pass, said nothing. Margaret, however, chattered on and on, mostly about nonsensical matters.

"When you are well we shall have to see to it that you practice the piano. No young woman should fall behind in her musical skills. I think, too, that Maryland, although she is quite young, should probably be encouraged to begin her piano studies as well."

Virginia frowned. It was difficult to speak with her mother on anything of real substance. She had so few moments of clarity, and when her mind did allow her to think sanely, Margaret Adams was deeply depressed and grief stricken over the death of her precious four-year-old.

"Mother?" Virginia called out.

Margaret turned and raised a brow. "You mustn't raise your voice, Virginia. You'll wake Mary."

Virginia grimaced and threw down her handwork. "Mother, we have to talk. There are matters going on of which I feel you should be aware."

"What things are you talking about?" Margaret came to the end of Penny's bed and gave Virginia her attention.

For once, Virginia felt that perhaps her mother's senses had returned. Her dark brown eyes seemed alert and clear, and her face was no longer pinched in worry but seemed openly curious.

"Carolina is courting Hampton Cabot. I fear they are quite serious and, well, that will lead to them wanting to marry." Virginia tried not to sound as indignant as she felt. It was bad enough that Carolina's incessant nagging had caused James to renew his interest in the railroad, but now she was actually closing in on a husband—the one thing that seemed to elude Virginia Adams.

"Marriage is a biblical institution," Margaret said rather piously.

"Yes, but, Mother, you have always insisted on the family tradition of the eldest daughter marrying first. I have not yet married, and therefore we cannot allow Carolina to marry. We should probably even put an end to the serious nature of her courtship with Mr. Cabot."

Margaret seemed to consider this for a moment. "I don't suppose Mr. Cabot understands much about the fever."

"What?" Virginia was thoroughly confused.

"The fever. Yellow-jack," her mother said thoughtfully. "Mr. Cabot might well be bringing the fever into this house, and I simply cannot have it. Mary is too young and Penny too fragile. We must speak with Mr. Adams about this and see to it that Mr. Cabot is not allowed to bring any animals onto the premises."

"Animals? Mother, whatever are you talking about? Mr. Cabot doesn't have the fever, not that it would matter."

"How dare you talk back to me?" Margaret's eyes widened in anger. "You are being disrespectful, and I insist that you go to your father at once and confess your sins." She pointed Virginia in the way of the door, and seeing there was nothing to be gained in continuing the conversation, Virginia left the room.

All she could think about was a drink. A nice glass of sherry would do wonders to soothe her shattered nerves. At one time, her mother had been a great source of help, but now Virginia knew she was on her own. There were very few people in the household, even among the slaves, whom she could call friend or confidant.

Entering the main drawing room, Virginia quickly went to the liquor cabinet and poured herself a generous portion of sherry. She gulped it down, fearful that someone might catch her, and had just replaced the glass and bottle when her father came unannounced into the room.

"Virginia, I didn't expect to find you here."

"Yes, well, Mother dismissed me. She thought I was being sassy and told me to confess my sins to you."

Joseph smiled sympathetically and came to embrace his daughter. Virginia allowed the hug but didn't encourage it to last lest her father detect the alcohol lingering on her breath. Instead, finding her father tenderhearted toward her pain, Virginia feigned tears and took a seat on the sofa.

"I'm so distraught," she said, hiding her face behind the dainty lace edges of her handkerchief. "Mother is so difficult to talk to, and I fear that should Penny pass on, she will lose her mind completely."

"I know, Virginia." Joseph sat down beside her and tried to offer comfort. "Your mother's one fault might be that she loved her children more than anything else in the world. More so even than her own sanity. I've tried to help her, but my prayers seem the only hope for her recovery. The doctor suggests a half-dozen remedies and, of course, bed rest, but Margaret will have no part of it. She desires only to stay beside her children, and because of this, her mind and body have been greatly weakened."

Virginia said nothing but held the handkerchief to her lips so her father wouldn't smell the liquor on her breath. She wondered silently if there might be a way to manipulate him to do her will.

"I'm glad York took Carolina to Washington," Joseph finally said, sounding completely spent by the conversation regarding his wife's mental health.

"Yes, perhaps that was good for Carolina, but what of Mother?"

"Your mother scarcely remembers that any of us are here, outside of Penny and"—he paused as his face contorted with the painful memory—"Mary. Poor woman cannot imagine that her baby is truly gone."

"Mother was asking for Carolina just this morning," Virginia lied. "I think she knows very well that Carolina is gone."

Joseph shrugged. "It's of little matter. She'll return after Christmas and then perhaps—"

"What do you mean, after Christmas?" Virginia interrupted. "Isn't Carolina coming home today?"

"No, a messenger arrived just an hour ago. York sent word that Carolina has been invited to be the guest of Congressman Alexander and his daughter, Lucille. It seems Lucille has captured the heart of your big brother. But that aside, she and Carolina have struck up a friendship, and she has requested that Carolina spend the holidays with them in Washington."

"But that will never do!" Virginia exclaimed, jumping to her feet. The sherry made her head swim momentarily, but she quickly recovered and continued with indignation. "Have you no consideration for Mother? Christmas with her family is exactly what she needs to help mend her mind. I had great plans for surprising you with a perfect Christmas dinner." Again she lied, and this time desperation was in her voice. "I've already laid plans for two corn-fattened geese to be prepared for our dinner. Why, Naomi is already cooking up a variety of side dishes and desserts. You can't let Carolina's selfishness ruin my surprise for Mother."

Joseph looked at Virginia in complete amazement. "I had no idea. With the sorrow and mourning this house has been given over to, I presumed the holiday would pass without much to bid it welcome."

"But don't you see, Father," Virginia said, this time lowering her voice to a more childlike timbre, "Mother needs us to rally around her. Otherwise, there will be no Christmas joy for her. With Mary dead and Penny so very ill, to allow Carolina and York to spend the holidays away from home would be unduly cruel."

"I honestly hadn't considered it as such, but I see where you may well be right," Joseph replied thoughtfully.

"I feel confident that I am." An angelic smile was plastered to Virginia's lips. "I prayed about it, Papa."

Joseph smiled and got to his feet. "I suppose, then, I should get a post off to York and Carolina. I'll have someone take it out in the morning. We shall bid your brother and sister return home for the holidays, and together we shall join forces to rally your mother's spirits."

Virginia watched him go and felt as though a single thread of victory had been woven into the otherwise blackened tapestry of her life. Another sherry to celebrate seemed in order, and going to the cabinet, she smiled. Then lifting her drink to the air she proposed her own toast.

"To breaking hearts everywhere. May Carolina's soon join the numbers."

Twelve

What Might Have Been

*C*arolina found herself excited at the prospect of attending a play with York and Lucy. They were to see James Hackett perform *Rip Van Winkle*, and on this, her second night in Washington, Carolina had already caught a fever of excitement in city life. But as she put the finishing touches on her hair, Carolina couldn't keep from wondering what was happening at home.

Oakbridge was such an important part of her, and yet Carolina knew she would gladly leave home to tramp around the world should the opportunity ever offer itself to her. She was connected to Oakbridge, the land and her family, but she also knew her father's wanderlust. A wanderlust that had caused him grief and sorrow because he'd never seen it fulfilled.

Carolina caught her reflection in the dresser mirror and was startled for a moment by her expression. Her brows were knitted together, her forehead furrowed in worry, and her brown eyes seemed to search out images that did not exist.

She thought of her mother, a woman of stern but loving nature. Carolina longed for her mother's grief to pass and for things to slip back to their old ways. She thought, too, of her father's suffering. She'd seen him age right before her eyes, and now there appeared more gray than black in his hair, and his face was always downcast and worried.

Her family had suffered greatly from the loss of Maryland. But Carolina could see it wasn't the death of the child that had caused the problem. It was the loss of their mother. Margaret Adams was in some ways dead to them all, and whether or not she'd ever return was entirely questionable.

"I'd love to leave and never return," she whispered to her image and instantly felt guilty for having said the words. It was so easy to

83

imagine going away and remembering things as they had been rather than standing by helpless to watch them further deteriorate.

Hearing the chimes from the clock in the hall, Carolina knew it was time to meet the others downstairs. She took up her gloves and handbag and checked her reflection one last time before descending the stairs.

"Ah, here she is," York replied and held out a hand to steady her down the final two steps. "You look wonderful."

"It's the gown," she replied. "I can't thank you enough, Lucy, for lending it to me."

Lucy Alexander, herself quite lovely in ice blue silk, smiled. "You do the dress more credit than I. I can't say that amber ever looked right on me."

Carolina glanced down at the dark golden gown. "I've never seen anything quite so lovely, and I've never worn a French gown before. Not that it feels any different from an American gown, but I feel different wearing it."

Lucy nodded. "Of course. That's the attraction. It's all up here," she said, touching her hand ever so lightly to her head.

York laughed and brought Lucy's cape. "I rather like the way it appears elsewhere. When I look at you, I don't even once consider what's up there."

"York Adams, how very unchivalrous of you," Lucy said, feigning a pout. "You told me you loved my mind."

York grinned. "And other things."

Carolina allowed the servant to help her into her coat as she spoke. "You two are scandalous."

Lucy giggled in a most becoming way, and York merely sighed and clasped his hands to his heart in a melodramatic pose. "Alas, she has captured my heart."

"Yes, and he's been practically worthless ever since," Lucy replied, taking hold of Carolina's arm. "Come along. Mr. Adams seems to have found a partner in himself."

The evening passed in the same lighthearted manner, and Carolina found herself completely captivated by York's and Lucy's behavior. They were like children in their teasing, but both were very aware of the power they held over the other. Lucy, for all of her heady speeches about women being independent thinkers, seemed quite content to gaze longingly into the eyes of her beloved York. She hung on his every word yet managed to assert her own opinion when she disagreed with his conclusion on a matter.

Carolina watched them more than she did the play itself. After all, she reasoned, the story was one she was already familiar with, and she could read it anytime. But watching York and Lucy was something she might not get another chance to do for a very long while, and they quite fascinated her.

But the play did evoke a haunting memory from the past—the night of her coming-out party. That night she had accidentally stirred up a fight with talk of the railroad, and when her brother put his fist into the face of one of their neighbors, Carolina found herself rescued by James and whisked away to the garden. It was here that she made mention of wishing to sleep away the years as Rip Van Winkle had. James had said he'd miss her if she did that, and Carolina grimaced even now as she remembered trying to push him to expound on that theme. Sadly, she recalled it was that very night he proposed to her sister. She tried to thrust away the memory, but her mind continued to wander into areas she'd forbidden it to go.

Arriving home after a late supper at Gadsby's, the trio was surprised to find a message on the entryway table addressed to York.

"It appears to be Father's handwriting," York replied, tearing into the envelope. He scanned the single sheet and handed it to Carolina. "Father wishes us to return home for Christmas. He believes it will help Mother's spirits to have us all around her for the holiday."

"Of course, he's right," Lucy said, without betraying any emotion. "I was thoughtless to not consider the situation."

"Nonsense," York replied. "You gave generously of your heart, which is what you do in most every situation. You merely acted on your nature."

Carolina handed the letter back to her brother. Disappointment was rapidly overwhelming her, but she knew it would be callous to suggest doing anything other than her father's bidding. "What shall we do?"

York smiled sympathetically. "It's too late to return tonight. We'll start out first thing in the morning." Then, as though suddenly struck by an idea, he waved his hands in the air. "Wait, I know. Lucy, why don't you come home with us? Company would do Mother good, and it's about time my family got to know you."

"I couldn't leave Father here alone in Washington."

"Bring him along. He's more than welcome. After all, we will one day be of the same family anyway." Carolina's eyes widened at this statement. York gave her a wink, and Lucy blushed and lowered her head.

"I believe Father already has plans made for the holiday. No, I must stay with him, but"—she paused to raise her gaze to meet York's—"why don't you both return after Christmas? You can bring in the new year with me."

"That sounds perfectly acceptable," York said, not giving it even a moment of consideration. "I'm certain that we could work it out. Are you interested, Carolina?"

"You know better than to even ask," replied Carolina. She felt a tiny bit of her disappointment fade.

"It's settled, then," Lucy said with a confidence Carolina was coming to admire in the woman. "Your room will stand waiting."

York seemed pleased with the compromise and looked upon Lucy with such love that Carolina instantly felt uncomfortable.

"I'm very tired and believe I'll excuse myself." Carolina paused long enough to give York a peck on the cheek and to embrace Lucy in a sisterly fashion. "Good night to you both, and thank you for a lovely evening."

She made her way up the stairs, longing for a love of her own. She paused at the top and, looking down, found York and Lucy in a tender embrace. As her brother kissed Lucy, she remembered Hampton's lips upon her own. It was then that Carolina realized she'd not thought of Hampton even once that day. It gave her a bit of relief to make that discovery and, somehow, remembering his kiss just now did not bother her in the same way it had previously.

York was speaking to Lucy in low whispers, and Lucy contentedly put her head against his shoulder. Carolina instantly remembered doing the same thing when James had comforted her after the death of Mary. She could still feel the coarseness of his coat beneath her cheek. She could still smell the scent of him and remember the way his fingers had touched her hair.

Turning away, she ran the rest of the way to her room and closed the door behind her as if she could shut out the images in her mind. Hampton's kiss. James' touch. James' tender expression.

James.

She crossed to the window and pulled back the drapes to stare into the darkened night. James was out there somewhere. She hugged her arms to her body and wished it were James in her embrace.

You said you would miss me, she thought. Do you miss me now?

"Oh, God, I love him so," she uttered the prayerful declaration and sighed. "Where has he gone?" She looked down on the street and tried to imagine him there. She could envision him in his black petersham coat and top hat staring up at her with a loving smile.

"Is it selfish to pray that you might come back to me?" she whispered against the frosty pane. "Is it wrong to love you when you gave your heart to my sister?"

With a sigh, Carolina moved away from the window and tried to force the picture of James from her mind. James is gone, she reasoned. Virginia released him and he went away. If he'd cared for me, surely he would have stayed.

A single tear trickled down her face, and Carolina quickly wiped it away. "I won't cry for what might have been," she chided herself, her heart breaking into a million pieces. "I won't cry for what never was."

Thirteen

Christmas Disaster

*H*ere, Mother, come see what we've done," York said, leading Margaret Adams into the main drawing room.

Inside, the rest of the family was happily assembled, including Penny, who had been carefully positioned on a lounging couch with copious numbers of quilts over her thin frame.

"Merry Christmas!" the children cheered in unison.

Joseph was lighting the last of the Christmas tree candles and beamed down a smile from where he stood atop a chair. "Merry Christmas, Mrs. Adams."

"My!" Margaret exclaimed and held her hands to her face. "It is glorious!"

Carolina gave Georgia's slender shoulders a squeeze and whispered, "Maybe things will go well, after all."

Georgia rolled her eyes. "I could have been at the Blevens' party tonight."

"Hush," Virginia said snidely. "Think of someone besides yourself."

"Oh, you mean like you do?" Georgia sneered from behind an angelic smile.

Virginia reached out and pinched her arm, but it was Carolina's arm and not Georgia's that she reached.

"Ow!" Carolina exclaimed, bringing everyone's questioning gaze upon her. She tried to think of something to say. "Virginia just offered to play Christmas carols for us," she finally managed.

"That would be grand," York said enthusiastically. "We haven't sung Christmas songs in a very long time."

"At least since last year," Georgia replied with undisguised sarcasm.

Virginia smiled amicably at Carolina, who was still rubbing her sore arm. "But of course I'll play." She swept across the room and took her seat at the piano.

"I must say, this is quite lovely," Margaret suddenly said, taking the arm of her husband.

"Look out," York said, pointing upward. "You've walked beneath the mistletoe."

Joseph smiled. "So I have. Dare I kiss my beautiful bride in front of all these witnesses?"

"Kiss! Kiss!" York declared, and Carolina picked up the chant with Penny following suit in a barely audible voice. Only Virginia and Georgia stared on in bored indifference.

Margaret blushed but nevertheless allowed her husband's embrace and kiss. Afterward, York and Carolina cheered while Virginia began the strains of "Joy to the World."

Carolina felt a certain amount of relief in the wake of this wonderful picture of normalcy. She'd feared all kinds of problems and disastrous beginnings, but all seemed well so far and it gave her comfort. This was as it should be, she thought. A wave of sadness touched her briefly as she remembered the way Mary would dance around the tree. They could never light Christmas tree candles with Mary in the house because she wanted so badly to touch the fire. Smiling to herself, Carolina reached out a finger to gently touch one of the candles.

"For you, Mary," she whispered, but the singing easily drowned out her words.

York led them in two more choruses before Joseph suggested they take their seats. "It's time to read the Christmas story," he said, taking up the family Bible from where one of the servants had placed it.

Everyone took a seat, and while the fire warmly crackled and popped, Joseph began to read. "And it came to pass in those days, that there went out a decree from Caesar Augustus, that all the world should be taxed. . . ."

Carolina's mind began to wander. She tried to focus on the retelling of Jesus' birth, but her mind was consumed with so many other things. Virginia's attitude still confused her, and she was determined after the celebration to have it out with her once and for all. I didn't drive James away from here, she told herself. I might have helped him renew his love of the railroad, but I didn't give him that passion in the first place. He would have eventually come back to it on his own. Her reasoning seemed logical, but what did not was that Virginia would throw away a perfectly good marriage proposal, all because her would-be husband desired to work on the railroad.

"And she brought forth her firstborn son, and wrapped him in swaddling clothes, and laid him in a manger; because there was no room for them in the inn." Her father's voice broke through her thoughts, and Carolina smiled. She'd always loved this story, and she especially loved the telling of it with her family all gathered round and Christmas cheer brightening otherwise dismal spirits.

There was so much to feel sorry about, but Carolina tried hard to put it behind her. Maryland was gone and Penny was desperately ill. Her mother was seemingly better but still had long spans of deep depression. Virginia was bitter and Georgia was out of control, while York was seldom home, and her other brother Maine was a world away in England learning to preach the Gospel.

That left only James. The one name she'd tried not to conjure to memory. The one person who was seldom far from her thoughts. He should have been here, she mused, and just as quickly as the idea came to mind it pained her. If he were here he would be at Virginia's side and not her own. Wasn't it better that he should be gone altogether than to have to watch him gaze lovingly at her sister? Could she have stood to watch a tender scene between them, such as she'd observed between York and Lucy?

Her father was concluding the Scripture reading, and Carolina felt marginally guilty for having paid so little attention. She knew the story by heart, yet seldom had she given it much thought. But this year was her first year as a true believer. She'd given her heart to Christ only days after Mary's death, and now she struggled to build on that spark of faith and find peace.

"Who wants to open presents?" Joseph asked with a gleam in his eyes that took away the worry of the past months.

"I do," Georgia said, finally seeming to get into the spirit of things.

"Me too," Penny called from her makeshift bed.

"Yes, let's open presents now," Carolina agreed and went to sit beside Penny.

"York, perhaps you should pass the gifts out. First bring your mother that red and silver one." Joseph pointed to the small flat package.

York quickly complied and brought his mother the gift. Placing it in her hands, he kissed her cheek. "Merry Christmas, Mother. I believe this package is from Father."

Margaret eyed the gift with genuine surprise and then tenderly opened it as though unwrapping something fragile. Inside, a necklace of rubies and diamonds glinted up at her.

"Oh, Mother, it's beautiful!" Virginia exclaimed in characteristic fashion. "I hope you'll let me wear that one day."

Margaret looked up to find Joseph smiling down at her. "I do hope you like it," he said softly and helped her place the jewels around her neck. He fastened the clasp, then stood back to admire them. "You do them justice, Margaret dear."

"Thank you," she whispered and seemed too overwhelmed to say more.

"Here's one for you, Penny," York said and handed her a brightly wrapped box.

Penny, with Carolina's help, opened the package to find a music box. Music tinkled out in a metallic melody, which Carolina instantly recognized as a popular lullaby entitled "Good Night." Carolina could remember singing the song at the close of a school program once when she was younger.

Good night to you all, and sweet be thy sleep;
May angels around you their silent watch keep,
Good night, good night, good night, good night.

She could almost hear the voices singing, and the memory brought tears to her eyes. Would life ever be so sweet again?

They shared gifts all around, each one delighting in the thoughtfulness of the others. Virginia quickly appraised Carolina's gift to her of a new navy and peach colored bonnet, then discarded it to one side without offering any thanks or comment. Carolina tried not to be offended and focused instead on the new book York had given her. The leather-bound copy of Washington Irving's *Astoria* instantly captured her attention.

"It's all about traveling westward to the Pacific Coast and setting up a trading establishment. The descriptions are most invigorating," York commented. "I think you'll find yourself quite caught up in it."

Carolina smiled. "I know I shall. Thank you so very much."

The room fairly buzzed with excitement and joy. Voices were raised in exclamations of delight and gratitude, and all seemed exactly as it should be. When it was time for refreshments, Naomi, Oakbridge's longtime cook, entered the room followed by several house slaves. Each carried a tray of succulent Christmas treats, while Naomi herself bore the Christmas pudding.

Carolina's mouth watered hungrily at the sight of such fare, and she was about to offer her assistance when Margaret jumped to her feet.

"But where are Mary's gifts?" she cried out in a fretful tone. "Have you all forgotten your sister?"

Joseph reached out to pat her reassuringly. "Margaret, you must remember that our Mary is with the angels in heaven. Her gifts there are far more grand than any we could hope to provide on earth." His voice was tender and gentle, but Margaret would have no part of it.

Wrenching away from him, she ran to the tree and inspected the empty floor beneath it. Next she went over each and every branch for some gift that might have been overlooked.

Carolina exchanged concerned looks with York, who was even now approaching their mother. "Mother," he said, reaching out to take hold of her arm. "Come rest by the fire."

"I will not! You won't treat your sister with such disregard!" She pushed him away and continued to search for Mary's presents.

"Margaret!" Joseph exclaimed, having reached the limit of his patience for such matters. "You must not do this to yourself, nor to the children who are still living."

This caused Margaret to halt and face him. "You do not know what you say, sir. Our Mary will be quite hurt."

"Our Mary is beyond hurt, my dear." He touched her shoulder gently and tried to urge her once again to sit. "Come rest. Do not let Mary's death spoil the night for the others."

"Mary is not dead! How dare you be so cruel!" Margaret screamed the words and flailed her arms. "You have all caused this!"

Joseph tried to take hold of her, but Margaret pushed him away and, in doing so, also pushed over the Christmas tree.

Carolina saw instantly that the lighted candles of the tree were now about to set off a fire of grand proportions. Grabbing up one of the quilts that covered Penny, she rushed forward just as York did the same. He pulled the quilt from her hands and beat at the tree until all of the candles were extinguished, while Margaret raged around the room, pushing over plant stands and serving tables.

"You have all done this!"

She was clearly beyond reasonable thought, and while Virginia looked on in stunned silence, Georgia began to cry openly. Carolina went quickly to Georgia and pulled the younger girl into her arms. Georgia buried her face against Carolina's shoulder, while Carolina sent a pleading expression to Virginia.

"Don't just sit there, Virginia," she admonished. "Help Father."

But Virginia made no response. She sat there staring at the melee with an odd look of dismay on her face.

A teapot of steaming water clattered to the floor in a resounding crash, causing Penny to whimper tearfully. Carolina pulled Georgia with her to where Penny lay and forced Georgia to sit beside her.

"Georgia, you must comfort Penny while I try to help Father."

Georgia said nothing but wrapped her arms around Penny and continued to weep. Carolina knew it was the best she could do. Crossing to York, she offered to see to the tree while he helped with their mother.

"Father cannot hope to calm her by himself. I think we are going to need the doctor as well." York nodded and got to his feet.

Together, Joseph and York managed to bring Margaret under control, but it wasn't a pleasant scene, and Carolina would forever remember the hateful look on her mother's face as they took her away from the party.

Later that night, when Margaret was asleep, aided by a heavy dose of laudanum, and Joseph had returned to the drawing room to survey the damage, Carolina found a moment to speak with him.

"Your quick thinking saved Oakbridge from going up in flames," he told her wearily. Plopping down in a chair, he buried his face in his hands.

Carolina came to where he sat and knelt beside him. "Papa, do not fret so. I cannot bear to lose you both."

Joseph lowered his hands and reached out to cup her face. "You haven't lost me. I may be worse for the wear, but I'm still here and here I will stay. But you . . . I think I did you a grave injustice by bringing you home. Virginia was so certain that such a celebration could benefit your mother, and for a time it looked as though it had. Now I'm grieved beyond words. According to Miriam, Georgia has cried herself to sleep, and Penny wants nothing more to do with her mother."

"Tell me what I must do to help, and I will gladly give my all," Carolina said softly. She took hold of her father's hands and held them tightly.

"I want you to return to Washington. York told me of Lucy's extended invitation. I want you to go immediately. Virginia will care for your mother, as she has from time to time, and I'll see to it that Miriam is relieved of her other duties in order that she might care for Penny."

"Yes, Penny loves her so," Carolina agreed.

"Georgia is so distraught and"—he paused as if the next words were too painful to say—"she needs a stronger hand than I can give her. I'm going to locate a finishing school for her immediately. The stricter the better."

"I think she will benefit from that," Carolina replied. "The rumors surrounding her are less than flattering, and with much more said, her reputation will be in tatters. But honestly, Papa, I don't need to go back to the city. I'll stay here and help you with the house."

"No. I absolutely insist that you return." He drew her to him, and Carolina laid her head on his knee as she had done as a small child. "You are meant for greater things, Carolina. I've always known this, although I can't say why. I feel it imperative that you spend some time away. I see a restlessness in you that once inhabited my own heart, and I won't see you stuck here to watch your mother as she is."

"But I love you both, and I want to be near you."

"No, you want to be near the people we used to be. I can't say how much worse your mother may get, and I may well have to heed the doctor's suggestion and remove her to a place that can better guard her from harm."

"An asylum?" Carolina questioned, raising up shocked eyes.

"It may come to that." Joseph's words were given with such grim resignation that Carolina refused to push him further.

"I'll do whatever you tell me, Father. Whatever will make things easier for you."

Joseph smiled for the first time since entering the room. "Then go with your brother. Go back to Washington and live for us both."

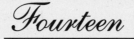

Fourteen

Love Letters

$\mathcal{P}$assing through the White House and into the French decor of the Blue Room, Carolina felt as though she were seeing it all for the first time. At Christmas, she'd been much too preoccupied with the glamor and festivities of the holidays and people. But now, having been summoned for a private dinner, Carolina took the time to study every detail.

Overhead, the opulent gilt-bronze chandelier cast down a warm glow. Carolina was notably impressed with the Pierre Antoine Bellange furniture. It was said that the Frenchman had created the gilded furniture for President Monroe because ordinary mahogany was not suitable for even a gentleman's house. Carolina smiled, remembering the vast quantities of mahogany at Oakbridge. Perhaps it was a different time, she reasoned, and followed her brother through the doors and into a room of red damask.

The Red Room was a lovely parlor and music room, and it was here that President Jackson greeted York and Carolina with warm regard.

"I'm so glad you could come. We have a rare night together. Mr. Van Buren is away with family and won't be joining us for dinner. Also, I have dismissed numerous dignitaries and holiday well-wishers in order to have a bit of peace and quiet. Of course, that isn't to say someone won't come straggling in and expect my undivided attention. This is a public house, after all."

Carolina curtsied and extended her hand. "The pleasure is all mine, I assure you, sir."

York took a more casual stance. Both the man and the house were his daily companions, and while neither had lost their charm, York appeared clearly comfortable with it all.

"You might have found your way into this room during the Christmas party," Jackson said, taking Carolina in hand. He tucked her arm against his waist and pointed to a portrait of Dolley Madison. "When Mrs. Madison held her illustrious social gatherings on Wednesday nights, this room was actually called the Yellow Room. It was said that the glittering of ladies' gowns and gentlemen's snuff cases literally made the room glow.

"You will note the piano and harp in the corner," he continued. "Many a famous person has given me entertainment in this room. Would you care to lend your skills to such an endeavor?"

"Mercy, no," Carolina said with the slightest shake of her head. "I'm not at all skilled in that area. I can play some, but believe me, it would be to both our benefits if I did not."

Jackson laughed, and Carolina wondered if the hacking cough would follow. When it didn't, she could only presume that he had recovered his health just as he'd assured her he would.

"We will dine in the back room," he told her conspiratorially. "In the family dining room. I wanted the evening to be personal and private and have instructed the staff to seat you at my right."

Carolina blinked several times in amazement. "I . . . I don't know what to say. I'm honored."

Jackson smiled. "No doubt, ten minutes into the dinner you'll be so bored of my old stories, you'll be pleading with your brother to take you home."

"That would be quite impossible," Carolina replied. "I would never grow bored with your stories."

Jackson paused and gave her a look of genuine affection. "My Rachel often said the same. How I miss her." His expression was bittersweet as he drew a deep breath and sighed. "She never wanted to come to the White House and, of course, she didn't. She died shortly before I made the move. Leaving her in Tennessee was the hardest thing I've ever done. A part of me died when she perished."

"You must have loved her a great deal," Carolina replied, not knowing what else to say.

"Indeed. Indeed." He remained thoughtfully distant, as though conjuring ghosts from the past. Then, just as easily as he'd grown solemn, he turned jovial again. "York, we have some very fine wine just in from France. Help yourself to it. Miss Adams, would you care for something before dinner?" He motioned to several tables where a variety of refreshments lay awaiting their attention.

"No. Thank you very much."

"Would you care for something, sir?" York asked, helping himself to a drink.

"Not just yet. I thought I might sit for a bit and enjoy your sister's company. Miss Adams, I do not remember when I've met a more entertaining and intelligent young woman. Your father and brother have often talked of you with great pride. I still laugh about the story of how you would sneak into your father's office to read my cabinet papers."

Carolina felt her face grow hot. She took the seat offered her by Jackson and folded her gloved hands daintily against the dark blue velvet of her gown. "Father has always said if you wish to know the truth of a matter, check it out for yourself."

"What a cracker you are!" Jackson said, slapping his knee. "You will keep some young man on his toes. Have you a beau, Miss Adams?"

"No, sir," she told him, not wishing to explain her relationship to Hampton Cabot.

"I find that unbelievable."

"It isn't for lack of their wanting to court her," York chimed in. He brought his wine and joined them by taking a seat beside his sister. "I've had half a dozen young men inquire as to my sister's willingness to be approached by suitors. I've managed to stave them off for a time, but I'm afraid sooner or later they'll avoid coming to me altogether and seek Carolina out on their own."

Carolina knew she was blushing furiously and could only lower her face in deep embarrassment. She had hoped the subject would remain far removed from her social life.

"So why is it you are holding all of these young men at arm's length?" Jackson asked her with a hint of amusement in his voice.

Carolina twisted her hands together. "I suppose it is because a man would expect me to take seriously his intentions of courtship. He would expect me to consider marriage, and I'm not of a mind to do that just yet."

York sipped his drink and added, "Carolina is afraid a husband would expect her to forget book learning and concentrate on the doldrums of running a household."

Jackson nodded. "It's likely they would at that. Still, I cannot imagine a beautiful young woman such as yourself remaining single for long." As if sensing her discomfort, Jackson turned to his young aide and asked, "And what of your courtship to Miss Alexander? Have you asked the young lady to marry you yet?"

"Not exactly," York replied, reddening slightly at the collar. "But we have an understanding."

"Ah yes. I remember having understandings with young ladies," Jackson grinned. "I will admonish you with the same words I gave my young ward and namesake, Andrew Jackson Hutchings, several years back: Seek a wife who will aid you in making your fortune and will take care of it when made. Simply put, you will find it is easier to spend two thousand dollars than to make five hundred. Look at the economy of the mother, and you will find it in the daughter."

"Wise words indeed, except in Miss Alexander's case her mother is deceased."

"Yes, I do remember that," Jackson answered. "But I can tell you from personal experience your young woman is most remarkable. I have been to the Alexander home in Pennsylvania, and she entertained me quite regally. I felt I'd become the spitting image of the King Andrew that some of my enemies would make me out to be."

"She is quite talented and very capable," York agreed.

"And beautiful," Carolina added, relieved the conversation had veered away from herself. "I have very much enjoyed her companionship, as well."

"York tells me you've been staying with her these past two days. Are you enjoying your time in Washington?"

"Very much, Mr. Jackson. York has made a wonderful guide, when time permits, and when he is away, Lucy—that is to say, Miss Alexander—keeps me quite busy. Tomorrow we are to attend a lecture by Mr. Sylvester Graham."

"Who is he?" York asked curiously.

"I can't really say," Carolina replied. "Lucy tells me he holds speeches for ladies only and talks of health and diet."

York frowned. "I'm not entirely sure I approve."

Jackson laughed. "Maybe you should acquire a wig and bonnet, Mr. Adams, and spy on the meeting."

Carolina gave her brother a mischievous wink. "York is only afraid that Lucy will find someone else more interesting than he. But"—she leaned toward the President—"I have it on good authority that the lady in question is quite taken with my brother, and, therefore, I feel he has nothing to concern himself with."

Jackson nodded. "I'm confident of that opinion, as well."

York's previous expression of worry was swallowed up in a smug, self-assured smile. "I told you she was smart."

Later, after a succulent dinner of wild turkey and side dishes too numerous to count, Carolina found her heart further endeared to the aged president.

"You must never feel rushed into matrimony, Miss Adams. It is im-

portant that a man and woman come to an understanding before ex-
changing vows."

"I heartily agree," Carolina replied. "But you must admit, in proper
society a woman's place is clearly in the home and under the protection of her father or husband. Few women are given the opportunity
to expand their education or to experience anything of the world without one of these men to accompany her."

Jackson smiled sympathetically. "You must forgive us for desiring
to protect those whom we cherish above all else."

"I do indeed forgive that overprotective nature, but I also would ask
for tolerance. It seems a small thing to ask that a man would allow a
woman to study and educate herself."

"Still, my dear sister," York added from where he'd sat in rather
stoic silence, "there ultimately remains the fact that such an education
cannot be used to any purpose."

"I beg to disagree, York." Jackson seemed to consider the matter for
a moment before continuing. "I see no harm in educating all people.
It is ignorance that renders a man dangerous. Why, then, should it be
any different with women? I would not find it offensive for a daughter
or wife of mine to read and better her mind. I would, however, draw a
line at her insistence upon complete independence. After all, such
women do not maintain genteel reputations for long."

Carolina sighed. "But shouldn't a woman be allowed to marry for
love and not for obligation?"

"Of course, Miss Adams, and I would fight any man who said otherwise." He dabbed his mouth with a linen napkin and cast it to the
table. "I would admonish any woman to marry for love and love alone.
To do otherwise would only create bitterness and regret."

"But most women are not given such leniency. Most marriages, in
proper society, are still arranged for profit and status. I remember one
of the first things my mother insisted for her daughters was that they
seek only a man of wealth and means. 'You will never worry about
empty platters,' she would tell me, 'if you marry a man whose affairs
are in proper order.' "

"And she is right," Jackson replied. "But you can certainly find a
man of proper means and fall in love."

Servants began clearing away the dishes, and Jackson got slowly to
his feet. "York, I beg your indulgence for a moment. I would like to
show your sister some very special letters. If you would care to retire
to the Red Room, we will join you there shortly."

"Of course," York answered, helping Carolina from her chair.

Moments later, in Jackson's private study, Carolina received a bundle of ribbon-tied letters.

"These are letters written by my Rachel and the answers I sent her in return. I am lending them to you so that you might better understand what I'm speaking of." His tender expression touched something deep within Carolina's aching heart. "I could never offer you better advice than to say, marry for love and love alone. The world may give itself over to wars and tribulation of all manner, but if you face it beside the one you love, you will see that anything is endurable. Anything is possible with love."

Carolina held the letters in a state of awe. "I can't take these. What if something were to happen to them?"

"The world has condemned me a hundred times over, and they murdered my beloved Rachel with that same condemnation. I want you to know her as I did. I want you to understand that our love was more than harsh remarks and innuendos upon newsprint."

"I would never imagine it anything less than perfectly ordered," Carolina replied. She hugged the letters to her bodice and reached up her hand to touch the President's weathered cheek. "Your Rachel was a lucky woman."

"Luck had nothing to do with it," Jackson said, sounding suddenly very old. "If it were for luck, she might still be at my side. Rachel once said she'd rather be a doorkeeper in the house of God than to live in that palace at Washington." He sighed heavily. "I pray God cherishes her as much as I did."

Later that night, after telling Lucy all about her evening at the White House, Carolina climbed into bed and began to read the Jackson letters.

"My Love," began one of Jackson's missives to Rachel, "The separation, so unlooked for, from you has oppressed my mind very much, still I hope that your mind is become calm." The tender affection of a husband for his wife was clearly penned. ". . . my heart is with you and fixed on Domestic Life . . ." Carolina could imagine the joy of a woman to receive such a letter from her adoring husband. ". . . I hope in God we will never be separated again until death parts us . . . May Jehovah take you in His holy keeping is the prayer of your affectionate Husband."

Letter after letter portrayed the same devotion and love.

"Beloved Husband," Rachel's feathery script opened, "I count the days until you are here with me again. The house seems quite empty without you." Carolina knew very well that feeling. Hadn't Oakbridge seemed empty when James went away?

Feeling her eyelids grow heavy, Carolina put the precious letters away for the night. She snuffed out the candle and lay back in the darkness. Hugging the pillow close, Carolina wondered for the hundredth time if she would ever know a love such as the Jacksons had shared.

Fifteen

When God Calls

*N*ew Year's Day, 1837, dawned cold and snowy. It had been agreed upon at breakfast that the family would brave the weather and go en masse to the small church favored by the Alexanders. Carolina had hoped they might attend one of the larger churches such as St. John's, which was noted for being the "Church of the Presidents." She had thought to catch another glimpse of Jackson, but York had assured her the President would not be in attendance. Carolina wondered at this, knowing the regard Jackson had seemed to hold for God in his letters to Rachel.

"His health isn't good," York told her as they entered the church behind Lucy and her father. "He's taken to his bed again, and I don't expect him to revive until he's able to leave Washington once and for all."

"Is he gravely ill?" Carolina asked in a whisper.

"I believe his heart is completely broken. Not only by the pain of life without Mrs. Jackson, but because the country is still in such turmoil. He's pressed in on all sides and has made some pretty fierce enemies."

"I can't imagine anyone hating him," Carolina said, taking a seat beside Lucy.

"He stirred up a hornets' nest," York replied. "I only hope Mr. Van Buren is able to take over the fight."

The church was very plain and simple. A small organ stood behind a decorative screen and groaned to life as the organist began to play. The stove at the back of the room did little to ward off the reminders of winter. Carolina found the chilly dampness penetrated the layers of wool petticoats, and even the heavy shawl Lucy had lent her was no protection against the cold.

Lucy seemed to feel the same way, because she kept her hands buried in her fur muff and leaned a little closer to Carolina, as if for warmth.

The congregation was called to stand and pray, and after that there was the singing of hymns and more praying. Carolina considered it a quaint, comfortable service until the snowy-haired Reverend Boswell took the pulpit.

"Now the Lord had said unto Abram, Get thee out of thy country, and from thy kindred, and from thy father's house, unto a land that I will show thee," the minister began reading from Genesis.

Carolina listened diligently, at first only vaguely aware of the comparison she placed between Abram and herself. Abram was called upon by God to go into an unknown land. She thought of the railroad and the endeavors of so many to delve into the unknown lands of America. She felt a longing surge within her soul. Her mother would call it wanderlust, but in spite of giving it a name, it wouldn't be ignored.

Shifting uncomfortably in the pew, Carolina thought of James and his desire to go west with the railroad. Had God called him to such a task? She'd never really heard James speak much on the matter of God, and because spiritual matters on a personal level were still so new to her, Carolina had never pursued such a conversation.

Then an even more intriguing idea came to Carolina. Was God calling her west? Was He in fact saying to her, "Leave your father's house and I will show you a new land"?

With a fierce scowl, Reverend Boswell rained down the Scripture as though it were a torrential storm from on high. And Carolina's discomfiture grew. The minister read from Genesis for over half an hour before pausing to cast an accusing eye on the congregation. Carolina wondered if he was checking up on the crowd for those who'd somehow managed to doze off during the Bible reading.

Then with penetrating eyes that seemed to be fixed on her alone, the minister boomed out in a loud voice, "When God calls you, will you obey?"

Carolina felt a trembling that began in her heart and seemed to wash over her in waves. Are you calling me, Father? she wondered silently.

She cast a wary glance toward her brother. York seemed completely unaffected, even bored by the long narration of Scripture. Lucy, too, sat without any notable expression of interest. Carolina lowered her eyes, afraid to look into the face of the minister.

"God called upon Abram," came the booming voice again, "and he took up his wife and all of his possessions and went out from the land of his knowledge into a place he did not know. God called him forth, and Abram went obediently, even unto the possibility of his own death. And why? Because it was well with him and the Lord, and he was an obedient man.

"And in this, God gave unto him a covenant. God blessed him and declared that he would make of him a great nation, and indeed we see today that we are a part of that nation. We are descendants of Abram, and we will each and every one of us face the calling of God.

"Will you go forth into obedience when God speaks?"

Carolina clasped her hands tightly together. Her heart fairly leaped at the anticipation of answering God's call. Was God calling her west? Had it been God's direction for her all along that she fall in love with the railroad and a man of like-minded determination, and see the West settled and developed?

After church, she rode in silence beside Lucy, who was sharing an animated conversation, mostly with York, about that afternoon's celebration. It was New Year's Day, and the Alexanders had placed an ad in earlier newspapers to announce they would receive visitors on that first day of the year. Even now, Lucy was giving an orderly account for the festivities and refreshments they would offer. But it was of little concern to Carolina, in spite of the fact that Lucy hoped to introduce her to several very eligible bachelors.

Carolina's thoughts were turned ever inward. How she longed to talk with James and explain her heart. Would he understand? Would he know her desires and believe her accurate in feeling led to go out of her father's house and into the unknown?

God, if you are calling me to leave my home, please open the door wide and show me the way, Carolina prayed.

The carriage bounced and jostled back and forth until they drew up in front of the three-story brick house.

"Oh, look, Father," Lucy cried in delight, "a mumming parade."

Carolina could see that indeed a line of masqueraded merrymakers were singing and dancing down the street. Mumming was something she'd only heard of and never in her short life had actually experienced. Folks of every shape and size would cover themselves in layers of clothes and mask their identity in order to fool their friends.

Carolina looked upon the mummers with interest. Some wore costumes that were little more than sheets and blankets held together with rope, while others were elaborately gowned. All wore masks of cloth or paper, and some played instruments while others sang songs.

York assisted Carolina and Lucy from the carriage just as the mummers drew closer and began to surround them.

"Good year to you, sirs and madams," one of the mummers announced.

Lucy pulled at Carolina's coat. "Come, we must guess who these kind people are. I think that one over there might well be Mr. Oneida."

Carolina's gaze followed to a portly figure whose paper mask resembled a brilliant gold star. "What makes you so sure?" Carolina asked, seeing nothing recognizable in any of the players.

"I'm certain I saw that star among his Christmas decorations. Mr. Oneida, is that you?" Lucy asked, quite seriously.

"I must confess you have a good eye, mi'lady." The man bowed low over Lucy's hand.

"You must all come in from the cold and play and sing for us," Lucy commanded. She turned and led the way to the door. "We have refreshments and gifts for you all."

Carolina followed at a slower pace.

"You seem preoccupied, little sister," York whispered against her ear.

Carolina smiled up. "Just considering the future."

York smiled and his gaze followed Lucy. "Me too."

"Are you going to make the holidays complete and ask for her hand?"

"I very well may," he answered with a determined look. "Would that meet with your approval?"

"Most assuredly," Carolina replied. "I already love Lucy as a sister. It seems only fitting that she join our family."

They brought up the rear, allowing the mummers to make their way into the house first. Carolina was just undoing the buttons of her coat when Henry Alexander appeared in the entryway.

"It seems this was delivered by one of your slaves while we were in church." He handed York an envelope. "The boy is even now having refreshments in our kitchen."

"Father is probably wishing us a good year," York replied, breaking the seal. He scanned the message then raised his eyes to meet Carolina's.

Carolina could instantly see the change in her brother. "What is it? What has happened?"

"Penny has died," he said simply.

In the front sitting room, the revelers were breaking into an enthusiastic song, but the noise was instantly muted in Carolina's ears. Penny was dead. It didn't seem possible, and yet she'd feared all along that her sister would never recover.

"Come," Henry replied. "You must have a chair and some peace.

I'll see to it that the house is emptied."

"Don't bother on our part, Mr. Alexander," said York. "Carolina and I must leave immediately for home."

"I understand. I'll have your horse readied. My driver will take your sister, and your slave can ride atop with him."

"Thank you, sir," York replied.

It all seemed so reasonable and easily settled that Carolina had no other choice but to go along with it. Her mind was a mass of confusion, and her heart was broken and shattered at the thought of the eleven-year-old girl who would never again climb trees or sing to her dolls.

"Poor Mother," Carolina whispered just as Lucy came into the room laughing.

"I feared you were all—" She fell silent and instantly sobered when she saw their grim faces. "What is it?"

Henry put an arm around his daughter. "I'm afraid Penny Adams has passed away."

"Oh, how terrible. Carolina, York, I'm so sorry." Her eyes conveyed a sincerity that said more than words ever would.

"We must take leave of your company," York replied, taking Lucy's hand gently in his. "I pray we will not long be parted."

Sixteen

Annabelle Bryce

"The drifts are impassable," James Baldwin told his traveling companion, Ben Latrobe. "I'm afraid the railroad is completely shut down at this point. We can take a sleigh into Harper's Ferry, but beyond that choice we'll have to turn back."

Several days earlier they had set out for Harper's Ferry to inspect the new bridge. There had been discouraging reports about the structure, and Latrobe had asked James to accompany him so they could see for themselves if the reports were true. But the trip had been a difficult one almost from the beginning, hampered by a snowstorm that seemed to be getting worse rather than better. A simple two-day trip was easily going to take five.

Ben Latrobe cast a discouraged glance out the train car window, then nodded and sighed. "I suppose it must be. We've been slowed down at every point."

"Must we go to Harper's Ferry at this time?" James asked. "I realize there are problems with the bridge, but could it not wait?"

Latrobe shook his head. "We can't risk it. What if the bridge collapses?" His wondrous seven-span structure crossed the river at Harper's Ferry and was their key to westward expansion.

"Do you believe the situation to be truly that serious?" another of their companions, Charles Stewart, asked.

"I do. I knew from the very beginning there were problems. The bridge was not built to my specifications. When I viewed the building of it last May, I could see that the masonry was shoddy. I brought it to the attention of the contractors and was assured that in spite of the rough work, the design would meet every important detail listed. Now, however, it looks as though I misplaced my confidence in the builders. There's a great deal of concern with the pier structures that come out

107

of the river itself. I was recently advised that we might have to rebuild. Then, too, there is a worry about the abutment connections. I only pray I may find a reasonable and economical solution."

The conductor appeared at that moment and ushered the three men into an awaiting sleigh. "I hope you gents don't mind, but I have several female passengers who will need to ride along with you."

"Not at all," Latrobe replied, then noticed the woman who was trying to navigate the icy train steps. "Be a good man, Baldwin, and offer up some assistance."

James picked his way back through the snow. His own footing was precariously awkward, and he found himself holding his breath as his foot slipped first one way and then the other. He reached the train car just as the woman moved to the final step. Ice had re-formed on the surface, and when she touched her boot to the platform, she lost her footing altogether.

With one quick, fluid motion, James caught her in his arms and saved her from plunging into the snowbank. However, the ice beneath his own feet kept him from retaining his balance, and he sat down hard on the snowy path.

"You, sir, should become an actor," the woman said in a refined English voice. "Your timing is impeccable."

James laughed, meeting eyes that were very nearly violet in color. "Your servant, ma'am," he said rather formally. "However, were my footing as secure as my timing, we might be seated in the sleigh rather than this wet snowbank." He waited until the conductor came to their rescue.

"Let me offer you a hand," the conductor said, reaching out to lift the woman from James' arms. He deposited her into the sleigh just as James got to his feet and dusted off his backside.

By the time he made his way to the carriage, the conductor had returned to help the other two women, both of whom appeared to be traveling companions of the first. Seating the three women on one side and the gentlemen on the other, James found himself matched up opposite the woman he'd attempted to assist.

"I should introduce myself," she said with a smile that was all charm and sophistication. "I'm Annabelle Bryce."

"The actress?" James asked. He'd heard of her performances in New York and Boston.

"The very same. I'm honored that you have heard of me."

"I doubt seriously there are many who haven't. You are highly regarded as one of the best actresses in the world."

"I don't know that I would go that far," Annabelle replied. She passed her gloved hand through the air. "These are my conspirators and constant companions." The two women at her left smiled as the wind blew down on them. "Miss Davina Richards is my understudy, and Gretta is my maid."

"Ladies," James said, "I'm pleased to meet you. I am James Baldwin." Then motioning to the gentlemen on his right, he added, "And this is Benjamin Latrobe and Charles Stewart."

There were nods of acknowledgment and greeting as the conductor loaded several pieces of luggage on the sleigh.

"Hope your journey's a safe one," he told them, then signaled the driver that they were ready.

A crack of the whip sent the team into motion, and James felt the stinging bite of the icy wind against his face. At least it had stopped snowing, although the sky remained heavy and threatened to resume the onslaught at any moment.

"So what brings you ladies to this part of the country?" Ben asked.

"We are performing, of course," Annabelle replied. She seemed not to notice the cold and refrained from huddling with the other two women. Davina and Gretta had all but buried themselves beneath heavy carriage blankets, while Annabelle actually appeared to thrive from exposure to the elements.

"A few of us agreed," Annabelle continued, "to perform in Harper's Ferry as a favor to an old friend. And since I have a sister who lives up the hill from the arsenal, I figured to kill two birds with the same stone."

Davina popped her head up at this. "We had no idea we would meet with so many obstacles, and were it not too late to back out, we might never have braved the trip."

"Yes, well, it might have been more pleasant traveling had the drifts not shut down the railroad." Benjamin Latrobe's voice betrayed the disappointment he obviously felt.

"It is of no matter," Annabelle declared. "I've never been one for convention. When plans change, I simply see them as new challenges and go about my business."

James smiled and nodded. He thought of Carolina and her spirit of adventure. That was exactly how she was. Whenever challenged with the impossible, she merely put her best foot forward and plunged headlong into the matter with all the enthusiasm she could muster.

"I see you approve," Annabelle said, directing her amused expression at James.

"I do indeed. Too often we are stifled by the obstacles before us. This railroad is a perfect example. Were it not for hearty men with visionary dreams and unquenchable spirits, riding the rails might not ever have been an option."

"Are you gentlemen with the railroad?" Annabelle asked.

"Yes indeed. We are even now on railroad business," Benjamin answered before James could reply.

"How exciting." She smiled sweetly.

"It can be," James agreed. He returned her smile and fell silent. Annabelle Bryce completely captivated his attention. She wasn't all that beautiful. Her nose was a tad too large for her face, and the years had given her a number of wrinkles around the eyes and mouth. But there was something unique about her that James could not quite define. Something that intrigued him and made him desire to know her better.

They were forced to stop six different times, not only to rest the horses but to warm the passengers from their frozen states. James kept mostly to himself during these times of respite, but on the final stop before reaching Harper's Ferry, he found himself the center of Annabelle Bryce's attention.

"You aren't like your companions," she said, instantly focusing her eyes on his face. "You are an outsider."

James knew his face registered surprise. His brows raised silently even as he asked, "And how would you know that, Miss Bryce?"

"Because like knows like." She reached her hands out to the woodstove and grimaced. "This is not nearly as warm as the fireplace."

"Yes, I know," James replied. "It's also not nearly so crowded." He glanced to where no fewer than ten people stood huddled around the crackling flames in the hearth.

Annabelle seemed to consider this a moment before asking, "Are you staying long in Harper's Ferry?"

"I'm not sure. There are some railroad problems, and I've come with Mr. Latrobe to see what can be done. If this blizzard insists on continuing, I suppose I might well be there until spring."

Annabelle laughed. "Pity us all then, for we might well grow tired of each other if that be the case."

"I doubt seriously people tire easily of you," James said without thinking. He watched her face take on an expression of sheer delight.

"You are quite the charmer, I think," she said, rubbing her hands together. "Have you a wife and children or maybe a string of admiring young ladies?"

James frowned and tried not to think of his broken engagement to Virginia Adams. Quite easily, he pushed the image of her face aside and found the void filled with the memory of Carolina. "There is no one," he answered, feeling as though he'd lied.

"I find that impossible to believe. But I will not pry. I myself have been married twice. My first husband was an actor. He died in a carriage accident only two years after we married. My second husband was a patron of the theater. He didn't care for his wife continuing to travel around the world. We actresses are not always held in high regard, and so he wished only that I would allow the notoriety of my past to disappear from view and memory. We parted company two years ago, and he instantly sought a divorce."

"I'm sorry."

"Don't be. My reputation was already questionable." She straightened her shoulders and jutted out her chin ever so slightly. The action instantly reminded James of Carolina. How stoic she could pretend to be when the need arose.

James didn't know quite what to say. "So now you are alone?" he asked hesitantly.

"Hardly that!" she exclaimed, pushing aside any hint of melancholia. "I don't think I've ever known a time in my life when I was alone."

"Truly?"

"Truly. I grew up in a house of wealth and plenty. My father was a land baron and knew his business well. He could make money at anything; he had but to touch his hand to the matter, and it turned to gold."

"King Midas, eh?" James asked with a chuckle.

"Exactly." Her eyes took on a faraway look in her reflection of the past. "We were eight girls and three boys, and our parents were very loving and generous. There was never a moment of solitude to be had. When I fell in love with the theater and my actor-husband, my father and mother were appalled. No member of the Gainsborough family would dare to lower themselves to the level of becoming theater people. So I was disinherited by my old family, and the acting troupe became my new family."

"So you married and changed your name as well?" James was already thinking of his own family problems. He had little doubt that his father had already disinherited him for his actions of the past.

She shook her head, causing strawberry blond curls to bob from side to side. "Annabelle Bryce is my name. I simply omitted the use of my last name."

"I see."

"I don't think you do, or you'd not take on such a sorrowful tone," she said softly. "I'm not unhappy with the way things have turned out. My husband and I had two happy years, and I've never known more pleasure and happiness than that which I've found with the theater.

And I'm never alone, just as I told you. I have friends all over the world, and I have but to appear before them, and I'm treated as royalty."

James had known similar welcomes. The Latrobes had taken him in for Christmas dinner and treated him as though he were one of the family. But the bur in his side remained that the very people he wanted to be welcomed by were the ones who despaired of him ever sullying their doorsteps again.

"Will you be staying with your sister?" he asked, suddenly realizing that he wanted to see Annabelle again.

"Yes, I suppose I will. She lives with her husband and four children, and she, like me, is an outcast in our family. Married beneath herself, don't you see?" She raised this question with a glint of amusement. "Royalty must never stoop to marry a commoner. Even if you're only pretend royalty." She laughed and gave her head a little toss. "That's really the funniest part of all. My parents are far better actors than I could ever hope to be. For you see, they have the entire world believing them to be something they are not. King and Queen Gainsborough and their little princesses and princes."

Their sleigh was now ready for departure, and as the others moved outside, James smiled and offered his arm to Annabelle. "Your highness," he said in mock respect, "might I escort you to your carriage?"

Annabelle's laughter was like the tinkling of glass chimes. She tied the ribbons of her bonnet before linking her arm through James' and simpered, "But of course, good sir. How very kind."

"Perhaps when we have arrived in Harper's Ferry, you will give me the honor of escorting you to dinner," James said rather boldly. He liked this woman, and he found her company to be far more appealing than the isolation he'd imposed upon himself.

"The honor would be mine, sir."

Seventeen

Fragile Faith

$\mathcal{T}$he funeral of Pennsylvania Adams was at first a quiet, somber affair. The cold weather had made digging the grave a difficult and nearly impossible task. Four of the larger male slaves had alternated with shovels and picks to penetrate the frozen earth. Carolina remembered watching the slaves work from her window and feeling a deep, abiding sorrow. Now as she stood beside the coffin that held her little sister, Carolina didn't even try to hold back her tears. They were burying another child. A child who should have grown into adulthood and lived a life of many more years. A child who had brought to the family smiles and tears, pleasures and fears. A child who would be sorely missed by all.

Carolina stood several feet away from her mother and father, but her eyes were ever on them. Her mother's face remained emotionless as the minister spoke of the hope of resurrection in Christ. Her appearance at the funeral had been uncertain, and Carolina was still rather surprised to find her in attendance.

When the slaves had come to dress Penny's body for the laying out and burial, Margaret had adamantly refused to allow anyone near her little daughter. She remained, as she had for the months prior to Penny's death, rigidly positioned at her daughter's side. It had taken Joseph's insistence that Penny be bathed and dressed to finally convince Margaret to leave the room.

What had followed afterward had been a confusing scene of hysteria and accusation. Margaret had returned to the nursery and, upon finding Penny gone, proceeded to tear the house apart in search. Finding her in the first-floor drawing room, laid out in a beautiful handmade coffin, had caused Margaret to fall away in a dead faint.

She seems not to even hear the words, Carolina thought, all the while watching her mother. The wind whipped at them mercilessly, causing the minister to hasten his eulogy.

"We commend the spirit of Pennsylvania Adams into the hands of Almighty God. Ashes to ashes. Dust to dust." The minister spoke these words and tossed a handful of frozen dirt upon the casket.

"What is he saying?" Margaret suddenly questioned aloud.

All eyes turned to the woman, and without any embarrassment for this interruption, Margaret tugged at Joseph's coat. "Where is Penny? Where is Mary?"

Joseph, eyes filled with compassion and tears, patted her hand gently. "They are no longer with us, my dear. Do you not remember?"

"What are you saying?" Her voice rose another level. She spied the casket as if for the first time. "You certainly haven't put our daughters in there, have you?" She rushed forward before Joseph could stop her.

Margaret tried to lift the lid of the box, but it had already been nailed down. "Open this at once and let my babies out. Are you mad? They cannot hope to breathe for long in there. Mr. Adams, open this at once!"

The small congregation of friends and neighbors grew uncomfortable with the scene. Lucy Alexander, who had stood supportively between York and Carolina, reached out to pull Carolina closer. It was almost as if she hoped to shield Carolina from the reaction of her mother. Georgia broke into sobs anew and seemed to cry harder with each of Margaret's words.

"You must open this box now!" Margaret screamed.

"My dear," Joseph answered, putting his arm around her small shoulders. "Our Penny is gone. She cannot come back to us, and the funeral must be allowed to proceed."

"Funeral! We cannot have a funeral!" She began to push away from Joseph and at the same time seemed intent on shedding her bonnet and coat. "I cannot believe you would do this," she said, struggling with the knotted ribbons of her hat. Finally, she ripped the thing from her head and threw it to the ground.

By this time, York had left Lucy's side and had joined his father. "Mother, you must calm down. Why don't I take you upstairs?"

"I'm not leaving the children!"

Carolina felt Virginia's gaze upon her and turned to find an expression of sheer hatred. There'd been no time to confront her sister with whatever injustices she held against Carolina, and it was clear that matters were no better now than they had been at Christmas. Had Virginia thought of a way to blame Carolina for Penny's death as well as everything else?

Margaret's screams filled the air, causing Carolina to quickly forget about Virginia. York and Joseph were trying to lead her from the services, but she would have no part of it. Fighting them both while hurling accusations and reprimands, Margaret was totally unaware of the spectacle she'd created.

Georgia was now quite hysterical, so Carolina left the comfort of Lucy and went to her sister. Pulling her into her embrace, Carolina sensed that Georgia was close to collapse.

"Come, we'll get you inside."

She led Georgia around to the back of the house in order to avoid their mother's hideous display of grief. Georgia's cheeks were reddened from the cold, and by the time they entered the kitchen, both girls were nearly frozen.

"I cannot bear it anymore," Georgia said as Carolina helped her into a chair. "Mother is crazy and I fear her and I fear that I'll die next. First Mary, then Penny, don't you see? I'm the next in line. I'm only fourteen, Carolina!"

"Shhh. You hush now," Carolina said, peeling off her bonnet and coat and soaking in the warmth of the kitchen stove. "You aren't going to die. Penny has never been of a strong constitution. Even as a baby she was sickly. The fever was just too much for her. She was too little and frail."

"But I'm not very much bigger," Georgia protested. "I can't stand it!" She put her gloved hands over her bonnet and clasped both to her ears. "Make it all stop!"

Carolina knew there were no words to comfort Georgia. She wrapped her arms around the quaking girl and held her tightly against her body. At first, Georgia remained stiff and unmoved, but gradually there was a softening of her body, a relaxing that signaled acceptance of the offered comfort.

"We must be strong for each other," Carolina whispered. The only other sound was that of the crackling fire inside the stove. Naomi was still among the funeral attendees, and they had the kitchen to themselves. Dropping to her knees, Carolina wiped Georgia's eyes with her kid gloves. Sorrowful blue eyes looked to Carolina with unspoken questions.

"It will not be easy with Mother," Carolina finally said. "She might not even survive this. We will have to be steadfast, or the pain will be too much to deal with. Rest assured, Georgia, God will help us through."

"I can't rest assured in God. He seems so far from this house," Georgia said bitterly.

"I know." And indeed she did. Carolina thought of her own fragile faith—faith she'd only months before come to accept. If God truly loved them and was as merciful as her father claimed, then why were they burying an eleven-year-old child? And if God was almighty and all-knowing, why had their mother reacted the way she had? Why couldn't God stop the demons that seemed to have taken over their mother's weakened mind?

"I want to go away, Carolina. Please help me. If you don't, I shall run away."

The words were spoken so softly that Carolina almost missed them altogether. Georgia had never been one to ask for help, and now her request betrayed a sense of desperation.

"Would you talk to Father?" she went on. "I want to go live with Aunt Clara in her new house in Georgia. Or maybe even go abroad and be with Maine and Aunt Bertha in England."

"Father has plans for finishing school," Carolina offered. "There are some very fine finishing schools in Virginia, and perhaps we could suggest one that would take you away from this area."

"Yes! That's it! Father will never say no to that idea. Oh, please tell me that you'll talk to him, Carolina. Please?"

"Of course I will. As I said, Father already has considered your need in this matter." Georgia seemed to breathe a sigh of relief, and Carolina hugged her close again. "See there, it will all work out to everyone's benefit."

"Everyone except Mother," Georgia added.

Carolina sighed and nodded. "Yes, everyone except Mother."

Hampton Cabot's arrival did little to comfort Carolina. Finding herself busy with the household running of Oakbridge Plantation, Carolina resented the demand Cabot represented on her few free hours. Still, she knew she couldn't protest. Her father was definitely not himself these days. Not only were there the continuous problems with Mrs. Adams, but her father was battling to obtain the railroad charter for the Potomac and Great Falls line, as well as deal with the economic uncertainty of the future.

Hampton's actions were considerably more subdued than his last visit. He seemed genuinely concerned for Carolina's state of mind in the wake of her sister's death. He spoke sympathetically and offered tender reassurance of his devotion. After a while, Carolina found his mannerisms to be comforting, almost welcomed. She couldn't say she was glad for all of his interruptions, but there were times when her own loneliness was too much. It was then that Hampton's companionship seemed not only acceptable, but a solace to be sought out.

"I wish I could have brought your father better news," Hampton said, leaning casually against the fireplace mantel.

"I'm sure your presence is reassuring to him," Carolina offered.

"The affairs of this country are in a sorry state," Hampton said, almost as if he hadn't heard her. "There is a time coming—nearly upon us, in fact—when we may find ourselves with very little to show for our efforts this past score of years."

"Is it truly all that bad?"

"Bad enough that this country has become so deeply indebted to England that we might as well be subjects of the Crown again."

Carolina's mouth dropped open and a tiny gasp escaped her lips. "That will never be!"

Hampton smiled tolerantly. "I've picked a bad topic to discuss with one of such a gentle and fragile nature."

Carolina actually laughed at this. "I assure you, fragile is not a word to use in describing my constitution. I handle surprises quite well. Politics and economic failures are things that have always been discussed at great length in this house."

Hampton left the window and came to sit beside Carolina. She started to move away, but he held her hand fast and pleaded with her to stay.

"I promise to do nothing that might cause you displeasure," he said with such sincerity that Carolina remained in place. His thumb gently stroked the top of her hand, causing goosebumps to form on her arm.

I will not fall in love with him, she chided herself. Yet, in spite of her resolve, she found her gaze drawn to his ruggedly handsome face. He was so very different from James. James' face held a noble, almost aristocratic appearance, while Hampton's physique could equally be at home in the coal mines of western Pennsylvania or in the stately grace of Oakbridge.

"You appear tired," he said gently. "Perhaps I have taken you away from your rest."

"No, not at all," Carolina answered. "It is kind of you to care, though."

He seemed about to speak on another matter when Lucy and York glided into the room, their arms entwined, their eyes filled with love for the other.

"We had hoped to find you here," York said, then sent Lucy on ahead while he closed the door. "I . . . that is we . . . want to tell you something."

Carolina could easily guess what their announcement might be, but she waited patiently for York to continue.

"Lucy and I are to be married." He smiled broadly and took the seat beside his bride-to-be.

Lucy flashed a radiant smile at Carolina. "We are to be sisters!"

"I'm so very glad," Carolina replied and felt her heart truly soar above the pain of Penny's death. "Will you have a long engagement?"

York seemed embarrassed at this and stammered a reply. "No . . . well, that is, I mean to say . . ."

"He means to say that we are going to marry next month. Neither of us wants to wait, nor do we see the benefit of a large wedding. President Jackson has offered us the use of the White House, but I prefer our quaint little house in the city. Will you stand with me, Carolina?"

Carolina felt honored by the invitation. "With pleasure." Then turning to her brother she beamed a smile of genuine affection and pride. "Congratulations."

"Yes, congratulations, Adams, Miss Alexander," Hampton joined in.

"We've told no one other than Lucy's father. I spoke with him in order to receive permission to ask her, but other than that, no one has been approached in regard to the matter. I was hoping you might help me with our family." York grew silent and reached for Lucy's hand. "Penny's death has made me see that time is not to be wasted where matters of importance are at stake."

Carolina knew very well what he meant. Hadn't her own thoughts led her down that very same path? "Father will be pleased," she replied. "As for Virginia . . . well, nothing seems to make her happy these days, and Georgia will be happy for the diversion and the excuse for a trip to the city."

"That leaves only Mother," York stated flatly.

"Yes, well, I don't suppose Mother will approve no matter what happens. You do realize that she will probably be too ill to attend?"

"Yes, and frankly I'd rather have it that way. I certainly want no repeat of the scene at Penny's funeral." He stood abruptly and took on a look of determination. "I'm going to go speak to Father right now. I must explain to him before he hears it from someone else. Will you excuse me?"

"Of course," Carolina and Lucy said at once.

Hampton, too, got to his feet. "I would ask that you also excuse me, ladies. I'm afraid I must get back to some important papers."

After both men had gone from the room, Lucy looked quite seriously at Carolina and asked, "Are you in love with him?"

The question startled Carolina. "Not at all." She paused for a moment, giving further contemplation to her words, then added, "But he is apparently in love with me."

Lucy's gaze darted from the closed door to Carolina. "That relieves me, Carolina—the fact that you don't love him."

"Why do you say that, Lucy?"

"I can't explain, but I feel there is something not quite right with Mr. Cabot. He seems sincere enough on the exterior, but I question his motives."

"Have you some reason to feel this way?" Carolina asked.

"Nothing I can put to proof," Lucy admitted. "Mostly it is just a hunch—woman's intuition, you know. But please promise me you will be careful. Take it slowly with him. He is worldly-wise and perhaps spiritually dim-witted. I see nothing in him to suggest otherwise."

"I'll be careful," Carolina promised, wondering what it was about Hampton Cabot that caused someone like Lucy to take notice and issue warnings.

Eighteen

A House of Cards

With a heart bound in sorrow, Joseph Adams rode out across the snow-covered meadows of Oakbridge. This was his land. His home. Yet he would trade it all away if it could only bring back the lives of his dead children and restore his wife's sanity.

Reaching the top of a ridge, he reined back the ebony gelding and surveyed his kingdom. This land was Adams land for as far as the eye could see. The orchards, now devoid of leaves and fruit, the snowy fields where corn and cotton once grew, the stand of woodlands where a small mill kept the plantation in lumber—all of it bore witness to his labors and years of perseverance. It also stood as a reminder of the price he'd paid for family obligation.

The world was blanketed in silence, but not so Joseph's heart. He warred within himself for answers that would not come. He knew the uncertainty of the future, and it terrified him like nothing ever had before.

The horse whinnied, as if anxious for his rider to move on, but Joseph was not interested in pressing ahead. His mind and soul were turned backward. Back to happier days when his children had been small and his beloved Margaret had wielded control over the plantation like the shrewd businesswoman she could be.

"Oh, Margaret," he sighed, sending puffs of white breath into the air.

He remembered the enchantress he had married. Theirs had been an arranged match, but love was far from absent. Joseph had lost his heart to the dark-eyed beauty from the first moment he'd seen her. And while she could be a bit stern at times and perhaps a little too heavy-handed in some matters, Margaret was all that he wanted and needed in a wife.

Now it seemed it was no longer to be so. She would stare at him with eyes that showed no sign of remembering the past and what they had shared together. She acted as though he were a stranger. But worse yet was the way she would look at him with her accusing eyes, as if to say, "You are responsible for my pain and loss."

The wind echoed mournfully in the valley, groaning through the trees as though joining Joseph in cries of regret. As it blew up over the ridge, Joseph hardly felt its bite. He was numb in his grief. Numb, yet not nearly enough to stop feeling the responsibility of it all. What was he to do? His entire world was falling apart, and as the crumbled bits seemed to move beyond his reach, Joseph knew an emptiness that would not be filled.

Yesterday, York had advised him of his upcoming wedding to Lucy Alexander. Joseph could still remember the anticipation of concern in York's expression.

"If you do not disapprove," York had told him, "we will be married very quietly in Washington."

Disapprove? How could Joseph disapprove? His son had found a woman to love, and with hope for a future together, they had laid out their plans. How could he, loving his son as he did, suggest they wait until a longer period of mourning had passed? How could he, desiring only the very best for his child, demand that they wait until his mother's sanity had returned? Especially when her sanity might never return.

Joseph shook his head. York would marry and begin a family, but not for the sake of Oakbridge. York wanted nothing to do with running a plantation, and he had reiterated that point yesterday. He wanted a life of politics, and he wanted to spend time with Lucy's father in order to learn more of the dealings of such things. He believed that he would be retained by Van Buren when he took over the presidency in March, but even with that carrot being dangled before his nose, York also desired to seek his own political gains. He'd even relayed the hope of one day running for office.

Remembering a letter that had arrived only that morning from Maine, Joseph felt a deeper despair. His only other living son had been called to the ministry. The young man was convinced, without the smallest doubt, that God would use him as a missionary to the Indians. He had this freedom as the second son, Joseph thought. He could make his plans for the future quite free of concern for family. Of course, Maine had no idea that York had rejected the responsibility of Oakbridge. Perhaps if Joseph offered Maine the choice of Oakbridge or the ministry . . . but just as the thought came to him, Joseph knew he would never tell Maine of his circumstance. He would never risk having his son give up on the dream God had led him to in order to run a plantation. Freedom would be Joseph Adams' legacy to his sons. Freedom to follow their hearts.

There seemed little recourse but to seriously consider Hampton's suggestion that should he marry Carolina, he might be allowed to run the plantation. Hampton Cabot had proven himself worthy of such a task, and if indeed what he'd said about Carolina feeling obligated to Oakbridge was true, then bringing him on board would make a great deal of sense. Of course, Virginia would hate him for such a thing.

Virginia was an entirely different matter. In their family, Joseph alone knew of the letter James Baldwin had sent her, breaking their engagement. James had tried to be an honorable man, and in many ways Joseph admired his decision. He wanted his children to marry mates who would love them. James did not love his Virginia, and therefore it seemed wise to dissolve the betrothal. Still, there was the matter of Virginia's heart. She had seemed completely broken by the news. Joseph had privately questioned whether his daughter really loved James or was merely saying yes to the first man who asked her to marry. But now he could see she was truly devastated by James' departure. If it wasn't love, then it was a form of devotion that merited as much regard.

He didn't know how to reach Virginia, nor did he have time to figure it out. She was angry and hostile, taking most of her misery out on Carolina. Poor Carolina. She had no idea of the blame Virginia placed on her shoulders. Joseph himself had seen the relationship blossom between Carolina and James, and while in the early months he'd told himself that it was nothing more than a sharing of like interests between a tutor and his student, he soon came to think otherwise. Now he felt certain that Carolina had acquired feelings for young Baldwin. However, she had kept them to herself in that he belonged to her sister. Joseph had watched her put aside her own feelings for the sake of Virginia. Albeit, Virginia would never admit to such a thing. Virginia saw only that Carolina had encouraged James' interests in the railroad, and the railroad had taken her intended away.

Joseph wondered now, however, if it hadn't been more James' love of Carolina that had caused him to break the engagement. His letter had relayed that his heart and interests lay elsewhere, and Virginia had assumed for the most part that this interest had to be the railroad. Joseph, on the other hand, believed the railroad was only one of the interests of James' heart.

This brought his thoughts back around to Carolina and Hampton.

Did she love Hampton, as he seemed to believe? Joseph clearly saw nothing of the admiration and respect Carolina had held for James Baldwin. Her face didn't light up when Hampton Cabot's arrival was announced, nor did she go out of her way to seek his company when he was in residence at Oakbridge. If anything, Joseph thought she sought only to avoid Hampton.

Lastly, there was Georgia to consider. The child was quickly becoming a woman and in two years would come out into society. But there was a wildness about her, an untamed spirit that seemed to drive her into completely unacceptable behavior. Joseph had heard rumors and feared that, should those things be true, two years might not pass before Georgia would have to settle down to marriage.

He knew there should be something he could do to better control her, but he was so tired. The only reasonable suggestion was one Carolina broached after Penny's funeral—to send Georgia to a finishing school. Carolina had even offered up the name of a rather strict home in Richmond where young ladies were properly turned out to the laud and praise of all who knew them. It appeared to be the answer to all of his problems with Georgia, and yet there was a part of him that felt guilty over sending her off to be dealt with by someone else.

But he was only one man. He could only do so much, although there seemed to be a never ending roster of responsibilities and only he himself to see to them. His shoulders sagged a bit lower, and his eyes blurred with unshed tears. It was as though he stood amid a house of cards, and piece by piece the thing was tumbling down around him.

He sighed again and gave the horse his head. Picking a slow path back down the ridge, Joseph felt more burdened than ever before. He considered each of his children and knew there was nothing he could do to ease their pain and suffering. He saw them each going their own way. Some by choice, others by his hand. York would marry, Maine would serve God, and he would soon send Georgia to Richmond. That left only Virginia and Carolina to deal with.

"Father, I have no clear path before me," Joseph prayed aloud. He looked skyward, as though hoping the throne of heaven would be revealed. "My family is deteriorating before my eyes. My hope is in you, but my heart is ever on them."

The horse stumbled, regained his footing, and moved on at a steady pace. Joseph, tightening the reins in his gloved hands, wondered seriously about the fate of his home and family. If only he could see some answer for their state of affairs.

"Help me, Father. Help me to know what is best for all of them. My Margaret needs your healing touch, and should she not be able to have it, I don't know what I will do." His chest constricted with the anguish he felt. He choked back a cry as he continued. "She is my world, my heart and soul, and now I feel such dread and loneliness that I cannot bear to face the days ahead. She has left me, left her mind and journeyed to a place where I cannot follow." He pulled back on the reins just as they settled on the path for home. Then with an imploring voice, Joseph lifted his gaze heavenward once again. "Please bring her back to me. I've already lost those who were so dear. Don't let me lose my beloved as well."

PART II

February 1837–
January 1838

*The train calls at stations in the woods, where the wild
impossibility of anybody having the smallest reason to get
out is only to be equalled by the apparently desperate
hopelessness of there being anybody to get in.*

—Charles Dickens

Nineteen

Impenetrable Walls

*O*n the fourteenth of February, 1837, Lucy Alexander became Lucy Adams. Her dark hair and eyes made a sharp contrast to the white brocaded satin of her dress. The gown, a creation from France, had been a gift from Lucy's father, while the veil, a gossamer piece with scalloped lace, had been her mother's bridal veil.

Carolina thought there had truly never been a more beautiful bride. The snug bodice of the gown set off Lucy's tiny waist, while the deep rounded neckline left her milky shoulders bare. She wore a strand of diamonds and pearls and carried her mother's small black Bible. She was confident and graceful and all things that a woman should be. At least, all manner of things that Carolina wished to be.

But while Lucy looked confident, York appeared pale. He seemed less sure of himself, almost nervous. Carolina had caught his gaze only once and thought instantly of a raccoon she'd once cornered in the stable. The surprise and fear that had registered on the animal's face was very nearly the same as that on York's. Normally, York would be the one to take charge of matters, but this time it was clearly Lucy who held the advantage.

The ceremony itself was short and simple. York and Lucy stood before the Reverend Boswell and pledged their lives and love to each other for all time. Carolina stood beside Lucy, while York, being without any close friends since the departure of James Baldwin, requested his father stand as witness to the union. The only other people present were a few mutual friends of Lucy and York, and of course, Virginia and Georgia Adams.

Carolina had known the intensity of Virginia's spiteful nature from the moment they departed Oakbridge for Washington. Virginia had protested such an event while citing that the family was in mourning.

This declaration was offered up at least a dozen times until Georgia threatened to be quite ill if Virginia didn't cease her complaints. This, of course, sent Virginia into a sulk, which Carolina readily felt was more endurable than her whining.

Once they'd arrived at the Alexander house the day before the wedding, Lucy, too, had picked up on Virginia's bitterness and went out of her way to extend the utmost courtesy. Nothing seemed to work, however, and Virginia had bid them all an early evening to seclude herself in the room Lucy had provided. She stayed practically out of sight until the wedding ceremony the next afternoon.

Now, sitting down to the wedding supper after the ceremony, Carolina wondered seriously how she might resolve the situation with her sister. Virginia refused to speak to her, and even when Carolina had tried to force the issue, she'd made little progress. Virginia clearly wanted no part of Carolina's comfort.

Laughter rang out from the far end of the table where Lucy and York toasted each other and tried to share sips of wedding punch from the same goblet. Lucy was careful to raise the linen tablecloth to cover her gown, as everyone knew it was bad luck to stain one's wedding dress.

Virginia came late to the table, and while such rudeness would ordinarily bring about a harsh reprimand from their mother had she been present, Virginia seemed completely unconcerned. In fact, Virginia seemed to have relaxed a great deal, Carolina thought, as she picked at the roasted duck on her plate. She watched Virginia out of the corner of her eye and instantly knew that something was amiss. Virginia's hand seemed incapable of doing what she wanted it to do. She nearly knocked over her wedding punch at one point, and brushed her sleeve against the candle flame at yet another. The coup de grace came when Virginia, laughing with rather too much zeal over a trivial amusement, nearly fell out of her chair.

"Virginia, are you all right?" their father asked in a tone of worry.

Carolina, sensing a scene was about to be created, quickly got up from her chair and moved to the end of the table. "Virginia hasn't been feeling well today. It's just all the excitement and such. I'll help her to her room."

Carolina reached out to steady Virginia's swaying form and helped her to her feet. Virginia turned and struggled to focus on Carolina's face.

"I don't need help," she said flatly.

Carolina smelled the liquor on her breath and took a tighter hold on her sister's arm. "Come along, Virginia. You'll soon be right as rain."

Virginia made only a minor protest to Carolina's insistent tug. As they exited the dining room, Joseph came up behind them to inquire as to the problem.

"Is Virginia all right?" he asked Carolina.

Carolina knew there would be nothing but trouble if their father learned that Virginia was drunk. She hated to lie but felt somehow responsible for her sister's actions.

"It's just female troubles, Papa," she told him in a hushed voice, all the while pushing Virginia toward the stairs.

"Ah, I see." Joseph's face instantly relaxed. "You take good care of her. I'll have one of the servants bring your meal up to the room."

"Thank you, Papa," Carolina replied. She was grateful Virginia hadn't attempted to offer her own account of the circumstance.

With her hand to the small of Virginia's back, Carolina followed up the stairs wondering what she would say to her sister once they were alone. It wasn't like anyone in her family to be given to strong drink. And it was especially unacceptable because Virginia was a woman. Their mother and father both abhorred drunkenness, and it was well known in the community that such actions weren't to be tolerated at any Adams' affair. So what had possessed Virginia Adams to break those rules?

Slipping into the bedroom at the far end of the hall, Carolina was unprepared for Virginia's sudden move. Whirling around, Virginia pushed Carolina backward with such force that Carolina fell against the door.

"What is wrong with you?" Carolina asked more harshly than she had intended.

"You!" Virginia spat out the word venomously. "You are what's wrong with me." She staggered to her trunk and opened it with dramatic flourish. Pulling a silver flask from beneath layers of petticoats, Virginia unscrewed the top and lifted it to her lips.

Carolina grimaced. "Haven't you had enough of whatever is in there?"

"No." Virginia took a long drink, then lowered the flask. "I haven't had nearly enough. I can still see you and hear you and be reminded of everything you did to me."

"What is it you have against me? Tell me that I might at least try to seek your forgiveness."

"Forgiveness? Never!" Virginia laughed maniacally. "You will never hear that word from my lips." Her speech was so slurred it was nearly incomprehensible.

Carolina shook her head. "What did I do to you? If you won't forgive me, why not at least explain what imagined wrong I've performed?"

"Imagined?" Virginia actually seemed to sober at this word. "You think I've imagined my injustices?"

"I just suggest that perhaps the situation isn't as it seems. I've no recollection of doing you any injustice, let alone one of such immense proportions."

Virginia swayed, nearly falling backward onto the bed. As if considering the idea for a moment, she paused in her tirade and looked down at the wedding-ring quilt that covered the top of the bed. Then without further ado, she plopped down in rather unladylike fashion and took another drink.

Carolina waited for her to say something more. Virginia's face contorted at the realization that the flask was empty. She tossed the thing aside, then looked at Carolina as though remembering for the first time that she was there.

"I hate you," she said, barely whispering the words. "I will always hate you."

Carolina stepped forward cautiously, feeling only marginally safe because Virginia was seated. "But why? What have I done?"

"Don't play the innocent with me." Virginia scowled and curled her lip as if to snarl. "You are the reason I'm alone. Do you know how it feels to attend the wedding of your brother, knowing that it should have been your own?"

"But you broke your engagement," Carolina responded, still not understanding. "How am I responsible for that?"

"You gave James his interest in the railroad."

"No, he already had an interest in the railroad," Carolina corrected. "I merely helped him to see it through his grief. I can't be blamed for that."

"Oh, yes you can be. I would be a married woman by now if not for your meddling. James was perfectly happy to take up banking until you kept forcing the issue of locomo . . . loco . . ." she stammered and put a hand to her head as if trying to remember something very important. When the word refused to come to her she shrugged her shoulders. "If you and that blasted railroad would have just remained out of sight, James would have stayed on as a banker."

"But for how long?" Carolina questioned. "Isn't it better that you know of his desires before marrying him than learning of it later?"

"But *I* was his desire!" she exclaimed, getting uneasily to her feet.

Carolina backed away cautiously, wondering if Virginia would attack her again.

"I was his desire, and he was happy with me. You ruined my life, Carolina Adams, and I will never forget it."

Carolina knew it was senseless to argue with Virginia, yet she was desperate to vindicate herself. "If you loved James, why didn't you support his desire to be a part of the railroad? Any other woman would have followed her intended in his duties, not demanded he give them up."

"What do you know? You're a child!" Virginia swayed and grabbed on to the bedpost. Her eyes rolled from side to side for a moment.

Carolina felt it futile to continue the conversation. "Why don't you let me help you into bed, Virginia? You don't want Father to find out about the drinking." She moved toward Virginia rather hesitantly.

Virginia fell backward against the bed. Rising up on her elbows, she shook her head. "I don't want your help."

"Is there nothing I can do to set things right between us? You know this will break Father's heart and only add to his worries."

"There is nothing you can say or do. . . ." Virginia's words trailed off. Then, as if a sudden revelation had come to mind, her eyes widened. "You could leave Oakbridge so that I never have to lay eyes on you again."

"My leaving is the only thing that will allow you to forgive me?"

Virginia laughed. "Oh no. I said nothing about forgiveness. I just want you out of my life. Why don't you marry that simpering bore, Hampton Cabot? Yes, that's it. Marry Mr. Cabot and move to New York and leave me alone." Then without warning, Virginia dizzily fell back against the mattress and passed out.

Carolina called to her several times, but seeing that she was in a deep state of alcohol-induced sleep, she pulled off Virginia's shoes and stockings. She then wrestled Virginia's body around the bed in order to strip her of the cumbersome velvet gown and corset. Leaving her with petticoats and chemise, Carolina managed to position her lengthwise.

She covered Virginia in a tender, almost motherly way and sighed. Maybe leaving was best. Hadn't she herself considered such an idea? Georgia's desire to leave home had only stirred up Carolina's own unspoken wishes. Oakbridge was no longer a haven to her, and distancing herself from it seemed to fit hand in hand with her belief that God was sending her west with the railroad.

She contemplated Virginia for a moment and considered her suggestion that she marry Hampton Cabot. It was true enough that doing such a thing would remove her from Oakbridge, but it wouldn't allow her to take up an active role with any railroad, much less her beloved Potomac and Great Falls.

"I'm not the reason James left," Carolina whispered to Virginia's now peaceful face. "I'm not to blame for your choices."

Then she turned to go, not completely certain of the truth of her words, because all her denials would never change the fact that Carolina had fallen in love with Virginia's fiancé.

Twenty

Heart and Soul

Carolina was still contemplating her future the following week when she visited the White House. President Jackson had opened his home to the public in celebration of Washington's birthday. The entire city was a mass of confusion and revelry during that holiday, and Carolina found herself actually quite anxious to return to the quiet of country life. But she wanted to see President Jackson once more before returning to Oakbridge.

She was received warmly by the staff, who by this time recognized the young woman whom their President had come to admire. She carried with her Jackson's letters and felt a lingering sorrow as she pushed through the crowds to make her way to the staircase. These people had little idea the anguish and pain that had been inflicted upon Rachel and Andrew Jackson. Nor did they know of their deep abiding love— a love that had suffered through many separations.

Throughout the house were tables laden with gifts. Pipes, ornate walking sticks, a small wagon made of hickory, hats, and other personal articles all came from the people who loved Jackson and wished to bid him a fond farewell from public office. The strangest gift of all came in the form of a huge wheel of cheese. Said to weigh fourteen hundred pounds, the cheese was four feet in diameter. At least it had been at the start of the day. Now there was little left of it given that every visitor to the White House had taken for himself a memento of the day. The smell of cheese lingered in the air, however, and Carolina smiled to think of the onslaught that must have ensued to so diminish the thing.

Jackson's mulatto, George, stood at the top of the stair awaiting her ascent. He bowed slightly and led the way to the President's bedroom. It was said that Jackson had only come downstairs five times since the December elections. His health and spirit were failing him fast, and

Carolina felt honored that he'd given her so much of his time and strength.

Passing through, she silently contemplated the upstairs hallway. There were packing boxes and trunks everywhere. The eight-year accumulation of Jackson memorabilia had to be readied for the move to the Hermitage, Jackson's beloved plantation in Tennessee.

George paused to open the bedroom door, then stood back to allow Carolina entry into the room. The drapes were pulled against the harsh winter light, and only two candles were lighted.

"Miss Adams," the aged Jackson called from his bed, "what an honor to receive you. Please take off your coat and stay with me a while."

"The honor is mine, sir," she said. Untying the ribbons of her bonnet, Carolina set it aside and quickly shed her coat as well. She took her place on a straight chair beside the bed and smiled. "I don't blame you for hiding out here. The crowds downstairs are quite unruly."

He smiled, the weary lines of his wrinkled face lifting for a moment. "There is nothing quite like a party to fetch in the prettiest of women. I must say, you grow more lovely by the day."

Carolina felt herself flush, but she kept her gaze firmly fixed on Jackson. In her heart, she wondered if he would live to see his successor take the oath of office in March.

"I read worry in those lovely brown eyes," he said before she could voice her thoughts.

"It is my prayer that you recover your health," Carolina replied softly.

"I will recover when I'm once again returned to my home." He spied the letters in her hands. "Ah, I see you've returned my youthful prose."

Carolina smiled and handed over the bundle. "I was most impressed. I laughed and cried and felt as though I knew Mrs. Jackson as a personal friend. You were truly blessed in your love, and I can only pray to find such a love myself one day. If such things are not reserved only for a lucky few."

Jackson coughed fitfully for a moment. Carolina thought the rasping sounds of his gasping breath could be compared to death rattles, but she pushed such an idea from her mind and tried to concentrate instead on the letters.

Finally calming, Jackson shook his head. "There is true love for you, Miss Adams. Of this I am sure. But you mustn't settle for anything less than the purest heart. There will come many men to woo you, and their charms may well lead you to the altar, but God alone knows who the right one will be. Trust Him for that direction."

"You speak as one who knows, yet I've heard it said . . ." She paused, suddenly realizing her boldness.

"Heard what said?" Jackson asked. "Surely we are good enough friends that you may be honest with me."

Carolina smiled. "I've heard it said you do not attend church and that you hardened your heart toward God after Mrs. Jackson's death."

Jackson's expression grew rather pinched. His snowy brows knitted together, further wrinkling his forehead. "God knows my heart and that it is not hardened toward Him, but rather toward those who killed my Rachel. You see"—he coughed for a moment, then continued—"my Rachel was sorely used and abused by her first husband. They divorced and we married, and folks have never forgiven her or me for such a deed. I always presumed God would be my judge, but instead I find it the pastime of a nation." He paused, his eyes filled with sorrow, as though painful memories haunted his every waking moment.

"Rachel was a lovely woman," Jackson continued after a moment, "as I'm sure you found out in the letters. She wanted only that we would share a quiet life together, but it was not to be. I was called upon to serve my country, and given that it was my duty, I could not trade one responsibility for the other. Rachel always supported me, however, and she fully planned to make the trip to Washington when I was elected President." His eyes grew misty. "She was buried in the gown she'd chosen for the inauguration. She was a vision, Miss Adams, an angel in white. She was buried on Christmas Eve, 1828. Almost ten years have gone by, yet it feels as though it were only yesterday that I watched her pass from this earth. Pass to a place where they couldn't hurt her anymore."

Carolina couldn't think of what she could possibly say that would offer comfort, and so she simply placed her gloved hand upon his bony one. He smiled in appreciation and brought his free hand to rest upon hers.

"Rachel would have loved you," he said.

"And I would have loved her," Carolina replied, knowing it was true.

He sighed and drew a ragged breath. "So you see, with my Rachel in heaven, how can I hate God? No, I assure you, Miss Adams, the matter of heart and soul is not one I treat lightly."

"But why is it that you refuse church? I've heard it said that you used to attend with Rachel in Tennessee."

"True enough, but I always feared that folks would see it as a political ploy. Rachel always wanted me to make my confession before the congregation and become a member of our church, but I knew the newspapers would catch wind of the fact and make a circus out of it. The cartoonists would no doubt have had me nailed to a martyr's cross, mocking our Savior's crucifixion. I couldn't bear the thought of bringing that about, but now that it's finished, now that I can return a free man to my home, I will honor God and Rachel and make such a declaration."

Carolina felt her heart soar. "That's wonderful!" She remembered something her father had said and offered it up. "God knows each heart, Mr. President. You have but to confess to Him, and He will honor your faith. To declare Him publicly is important, for it shows that you are unashamed to be associated and called one of His children, but even in private He hears you."

Jackson nodded. "I believe that, too. It's never been a problem accepting what God has to offer. The problem has come in forgiving the wrongs."

Carolina felt an instant pang of regret. Virginia would never forgive the injustice she held Carolina responsible for. Jackson had already declared on many occasions that he would never forgive those who'd robbed him of his wife. She braved the question that arose in her heart. "What of forgiveness? Will you forgive everyone?"

Jackson's expression remained rather stoic. "For those who've wronged me, I will forgive. But for those who wronged her . . . they must answer to God."

Twenty-One

First Step

With the coming of April and the spring thaw, memories of the crippling blizzard of 1837 were quickly forgotten by the small but thriving community of Harper's Ferry. James found himself calling this place home more and more, yet his heart was not really here. It had been six months since he'd spoken to any of his family, and he hadn't found the courage to even drop them a letter and assure them of his well-being. He was ashamed. Deeply and undeniably ashamed.

His actions hadn't been those of a man, but of a spoiled child who, upon seeing that the game wasn't being played his way, had taken his leave and refused to play on. Now, toying with the last of his supper and considering the next day's work, James found his heart turning ever homeward. The evenings were always the worst. When the work-day was done and everyone went their separate ways, James then realized just how alone he truly was.

It wasn't a lack of friends that left him feeling so isolated and rejected. He'd managed to make many new acquaintances, among those, the sister of Annabelle Bryce, Mrs. Letitia Martens, and her family. But it wasn't the same.

Lost in his thoughts over dinner in the hotel where he resided, James didn't react to the feminine voice that called his name until he felt a gloved hand on his shoulder and heard the voice again.

"Mr. Baldwin. How good to find you here."

He looked up and found Annabelle Bryce's amused expression.

"Miss Bryce, what a surprise." He got to his feet and gave a bow before pulling out a chair for her. "Won't you join me? I was nearly finished, but I would happily keep you company." In truth he'd hardly touched his food.

"I've dined already, but perhaps you would honor me with a walk about town?"

"With pleasure," James replied, tossing several coins down to pay for the meal even as he extended his arm to Annabelle.

Once they were outside, Annabelle's formality broke down. "So how are you? It seems like forever since we endured that snowstorm together."

James smiled and secured his top hat before answering. "It has been forever, but I'm faring well."

"James, this is me, Annabelle, remember?" She used a familiar tone and looked upon him with the tolerant expression of a mother to her child. "You look awful. You've lost weight. Your face is positively gaunt, and there are dark circles under your eyes. You haven't gone and caught consumption, have you?"

Rather than being put off by her attitude, he was curiously drawn by it. "No, nothing so manageable as that."

She laughed. "You must be in a bad way to suggest consumption as manageable. Now, tell me what is wrong."

James shrugged. He'd never allowed himself to be completely honest with anyone since leaving Carolina back at Oakbridge. It seemed awkward to share his heart, and so he took the conversation in another direction. "Would you care to climb the steps to Jefferson's Rock?"

"I'd love to, and afterward we can visit Letitia and beg some refreshment."

Forty-four stone steps had been carved out of the solid cliff to the upper levels of the Harper's Ferry community. It was said that Laura Wager, niece of the town's founder, Robert Harper, had overseen this ambitious task in 1817, and now the steps were used with little consideration to their origins.

While the scenic view from Jefferson's Rock was impressive—Harper's Ferry was less so. It was rapidly becoming the most important factory town in the Potomac valley, but because of this the air smelled of coal smoke, and a constant clatter of hammers, machinery, canal barges, and trains disrupted the pleasantries of this secluded valley.

Annabelle, barely winded from the excursion, took off her bonnet when they reached the top and let the wind blow through her strawberry blond curls. James thought she looked a bit pale, but considering that winter was just now behind them, it wasn't unusual to find people in such a state. He also knew her penchant for overworking. Articles announcing Annabelle Bryce's performances were never hard to come by, and if James had rightly calculated, Annabelle had starred in continuous nightly performances since her departure from Harper's last January.

They enjoyed a companionable silence while James' thoughts drifted back to his dismal life. He was glad Annabelle seemed intent on the scenery. After a time, however, she turned to him and questioned, "So, aren't we good enough friends that you can share the heavy burden you carry?"

James knew she would ask this before the words were even out of her mouth. "I do not like to burden my friends," he replied, his gaze fixed on the river below.

"I see," she said and turned to walk away.

"Wait! Where are you going?" James asked, hurrying after her.

Annabelle's violet eyes widened. "You don't want to share your bad times . . . your heartaches. So, therefore, I want no part of your good times. Friendships are not to be based on such superficial foundations."

"I'm sorry. Please don't go."

Annabelle adjusted her knitted shawl and squared her shoulders. "Will you deal honestly with me?"

"I'll try."

She appeared to consider this for a moment, then turned again as if to leave. "Not good enough, Mr. Baldwin."

James sensed she would not back down, and besides, perhaps he did need a friend right now with whom to unburden some of his heavy load. "All right, but if you should hate me for my confession, let it be on your shoulders."

Annabelle turned with a mischievous grin. "Me, hate you? Should I stand in judgment of another when my own actions have been considered so questionable?"

James felt immediately relaxed at this. Perhaps the only one to truly understand such indiscretions as his was one who had had similar experiences. "It isn't a short story."

"The weather is pleasant and I have all day." She walked to a rather large, flat boulder and took a seat. "Pray continue."

James looked out on the river valley below and sighed. "You see that railroad bridge below us? It was weakened by improper construction. The master plan was good, but the man in charge of construction refused to heed the instructions. He substituted cheaper materials, and now the pier headings have cracked and the bridge is unsafe. Shoddy workmanship and poor materials are to blame for the failures, but the one who is mostly to blame is the man who made such choices."

"And were you that man?" Annabelle asked softly.

"Not in as much as the bridge is concerned." James turned to her. "But where my own life is concerned, I alone am responsible for the demise."

"What is to be done with the bridge?" she asked.

"It will have to be rebuilt, at least the five piers in the river will be. There is nothing else to do at this point; it's simply too late to merely brace it up."

"And is it too late to merely brace up your life?"

"I fear so." The simple reply was filled with emotion.

"So shoddy workmanship and poor materials are the culprits on the bridge," Annabelle stated, "but what of your own life? What happened there, and what has been destroyed that must be rebuilt?"

James studied her for a moment. He searched her expression for any hint of condemnation, and finding none he began his story. "There was a girl. I was hired to tutor her, and because my parents desired I marry a wealthy woman, I was to consider such a match to this young woman's older sister. Which I did, albeit not as willingly as I should have. To draw things to a conclusion, I agreed to marry the older sister, but . . ." His voice trailed off as though even speaking the words would forever condemn his soul.

"But you fell in love with the younger sister," Annabelle finished for him.

James looked at her, knowing the anguish of his soul was surely conveyed in his eyes. "Yes. I didn't think I had. I thought it was simply that Carolina—that's her name—had inspired me to return to the railroad. I was grateful to her for her encouragement, and I highly admired her intelligence and eagerness to learn. She isn't like any other woman I've ever known, perhaps with exception to you."

Annabelle smiled but remained silent.

James pulled his top hat from his head and twisted the brim in his hands. "She doesn't even know I care for her, and now that I've broken the engagement to her sister, Carolina Adams would never consider me for one moment. I've acted in a completely unforgivable manner. I broke an engagement, although I allowed her sister to appear the one who had done so. There was a death in the family, and it made postponing the wedding quite convenient. I simply took undue advantage of the moment and penned a letter of dismissal. I broke the hearts of my parents in doing so, as they were quite desperate for me to bolster the family's failing economy with an advantageous union, and I left without saying a word to them."

"You said nothing?"

"I left a letter. I tried to explain, but you must understand I wasn't even sure what it was I felt at that point. I was still convinced that it had to be a simple infatuation with Carolina. Not that I would have admitted to them my feelings at all."

"No you wouldn't," Annabelle said quite seriously. "But you knew it was love, real love, or you'd have never acted in such a manner."

James' mouth dropped open, about to reply, but then he closed it. She was right. A part of him had known from the moment he'd first bumped into Carolina at a party in his home. Yes, even then he'd given a part of his heart to her. It had taken very little to offer her up the remaining portion.

Annabelle got up and walked to where James was still pacing and considering the matter. "You have faulty pier headings, and they must be rebuilt. How will you do it?"

James shook his head, trying to figure out if she meant the railroad or his life. "I suppose we must take one pier at a time. Tear out the old faulty pieces and reconstruct the new."

"And you won't destroy the whole bridge by working these little things out, will you?" She placed her gloved hand upon his arm and looked up at him with an expression of complete understanding.

"No," James replied, seeing her meaning. "It won't be easy."

"Good things seldom are," she said with a smile.

"So where should I start?"

Annabelle looked skyward and pursed her lips ever so slightly. "Hmm . . . I think forgiveness is the very best place to start. Although I must admit I'm not very good in accomplishing such matters myself, but I know good advice when I give it, even if I can't always follow it myself. I think you must first seek to forgive yourself, then ask it of those you've wronged."

"What of God?" James asked. Several spiritual conversations with Ben Latrobe had also been haunting him lately, and soul-searching was rapidly becoming a full-time consideration for him.

"Have you wronged Him, too?"

"I believe I have."

"Then maybe that is where you should start." Her words were simple and without condemnation. "After that, you should send a letter to your mother. Her heart must surely be broken by your absence."

James nodded. "I suppose you are right. It's just that I felt so confident they would want nothing more to do with me."

"Then let them be the ones to say so," Annabelle replied. "They should at least be given that chance."

James felt a surge of hope. "You are wonderful, Annabelle. I wish I had met you long ago."

"Does that mean you'll write that letter?" she asked in coquettish fashion.

James laughed and linked his arm with hers. "Yes. I'll write the letter. Now, didn't you suggest we impose upon your sister for refreshments? I'm very nearly parched from all this talking and famished from the walk up here."

"Confession is hungry business," remarked Annabelle with a grin. "Perhaps now you can eat properly and put some flesh back on your bones. You don't want to look shabby when you go back for your Carolina."

James startled at this. Could he go back for her? Would there ever come a day when she would welcome him into her life again?

Annabelle sensed his concern and patted his arm. "One pier at a time, remember?"

James drew a deep breath. "Yes. One pier at a time."

Twenty-Two

Battle Lines

$\mathcal{I}$t's a lovely party, don't you think?" Julia Cooper asked Carolina.

"To be sure." Carolina turned to Lucy and drew her into the conversation. "Sarah Armstrong will make a beautiful bride, but not quite so beautiful as you were, Mrs. Adams."

Lucy laughed and Julia smiled conspiratorially. "You don't suppose she'll wear those awful feather contraptions on her wedding gown, do you?" Julia asked in a low whisper.

Sarah was notorious for dressing a bit ostentatiously, and even now at her bridal shower she was decked out in a bold, if not overwhelming, red gown complete with ostrich feathers.

"I don't suppose Randolph Buford will care what she wears so long as she continues to look beautiful. He's quite wealthy, you know"— Julia offered the gossip as if it were news—"but very much one who cares about appearances."

"Wealth may not be enough to weather the coming storms," Lucy said. "My husband tells me we may well see a complete failure of the monetary system."

Julia looked at her rather strangely. "Do you really have an interest in such things?"

Carolina answered before Lucy could speak. "Lucy and I both see it as a responsible matter for women to be informed as well as men. We are, after all, the ones who will figure out how to make things stretch to meet the household needs, are we not?" She didn't wait for Julia's response but continued. "And while I'm not yet responsible for my own home, I see a great deal to be gained by keeping myself informed. Lucy and I attended a lyceum not long ago that addressed the need for better educating women. Did you know that Oberlin College in Ohio is now offering college degrees to women and negroes?"

143

"How shocking," Julia admitted. "Tell me you aren't considering such a thing."

Carolina shrugged. "I've long held a desire for furthering my education, as you well know, Julia. College has been uppermost in my mind, and now that such opportunities are starting to present themselves to women, it just might make my dreams come true."

"It seems to me that the idea of a young woman, unchaperoned in an unfamiliar place, is asking for trouble," Julia said, fanning herself thoughtfully. "What if it turns out to be more than you can endure?"

"Women can often endure a great deal more than they give themselves credit for," Carolina said.

"I'd like to see men endure the travails of childbirth," Lucy interjected with a twinkle in her eye.

Julia gasped, then giggled at the ridiculous picture Lucy's words conjured.

"I believe keeping us ignorant makes men look better," Carolina said with a mischievous smile.

"Of course, we mustn't let on that we know what they're up to," Lucy added.

Several other young women joined them, including Sarah Armstrong, whose dress made enough noise to bring an awkward halt to the conversation.

"We simply had to ask you something, Carolina," Sarah said, glancing behind her and then to either side. The other women nodded, as if to prove agreement.

"Ask me what?"

"Well, while Virginia is in the garden with Kate, I thought you might dispel the rumors about her."

"What rumors?"

Sarah gave her a look of disbelief. "Surely you know what I'm talking about."

"No." Carolina looked to Lucy, who shook her head.

"I believe Sarah wants to know about Virginia's broken engagement to Mr. Baldwin," Julia said, looking rather peeved with Sarah for bringing up such a delicate matter.

"What of it?" Carolina asked defensively.

"It is thought that perhaps your sister was jilted. My brother Daniel suggests that James, and not Virginia, dissolved the agreement."

"That's utter nonsense," Carolina replied. "I can't imagine how such a rumor could get started. James is a man of honor, and Virginia was overwrought with grief. Our mother has been quite ill since the death of our sisters, and Virginia felt it her obligation to care for her."

Lucy added indignantly, "It is scandalous that anyone would seek to bring further grief upon a family that has already suffered so much."

Sarah wasn't deterred. "There are servants to care for your mother. And everyone knows Virginia isn't exactly the devoted type. Besides, why else would Mr. Baldwin completely disappear from Washington? His parents haven't even had so much as a letter from him, and my mother told me that Mrs. Baldwin is sick with grief. If James Baldwin is so honorable, why has he left his mother to fret over his whereabouts?"

"I can't believe James . . ." Carolina paused, feeling her face grow flushed. "Mr. Baldwin would never do such a thing willingly. Perhaps he is ill or unable to write."

"Perhaps he is simply too ashamed," one of Sarah's companions offered.

Carolina caught sight of Virginia and Kate Milford Donnelley as they entered the room. She wanted nothing more than to shut Sarah Armstrong's mouth on the matter, but before she could change the subject, Sarah continued.

"Virginia dare not wait much longer for a husband. She's getting terribly old, and no man will want her once she passes twenty. Perhaps there is something wrong with your sister that made James want to break the engagement." Sarah, obviously still unaware of Virginia's presence, drove home her point. "Maybe your sister is . . . well . . . perhaps she's compromised."

Carolina saw the expression on Virginia's face. The look contorted from one of disbelief to sheer rage. Hoping to avoid an ugly scene, Carolina hurried to her defense.

"How dare you!" Carolina retorted. "My sister is an honorable woman. Mr. Baldwin did not break the engagement, she did! And she only did so in order to put our family first. I think you positively mean-spirited, Sarah Armstrong, to suggest anything other than the truth."

———

Virginia had heard most of the conversation and felt a seething rage overcome her. It was bad enough to be the center of such nasty gossip, but to have Carolina support and defend her was too much. She wasn't about to stand by and say nothing in her own defense, nor was she about to allow Carolina to come out of the situation looking like a heroine. No, Carolina and James had neither one paid the price for double-crossing her. But perhaps it was time to start.

Feeling Kate's hand tighten upon her arm in a supportive way only stirred Virginia's anger. She didn't want anyone's pity, nor did she want to be regarded as a spinster. What she really desired was that Carolina suffer as much as she had. Instead, she had a beau who was quite devoted and spoke of marriage at every turn. How Virginia would love to find a way to put an end to that adoration!

Feeling the effects of the sherry she'd managed to sneak sips of throughout the day, Virginia felt her courage bolstered. An idea sprang to her mind—an idea that just might see Hampton Cabot packing his bags forever. Glancing around at the small gathering of women, she smiled to herself. This was the perfect setting for her first strike against her sister.

A hush fell over the room as it became evident to the others that the object of their discussion had come to join them. Virginia exchanged a glance with Carolina and hated the sympathy she read in her sister's expression.

"Perhaps in the interest of truth, sister dear, we should be wholly honest," Virginia said.

Carolina looked at her with such an expression of confusion that Virginia actually laughed out loud. The other women looked at her strangely, and even Kate pulled away. Virginia didn't care. Let them all think what they would. It couldn't get much worse anyway.

"The truth," Virginia stated calmly, "is that my sister played a bigger part in the destruction of my engagement than she would ever want you to know about." All gazes moved from Virginia to Carolina, who shook her head in confusion.

"What are you talking about, Virginia?"

"Yes, Virginia, please tell us," Sarah added eagerly.

Virginia felt the power of holding the room captive. She thrilled to know the anguish she was about to impose upon her goody-goody little sister. Carolina would no longer be considered the belle of the county when this news hit the streets. And Hampton . . . well, poor Hampton Cabot just might need another source of comfort. Instead of sending him packing, Virginia was already imagining herself as the comforting heroine in his life.

"I'm sorry, Carolina, but I can no longer protect you," Virginia began in a rather regretful tone. She offered what she hoped was a truly mournful look before plunging ahead to destroy her sister's reputation. Feigning tears, Virginia slipped down in the nearest chair and pretended to be overcome with emotions.

"I tried to keep others from knowing. I tried." Virginia's stirring scene caused Kate to hurry to her best friend's side.

Lifting her face and dabbing at her eyes, Virginia gave her head a little shake. "I suppose because she is so young and"—Virginia looked up at Kate—"because she insisted on reading those books . . ."

"What books?" Sarah asked.

"Totally inappropriate books," Virginia answered. "She and my Mr. Baldwin—oh, but I mustn't call him that now." She sighed heavily and dabbed again at her eyes. The entire room was hers to command. Even Lucy and Carolina sat completely mesmerized by what she might say next.

"Mr. Baldwin and my sister began their relationship as tutor and student. My sister wanted to learn all manner of study, and my father, bless his soul, didn't understand just exactly what manner of study she had in mind."

"Do tell," gasped Sarah, now sitting on the edge of her seat.

"Yes, tell us, Virginia," Kate encouraged.

Virginia smiled to herself from behind the veil of her handkerchief. "Carolina wanted to learn about, well—" She looked intently at each of the women. "Carolina wanted to learn about science . . . if you understand my meaning."

Carolina stared openmouthed at her while the others were abuzz with chatter about the implications. Virginia fixed a stony stare on her sister and waited for the comments to die down.

"I believe if you asked my sister, she would have a hard time denying that she and Mr. Baldwin shared a very close friendship. They were given to late-night discussions and . . . well, perhaps the only word I might speak in delicate company is . . . experiments."

"No!" the women cried in unison, with exception to Lucy and Carolina, who were obviously too shocked to speak.

"It's true. I even managed to come upon them in a most intimate embrace," Virginia said, then looked away, as though trying to regain some lost composure. The expressions on their faces made her want to laugh. This was the perfect revenge. No proper family would accept Carolina as a potential daughter-in-law after she finished with this little performance. The only thing that would be left to accomplish after this would be making certain Hampton heard the news as well.

"I can't reveal what else took place. She is, after all, my sister. But I feel I simply cannot live a lie any longer."

"Oh, you poor thing," Kate said, patting her gently. The others murmured in agreement. "To think that your own sister would dally with your intended."

Accusing eyes turned on Carolina.

"I never!" she finally managed to exclaim.

"You never what, Carolina?" Virginia questioned. "Is it not true that you and James would sit side by side, often late into the night, discussing heaven only knows what?"

"That is true, but you were . . ."

"And is it not true that I found you embraced in James' arms?" Virginia interrupted.

Carolina shook her head. "You know very well that he was only comforting me after Mary's death."

"Yes, of course. Did he also come to you in the night, to offer . . . comfort?"

Carolina jumped tearfully to her feet. "I am innocent of these accusations."

Lucy stood beside Carolina, placing an arm around her trembling shoulders. "Enough of this!" she said in such a commanding tone that even Virginia was sobered. "I don't know what Virginia's game is, but if anyone here chooses to believe *any* of these nasty accusations, they are far worse off than either of these two fine girls. If you relish lurid stories, then read fiction—do not seek to ruin your friends—!" Lucy's voice broke off as she was overcome with her own emotion.

"We just want to know the truth," said Sarah lamely.

"All you want to know is silly gossip, and you don't care who you must hurt to find it," countered Lucy, swallowing her emotion.

"Well, I—"

"She's right," said Julia, obviously gaining courage from Lucy. "And I, for one, want to hear no more of it." She strode to Carolina and placed an arm around her other shoulder.

"What about me?" cried Virginia, stamping her foot as real tears fell from her eyes.

Now Lucy left Carolina and went to Virginia. "We know you are distraught and unhappy, Virginia—only that could make you say such untrue things." She tried to lay a comforting hand on Virginia's shoulder, but she shrugged it away.

"No one ever believes me!" Virginia sulked.

"We believe you when you said you desired to put off your marriage because of your family's grief. We know that's the truth, and only your fears for your future make you try to hurt others."

Realizing she was only going to end up looking worse than before, Virginia dabbed at her moist eyes with her handkerchief and, though it wasn't hard, tried to look quite pathetic. "Maybe so . . . but I don't want to be"—a real sob broke through her lips—"an old maid!"

"There, there," said Lucy. "You won't be. You are a beautiful young woman, and there will be other men for you."

The others offered up similar encouragements. All except Carolina, who still stood by in stunned silence. Virginia wondered why she should still be taking on so—her plan had fallen flat, thanks to that other goody-two-shoes, Lucy. But at least Lucy had managed to keep her from looking bad.

No, I don't look bad, she thought dismally. Now they just feel even more sorry for me. And I hate it! Why can't I just once feel some victory in my life? Why does everything have to go wrong for me?

But the group was still quiet and tense, and Virginia was almost glad for what Lucy did next, because it took all their simpering, sympathetic attention off her.

"Perhaps this would be a good time for me to make a happy announcement." Lucy paused and glanced at Sarah. "I hope you won't think me trying to take away from your day, Sarah."

"Do continue," said Sarah. "I think we could use some good news about now."

All eyes turned to meet Lucy's now smiling face. "I wanted all of you to be the first to know my news. York and I are expecting a baby."

This new focus was eagerly accepted by all, and while everyone sought to congratulate Lucy, Virginia quietly slipped from the room. Telling herself that no one would miss her anyway, she pulled out a silver flask from her skirt pocket and drained the contents.

There had to be a way to pay Carolina back for what she had done. There had to be a means to hurt her sister as she herself had been hurt. But more than anything, there had to be a way to accomplish all that and find her own husband besides. Maybe there was something to her earlier thoughts of stealing Hampton Cabot. All she had to do was pour on the charm—

Suddenly Virginia hiccuped.

"Oh, goodness! I'll need more sherry for that."

But the sherry already in her system gave her enough false bravado to believe her own praises. Mrs. Hampton Cabot did have an acceptable ring to it, and with little difficulty, Virginia knew she could take that name for herself. And should Hampton prove more loyal to her little sister than she suspected . . . well, Virginia would just have to handle that in her own creative way.

Either way, the battle lines had been drawn, and soon she could sit back and count the casualties.

Twenty-Three

The Baring of Souls

*L*eland Baldwin sat in his richly furnished office at the National City Bank, gazing out the window at the impressive view of the Capitol building, its pure white facade gleaming brilliantly in the spring sunshine. A self-satisfied smile spread across his face. His plans were finally taking shape, and he found the excitement nearly too much to contain. The Virginia legislature had granted the Potomac and Great Falls a charter for their railroad, established in effect for ten years. Leland's imagination began to run away with him at what this would mean.

He studied the list of investors and felt the surge of elation double. He had more than enough money to divert into a dozen other projects and still make it appear as though work was actually proceeding with the P&GF. His only problem would be in keeping Joseph Adams satisfied.

As if on cue, Joseph appeared at his open door and knocked lightly. "May I see you for a moment?"

"Adams! I had no idea you were to be in town today," Leland said, quickly sweeping the evidence of his plans into a desk drawer. "Come in. I was just preparing to drive out to Oakbridge." He held up a paper and smiled. "Our charter has been granted."

"That is good news," Joseph answered, but Leland thought his mind sounded far from the issue.

"What can I do for you?"

Joseph took a seat and stared at the top hat he held in his hands. "I'm afraid matters at Oakbridge have caused me to rethink our working relationship in regard to the railroad."

Leland felt his chest tighten. "Surely you don't plan to back out now. Not with the charter in place."

"No, not actually back out," Joseph said thoughtfully. "Leland, may I be quite frank?"

"Of course. We've been friends too long to presume upon any other method."

"Mrs. Adams is gravely ill. I fear for her, and I find that much of my time is consumed in seeking help for her. I may even have to take her to Boston. A doctor there has had much success with the very distraught."

"I'm so sorry," Leland said and genuinely meant it. His own wife was suffering through bouts of despondency due to their son's disappearance, so he had some understanding of his friend's suffering. "Is there anything I might do to ease your burden?"

Joseph nodded. "That's why I'm here. I know I'm imposing a great deal of responsibility on your shoulders, but I must ask that you take over the running of the Potomac and Great Falls Railroad. At least for a short time. I will, of course, continue to invest and promote the line, but I need time away from the business end of matters."

Leland could scarcely believe his good fortune. "Don't give it another thought. I will be happy to help you in any way I can."

Joseph seemed quite broken on the matter. "I don't intend for it to be long. I suppose my hope is that Mrs. Adams will regain her composure and find life worth living again. However, in the meantime, I must do whatever I can to get her proper care."

"Of course. To be certain." Leland seemed to consider the charter for a moment. "The charter is for a ten-year period. We can easily put off actually building for another year. That will also allow us to secure additional investors and make a more complete survey of the area."

"Yes, that perhaps does sound wise."

"Then, too, it is my hope that James will have fulfilled whatever obligations he holds with the Baltimore and Ohio. When he has returned, perhaps he will be able to offer us further insight that can guide our steps."

"How is your son?" Joseph asked with marginal interest.

Leland studied Joseph for a moment. His hair was grayer and so, too, his complexion. His eyes were sunken and his expression rather hopeless. The unspoken past seemed to hang between them.

"Joseph, I must reward your honesty with my own." He was given Joseph's immediate attention. "I've not heard from James since learning that he'd broken off with Virginia. I've wanted to broach the matter with you on several occasions, but I was, well, quite frankly, too ashamed."

"But why? You had nothing to do with it." Joseph seemed to take on a tone more like his old self.

"Oh, but I did." Leland played the part of mournful father. It wasn't a hard part to play, for in fact he was quite grief stricken over his son's behavior and disappearance. "I pushed the boy too hard. I insisted that he find a woman of virtue and settle down to a life of banking and raising a respectable family."

"No father could want less for his only child."

"Perhaps, but I feel that your family has suffered because of my desires. I know that James felt honor bound to his proposal, but I also know he's driven by some unseen force. It's taken him away from his mother and me, and it's changed him."

Joseph smiled sympathetically. "He didn't love her."

The statement seemed to come from nowhere, and Leland was quite taken aback. "What do you mean?"

"I mean, James never loved Virginia. Virginia is a determined young woman, and she clearly set her cap on James from the first moment he paid her court. But I never saw James' eyes light up with love for her."

"Love is too frivolous an emotion to plot an entire life around," Leland said rather authoritatively. "You and I both know that some of the best marriages are arranged ones. Love follows in time. The boy would have learned to love."

Joseph shook his head. "I didn't say James couldn't love. In fact, I believe more strongly than ever that he was in love. But not with Virginia."

"If not Virginia, then who?" Leland felt a hopefulness course through him. Perhaps there was another prestigious family who would see his James as a suitable match.

"Between you and me?" Joseph questioned and Leland nodded. "I believe James was in love with Carolina."

Leland gasped. "Your Carolina?"

"Yes. I believe further that Carolina was in love with James, although neither one ever acted anything but completely proper. I doubt they even realized their feelings were mutual."

"I've heard rumors," Leland began, then shut his mouth tightly.

"As have I, but they are unfounded and untrue." He looked at Leland as if defying him to suggest otherwise.

"Of course." Leland fell silent, not knowing what else to say.

"It is of little matter now," Joseph said with a heaviness that matched his expression. "I don't hold malice toward James. I actually admire him for backing out of a situation that seemed wrong to him. He has great conviction, and perhaps charted in the right direction, he will go far. If you're worried that I somehow hold you responsible, then let your mind consider it no longer."

Leland exhaled loudly and nodded. "It has been uppermost in my mind."

Joseph got to his feet. "Then put it from you. I must be going. Thank you for helping me with the railroad. Oh, please don't hesitate to send the progress reports. Carolina goes over them with a fine-toothed comb, and I would very much like her to remain actively engaged in this matter. In fact, it would give me a great deal of happiness if you might continue to meet with her occasionally. She's a brilliant young woman, Leland, and I feel many of her ideas merit consideration."

"Certainly," Leland replied, not for once planning to go through with such a suggestion.

Joseph paused at the door and glanced around the room. "They say things are always darkest before the dawn."

"That's true enough," Leland agreed. "But the sun always rises, and it will for you this time, as well." He struggled to come out from behind his desk, his rotund body giving him pain as he crossed the room to shake his friend's hand. "Don't hesitate to call upon me if there is anything I can do for you."

"Thank you, Leland. You have been a true friend."

Leland managed to contain a grimace as Joseph departed the bank. Leland realized he wasn't a good friend at all. He wasn't even a good banker. It should bother him more that he was deceiving people who trusted him. And it did bother him, but the way things were playing into his hand, it also gave him a strange sense of exhilaration. Closing his office door, Leland began to smile in spite of himself, and he felt for all the world like a new man. Joseph would no longer be looking over his shoulder, and in his place, a seventeen-year-old girl would review the materials of operation. He chuckled and waddled back to his desk. If he couldn't pull the wool over the eyes of Carolina Adams, he might as well give up the business altogether. She might be intelligent, as her father said she was, but she was still a youngster and a female, and neither was much of a threat to Leland Baldwin.

Twenty-Four

A Day of Reckoning

The sign was tacked temporarily into place by Leland himself:

BANK CLOSED

Stepping back, he gave a last look at his former place of business and felt a surge of mixed emotions. Anger was high at the top of the list. Anger that the economy had failed him. Anger that the President and Congress had made success impossible. May 10, 1837, would forever live in his mind as the day the world went completely mad.

"What do you mean by this?" a customer yelled from the growing crowd. "What about our money?"

"Yeah? What are we supposed to do now?" another called out.

Leland faced them with a fixed expression. "I assure you this is only a temporary precaution. There is no reason to concern yourselves unduly."

Tucking his satchel under his arm and leaning heavily on his walking stick, Leland made his way to his carriage amid boos and name-calling. He ordered his driver home and fell back against the leather upholstery. There was a great deal to be considered. The banks had been suspended by prearranged agreement, but it didn't help matters at all. Leland still faced the inevitable audit, which would show his bank terribly out of order in the contrast of reserves versus loans. The previous summer's Distribution Bill had forced him to part with a great portion of the bank's solid assets. It had crippled the bank of legitimate moneys, but Leland hadn't allowed that to stop business. He merely produced false bank drafts through his brother Samuel's less-than-legal procedures. It was enough to see the bank through, but when the second distribution had come due in April, Leland barely remained solvent.

He wasn't alone. Most of the other private banks had positioned themselves in the same hole. The federal government had put deposits on hold with a variety of private banks, but these deposits were to remain as reserves. Everyone, including the President and Congress, had looked the other way as the banks did business with federal moneys. It was thought of as harmless, and the private banks felt they were entitled to such usage. But within two years the United States had gone from being completely debt free to hopelessly entangled in an economic crisis.

Bankers were running scared and desperate, doing whatever they had to in order to face the fewest consequences. Loans were called in, stock dividends were suspended, bank-draft usage was restricted to those notes that were written against well-known institutions of finance. But there was no apparent way to stop the downward spiral. Leland doubted that very many legitimate bankers would have finagled the same resources and solutions as he had. Counterfeiting and fraud wasn't a game for the faint of heart.

As one bank after another was forced to admit defeat, many began to cry out for the guidance of Nicholas Biddle, president of the now state-owned Bank of the United States. Despite the fact that Biddle was looked upon as the savior of the country, having pulled the nation out of great economic turmoil following the War of 1812, Biddle's bank was now doing just as poorly. Having made a last attempt at remaining chartered and solvent, the Bank of the United States had brought itself, in March of the previous year, under the protection of the state of Pennsylvania. This appeared to be the answer for keeping Biddle in a position of power, and the bank appeared to have thrived. But that was before the Distribution Bill had demanded the redistribution of some forty million dollars in surplus federal funds to the states.

Biddle is probably having a good laugh right now, Leland thought as the carriage came to a stop. Biddle had warned the public that destruction of the Bank of the United States would render the country in crisis. He had warned too that it was not only unconstitutional, but foolish banking to redistribute the federal moneys.

It was even said that Biddle had visited President Van Buren on more than one occasion to convince him of the wisdom of reinstating the Bank of the United States, in the hope that he could turn this new economic crisis around. Leland doubted it would result in anything Biddle wanted to hear. Van Buren was Jackson's man through and through. It would matter very little that the merchants of New York had banned together to request Biddle assume leadership of the bank once again. It would probably not affect Van Buren's decision either to know that the general public saw the banking troubles as something the President had complete control over.

So long as Jackson continued to write letters advising Van Buren to preserve the Specie Circular—Jackson's emergency action to put an end to paper money purchases by land speculators—Biddle didn't stand a chance. It was, for all intents and purposes, Jackson's third term in office, via Martin Van Buren.

To Leland it didn't matter who was in charge. He could become friendly with either side when it suited him. He could become bosom companions when it profited him, or mortal enemies if such folk crossed him. His main interest was to find the most advantageous position and execute it to the fullest. He could see this newest crisis as both a blessing and a curse.

His footman opened the carriage door and stepped back. Leland struggled to descend and make his way into the house. The gout was ever present in his right foot and crippling him so that without the use of a sturdy walking stick, he was nearly incapable of passing from one room to the next. Even so, it was of little consideration at the moment. There were plans to be made and a future to be decided.

"Mr. Baldwin," Edith called out as her husband entered the house. "Is it true? Have the banks closed?"

"True enough," Leland replied, tossing his hat onto the entryway table.

"I dared not to believe such hideous gossip," Edith said, sounding quite shaken. "Whatever will we do? Are we completely without funds?"

Leland looked at her worried expression for a moment, then shook his head. "Not at all, Mrs. Baldwin. Have you ever known your husband to be without proper assets?"

Edith smiled weakly. Leland offered her his arm and led her into the front sitting room. "I have a great deal of work to be done in my study. Will you see to it that I'm not disturbed?"

"Of course," Edith replied. "Would you like any refreshment?"

"Perhaps later," he said, helping her to a chair. "I must go for now, but perhaps this evening we will find time to talk."

He left Edith to stare at him in some confusion and sought the solace of his study. Locking the doors behind him, Leland tossed the satchel onto his desk.

It wasn't as if the demise of the banking system was a surprise. There was no way of predicting exactly how long it would last, or what the ultimate outcome would be, but it wasn't a surprise to those involved in the industry.

His chair groaned in protest as he settled his enormous mass upon it. One thing would work in his favor. With a depressed economy and the banks having closed their doors, Leland knew he was in the perfect position to postpone the progress of the P&GF Railroad indefinitely. Investors would be notified that most of their investment moneys had been devalued or lost in the wake of the panic.

He smiled at his own genius. Months ago he had meticulously plotted to turn his paper money investments into coin, particularly gold. Taking a letter opener from his desk drawer he went to the fireplace and thrust the opener between two loose bricks. They came apart slowly, and while Leland inched them from position, his smile only broadened.

With the two bricks removed, Leland could reach into the opening and feel the multiple bags of gold. His investment. His future.

A scream broke the morning silence, and Leland felt his heart race in dread. Edith! He quickly replaced the bricks, double-checking to make sure they were secure before going in search of his wife.

Hurrying to the front room, Leland stopped in stunned surprise. The letter opener he'd used to tap the bricks back into place fell from his hand and clattered noisily onto the oak floor.

"James!"

Twenty-Five

A Stranger's Rescue

*I*n spite of the failing financial structure of the country's business world, Washington society moved forward to forget its troubles in any way it could. Edith Baldwin had seen the summer charity ball as the perfect way to reintroduce her son to genteel company, but James was uncertain.

Home for less than a week, James had struggled through the days trying to make his parents understand his decision to break his engagement with Virginia Adams. From his mother came complete absolution of guilt and sin, but from his father came another attitude entirely. James had not only disobeyed his father's instruction, but knowing full well the impact it would have on his family, he had chosen his own way over the well-being of his parents. This was something for which Leland would probably never forgive him. And James found himself crumbling in the face of his earlier resolve. Making things right wasn't going to be easy.

"James, you must stop hiding back here," his mother said, pulling him from one of the side rooms into the main ballroom. A full orchestra sent up the rhythmic melody of a waltz, while hundreds of people danced beneath the crystal chandeliers of the Gadsby Hotel.

"I can't say that I'm comfortable with this situation," James replied. "No doubt there are going to be questions, which I hardly feel like addressing publicly."

"Then don't," Edith replied and, spying Julia Cooper standing alone, thrust James forward. "Julia dear, have you had a chance to greet my son? He's just returned from duty with the railroad in the far frontier."

Julia Cooper's dark eyes expressed surprise. "Why no. I hadn't realized Mr. Baldwin was in attendance."

James was rather confused by the expression on her face. She seemed to be studying him as if weighing a serious matter. Since she was Carolina's closest friend, perhaps she'd been privy to more information about James' departure than most.

Bowing before Julia, James was unaware that his mother had slipped away, until turning to speak with her, he found her gone.

"I believe my mother fears the party will suddenly stop if she pauses for even a moment."

Julia smiled. "Well, Mr. Baldwin, how long have you been back?"

James took a deep breath. "Nearly a week. Mother felt it absolutely necessary that I accompany her here this evening, especially in light of my father's illness."

"Oh? I did not know he was sick. I pray it is nothing serious."

"As do I," James replied. "I feel his worry about the economy is taking its toll upon him." He used this in place of the real reason. His father refused to attend any function with James, and since Edith wanted to use this particular soiree as a way to expose her son in a popular light, Leland declined to attend.

"So no one has yet been informed of your return?" Julia asked, daintily fanning herself.

"No." James' eyes scanned the dancing partners and found a dozen or more people he knew. "I suppose it will be a shock to everyone."

"No doubt," Julia replied. "Especially to Carolina Adams."

James felt his body tense at the name. It was true that she was part of the reason he'd returned to Washington, but he wasn't prepared to see her here tonight. "Is she here?" he asked, hoping against all odds that she wasn't.

"Why yes." Julia waved her fan to James' right. "She's over there."

James steadied his nerves and forced himself to look. Then catching sight of her, he felt his breath nearly knocked from him. Carolina.

She had grown up in his absence, and on her arm was a gentleman who seemed quite intent on her attention. James ignored the tall, broad-shouldered man and instead studied the woman who'd haunted his sleep and daytime dreams. Carolina.

He wanted to rush to her—beg her forgiveness—declare his love. Instead, he was frozen in place. He watched her dance, whirling and swaying in time to the music. She wore a brocade gown of peach, cream, and green with pale beige lace that was nearly the same color as her skin. Deep brown curls bobbed up and down as her partner turned her first one way and then another.

"She will be surprised, won't she?" Julia asked.

"I suppose she will," James whispered. "Who is the gentleman she is dancing with?"

Julia raised her chin a bit, as if Hampton Cabot's towering frame could not be seen from where she stood. "Why, that is Mr. Hampton Cabot. He is Mr. Adams' commission merchant from New York City."

James turned away from the dancers and looked down at Julia. "Are they good friends?"

"You might say so. Carolina confided in me earlier this evening that she suspects Mr. Cabot will ask for her hand tonight," Julia answered smugly.

James felt as though she'd just twisted a knife in his gut. He wanted to remain calm, but suddenly the plans he'd once considered were falling apart. "And did she also express her feelings on the matter?"

Julia nodded, then smiled at her approaching husband. "Indeed she did. It would not surprise me to learn that they are already engaged. Oh, William, look who has come back to Washington."

William Cooper gave a stiff bow of greeting, then took a possessive hold on Julia's arm. "Mr. Baldwin."

"Mr. Cooper." The words were offered formally and without emotion by either man.

"Come, Mrs. Cooper, I should enjoy a dance. If you'll excuse us, Mr. Baldwin."

James barely heard the words, nor concerned himself with the obvious snubbing he'd just received from his former friend. Carolina might well be engaged. He'd come too late!

The musicians built the melody into an impressive crescendo, then let the refrain linger in the air only moments longer before striking the final note. As the dancers came to a halt, James found his gaze settle on the flushed face of Carolina Adams. He stared at her as if willing her to see him. And then, without warning, she looked up and caught his glance. A stunned look of what could only be described as dismay passed over her expression as their gazes locked.

Don't hate me, he prayed, seeing the dismay grow rapidly into panic. He watched her turn to the tall, blond Mr. Cabot and say something, and when the man nodded and led her from the room, James knew that his prayer had gone unheard.

She despises me, and with good cause, he thought. But the anguish was still nearly too great to bear. He had never known such pain as this. It ripped through him like a hot knife—scorching—burning every part of him.

He wanted to go after her and plead with her to listen to his explanation, but what could he say that would make any sense? He'd acted in complete foolishness. His departure had been born out of selfishness and indecision. He could see that now, but he could also see that he'd fled confrontation and heartbreak. He might have gone about it in the wrong way, but it had been the right decision to refrain from marrying a woman he didn't love.

Clenching his fists to his side, James forced himself to remain in place. He couldn't go after her. She'd made it clear that she wanted nothing to do with him. Otherwise, she would have waited. Waited for him to come to her from across the room. Waited for him to return from Baltimore. Waited to say yes to him, instead of Hampton Cabot.

———

Carolina felt she could barely breathe through the tightly corseted gown. It was bad enough to know that she was the brunt of so much gossip. But to find James actually here, after such a long absence, was more than she could bear. She wanted nothing more than to forget him, yet his image followed her from the dance floor; and while it was Hampton Cabot at her side, it was James who filled her thoughts.

"You look unwell, my dear," Hampton said, leading her into an empty side room.

Carolina knew it was unwise to be alone with Hampton, especially in light of her confusing emotions. James! She couldn't even think his name without feeling the tightening in her chest. "I'm just a bit winded," she finally offered Hampton, whose worried expression seemed most sincere.

"Here, sit for a moment." Hampton helped her to a small settee.

"Thank you." She bowed her head, unable to look him in the eye. Earlier that evening she'd discussed Hampton with Julia Cooper. Carolina had done a great deal of soul-searching and had come to the conclusion that perhaps the only thing she could do to rectify things between her sister and the rest of the world was to marry Hampton and move quietly away. At least then, the gossip might die down.

Julia had agreed. She'd even encouraged Carolina to promote Hampton's proposal by leading him away from the crowd and into a room such as the one they were in now. Would Hampton believe that to be her reasoning? She had thought herself capable of accepting marriage to him, even knowing that she didn't love him. He could take her away from Oakbridge and Virginia's hatred, away from the misery of seeing her mother go completely insane. Julia had promised her that love would come in time. All she had to do was accept his marriage proposal.

And that was what she'd intended to do, but now all of her plans lay shattered. With one look at James Baldwin, Carolina knew her heart could never be in such a union. Hampton would demand her love and devotion, and rightly so, but how could she give him what clearly belonged to another? Carolina put her hands to her head, longing to force the thoughts from her mind.

"Should I send for a doctor?" Hampton asked.

Carolina shook her head and folded her hands again in her lap. "No, I'll be fine in a few moments. Please return to the party if you like." She looked up at him and found him smiling.

"I wouldn't dream of it," he said, slipping into the space beside her. His large frame pressed closely to hers to accommodate the small settee. Carolina instantly tensed and tried to move away, but Hampton would have no part of it. He pulled her into his arms and whispered against her ear, "Not after you went to so much trouble to get me here."

"I never—"

"Shhh," he said, lowering his lips to hers.

Carolina's mind raced in a hundred different directions. She pushed at Hampton and tried to turn her face away, but to no avail.

"Don't tell me that you didn't want me to do this," Hampton said, finally pulling back just enough to look her in the eye.

"You don't understand," Carolina began. "I know what you must think, but it isn't true."

Hampton relaxed his hold, and Carolina took advantage of his surprise to jump up from the settee. Somehow she had to convince Hampton she could never be the wife he wanted.

"You have to listen to me, Hampton." She used his first name, hoping the familiarity would calm the agitation she read in his expression. "I don't love you and I don't believe I ever could."

Hampton came to her but refrained from touching her. "All evening you have presented yourself in such a way to suggest that you were very much open to receiving my affections."

"I'm sorry. I am to blame. I thought perhaps I could." She paused, putting her hands to her head again. "I wanted to give you a chance, but I can't go through with this."

Hampton reached out and took hold of her wrists. "You're just scared."

"No." Carolina shook her head and tried to pull away. But instead of releasing her, Hampton pulled her toward him.

"I've no interest in games. You are a pampered little girl who doesn't know what she wants."

"You're wrong," she breathed. You are so very wrong, she thought silently. I know what I want, but it isn't you.

Without warning, Hampton pulled her forward, and Carolina lost her balance and fell against him. He crushed her to his body and refused to set her free. "You need to remember your place. You need to forget about your books."

"Let me go," Carolina demanded, rapidly losing her composure.

"Don't you know how much I want you?" He kissed her hard, bruising her lips.

Carolina stamped her foot down on the top of his, but her satin slipper made little impact against his boot.

"Stop fighting me and tell me that you'll marry me."

"I can't, Hampton. I don't love you."

"It doesn't matter. Besides, now that we're here alone, your reputation is probably finished. You already know the gossip around town. Virginia tells me that you—"

"Virginia admitted them to be lies to suit herself. I've done nothing to compromise my reputation, unless you count this."

Hampton leered. "In this day, the slightest unsavory gossip could find you forever unacceptable in polite society. You should be grateful to find a man who pays no heed to what you might have done with Virginia's beau. I've had plenty of other women in my life, and knowing that you dallied with your sister's fiancé is just proof of your youth. But here and now, the outcome could be quite different. You are no longer fifteen. Should they find us missing and locate us in a private hotel room, even a sitting room such as this, you could well be forced to marry me. Even your father would insist." Hampton seemed to consider his own statement for a moment.

Carolina choked back a sob. "My reputation has already suffered considerably." She couldn't help but think of the cold, calloused treatment she'd received that evening by the Armstrong family. Virginia's lies were still circulating among a few who wanted to think the worst of her. Who could know what the end result would be?

"Then cast away your inhibitions and come away with me tonight. Don't you see how much I want you?" Hampton buried his hands in her hair and bent her back to accommodate his height. "I desire you, Carolina. Nothing else is of any importance."

"Not even my feelings on the matter?" She turned her face to refuse the kiss he would have forced upon her. "Release me, Hampton. I want to go home!"

"It would appear your companion is less than interested in your attention, my good man." The voice of a stranger halted Hampton's actions and allowed Carolina to pull away.

Frightened beyond her wits, Carolina hugged her arms to her body and began to cry.

"Sir, you are not wanted here," Hampton said firmly. "I must demand that you leave."

"I defer to the lady's wishes."

Carolina lifted her face to meet the harsh gaze of her unknown rescuer. She bit her lower lip to keep from crying out in surprise. The willowy black-clad stranger was the same man she'd disturbed, nearly a year before, in a Baltimore cemetery. The recognition was instantaneous by both parties.

Hampton didn't seem to notice or care. He was obviously angry at the interruption. "The lady is with me."

"No I'm not!" Carolina said, suddenly finding the courage to speak. She moved toward the dark-eyed man, feeling the intensity of his stare upon her. "Thank you, sir, for your assistance."

A part of her wanted to offer him an explanation, while another part wanted nothing more than to seek solace in the arms of James Baldwin.

"Carolina Adams, this is far from over," Hampton declared as she moved to the door, putting the stranger between them.

"It must be. Good evening."

She gave the stranger a single nod and hoped that her feelings of gratitude were clear by her expression. She hurried from the room, wiping her tears as she went.

She wanted to go home and forget that this evening had ever taken place. She quickly scanned the crowd. York and Lucy had already departed for the evening with Julia's promise to see Carolina safely to their home after the dance. Julia, however, was dancing with her husband and seemed far too preoccupied to offer Carolina any assistance, and given Virginia's deceit, Carolina honestly wondered if any of her other friends would even consider helping her. Even James was nowhere to be found. Had he left when she had so rudely run from him?

"If I might be so bold, my driver would be happy to deliver you safely home. I'm staying here at the hotel, so I assure you it will not indispose me in the least."

It was the voice of the stranger. Turning to face him once again, Carolina knew there was no other answer. "Thank you, sir. I would be grateful."

Twenty-Six

Negotiating the Future

$\mathscr{B}$en Latrobe tells me you've been a valuable asset to this railroad," Louis McLane said, sitting back in his chair. James shrugged. His mind was far from the subject of the railroad. "And," McLane continued, picking up a letter, "Philip Thomas says here that you have offered creative solutions that have saved the B&O a great deal of money."

James did his best to focus on the new president of the Baltimore and Ohio. And in reality he was not a man easily ignored, with his striking appearance crowned by deep-set eyes that could make a man stand and reckon with his actions. Those eyes burned with such fierce intensity, James didn't know how his own mind could have wandered.

Louis McLane glanced over the letter once more before laying it aside. "I'm impressed with your references, Mr. Baldwin. As you know, I've been hired on with the sole purpose of pushing this line west of Harper's Ferry and on to the Ohio River. It won't be an easy task, especially now in light of the depressed economy. This country is suffering greatly," he noted, as if it might be news to James.

"You may not be aware of this," McLane continued, "but wheat crops in the surrounding areas are being devastated by some type of insect. I believe they've called it the Hessian fly, but it matters little what name they give it. What's important is that it furthers the depression of this country. Farmers are going to lose a great deal of money, and, in turn, people will have no food to buy. Obviously folks can't afford to invest in railroads when they have trouble putting food on the table."

McLane seemed to study the papers on his desk a moment before continuing. "I like what I see in you, Mr. Baldwin, but keeping you on for much of any kind of salary is going to be difficult at best. I don't know if you're aware of this, but just last week the Irish laborers on the

Chesapeake and Ohio Canal rioted."

"I had heard something to that effect," James replied.

"They've rioted before and usually over money, conditions, supply shortages, and general ill-will. I believe a shortage of everything has triggered this bout." He leaned forward; great lines of worry seemed etched permanently in his forehead. "The railroad is at a standstill; otherwise, we'd probably have more of our own riots to contend with. The B&O is barely running. But, of course, you probably know all of this."

James wearied of the battle raging within his mind. A part of him wanted to immerse himself in work and the future of the railroad, while another part kept bringing to mind Carolina on the arm of Hampton Cabot—the man she would marry! He fought to clear away every image but that of Louis McLane and the railroad.

"I don't understand one thing," James said, forcing the direction of his thoughts. "Other railroads are actually thriving in spite of the financial crisis. I've paid close attention to this through a variety of sources. Several small lines in New York and Pennsylvania, for instance, are running at a profit."

"Yes, but those lines are completed. They move from one place to another with a specific purpose, whether it is to haul coal or milk. The Baltimore and Ohio is not successful because it is not complete. We have not even reached our first real objective on the main stem, which is Cumberland. Cumberland represents the eastern terminus of the National Road, and it is from here where we can benefit by picking up the main flow of wagon shipments from the West and stagecoach travel."

"But the Washington Branch is doing well. The passenger traffic is up considerably," James offered.

"And do you suppose it will continue to do well when repairs cannot be made to keep up the line? Do you suppose when engines and railcars break down and repairs can't be made for lack of funding it will continue to do well? Not to mention that people must have money in hand in order to spend it on travel."

James was finally able to fully realize what McLane was saying. And his concerns over Carolina and her possible marriage to Hampton Cabot were overwhelmed by fear for his very job. His mind was now completely fixed on saving the B&O. "What is to be done?"

McLane seemed to sense James' change in spirit. "We must reach Cumberland. If not, then all is lost and the B&O will fail."

"And how do we do this without funding?"

"We will have to find new sources of support."

"Europe?" James asked, knowing McLane's reputation for international connections.

"Possibly, but it is doubtful. They, too, are suffering. Especially England. You must remember that, in a way, this all started with that country."

"How so?" James asked.

"They were heavily investing in American prosperity. Last summer, with Jackson's passage of the Specie Circular, England began to see the wisdom of curtailing trade with American companies. Their own banks refused to issue further credit to merchants who planned to do business with America. This, of course, caused problems for merchants on both sides of the Atlantic, and by March, financial panic in England caused banks there to demand payment in American gold.

"Naturally, draining this country of its resources created a plunge downward from which we couldn't hope to recover in time to keep from crashing into complete ruin."

James felt a hopelessness come upon him. He'd worked hard to see the Baltimore and Ohio become successful, and even though he was but one single man in the midst of many, he felt he owed her an allegiance in her time of trouble.

"I'll work for stock," James said, suddenly seeing a plan. "In fact, I would bet a great many men will work for food and stock alone."

McLane nodded. "That would save some expense. However, unless we can get the state to honor the pledge of financial support they made last year, we won't have any supplies to put in the hands of those workers."

"Still, it will take very few supplies to continue the survey to Cumberland. Once that is established we can put men to work clearing the road of trees and establishing passage for the rail. That will require little more than putting picks and shovels in their hands, at least to start. I do realize there will be areas that will require the blasting out of rock and the building of bridges, but it would at least set the beginning."

"I've already considered that matter, and I agree completely with you. Still, there is the problem of convincing the workers that they should give us their all, when the pay will be so very little. In fact, we may need to forego cash and issue script instead."

"Railroad script?"

"Yes. Company money. Certain stores would honor it in lieu of cash, at least for a time. The B&O's reputation is sound, and I've little doubt it could work. That is, if the men will work for script or even your idea of stock."

"I'll talk to them," James replied. "They know me and they know they can trust me. I'll explain the situation, and I just know they will see it our way. After all, what other job will they have to go to?"

"Those with families aren't going to be inclined to stay," McLane said, thinking through the matter.

"Probably not and rightly so." James paused, thinking of Carolina once again. "If a man is responsible for a wife and children, he cannot very well work for stock." He felt suddenly relieved that he'd not come back to Baltimore as an engaged man. He could never offer his services in such a manner if he was obligated to a betrothal. "But the idea of script might well intrigue them."

"Very well, Baldwin. I'll draw up the details of what we can offer, and you take it to the men. Agreed?"

"Yes, sir," James said, getting to his feet. He extended his arm and shook McLane's hand enthusiastically. "Agreed."

———

But the workers were far from enthusiastic about James' proposal. Most of the men were married, and many had already given up on the B&O as a means of support. Returning to Baltimore from Harper's Ferry, James was a defeated man. He hated the idea of facing McLane. The list of those who'd signed on to work under the new agreement was small, and James knew full well it represented less than a quarter of the men they needed.

Deciding to put McLane off until the following day, James stepped from the sweltering confines of the train and made his way to a local tavern. Drowning his sorrows in several glasses of whiskey, James was beginning to forget the pain of the railroad only to remember his anguish over Carolina.

Apparently, he thought, I've not had enough. He ordered a bottle to take with him and made his way home. Halfway there, steeped in pity for his past mistakes and present failures, he spied Annabelle Bryce.

"Miss Bryce," he called, and she turned.

Flashing a smile from her cherry red lips, Annabelle waved. "Mr. Baldwin, how very good to see you. How are you this day, or should I say, evening?"

"I wish I could say that all is grand and glorious, but it would be a lie, and I long ago gave up such contrivances with you."

Annabelle linked her arm through his. "For such honesty, I shall have to reward you."

James sighed. "A couple hundred railroad workers would suit me just fine."

Annabelle laughed in her lyrical way, but it did little to lift James' spirits. "I was thinking more along the lines of dinner," she said, then pointed to the bottle tucked under his arm. "Unless you plan to continue drinking yours this evening."

"Dinner? I suppose we could. There's a fine establishment—"

"No. No. I meant at my place. I have recently acquired a lovely little house just four blocks from here. If you don't mind the walk in all this heat, I shall happily extend a welcome to you and prepare for you a feast fit for a king."

"I couldn't impose."

"Nonsense. It isn't an imposition. I have to eat whether you are there or not, and my maid is there to help, so it really won't be that much work for either of us. Besides, you look as though you could use a friend, and I'm much better company than that bottle."

"Well, I don't know . . ."

"There's a wonderful pork roast in the oven that you might as well come help me enjoy."

James could think of nothing more appealing than the company of a lovely woman. Unless, of course, that woman could be Carolina Adams. Feeling his head spin with the effects of the liquor, he nodded. "All right. Lead the way."

Within the hour, Annabelle and James were seated at a small candlelit table in Annabelle's parlor, enjoying a succulent pork roast and dilled potatoes while she shared stories of her stage performances in Boston. When her plump German maid, Gretta, appeared with an apple cobbler for dessert, Annabelle told him of her decision to take a month's holiday away from the stage to relax a bit in Baltimore.

"So you see, you have saved me from an evening of boredom and misery," she said lightly and signaled for Gretta to leave the room. "Do you care for anything else?"

"I'm afraid I've had more than enough," he said, lingering on the features of her face. Her violet eyes seemed almost black in the flickering candlelight. Her hair was worn casually knotted at the back of her neck, and her dress was a soft printed muslin. He liked her like this. She seemed less Annabelle Bryce the actress and more what he imagined would be Annabelle Gainsborough, the English rose.

"You have a strange look on your face, James Baldwin." She held up the bottle of whiskey he'd brought and noted it was half empty. "Perhaps you have had too much."

James drew a deep breath. "Do you know how much I've come to care for you?" She shook her head slowly and set the bottle down as he continued. "I've thought of you often. I close my eyes and conjure your face to mind, and it makes my day brighter." He closed his eyes and smiled. "You are an important part of my life, and I cannot imagine not having you near me every single day."

James knew he was hopelessly lost in the effects of the alcohol, but his loneliness was getting the best of him. He needed someone to care that he was lonely. He needed someone to care that he longed for companionship. He needed someone.

Opening his eyes he leaned forward. "Why don't you marry me?"

Annabelle looked at him thoughtfully for a moment, then put her hand atop his. "Because I'm not Carolina Adams, and she's the one to whom you're truly speaking."

James was taken aback by her brutal honesty. "But we could be happy. You and I get along famously, and we see eye to eye on many things. You love your independence, and I swear I wouldn't interfere. I love the railroad, and I would be gone probably as much as you would be, but when we came back together we wouldn't have to be alone. Don't you see? It might work."

Annabelle smiled sympathetically. "No, James. I cherish your friendship, but your heart belongs to another woman. That is sacred and I would never interfere in such a precious thing."

"But I need you. I need—"

"You need her," Annabelle interrupted, and James saw for the first time there were tears in her eyes.

"Don't cry," he whispered, feeling his head swim from the whiskey. "I didn't mean to hurt you by suggesting something unthinkable."

"It isn't that, James," she replied. "It's that you are so very empty and lost inside, and it pains me to see you struggle this way. I know what it is to be lost and to feel that no one in the world cares."

"But the world loves you, Annabelle, and as you told me once long ago, you are never alone."

She wiped away the tears with her napkin. "I'm never alone, but not because of the world and the people who follow me. I suppose I led you to that belief, but it isn't so. I'm not alone because deep inside, I know a higher source of strength. Deep inside, I know God watches over me and loves me, and that, James, and nothing else, is why I can go through each day. You do not have a faith in God, and therefore you are only half a man. You struggle alone and the loss consumes you."

James startled at this. With his senses dulled he could not hide his reaction. Annabelle seemed to sense his disbelief.

"I know. I know. You see the actress and the wild life I lead. You know from my own lips that my husband divorced me and that my reputation is tainted beyond all belief. But, James, the world's view is not always right. Every day I lay myself out before God and realize how very far I've missed the mark of perfection. And every day I get up and try again. I might not be welcome among the pious people of the church, but in my own heart I know God forgives me and helps me to try again. Maybe one day you will accept this for yourself as well."

"Perhaps," James murmured, feeling too uncomfortable to continue with the discussion. "I'm afraid I should go," he said, getting to his feet.

Annabelle followed him to the door. "James, promise me to at least consider what I've said. I'm no saint, of that we both know, but God has the answers, and maybe, just maybe, He will show you the way to win your Carolina." She smiled sadly and reached up to touch his cheek. "I almost wish I could be her."

James felt a sadness wash over him, and the longing he felt was only magnified by the concern he read in Annabelle's eyes. "Me too," he whispered. He stepped into the night, then paused to look back at her. "I'll give it some thought, Annabelle. I do promise."

Twenty-Seven

Educating Enticements

"We've lost a great deal," Hampton told Joseph Adams, "as have many folks, but we're not as bad off as most."

"Thanks to you," Joseph said with a cursory glance at the financial ledgers Hampton had furnished.

"Well, it is my job. Of course, I'm more inspired than some." Hampton rubbed his chin thoughtfully. "Sir, there is another matter that I would like to discuss."

Joseph considered him for a moment. "My daughter?"

Hampton smiled. "In part, yes."

"Go on."

Hampton knew the delicacy of the situation. Somehow he had to win Joseph over to his side. If he could entice Joseph to see the merit of Carolina joining him in marriage, then he knew half the battle would be won. And it was an important battle to be sure. Too much was at stake to simply walk away in defeat.

He took a seat across from Joseph's desk and folded his hands. "I'm afraid Carolina is a bit hesitant to accept my proposal, and I had hoped you would perhaps speak to her on my behalf."

"I believe in allowing my children to choose their own mates. Arranged marriages have their good and bad points, but I'd like to believe my children are marrying for love and not position."

"I realize that, but I also believe Carolina loves me."

"Has she told you this?"

Hampton looked at the ceiling. "Not in so many words."

"Then what gives you this belief?"

Hampton lowered his gaze. "Perhaps this is the wrong thing to say to a father, and perhaps my liberties have been too great, but Carolina responds quite enthusiastically to my embrace and kiss." It wasn't a lie, Hampton thought. And even if it had been, he would have said it anyway. He would use whatever means necessary to win Joseph's assistance.

"I see. I pray you haven't pushed the bounds of proper conduct with this embrace and kiss."

"No, sir," he lied convincingly. "I wouldn't dream of such a thing. Actually, the situation came about by Carolina's prompting. Each time, she has arranged for us to be alone."

"Each time?" Joseph shifted and looked a bit more uncomfortable. "Just how serious has this thing become?"

Hampton smiled. "I would never dishonor her, of that you must believe. I want to marry her, but she is so concerned with the family that she refuses to give me an answer. She's told me again that she must refuse my proposal because she can't be parted from those who need her most. She is completely devoted to her family, but especially to you."

"To me? But why should she concern herself with me?"

Hampton knew he'd piqued his employer's interest and pressed the issue forward. "You see, I have offered Carolina not only marriage, but the promise that we could remain near to Oakbridge."

"And this didn't convince her to say yes?"

"She's convinced that Oakbridge and her father are wavering on the edge of complete destruction. She doesn't want to do anything to bring about the ruin of either her home or her beloved father. She won't hear of leaving you, because by staying on, she knows you will allow her to help you run the plantation, and she knows that you have no one else."

"That much is true. Carolina has been of great help to me."

"Exactly. And that is why she refuses to agree to our marriage. She's convinced that you would insist I return to New York and that she would have to leave her home and loved ones."

"So what is it you would have me do?"

"I would ask you again to consider allowing me to train at your side as the man who will see Oakbridge continue in prosperity. If Carolina hears from your own lips that you plan to do this, then I feel certain she will accept me as a husband."

Joseph considered this for a moment, then leaned back in his chair. "I have already given a great deal of thought to your suggestion, and I must agree it seems the most reasonable and responsible way to go. Maine assures me that he has no desire to take control of Oakbridge, and York has also admonished me to consider giving the reins over to another member of the family. Of course, York suggested Carolina be the one to run things."

Joseph smiled at this, and Hampton did his best to refrain from making a snide remark about women in positions of power.

Just then a knock sounded on the library door.

"Come in," Joseph called out, and to their surprise, Carolina appeared on the threshold. Both men rose as she spoke.

"Please excuse me, Father, but the Coopers' overseer is here to collect the grain you promised."

Joseph nodded. "Hampton, you will have to excuse me. We can pick up this conversation at another time." He turned to the door and, after kissing Carolina on the head, went downstairs to attend to business.

Hampton saw this as the perfect opportunity to play the humble suitor. As Carolina turned to leave, he called to her. "Please stay a moment. I feel I simply must apologize to you."

Carolina turned, the sprig muslin gown whirling around her legs as she did so. Her dark eyes beheld him as if trying to find any reason to do as he bid.

"Please . . . about the other night."

"There's nothing to say," Carolina snapped frostily.

Hampton strode closer. "But I believe there is. You see, I forgot myself and my manners. I saw a beautiful woman. A woman of such quality and refinement that I simply lost my head in passion." He took several tentative steps toward her, then halted. "I know it was wrong to push you, but you must know how very much I desire you. You haunt my thoughts day and night, and I'm nearly heartsick at the thought of returning to New York City without your promise to marry me."

"Mr. Cabot . . ."

"Please," he said, raising his hand, "hear me out."

"To what purpose?"

"To the purpose that you further understand me." Hampton stepped closer, but seeing her eyebrow arch suspiciously, he stopped once again. "I know it was wrong to force myself upon you, but I was simply overcome. Can't you see that what I feel for you is genuine?"

"I suppose I can, but I've already told you I do not love you."

"It doesn't matter. I'm offering you enough love for both of us. You will come to love me in time, of this I'm certain. And because I am certain of it, I'm willing to offer you a token of my trust and hope in that love."

"What kind of token?"

"A college education." Hampton held his breath waiting for her response. The look of disbelief on Carolina's face was enough to let him know he'd drawn her full attention. "There are several progressive colleges in New York that are allowing women to obtain degrees. I would allow you to attend and completely finance such an expedition, if you would only do so as my wife."

Carolina actually looked as though she might faint, and Hampton hurried to bring her a chair. "Here, sit down," he urged. "I didn't mean to shock you so badly."

"No, that's all right," she murmured and took the seat. "I must ask you something."

Hampton drew up a chair and sat on the edge of the seat. "Anything."

"Why are you so intent on marrying a woman who obviously doesn't love you? I've told you over and over I don't feel the slightest bit romantic toward you, yet you continue to pursue me and now offer me the choicest of my dreams if only I will agree to wed you. It doesn't make sense to me."

"I love you, Carolina. I know that may sound trite, but believe me, it isn't. I know you have dreams for an education and dreams of seeing yourself in an important role with the railroad. I find that, although women in such roles once offended my sense of propriety, my love for you is making a changed man of me."

"And you would marry me, knowing that I was only doing so in order to obtain a college education?" Her eyes narrowed and her brows knit together in anticipation of his reply.

"I would." He tried to appear as besot with her as he was with her father's power and money. "There would need be no secrets between us. Marry me for the schooling. Marry me for the railroad. Just marry me."

"My father could give me an education, too."

"Yes, but if you did so as a married woman, you would not risk your reputation."

He could see that the idea was intriguing to her and waited while she silently contemplated his proposal.

Several moments passed before she spoke again. "And what would you get out of this arrangement?"

Hampton felt a surge of self-satisfaction. He'd finally managed to break through her tough facade to at least get her to consider him as a prospective mate. Some women had to be wooed with diamonds and rubies, others with sweet words and acts of passion. But not so Carolina Adams. To woo Carolina, one had only to dangle a carrot marked "education" in front of her nose and she was instantly drawn in.

"I would get you for my wife," he said, leaning forward. He gently touched her hands with his, being careful not to appear aggressive. After all he'd gone through to reach this point, he didn't want to frighten her now. "I would be a good husband, Carolina."

"But I wouldn't be a good wife," she replied. "A good wife would give her heart to her husband, and I can't promise you that I could do that."

He read the turmoil in her eyes. "But you've been honest with me about all of this, and I'm telling you that I would take my chances. Besides," he smiled at her innocent expression, "I have confidence in myself. I believe I could make you learn to love me."

"I must say you've given me a great deal to consider." She stood and moved toward the door. "I'll give you an answer tomorrow."

Hampton watched her go with a sense of accomplishment. It was all too easy, and he chided himself for not having thought of it sooner. Education was the key to her heart, and little did it matter to him that it was all a lie. He wanted to assure himself a position in the family, especially a position that could well see him in charge within the shortest amount of time. Once he convinced Carolina to say yes, Joseph would follow suit by offering him Oakbridge. When Carolina saw how desperately her father needed them there, she would naturally see the folly in moving away. No, there would be no possibility of Carolina deserting her father for her own way. She was much too self-sacrificing to ever dream of it. He smiled. Then it would be Carolina herself, and not Hampton, who put an end to her dreams of college. He would be the sympathetic suitor who promised that one day it would all work out if only they patiently faced it together.

Gathering up the fabricated ledgers he'd brought for Joseph's perusal, Hampton felt himself very close to the power he so longed for. At least Carolina was beautiful, he mused. She might not come to him as a loving wife, but he would use her as one. Once she was saddled with three or four children, she'd soon enough forget any desire for college, and by that time, he would be master at Oakbridge.

Carolina brushed out her hair and further contemplated Hampton Cabot's proposal. Only this morning she would have found such thoughts impossible. But that was before Hampton had offered her college.

Laying the brush on her dressing table, Carolina crossed the room and sat down on the window seat. She pulled back the heavy draperies and felt the cool night air surround her. This was her favorite place to think things through, and snuggling down into her robe, she intended to think through Hampton's unusual proposition.

"I've been completely honest with him," she murmured. "He knows I'd only be doing it for the education."

But even as she said this, Carolina knew it wasn't a good reason to marry. Marriages were made for a variety of reasons, but she couldn't imagine her father sanctioning a union based on the mere profit of one party. Hadn't that always been his reasoning for refusing to force his children into arranged marriages? No, Father would tell me to marry for love, she thought, pulling the robe tighter about her.

"I don't love Hampton," she whispered and silently wondered whether she could ever learn to love this man as a husband.

She pressed her hands to her head, fighting against the fury of emotions that threatened to explode. Could she ever love any man save James Baldwin? And if she could never have the man she truly loved, then why not at least marry an amicable man whose kiss set her to trembling and who offered her the dearest desire of her heart? From somewhere deep in her memory, she remembered Lucy's warning to be careful of Hampton. Something about him had made Lucy uneasy, too, and Carolina had taken this caution to heart. After all, Carolina could easily attribute her own uneasiness around Hampton to his insistence on a physical relationship, whereas Lucy felt uneasy for reasons all her own.

"But Father thinks quite highly of Hampton," she reminded herself. She drew up her knees and hugged them close. "Father is the best judge of people, and if he believes Hampton worthy of trust, then why should I think any differently? Maybe I'm just being silly."

Hampton expected an answer in the morning. Sitting up all night wouldn't change that fact. She slowly replaced the curtain, stretched, and went back to her dressing table. Picking up the brush again, she eyed her reflection in the mirror and paused with the brush halfway to her head. Her dark hair fell in a swirling wave against her robe.

"I am a woman, nearly full grown," she told herself. "James is gone, and my family is quick to go forward with their lives without regard to me. Why should I remain behind? Why should I put off what will inevitably happen one day or another? At least with Hampton, I will get a part of my dream."

Twenty-Eight

The Seduction

*V*irginia listened to the sounds of the summer night while silently sipping her third glass of sherry. Through her open bedroom window she could survey the moonlit landscape and consider her plight. Time was passing by too quickly, and all of her schemes and dreams seemed to have failed her.

Turning from the window she looked at her bed and felt a twisting pang of regret. The heavy mosquito netting did nothing to block out the fact that the confines were empty. Most of her friends were married and sharing their beds with attentive mates. But she was alone and would remain so forever unless she did something to alter that state soon. Downing the sherry, she went to her dresser and took out the nearly empty bottle. She poured the remaining liquid into her glass and held it up in a mock salute to herself.

"I'm the only one who'll drink to me," she said, then tossed down the drink without even tasting the contents.

"Virginia?" a voice called from the other side of her bedroom door.

At first Virginia thought she'd imagined it, and given the amount of liquor she'd just consumed, it wouldn't have been unreasonable to consider. But just as she was about to take off her robe and slip into bed, the voice came again.

"Virginia, it's Carolina. May I come in?"

Virginia rolled her eyes and opened the door. "My, my. And to what do I owe the honor of this visit?" she asked, slurring her words despite her unmistakable effort to sound sober.

"Are you all right?" Carolina asked, seeming surprised at her sister's state.

"I'm as well as can be expected. Now, do you mind telling me why you've come?"

Carolina bit at her lip a moment. A number of expressions crossed her face before she settled on one that seemed most determined. "I wanted to share something with you. In fact, you'll be the first to know."

"I'm so honored," Virginia said, swaying only slightly. The effects of the sherry were starting to take their toll.

Carolina twisted her hands together. "You once suggested I could best help you by marrying Hampton Cabot and leaving Oakbridge. I just thought I would let you know I plan to do exactly that. Hampton has asked me to marry him and move to New York, and I have just decided to say yes. I haven't even told him, because I wanted to somehow set things right between us first."

Virginia felt the bottom drop out of her world. "Marry him? You're really going to marry him?"

"Yes." Carolina seemed eager to move away from that topic and insisted on bringing up the past. "Look, Virginia, I don't know why you said the things you did at Sarah Armstrong's bridal shower, but I want to assure you I never did anything improper with James. It is true I held him in high regard, and if that was wrong, then please forgive me. But I would never have done anything to interfere between the two of you. Can't we put the past behind us?"

Virginia knew it would do little good to cause a scene, but her mind raced with thoughts of how to put Carolina in her place once and for all. Revenge was still uppermost in her mind, and the link to destroying Carolina's happiness was Hampton Cabot. Somehow, she would have to put an end to their plans, but now didn't seem the time. Desperately needing as much information as she could get, Virginia swallowed her pride. "Of course we can. I'm very happy for you both," she lied. "I'm sure you will be very happy with Mr. Cabot. When will you tell him the good news?"

"After breakfast tomorrow," Carolina replied.

Virginia hated her for her serene expression. How dare Carolina be happy when she was so miserable! How dare her little sister plan a future when hers was so hopelessly mired in despair.

"And when will you marry?"

Carolina was rather taken aback by this. "Why, I don't know. I haven't given it much consideration."

"Certainly given the affairs of our home, you will want to do it with haste."

"I suppose you are right."

Virginia smiled. "Well, little sister, it seems as if fate has smiled down upon you. I'm sure your dreams will be sweet tonight."

Carolina's innocent countenance made Virginia want to rage, but instead she held her temper and fixed a sugary smile upon her lips.

"I'll leave you to go to sleep," Carolina said, opening the door once again. "I just wanted you to know. I didn't want there to be anything standing between us."

"Put your mind at ease," Virginia replied with assurance.

When Carolina had gone, Virginia reached for her bottle of sherry, only to find it empty. Curse her, Virginia thought and barely stopped herself from hurling the bottle against the wall.

Down the hall, Hampton Cabot would be sleeping. Virginia imagined him there and seethed. He wanted to marry Carolina, but for what purpose? He'd first looked upon Virginia, but Margaret had told him Virginia was intended for James. Now, however, James was gone, and Carolina was soon to announce her betrothal to Hampton. Somehow Virginia had to put an end to it.

Suddenly she became aware of a tiny thought in her clouded mind, and then it became a full-fledged revelation. Perhaps Hampton could be persuaded to redirect his interest if the proper incentive were given. Virginia went to the mirror and studied her reflection for a moment. She dropped the white lawn robe to the ground and appraised her figure through her nightgown. Smiling to herself, she imagined playing the seductress. She contemplated how she might use her female attributes to her advantage, conjuring up scenes she had seen acted out on stage, or had read about in the romance novels she so enjoyed. Reaching a hand up, she unbraided her hair and shook it out. As it tumbled nearly to her waist, Virginia was confident in her feminine wiles.

She waited until the house was completely silent, void of any wakeful person. When the chimes sounded one o'clock, she knew her moment had come. Taking up a single candle, Virginia tiptoed into the hall and made her way to Hampton's room. To compromise herself seemed a small price for revenge. She would steal Hampton away from Carolina, and whether he came willingly or with a fight, Virginia was determined there would be no marriage for her sister. If things went her way, however, Hampton would readily agree to marry her and forget Carolina. If not, Virginia would address them all at breakfast and, through fits of tears and embarrassing confession, admit to having spent the night with Hampton. That would definitely put an end to any future he had with Carolina, whether or not he cooperated with her plans for marriage.

The handle turned easily, and without a sound, Virginia pressed the huge oak door open and slipped into the room. She locked the door behind her and turned to see if her presence had been noted by the

180

room's occupant. Hampton was sound asleep.

Finding courage in her drunken state, Virginia pulled back the bed curtains and gasped aloud at the sight of Hampton's sleeping form. Gathering back her composure, she was glad he wasn't hard to look at. Dressed in long cotton underwear, Hampton's chest was exposed where the buttons had come unfastened. She leaned closer to better view his face, not seeing the candle wax that dripped onto Hampton's chest until it was too late.

"What in the . . ." he exclaimed, sitting straight up, rubbing the hot wax from his skin.

Virginia jumped back, nearly falling. "I'm sorry!"

Hampton stared at her as though trying to decide if she was real or a dream. "Virginia? What are you doing here?"

Virginia struggled for something to say. "I . . . uh . . . thought we should talk."

Hampton, who by now was fully awake and far less surprised, took account of Virginia's nightclothes and threw her a wicked grin. "You don't seem dressed for talk."

She fumbled with the ties of her robe. "Well . . . that is to say . . . it depends on what we talk about." She swayed dizzily, hating that she'd drunk so much sherry, yet knowing she would never have had the courage to approach Hampton otherwise.

Hampton's eyes narrowed. "And what did you have in mind?"

"You see," she said, twisting the robe ties, "my sister came to see me earlier this evening. She told me that you'd asked for her hand in marriage, and she was going to give you an answer in the morning."

"That's true enough. Did she tell you what her answer would be?" Hampton leaned toward Virginia, gazing intently at her.

"She did, and that's why I'm here."

"And what did she say?"

Virginia began to tremble. "She plans to refuse you." Seeing Hampton's expression change from desire to disbelief, Virginia continued. "She's in love with someone else. It wouldn't be proper for her to marry you and love someone else."

"I see." Gone was the tone of impassioned interest, and in its place Hampton sounded almost angry.

"But I thought maybe I could ease your disappointment. You see, Carolina might not be in love with you, but . . . I am."

"You're in love with me?" Hampton asked, sounding completely surprised. "You've never shown me the slightest bit of interest." He paused and got out of the bed. "Until now."

Virginia backed up a step. "I couldn't interfere in my sister's romance. I didn't think it proper to show an interest in her suitor. But now . . . now that she's made her decision . . . I felt I couldn't wait any longer. Oh, Hampton, you are the man I love. My sister won't marry you, but couldn't you bring yourself to settle for me?"

Virginia gasped as Hampton pulled her roughly into his arms, pressing his lips against hers. She stood stiffly in his sudden embrace, not prepared for his enthusiasm, nor for her own response. He was quite adept at stirring the fires of passion, and before she knew what she'd done, Virginia had wrapped her arms around his neck. Suddenly, revenge seemed sweeter than ever.

As Hampton pulled away, Virginia found her breath coming in ragged little gasps. "Marry me. Marry me tonight, Hampton."

Twenty-Nine

Startling Discoveries

*C*arolina came to breakfast convinced that what she was doing was right. Marriages of convenience happened every day for a variety of reasons. They were usually set up to make the most advantageous arrangement for both parties. Was agreeing to marry Hampton any more or less than this?

She frowned at the memory of Andrew Jackson admonishing her to marry only for love. James was the man she loved, but obviously he did not love her. It had been nearly a year since his departure from Oakbridge, and not once had he so much as posted her a letter. Then his reaction at the hotel ball had to be considered as well. Surely, if he had any real interest in her, he'd have remained at the party in hopes of talking with her. She knew she was the one who had turned and fled when she was startled to see him there, but why hadn't he pursued her? The matter nagged painfully at Carolina.

Staring at her father, who sat so wearily at the head of the table, Carolina wondered how he would react to the news. He liked Hampton and obviously trusted him with their financial affairs. Her father would most likely welcome Hampton as a son-in-law.

Just don't let Father ask me if I love him, Carolina thought.

With her mother confined to her bedroom and Georgia off to finishing school in Richmond, Hampton and Virginia were the only other people expected at the breakfast table. Carolina found it strange that Hampton should be so late in coming to the meal. He would be anticipating her answer, and Carolina had even thought she might have found him awaiting her in the hall that morning.

"Massa Adams," a negro child spoke, coming through the kitchen entry, "Miriam says to gib yo dis." The boy thrust a white envelope into Joseph's hands.

Joseph took the letter and opened it while the boy disappeared back into the kitchen.

"What is it, Papa?"

Joseph scanned the letter, then looked up with an expression that appeared both regretful and sympathetic. "I'm afraid you must brace yourself for some painful news, my dear."

Carolina couldn't imagine what possible news her father might share. Was it James? Had something happened to him? She felt her stomach tighten into a knot. "What is it?" she asked again.

Joseph drew a heavy breath. "It would seem Virginia has eloped."

"Eloped?" She let out the breath she'd been holding and asked, "With whom?"

Joseph seemed to wince as he folded the letter back into the envelope. "With Mr. Cabot."

The words barely registered in her brain. Carolina felt the breath knocked from her and fell back against her chair with one hand to her throat.

Joseph instantly got to his feet and came to her side. "I'm so sorry, Carolina. I know what a shock this must be. I can't imagine what Virginia was thinking, or for that matter what manner of game Hampton is playing. Let me get you something." Her father went to the sideboard and started to pour a glass of brandy.

"No, I'm fine," she barely whispered.

"I'm so sorry, my dear." Joseph recapped the bottle and took his seat again. "I know you and Hampton were becoming quite serious."

A sudden giggle spilled from Carolina's lips, startling them both. "I'm sorry." She tried to compose herself before continuing.

"It's quite all right to be grieved, Carolina," her father said sympathetically. "Virginia and Hampton's actions are reprehensible. I can't imagine what got into either one of them. Why only yesterday, Hampton pleaded with me to assist him in convincing you to marry him."

"He did?"

"Absolutely. He seemed quite sincere in his feelings for you, and I felt him rather noble in his desire to help me with Oakbridge."

"With Oakbridge?" Carolina questioned. "What do you mean?"

"Hampton hoped that I might train him to take over the running of Oakbridge in light of York's and Maine's disinterest. He felt that as your husband, he could assume responsibility from me and ease my load, while allowing you to stay close to home."

Carolina began to see the truth of the matter. Hampton had promised her an education, while promising her father that they would remain on the plantation. He was simply deceiving her in order to get the position of power he truly wanted. Anger began to replace shock, and remembering her conversation with Virginia the night before, Carolina realized how amply she must have played into both their schemes.

Joseph seemed to have run out of words of comfort, and before he could continue, Carolina got to her feet. "I must explain something, lest you worry overmuch about this turn of events," she said, now feeling a need to console her father. "I did not love Hampton Cabot. I am ashamed to say that I considered marriage to him, not because of what it might have done to assist your needs, but because of the things Hampton promised me." She stopped at denouncing Hampton any further. If he was only after a place in the family, then he was by now, in all probability, her sister's husband. What happened from this point forward need not involve her. Her father was no fool. He would reason through the entire matter and come to the right conclusions as to what he could or couldn't trust to Hampton's care. And with the tension of animosity and bitterness from Virginia, Carolina knew that to say anything against her sister would only serve to widen the chasm between Virginia and the family. Torn between making herself feel better by exposing their lies and protecting her father from further worry, Carolina chose her father and remained silent.

"But what things could he possibly have promised you that would entice you to marry for anything but love?" asked her father.

Carolina came to his side and put her hand to his shoulder. "I'd rather not discuss the matter further. I was a poor judge of character in both Hampton and myself."

"Don't feel too badly," her father comforted. "We were both fooled—you by his promises and I by my loyalty to his father's memory."

"I should have sought God more readily in my decision, but I confess it didn't even enter my mind."

Joseph put his hand over hers. "Are you truly all right?"

"Yes, of course. In fact, I'm rather relieved. I nearly made a hideous mistake, but God rescued me. We shan't despair of this, Papa, but rather give thanks for God's mercy."

Joseph smiled. "If you are certain."

"I am."

At that moment a voice was heard in the foyer. "Is anybody home?" York Adams called out. He strode into the dining room with a determined expression.

"York! What a pleasant surprise. What brings you all the way out here?" Joseph asked.

185

Carolina hurried to embrace her brother and pulled him with her back to the table. "Are you hungry? We were just about to have breakfast. Oh, and how's Lucy?"

"It smells wonderful. I'm starved, and Lucy is just fine." York took the seat at his father's right, and Joseph rang for the servants to begin dishing up the meal.

"So, how is everyone here at Oakbridge?" York asked.

"Your mother is the same," said Joseph, "Carolina and I are fine, and Virginia is . . . well, I don't know about Virginia."

"Now what has she gone and done?"

Joseph tossed his son the letter. York read it, shaking his head incredulously. "This is too much even for Virginia. How are you, Carolina?"

"I am perfect . . . really. Hampton and Virginia suit each other well. And we need not discuss it further."

"Nonsense," York said, eyeing her closely. "I'd say there's a great deal that needs to be discussed. Especially in light of the liberties Hampton took with you in the past."

"Liberties?" her father questioned, paling.

"Hampton only kissed me," Carolina responded quickly.

"Well, that is enough!" York declared. "He courts and woos you, only to run off in the dead of night with your sister. I'm telling you, this man is without honor."

"Still, Virginia can be very persuasive," Carolina added softly. "Perhaps her loneliness got the better of her."

"Indeed, that is possible. She's never quite recovered from losing James," Joseph said.

Carolina looked at her father while York picked up the conversation to denounce Virginia's actions. What did her father mean in saying Virginia had never recovered from losing James? Virginia had been the one to send James packing. Virginia had chosen her life of sacrifice. Hadn't she?

"Well, all I can say," York concluded, "is that the local gossips will have quite an affair with this one."

"That doesn't worry me nearly as much as dealing with family and friends," Joseph replied.

"And what will we tell Mother?" Carolina suddenly forgot her concerns about Virginia.

Joseph shook his head. "I don't know. I suppose we simply give her the truth as straightforward and delicately as we can."

"And how will you deal with the wayward couple when they choose to turn up here again?" York questioned.

"She's my child," Joseph answered, sounding suddenly aged beyond his years. "How can I send her from me?"

Carolina reached out to pat his hand. "Of course you won't send her away." She gave York a pleading glance. "There is no reason for you both to be up in arms about this. I didn't love the man, and I am not distraught to find him gone. Please believe me."

York nodded. "So long as you aren't hurt overmuch."

Carolina smiled. "I'm not. Now, why don't you tell us what is happening in Washington?"

York gave his sister a brief glance, as if weighing the honesty of her words, then said, "A great deal. The Whigs are making things difficult for President Van Buren. They are opposed to absolutely everything Jackson and Van Buren stand for. Primarily they feel the President should rid the country of the Specie Circular. Van Buren opened Monday's panic session of Congress supporting the need to continue with Jackson's 'hard-money policy.' "

"What is that?" Carolina asked, happy to have the attention away from Hampton and Virginia.

"Just another name for the requirement that land purchases be made with coin or authorized bank drafts," York replied. "Of course, this wasn't received well because the fact remains that land purchases out west have slowed considerably due to this policy. The western states are livid because they were just beginning to taste prosperity, and now they feel the reins have been pulled in on their plans."

"What does the President propose as an answer?" Joseph asked.

A servant offered York a platter of sausages from which he took a generous portion. "Van Buren proposes a federal treasury. He believes it will protect the government against business pressures where money is concerned. The President believes that the people of this country expect far too much of the government."

"How so?" Carolina questioned. "Shouldn't the government represent the people who created it? How can we be expecting too much when we are an intricate part of it?"

"But as Van Buren pointed out, it isn't the business of government to make people wealthy. What we see daily are various groups coming to Washington in search of funding for their pet projects. Be it railroads or orphanages, people simply believe it the responsibility of Congress to provide the moneys for whatever they deem necessary."

"And how is the idea of a federal treasury being received by Congress?" Joseph inquired.

"For the most part, it's being ignored. No one believes it can resolve anything to put all federal moneys under the protection of a treasury.

Even when shown the sensibility of proper gold and silver reserves backing one system of money, they simply scoff and make snide remarks. For instance, Senator Clay was indignant and told Congress that Van Buren's plans were cold and heartless and that Americans were a bleeding people. To Clay and the Whigs, paper money is important. Clay said, and I quote, 'It was paper money that carried us through the Revolution, established our liberties, and made us a free and independent people.' He doesn't stop to add that it was also fraudulent paper bank drafts written from hundreds of different banks that helped give birth to the panic we're now experiencing."

Joseph shook his head. "We should pray before our food gets cold."

He bowed his head and offered thanks, while Carolina silently thanked God for saving her from Hampton's deception. How could I have been so blind, Father? she prayed silently. How could I have given in to such deceit?

"Now, speaking of giving birth," Joseph said upon conclusion of the prayer, "when will my grandchild be born?"

"Next month, according to the doctor. That's another reason I've come today. Lucy and I have discussed it, and we'd really like our first child to be born here at Oakbridge."

"How marvelous!" Carolina exclaimed. "Oh, Papa, won't that be wonderful!"

Joseph smiled proudly and nodded. "Indeed it will be. How soon will you move her in?"

"Immediately, if that is all right."

"But of course. I'll have your room aired out and made ready."

"If you don't mind, I thought perhaps you could arrange for us to have the nursery and adjoining bedroom. Unless you think it will bother Mother."

Joseph considered this. "Your mother is scarcely ever out of bed and never out of her room. No, I don't believe it will be a problem. In fact, maybe a new baby will be the very thing to bring her back to us."

"Is she still not speaking?" York asked.

"Mother hasn't talked in months," Carolina answered for her father. "She just lies in bed most of the time, hugging the doll that Maryland used to carry around the house."

York seemed unable to deal with the reality of his mother's fragile sanity and concentrated instead on his plate. Carolina understood how he felt. She'd grown increasingly weary of her mother's condition and, in turn, only managed to feel guilty for her impatience. She wanted to grab her mother by the shoulders and shake her. She wanted to declare that while her little sisters might be in heaven, she was still on earth, along with her other siblings and their father, and all of them needed her to return to her senses.

"You must excuse me," York said, jumping up just as dramatically as he'd entered only fifteen minutes earlier. "I've got to get back to the city. I shall see you soon, however, and bring Lucy with me."

After he'd gone, Carolina turned to her father with a smile. "Two leave the house and two come back, soon to be three. How like God to bless us in adversity."

Joseph reached out and patted her arm. "Yes, it's very like our God to do just that."

Thirty

New Arrivals

*A*nd it was in the midst of adversity that Lucy Adams gave birth to a daughter on the second day of November, 1837. Amy Allison Adams was welcomed by all and pronounced the most beautiful baby in Virginia by her doting father. York's pride was clearly a matter of open regard as he held his daughter and praised his wife.

"My darling, you have made me a very happy man. She is absolutely perfect," he told Lucy, and Carolina readily agreed as her brother passed the sleeping baby into her arms.

Staring down at the infant, Carolina felt a twinge of envy and sadness. Amy looked a great deal like Maryland when she was born. A dark matting of brown hair and long black lashes gave the child an uncanny resemblance to her now departed sibling.

"Oh, Lucy, she is very pretty."

"Just like her mother," York said, squeezing Lucy's hand.

"I rather like her myself," Lucy said with a tired smile, then turning to her husband she asked, "You aren't overly disappointed that she wasn't a boy, are you?"

"Good grief, no!" York declared. "I wouldn't dream of being disappointed. Some of my favorite people in all the world are women. You, Carolina, and now Amy."

Carolina handed Amy to Lucy and braved the question, "Has Mother seen her yet?"

York shook his head. "Father thought it best if we presented her privately. Later this afternoon, he and I can take Amy to Mother's room, and that way if her reaction is bad, I can quickly bring the baby back here."

"I pray it goes well," Carolina told him.

———

Upon seeing the infant, Margaret was certain the child was one of her own. At first, calmly considering the sleeping child, Margaret had seemed at peace about the matter. Joseph had gently explained that the baby had just been born to Lucy and York, but Margaret seemed unconcerned with that information.

"Her name is Amy," York had told his mother. It was this statement that set her off.

"Nonsense! Why would you call your sister by that name? Her name is Maryland." They were her first words in some time.

"No, Margaret," Joseph tried to reason with her, "this is not our Mary. This is York's daughter, Amy."

Margaret exploded in agitation. "How dare you steal my baby and call her by another name! You cannot do this!"

Joseph turned to York, shaking his head sadly. "You had better return her to Lucy."

"No! Bring back my baby!" Margaret cried, her days of silence forgotten.

After that, Margaret seldom seemed in her right mind. Her few moments of lucid thought were now clearly relegated to the past. She cried for her children and raged at those who attempted to soothe her.

November grew into a month of unrest, both at Oakbridge and in Washington. The Whigs were up in arms and had actually taken to public scenes of protest. Placing themselves outside the White House grounds, they had fired several rounds of blank charges from a brass cannon. York had relayed the incident, which had resulted in much name calling and rock throwing, but no injuries.

It seemed as though the entire world had gone mad. Washington was divided, as it generally was, but the anger and animosity of the general populous caused York to remain at Oakbridge for an indefinite period. Even Lucy's father, after coming to meet his first grandchild, had made the decision to close up the house in the city and return to his home outside Philadelphia.

"Let them all settle down and realize that this depression is no one person's fault," he had told York.

"The President's house will be at the center of all manner of protest and riot," Lucy had said fearfully. "Do you have to go back into that den, York?"

"It is my job, love," he told her gently. "Knowing you're safe will allow me to give full consideration to my own welfare." And so it was settled, yet everyone remained on edge.

Carolina, too, felt a growing need to remove herself from Oak-bridge. She was discontent with every portion of her life, and had it not been for Lucy's company, she would have pressed the issue with her father.

Lucy, however, was a blessing, and Carolina clung to her like a ship's anchor in a storm. Ever the attentive mother, Lucy and Amy were seldom parted, and Carolina found both pleasure and pain in her time with them. The stirring desire to move forward with her life, even into marriage and motherhood, was something Carolina felt quite torn about.

"I wish I better understood myself," she admitted to Lucy one afternoon. "I find I am in such a quandary."

Lucy, quietly nursing Amy, arched a dark brown eyebrow in an unspoken request for explanation.

Carolina paced the room a bit and tried to collect her thoughts. "It's just that I find myself wanting it all. Does that sound selfish?"

Lucy smiled. "No, but it does sound familiar. I could have declared those words for myself."

"But you have it all. You have a completely devoted husband who respects your intelligence and isn't intimidated by your wisdom, and you have a beautiful child. Your future holds nothing but the very best."

"And yours is completely without hope, I suppose."

Carolina paused and considered Lucy's remark. "It isn't that I deem it without hope. It's that I'm uncertain what direction to move in. I know what everyone expects of me, but I don't know that I can be that person."

"And who would that person be?" Lucy asked, gently lifting Amy to her shoulder.

"The perfect hostess . . . lady of the house . . . wife . . . mother . . . ornamental figure."

"And who is it that you want to be?"

Carolina shrugged. "That I do not know. Someone once told me I had to find the truth within myself. A truth no one else can figure out for me. The problem is, I'm not so sure I can figure it out, either." She paused and walked to the window. Outside, the world had passed again into preparations for winter as December crept upon them. The stark land, devoid of greenery and flowers, seemed a perfect reflection of Carolina's heart.

"I feel as though the entire world is whirling around me, and I'm standing still—my feet stuck in mud. I want an education, but I also want a husband and family." She thought of James and felt a bittersweetness at the memory of his image. I want James Baldwin, she thought silently, but would never dream of uttering the words.

"You needn't trade off one in order to have the other," Lucy said, rocking Amy into a tranquil sleep.

"Are you certain of that?" Carolina eyed Lucy doubtfully, then continued. "Because I'm not. I see men who are intimidated by women who ask too many questions. I see men who find it offensive for a woman to have an opinion of her own, especially if that opinion crosses over into their masculine world. The men I know would demand I forget about college and the railroad and instead run a household and rear children. Which I want to do!" she exclaimed in complete exasperation. "But I also want the rest."

Lucy smiled and nodded. "Then that's what you should have. You'll never be happy settling for less."

Carolina came to Lucy. "But what if while insisting on having it all, I lose it all instead? What if I pass up the chance for marriage and family because I insist on going to college? On the other hand, what if I arrange to go to a university and find that it isn't at all what I wanted or am even capable of, and lose again?"

Lucy got slowly to her feet and placed Amy in her cradle. After tucking a blanket around the sleeping baby, she turned to Carolina.

"Carolina, no one knows what the future holds except God. I've not heard you mention Him even once in your considerations."

"I tend to forget that He has an interest," Carolina said with a sheepish smile. "I know He cares and I know I am to seek His will. But what if God's will is very, very different from mine?"

Lucy chuckled softly and led Carolina from the nursery into her adjoining bedroom. "Carolina, you know that God wants only the very best for His children. Why do you believe you might be an exception to that desire? Seek Him first, and the rest will follow in order. If you put God last, nothing else will stand the test of time, because you will have built on a faulty foundation. God can give you the desires of your heart, but your heart's first desire must be Him."

Carolina felt as though Lucy had just issued a startling revelation. "I know I've heard these words before, but it is so hard to remember. I mean, in the face of all that has gone on—Mary's and Penny's deaths, my mother's suffering, Virginia's hatred and elopement with Hampton, and now all this turmoil from the financial panic and such—I just feel so restless and anxious for my life. I desire to run away from it all. I long to be far removed from this place, yet Oakbridge is my home. How can I not cling to it and stay?"

"Pray and seek God's voice." Lucy put her arm around Carolina's shoulder and hugged her. "He will show you what is best. Just as He did for me. I thank God every day for allowing my marriage to make us sisters. You are so like me that I see myself in you. I know we will be good friends long after the trials and tribulations of these days pass away. Just trust God to guide you, Carolina. He is able, and you must believe in that."

Carolina left Lucy's room to consider all she had said. For once a small peace took hold of her thoughts, and Carolina believed that the answers were closer at hand than ever before. The restless need to leave home could well be a good thing. Perhaps she could travel—maybe even visit her aunt and brother Maine in England.

Reaching the top of the stairs, Carolina could hear her father in what sounded very much like an argument. It seemed to be coming from the entry hall, and making her way down the stairs, Carolina wondered what in the world had caused such a stir.

She reached the entryway and gasped in surprise at the scene. Her father was red-faced and quite agitated, while a humble-looking Hampton and Virginia endured his tirade.

Locking gazes first with her sister, Carolina found a smug sort of satisfaction in the returned stare. She then lifted her face to meet Hampton's eyes. His expression was startled for a moment, then fixed with a determined look of accomplishment.

Noting this exchange, Joseph turned to find Carolina. Her presence seemed to calm him instantly, and without giving thought to the fact that he was choosing one child over another, Joseph went to her and slipped his arm around her supportively.

"As you can see for yourself . . ." Joseph began, then let the words trail into silence.

"Yes," Carolina said, lifting her chin as a sign of strength and acceptance. "I can see for myself the newlyweds have returned."

Thirty-One

Reaching Limits

Carolina went over the list of figures and information sent her by Leland Baldwin. The Potomac and Great Falls Railroad was suffering no less than the rest of America. Depression had caused the failure of many newer rail lines and businesses, and from the sound of Leland's discouraging letter, the P&GF was desperately close to the same fate.

"I just don't understand," she murmured. Her father had assured her that the investments were solid and that even in the wake of the panic, they would have enough to begin clearing land.

Leland's letter said otherwise.

"And while I know you are as anxious as I am to put tracks down and see the realization of this line, the financial distress of this country makes such a thing quite impossible," she read.

"The cost of laborers will exceed what little remains of the initial investments, and this allows no consideration whatsoever for the purchase of supplies and equipment."

Carolina shook her head. "It just doesn't make sense." She calculated the losses Leland outlined and found discrepancies in the figures. Perhaps some detail had been inadvertently omitted. She studied the columns, rechecked the investment losses and equipment costs, and still found that the totals were off.

Puzzled at this outcome, Carolina pushed the paper away and tried to reason through the situation. Obviously a good portion of the investments could have been lost in the panic. People were scared, and it was natural for them to pull out of risky deals. But by her father's calculations and Leland's admission, most of the investment money for the P&GF came from Adams money. Carolina knew her father hadn't removed a cent of his support, nor had his investment been kept in the bank. So where had all the money gone?

195

She longed to go to her father and talk over the matter, but these days he was seldom open to such discussions. Her mother's insanity had taken a fierce toll on the family, but especially on Joseph. When he wasn't at Margaret's side, he was so lost in brooding and dismal thoughts that Carolina felt it would be insensitive to present her worries about the railroad to him.

"I could have bet good money on finding you here," Hampton Cabot said from the doorway of the library.

Carolina quickly stuffed the railroad report into a desk drawer and locked it before getting to her feet.

"Aren't you even going to bid me good morning?" he asked in a tone that suggested amusement.

Carolina looked at him for a moment, drew a deep breath, then spoke. "Good morning, Mr. Cabot."

"There, that wasn't so hard, was it?" He sauntered across the room and took residence in the chair opposite her father's desk. "I do believe you've been avoiding me."

"Believe what you like, it is of no interest to me, sir." She swept past the desk and headed for the door.

"So we are to be enemies?" he called out.

Carolina stopped and turned. "Enemies? Why, no. I wouldn't give you that much consideration. You simply are unimportant to me, Mr. Cabot."

"And well I know it. You act the part of the wounded maiden, yet I know full well you intended to reject my proposal of marriage. Are you merely put out that I rejected you first?"

"I have no idea what you are speaking of, but I am in no way distressed that you, as you say, rejected me. As you will recall, I told you on more than one occasion that I did not love you or care for the idea of marriage to you."

"Then why the avoidance? Why do you treat your sister with such scorn, if not for want of her position in my life?"

Carolina gave a haughty laugh. "I have seldom ever envied Virginia anything." She paused when an image of James came to mind. "Believe me, I do not envy her now, nor do I treat her with scorn as you might suggest. I have nothing but love and concern for my sister." She turned to leave but stopped abruptly at the door. "And perhaps pity."

"I assure you, there's no need of that, sister dear," Virginia said, pushing past her to join Hampton in the library.

Carolina shrugged, trying not to appear overly unnerved by Virginia's contemptuous stare. "Given time, you may feel otherwise."

She forced herself to leave the library in an unhurried fashion. Deep inside, all she really wanted to do was run as far away as possible from both of them, and yet she wasn't completely certain as to why she felt that way. She didn't love Hampton, and she didn't envy Virginia's place in his life. Still, there was something about the two of them living at Oakbridge that rubbed like a thorn in her side. With a sigh of exasperation, Carolina went in search of Lucy and the solace she knew could be found in her company.

"May I come in?" she asked, peering into the nursery's open door.

"Please," Lucy replied. "Amy is quite happily sleeping, and I've just picked up my sewing."

Carolina took the chair beside Lucy's rocker and stared dismally into the fireplace flames. "I want to leave Oakbridge," she announced without warning.

"Leave?"

Carolina turned to meet Lucy's dark eyes. "Yes. I can't abide staying under the same roof with Virginia and Hampton."

"I didn't think you minded that they married."

"I didn't think I did, either." Carolina folded her arms against her body. "In fact, I know that it isn't their marriage that bothers me. It's the feeling of living with such hostility and . . . well . . . evil. I feel as though evil has pervaded this house."

Lucy nodded. "I told you once before that there was something quite disturbing about Mr. Cabot. I still can't say what that something might be, but I agree with you."

"Granny would have said that evil spirits have invaded Oakbridge."

"Granny?"

"She was an old slave whom I dearly loved and used to confide in. She's dead now—in fact, probably turning over in her grave at the way the family has fallen apart."

Lucy leaned closer. "You mustn't fret so, Carolina. Things will work themselves out. At least your mother seems comforted by Virginia's presence, and Hampton is offering your father a great deal of help. Maybe we need only keep an eye on things and see how they come about."

"But I don't want to keep my eye on things." Carolina got to her feet and began to pace. "I don't want to remain here. I'm miserable and tormented, and I want to go as far away as possible." She stopped, arms akimbo. "Yet I know I mustn't leave you and Father."

"Don't be held here by my presence," Lucy admonished. "York is already making plans for my return to Washington. He's quite miserable being so far removed. It isn't convenient for him to come home as often as he'd like, so I've no doubt we'll be moving soon."

"Then I suppose Father is my only concern."

"Father Adams wouldn't want you to sacrifice your peace of mind on his account. But tell me this, where would you go?"

Carolina shrugged. "I don't know."

"I have a suggestion, although it might seem completely out of order."

"Tell me."

Lucy put down her sewing. "I have a friend . . . well, actually, he was married to a dear friend of mine. He's now a widower and father to a small daughter. He lives in Baltimore, and I have heard through mutual friends that he has immediate need for a nanny."

"A nanny?"

"I know that a woman of your standing and means need not consider such a position, however . . ."

"Social standing isn't of concern to me," Carolina interjected. "How old is the child?"

Lucy smiled. "Victoria is barely nine months old. She's been cared for by a string of maids and nurses, but no one has offered the child any permanency or stability."

"Why is that?"

"Her father is a difficult man to work for," Lucy said flatly. "Blake St. John is a very troubled man, but he is a good and honest man as well."

"Blake St. John," Carolina tried the name. "And he lives in Baltimore?"

"Yes. He lives there quite well, in fact."

"How did your friend—his wife—die?" Carolina asked, suddenly wanting to know everything.

Lucy grew very solemn. "No one knows for sure. Blake would never say much about the matter. All I know is that Suzanna died only days after Victoria's birth."

"How tragic."

"Yes, it was." Lucy looked to where Amy slept contentedly. "I cannot bear to imagine the anguish of being parted from a child."

"It's hard to lose someone you love," Carolina murmured, her mind dwelling on the death of her own sisters. "Were there other children in the home?"

"They had a son," Lucy replied and shook her head. "But he drowned. His death nearly caused Suzanna to lose the baby, but she took to her bed and safely gave birth to Victoria eight months later."

Carolina considered the matter for several moments. To move from Oakbridge was one thing, but to take on the responsibility for an infant was entirely different. How long could she offer her services? And would her father ever approve of such an idea?

"It is something to think about," Carolina finally said. "Do you think your friend would be open to the idea of my employment?"

"I can't think of any reason why he would not. Blake is a fair man, and while I can't say that we are very close, he would no doubt consider my reference to be valid."

Carolina nodded. "It would get me away from here, without removing me too far. The railroad would make it easy to return if there should be any real trouble or need." She pondered these things for a few moments before nodding. "I'll give it some prayerful consideration."

Thirty-Two

Amy's Disappearance

$\mathscr{I}$can't find my baby!"

Carolina, used to hearing the cries of her mother's anguished mind, paid little attention until she realized it was Lucy and not Margaret who now made the declaration.

Bursting into the second-floor sitting room, Lucy's pale face gave evidence to her despair. "Amy is gone!"

Joseph and Carolina looked up immediately, but Virginia went on with her embroidery while Hampton read a periodical.

"Gone?" Carolina came to Lucy's side.

"Yes! I awoke from my nap and went to feed her, and she wasn't there. Her cradle is empty."

"Did you ask Miriam?" questioned Joseph. "Perhaps the child woke up early, and Miriam thought to let you rest."

Carolina knew the slave woman would never remove the infant without permission but said nothing to counter her father's suggestion.

"I asked everyone. No one has seen her."

"We will help you look," Carolina said, taking Lucy in hand. "She must be nearby."

Joseph turned to Virginia and Hampton and, without questioning their willingness, issued them orders. "Hampton, you go to the slave quarters. Virginia, take the first floor."

Carolina saw Virginia open her mouth as if to protest, then shut it rather hastily at the look of insistence on their father's face.

"Come along, Lucy," he said, taking hold of her arm. "We will search out this floor while Carolina takes the third floor and the attic." He looked at Carolina as if seeking her approval, and she quickly nodded.

Darting down the hall in an unladylike fashion, Carolina couldn't imagine what had become of Amy. She had just reached the stairs when a miserable thought occurred to her. What if her mother had taken her?

Seeing her father and Lucy head down the opposite wing, Carolina decided to check it out for herself. She made her way to her mother's room and knocked very lightly before pushing back the door.

"Mother?" The room was empty.

Panic flooded her heart and soul. Margaret was not capable of caring for herself, much less an infant. Carolina tried to imagine where her mother might have gone. The nursery was the logical place, but that was just across the hall, and the open door there revealed its emptiness.

Hiking her skirt, Carolina bounded upstairs and made her way down the third-floor hall. There were several rooms here, used primarily for the house servants, while a huge portion of the floor was devoted to the ballroom.

Carolina made her way through each room, softly calling to her mother. There was no response. She strained her ears to hear even the tiniest cry or spoken word, but there was nothing.

A quick appraisal of the dark and empty ballroom revealed only chilled silence. The room had been shut up since Carolina's coming-out party almost two years ago. It wasn't hard to remember the musty room filled with dazzling guests and musicians. For a moment, Carolina could nearly hear the music and see the dancers, and then the images disappeared, replaced by the sound of a baby crying.

It was coming from the attic.

Torn between rushing ahead on her own and returning for her father, Carolina ran to the top of the stairs and called down.

"Papa! Papa, come quickly!"

"Carolina?" His voice sounded muffled and unsure.

"Yes, come to the attic."

She hurried away without waiting for his reply and made her way up the narrow attic stairs.

"Mother?" she called softly. "Mother, are you here?"

She could hear the baby's gurgling cries, but nothing else. Reaching the top step, Carolina glanced around the darkened room. The far window had been opened to allow the sunlight to filter in, and because of the winter wind being allowed in as well, the room was now freezing.

Picking her way through the shadowy room, Carolina called again. "Mother?"

"I'm rocking Maryland," came the reply.

Carolina swallowed hard and eased around a dressmaker's dummy to where she finally saw her mother seated on the floor beside the cradle that had once belonged to Maryland.

"She's fretful and I fear a little colicky," Margaret said. Her mother's nightgown billowed out around her, while her shawl had fallen away. Carolina picked this up and wrapped it around her mother's shoulders while Margaret continued trying to soothe Amy.

"You mustn't wear yourself out, Mother."

"Carolina!" her father called.

"We're up here, Father. I'm with Mother and . . . Maryland."

Margaret smiled up at her. "She's been up all night."

"Why don't you let me rock her while you get some rest?" Carolina said, kneeling beside her mother. "Papa can help you to bed, and I will care for Mary while you sleep."

Margaret stifled a yawn and nodded. "That would be very generous of you."

Joseph appeared at the door and stared in disbelief at the scene before him. Carolina, sensing her father's despair, quickly picked up the conversation.

"Father, Mother is very tired, and I've agreed to watch Mary while she rests. Would you help her to bed?"

Joseph instantly became aware of the ruse. "Of course," he said, reaching out to gently help his wife to her feet. "You have been working too hard again, Mrs. Adams. That is why we have servants, you know. You mustn't take everything on by yourself."

Margaret nodded, her mind peacefully in another world. As Joseph led her away, Carolina picked up Amy and held her close against the chill of the room. Following behind, she wondered if Lucy would ever forgive Margaret for this episode. She remembered the look of complete horror in Lucy's eyes and knew she would never again rest easy under the same roof with Margaret Adams.

She reached the third floor and found Lucy waiting anxiously for her child. Joseph was already leading Margaret down the back stairs, all the while talking softly to her about inconsequential matters.

"My baby!" Lucy sobbed, taking Amy in her arms. "She's freezing. Oh, Carolina, what if she grows ill?" She cradled the child to her breast and cried.

"Come, Lucy. Let's get her downstairs and warm her before the fire."

"How could she do this to me?" Lucy asked, seeking Carolina's face for an answer. "How could your mother do this?"

"Don't hold it against her, Lucy. Remember our earlier conversation about your friend. Losing a child can never be easy. Your own heartbreak just now is proof of how it strains the senses. I know Mother never meant to harm Amy. She truly thought Amy was Maryland."

"I don't care. I can't remain here to watch and worry as to whether your mother will snatch my daughter away again. Oh, what if she'd dropped her or completely lost her senses and tried to hurt her?"

Carolina helped steady Lucy as they walked. "I don't think Mother is capable of hurting anyone. But if it makes you feel better, I'll send a rider for York, and you can make your decision about leaving."

"Yes," she nodded. "Please send for my husband."

———

It was decided that Lucy and Amy would depart immediately for Philadelphia. Living apart from her husband would be sheer misery, but there was still too much chaos in Washington for her to return there. Lucy felt certain that life with her father would afford her greater peace of mind where Amy's safety was concerned.

York, reluctant to see his young wife and daughter slip away, agreed to the move, but not with the enthusiasm that Lucy seemed to hope for. He sympathized with his wife, but felt the conflict with his position as a presidential aide.

Their last morning together caused Carolina a great deal of sorrow. Lucy had become a trusted confidante, and her presence at Oakbridge made Carolina's life bearable.

"I shall miss you ever so much, Lucy," Carolina told her honestly. She tried to maintain a cheerful disposition, but her misery was quite apparent.

"And I shall miss you, but it won't be forever."

Carolina shook her head. "I can't imagine what this house will be like with you and Amy gone."

Lucy held open her arms and Carolina embraced her. "You will write, won't you?" Lucy asked, giving Carolina a gentle squeeze.

"Of course I will." Carolina felt tears come to her eyes but refused to give in to her sorrow. "I know I'm being selfish, but I can't help wishing you would stay."

"I know."

Just then Joseph entered the room and with a regretful expression came to where the two women stood.

"The carriage is ready and York says you must come along."

"Thank you, Father Adams," Lucy said and smiled. "It won't be forever, as I just told Carolina. I hope you understand. I have to protect Amy."

Joseph nodded. "I do indeed understand."

It suddenly came to Carolina that this might well be her last opportunity to introduce the idea of Blake St. John's need for a nanny. With Lucy's assistance and knowledge of the St. John family, Carolina had little doubt her father would consider the situation in a more positive light. And given the fact that everything dear to Carolina was slipping rapidly away from Oakbridge, moving to Baltimore held more appeal than ever before.

"Papa," she said, putting her hand on Joseph's sleeve, "before Lucy goes, I want her to tell you about a gentleman in Baltimore."

Lucy eyed her with an expression of puzzled contemplation for a moment, then she suddenly seemed to realize what Carolina's request was all about.

"Oh?" Joseph looked to Lucy for explanation.

"I have a friend, actually the husband of a now deceased friend," Lucy began. "His name is Blake St. John, and he does indeed reside in Baltimore. He is very well kept, and I believe a great deal of his business is in textiles and sugar."

"I am familiar with the name and the reputation of the man. But why is it that you bring him to my attention?" he asked Carolina.

"Because he has an infant child," Carolina explained. "He needs a lady of quality to come and care for the little girl. I thought perhaps you might consider allowing me to apply for the position."

"You?" Joseph's tone registered disbelief. "You're a young woman of privilege and social standing. Do you honestly wish to remove yourself from such a life and take up residence with a total stranger, all in order to become a nursemaid to a child you do not know?"

"I know it sounds strange, Papa, but I do wish you might consider it." Carolina threw a pleading look to Lucy.

"I assure you, Mr. St. John is from a fine family," Lucy explained. "However, he is alone in the world, save for his daughter. There is no other relative to come and care for the child, and he wants more than a nursemaid in the person he hires. He wants a young woman with exactly Carolina's social standing to properly train his daughter. Then, too, he is offering a substantial salary."

"See there, Papa? I could help out in the midst of the financial struggles."

"The women of Oakbridge need not hire out to put food on our tables!" His voice rose, but he quickly calmed. "We are well enough off without my daughter needing to take up a position of employment."

Carolina realized she'd touched a nerve. "Perhaps then I could put my money toward the development of our railroad."

Joseph eyed her suspiciously. "You desire to leave Oakbridge that badly? Badly enough to risk your reputation? You do realize what people will say. Not only about you, but about the family as well."

"You've always taught me not to fear what people say. My reputation has already suffered greatly in Washington, and we both know why. Even so, I've never cared to give much worry to such things, Papa. I'd just as soon put on trousers and bob my hair in order to explore the wilds of the West rather than hostess a gala event."

"I can't help but feel I've brought this on." He sounded suddenly tired. "I encouraged your independence and now you are discontent."

"No, not that so much." She read the hurt in his expression and wrapped her arm around his waist. "Papa, I need to be away for a while. I can't bear the way things are. Mama is so difficult these days, and Virginia and Hampton are . . ." She paused and thought better of drawing them into the list of reasons. "I just simply need a change. I feel that I'm stifled here and going nowhere. Even Georgia is enjoying a time of recuperation and growth while in Richmond. Is it so very hard to imagine the same need in me?"

"Of course not. I've been heartless to ignore your misery." Joseph kissed her lightly on the forehead.

"No, you've been an excellent father, but you carry too many burdens. Virginia and Hampton are already helping you with Oakbridge, and rightfully it is their duty. Virginia is the eldest daughter, and her husband should serve at your side in the absence of your own sons. There is really no place for me here, especially now that Lucy is going to Philadelphia."

"That isn't true. You will always be needed and wanted here," Joseph assured her. "You can continue to help me with the bookwork."

She shook her head. "That is Hampton's world, and he's made it clear that I do not belong in it. Try to understand, this isn't because of anything you've done. It's me. I need this, Papa. I need to sort through my thoughts and decide what kind of future I want. If I go away and work at something different, then perhaps I can know my own mind more rapidly."

"I suppose Baltimore is not all that far away, especially with the railroad in place." He seemed to consider the matter for a moment longer, then nodded his consent. "If that is what you wish, then I will allow Lucy to post a letter of introduction and make the suggestion that you would be willing to seek Mr. St. John's employment."

"Thank you, Papa. Thank you so much." Carolina threw herself into his arms and hugged him tightly.

"Lucy?" York called. He appeared in the doorway, holding a heavily bundled Amy. "Are you ready?"

"I suppose I am," Lucy returned. "Carolina, I will write Mr. St. John right away." She leaned over to kiss Carolina and Joseph, then joined her husband. They walked downstairs and outside to the awaiting carriage. York handed the baby to Carolina while he assisted Lucy.

Carolina touched her finger to the sleeping baby's cheek. "I shall miss you, little one," she whispered.

York took Amy again and handed her up to Lucy, while Carolina and Joseph huddled together against the cold.

"May God be with you," Joseph called out.

"And with you," Lucy and York responded in unison.

As they drove out of sight, Carolina felt the immediate loss of Lucy and Amy's departure. Looking back at the house, a chill overtook her. There would be no refuge and no one to shelter her from the darts and arrows of Virginia's wrath and Hampton's smug assurance of power.

Thirty-Three

Blake St. John

$\mathcal{J}$anuary 1838 came in with a surprise snowstorm and a letter from Blake St. John. The letter was addressed to Joseph and very properly commanded that Mr. St. John would receive Mr. Adams and his daughter on the tenth day of the month at precisely one o'clock.

The letter was her first introduction to Mr. St. John's demanding, no-nonsense nature. The second confirmation of this came in the stately St. John grounds in Baltimore. Taking her father's hand to descend the carriage, Carolina stared at the black iron fencing that encircled the yard. An arrangement of shrubbery had been trimmed back to face winter's wrath, but otherwise the front of the house was void of vegetation or life.

The two-story brick home, located near Federal Hill on the west side of the Baltimore harbor, seemed foreboding and unfriendly. Carolina wondered now at the sanity of offering to care for the child of a total stranger. What did she know of this man or, for that matter, of taking care of children?

She allowed her father to handle the introductions and was rather disturbed when a sour-faced housekeeper told them that Mr. St. John was not in. They were led to a front receiving room and told to wait until his return, but otherwise, Joseph and Carolina were completely ignored. It only added to Carolina's discomfort.

Trying to still her nerves, Carolina glanced around her. She was impressed by the wealth of imported porcelain and crystal figurines. The furniture, hand carved from the finest mahogany and cherry woods, gave the room warmth in contrast to the bric-a-brac. Supple velvet and brocade upholsteries, all in varying shades of red, furthered the effect of richness. Overhead hung a delicate crystal chandelier suspended by gilded rings of entwined gold. The dozen or so candles were not lit at this time, but Carolina could well imagine the beauty of such a scene.

Time seemed to drag by, and still St. John had not made his appearance. Her father glanced at his watch for a second time and met her questioning glance with a shrug of his shoulders. And still they waited.

"I suppose something has come up," her father suggested. Indeed, Mr. St. John was over twenty minutes late to the meeting he himself had initiated.

Then, without warning, a commotion could be heard in the front hall and a masculine voice boomed out orders.

"Mrs. Graves, see to it that the child is readied for our visitors, then tell Cook to prepare refreshments."

"It's already been seen to, sir," came the voice of the elderly woman who'd shown Carolina and her father into the sitting room.

"Very good. Ramsey, take these things to my room."

"Yes, sir."

Carolina listened, mesmerized by the commanding voice and the evident respect of the people who responded. What had she gotten herself into?

Sliding back the sitting room doors, Blake St. John entered the room without warning.

Carolina gasped at the sight of him. Tall, dark, and willowy, this was the same man who'd rescued her in Washington from Hampton Cabot's undesired advances. Moreover, it was the very same man she'd intruded upon in the small Baltimore cemetery not quite two years earlier.

"Miss Adams. Mr. Adams," he said, greeting the risen Joseph with a hearty handshake and casting a perfunctory bow in the direction of the still stunned Carolina. "I am Blake St. John."

"An honor to meet you, sir," Joseph replied and took his seat.

"I must say, I have the advantage. I feel as though I know a great deal about both of you." St. John gave Carolina a knowing glance, but there was no amusement in his eyes.

Carolina felt her cheeks grow hot. She'd never told her father of Hampton's advances, and now she prayed Mr. St. John would respect her circumstance and refrain from sharing the scene.

As if understanding her thoughts, Blake continued. "Lucy Adams, your daughter-in-law, has written me two very long and detailed missives, and I must say, I am quite surprised and honored that you would consider yourself interested in the position I am offering." He directed these words to both Joseph and Carolina, but it was Carolina to whom he directed his dark, disturbing gaze.

She dared to look into his ebony eyes, trying to bolster her confidence in his intimidating presence. But looking deep, she felt a foreboding sense of fear. While it was said that the eyes were the windows of the soul, Blake St. John seemed to have positioned walls of darkness where a flicker of understanding might normally have resided. Swallowing hard, Carolina forced herself to smile, hoping Blake's stern expression would soften. It did not.

"My daughter is intelligent, independent, and industrious," Joseph said, as though arranging the sale of a slave. "This is her choice to consider, and while I'll not interfere in it, I want to know what arrangements have been made to ensure her reputation will remain unsoiled."

Carolina felt a surge of embarrassment as her father touched on the subject of impropriety and how others might perceive her living arrangements should she be taken into the employment of Mr. St. John.

"I can well understand your concern, sir. I will seldom be in residence here. That is one of the reasons for my need. I have a great many business interests, and they take me both abroad and throughout the states. Mrs. Graves is in charge of the household and hasn't the time for an infant, nor does she have the education to rear a child and teach from books. The remaining staff, my man Ramsey, who will of course accompany me, and the cook, Mrs. Dover, are the only other people who will share residence with your daughter. Of course, she may bring her own maid."

"I see. So when you are in residence she will clearly be chaperoned by two older women?"

"That is correct. There should never be the occasion for questioning this arrangement. I cannot abide gossip; therefore, I see little reason for your daughter to be subjected to any ridicule or public questioning." St. John issued this so matter-of-factly that Carolina found herself voicing a question.

"Am I to remain a prisoner within these walls?"

He eyed her as if judging her value, then shrugged. "I suppose I cannot put that demand upon you; however, everything you have need of will be delivered to you upon request."

"But what of outings for your daughter? What of church on Sunday?"

"I do not hold with religious rhetoric and ceremonial fanfare. The church has afforded me very little comfort in the wake of my wife's and son's deaths, and therefore I see little reason to attend their sessions of hypocrisy."

Carolina was stunned by his attitude toward church. Raised among people who respected the institution of public worship, she found it unthinkable that this man was denouncing all that she held holy.

"Surely you wish for your daughter to be raised to know God?"

St. John narrowed his eyes. "No, I cannot say that I see a value in that."

"Then I am obviously not the woman you would seek to employ for this job. I am a Christian and I hold the Word of God to be holy. It tells us there to remember the Sabbath day, and I would emphatically insist on being allowed to do so."

He seemed to consider this for a moment, then shrugged. "I see no purpose in it, but I won't forbid it."

Carolina felt at that moment that no amount of money or promise of independence could make her see St. John's employment in a favorable light. She was nearly ready to insist on their departure when Mrs. Graves arrived with Victoria St. John.

"Ah, Mrs. Graves." St. John got to his feet and motioned. "This is my daughter, Victoria."

Carolina instantly lost her heart. The child was blessed with rosy cherub cheeks and an abundance of dark brown ringlets. With brown-black eyes, Victoria St. John eyed Carolina suspiciously. Mindless of the others, Carolina moved across the room to greet the infant.

"Hello, Victoria," she cooed and touched the baby ever so lightly on the nose. The tiniest smile formed on Victoria's lips before she shyly buried her face against the housekeeper.

"She don't take to strangers," Mrs. Graves announced, then as if to prove her wrong, Victoria raised her head and babbled at Carolina as though holding a conversation.

Ignoring the housekeeper's admonishment, Carolina held up her arms to see if the baby would come to her. "You are very pretty, Victoria. Would you like to come see me?"

The baby held off for a moment, then to everyone's surprise lunged fearlessly from Mrs. Graves' arms into the awaiting embrace of Carolina.

Murmuring softly to the child, Carolina remembered Maryland. Victoria had the same soft dark ringlets and pudgy baby cheeks. And while her eyes were much darker and more brooding than Mary's had been, the resemblance was still strong.

Suddenly realizing the silence around her, Carolina glanced up and smiled. "She's a beautiful child."

"I think she rather likes you, Carolina," her father said, chuckling. Turning to St. John he added, "She's a charming baby, Mr. St. John."

"Normally the child will have nothing to do with anyone. Even Mrs. Graves finds her unmanageable."

The woman harumphed at this but said nothing.

"How old is she?" Carolina asked.

St. John grimaced. "She'll be one year next month."

Carolina nodded. "I would like to know more about what you would expect of me," she said, coming to sit again. She bounced Victoria on her lap and played pat-a-cake to entertain her.

St. John seemed uninterested in the child, and Carolina found this very odd. She wondered if he had any love for the baby and then chided herself for such a thought. Of course he loves his own child.

"I would rather leave that to your management," he replied. "I will offer you a salary, room and board, and anything else you feel you need to provide for Victoria, including an allowance for clothes, toys, and whatever else a baby might need."

"That sounds most generous," Joseph said, watching Carolina with the baby.

In her heart, Carolina wouldn't have cared if the man had insisted she do the job for free. Her earlier fears and reservations crumbled. She couldn't explain why or how, but just looking into the face of Victoria St. John, Carolina felt a bond she couldn't ignore.

Meeting her father's gaze, Carolina smiled. Saying yes to the arrangements seemed very right, and having already prayed a great deal about the matter, she felt confident in what she was about to do.

"I would very much enjoy caring for your daughter, Mr. St. John, but on one condition."

He arched a dark brow questioningly. "And what would that condition be?"

"That you make no objection to my giving your daughter a religious upbringing. My faith in God is a living, daily thing. I won't hide it away or seek to keep it from her. If you want to acquire my employment, you must agree to this."

St. John's stoic expression changed very little, even as he clenched his jaw. Carolina could see a tiny tick in his cheek, but other than this, he remained clearly in control of any disagreement he might have felt.

After several moments of silence he nodded. "Very well, but in turn you must agree to my conditions as well. The first is that you never question me about the past, nor mention the names of my wife or son in my presence. You will keep yourself to those parts of the house that are allowed to you, and refrain from those that are forbidden you. And you will keep your religious views out of any conversation that includes me."

Carolina's gaze was locked with St. John's. She could sense his anger but see no evidence of it. Even his voice was passive and monotone.

She broke his stare and looked to her father. Joseph seemed to sense that she was seeking his approval, and at his nod, Carolina turned back to St. John.

"I accept. I will have to return home for my things, but—"

"No, that won't be necessary," St. John interjected. "I will arrange for everything to be shipped here. What you might have need of before that time, you should tell Mrs. Graves and it will be purchased for you."

"You intend for me to stay here . . . now?"

"If you would." It was the first time St. John had voiced anything even remotely close to a request. "Victoria has no one," he added, seeming to know it would seal Carolina's decision.

"Very well, Mr. St. John." She lifted the baby in her arms and gazed into her seeking eyes. "Well, Mistress Victoria, it seems I am to be your new nanny."

PART III

June – November 1842

The hopes of this nation, and of unborn millions of men of every clime, are bound by mysterious links to these highways of commerce. . . . The blows of fanaticism shall fall harmlessly upon a Union thus held together by the iron ties of interest, as well as by the more sacred bonds of affection and common nationality.

—Enoch Louis Lowe

Thirty-Four

Out of the Darkness

*I*n the years that followed America's most severe economic depression, the world changed greatly, and with that change came a new national spirit born of adversity. In England, a beautiful young queen, Victoria, took the throne. In America, the reins of presidential power were changed not once, but three times. Martin Van Buren and Jacksonian agendas were relegated to the past as William Henry Harrison won the nomination of the Whig party and came into office. His stay, however, was short-lived. Having caught pneumonia at his own inauguration, he served only thirty-one days as President before dying. John Tyler then became the tenth U.S. President in 1841, the same year Britain declared sovereignty over Hong Kong.

America exuded creativity and change perhaps more than any other country in the world. Despite the effects of a depression, an inventor named Charles Goodyear discovered the process of vulcanization, thus making a popular new market for the commercial use of rubber. Elsewhere, a relatively new game called baseball was off to a popular start, and portrait painter Samuel Morse exhibited his electric telegraph at the College of the City of New York.

It was a challenging age of growth for the country, and while westward expansion took on new possibilities for thousands of Americans, the railroad grew to meet demands. For James Baldwin, the summer of 1842 represented his fifth year of full-time service with the Baltimore and Ohio Railroad. During this service he'd watched the infant company assume a portion of maturity, but never to the degree that he and others fervently prayed for.

James surveyed the workmen from his vantage point on a narrow shelf of Maryland limestone and shale. At least the weather was with them. Spring rains had slowed their progress, but by May they had managed to reach Hancock, Maryland, a small community on the Potomac River. This town represented a point slightly more than halfway to Cumberland, and while there was great revelry and celebrating among the workers, the board of directors still gnashed their teeth and despaired of ever reaching the Ohio River.

"It ain't your responsibility!" a man suddenly yelled out, instantly capturing James' attention. The man, a burly, barrel-chested worker, affectionately nicknamed Two-Toes after a nasty blasting accident, was arguing with a wiry Irishman named Mahoney.

It was the third argument in less than twenty-four hours, and James knew that unless he attempted to defuse the incident, the two men would soon be brawling. Scurrying down the rock shelf, James reached the characters just as a third man entered the argument.

"Masterson, this isn't your fight," James admonished and ignored the man's growl as he pushed him back away from Mahoney and Two-Toes.

"I'm telling you there's too much black powder in that charge," Mahoney yelled, poking a long index finger into the chest of the heavier man.

"And I'm telling you that it ain't your concern. I know what I'm doing."

"Sure, just like the time you blasted off half your foot."

"Why, you . . ." Two-Toes pulled back a fist and would have made contact with the man's face except for James' intercession.

"Two-Toes, what's going on here?" James asked. Cautiously, he placed himself between the two men.

"Mahoney's trying to tell me my job."

"He's gonna blow us all to kingdom come," Mahoney said, spitting tobacco juice across James' well-worn shirt.

James ignored the stain and turned to face Two-Toes with a smile. "You aren't trying to avoid a full day's work by rushing off to see the good Lord, now, are you?"

The man refused to be placated with James' good-natured question. "I know my job and I cain't do it standing here a-jawing with you."

By this time the other workers had gathered around to see what the commotion was, and even Benjamin Latrobe was making his way across the ridge to see what was holding up the final blast of the day.

James hoped to put everyone at ease and return the men to work, but just as he turned to speak, Two-Toes headed off in the direction of the blasting charge, tamping rod in hand.

"Just keep that Mick away from me," he called over his shoulder.

Mahoney had taken all he was going to stand for and, with a slight lowering of his shoulders, charged after the heavier man and plowed into his back at a full run. It took only moments for the matter to get completely out of control. A full-blown free-for-all ensued, and even James was not spared in the onslaught that followed.

Nursing a sore jaw, James tried to maneuver himself out of harm's way when a tremendous explosion knocked him off his feet and sent a rain of rock and dirt pelting down around him, leaving James little recourse but to bury his head under his arms. Another explosion followed the first. Rock hailed down on his back, biting and piercing his flesh. When the ground stopped shaking, James was one of the first to get back on his feet. All around him smoke and dirt filled the air, making it impossible to see.

Groping at the air, James coughed and wiped at his watering eyes. "What happened?" he called out, as though it weren't already apparent.

"We've got men buried over here!" came a voice through the haze.

"James, are you here?" It was Ben Latrobe's voice.

"Over here, Ben. Are you hurt?"

"No, I was back far enough, but I thought surely you were buried alive." Latrobe reached James through the hazy air. The commotion around them added to the confusion.

"Not me, but apparently others weren't so lucky," James replied. "We need to get this thing organized and dig those men out."

But the uninjured workmen were already digging at the massive pile of dirt and rock that had seemingly appeared from thin air.

James took up a shovel and began working beside two other men. His mind filled with hideous images and disheartening thoughts. How many men would he find dead beneath the rubble?

"I've got one!" yelled a man.

James glanced up only momentarily to see the workers pull the limp body of a man from the dirt.

"Is he alive?" someone called.

"Barely."

James wanted to pick up the pace and rake the shovel across the debris, but he hesitated digging into the mess, fearing that he might accidentally dig into an injured man.

"Who's missing?" James heard Ben Latrobe ask the surviving men.

A quick head count revealed that an additional five men, including Two-Toes and Mahoney, were still unaccounted for. James scraped away layer after layer of gravel and dirt, but as the minutes passed he grew more desperate. A man had to have air to survive, and buried beneath the mounds of rubble, five souls were being denied that very element.

He tossed the useless shovel aside and began clawing at the dirt with his hands. Razor sharp pieces of rock bit into his flesh, but James ignored the pain and continued to work.

"Here's Mahoney!"

James glanced up to see two men hoist up Mahoney's lifeless body. "He's dead," one of the men announced.

James felt sickened. Bile rose in his throat, and he fought to keep from expelling the contents of his stomach. Dig, he told himself. Dig and think of nothing more than finding the other missing men alive.

His hand met with resistance as he pulled at the dirt. Brushing aside the debris, James spotted a hand. "Here's one!" he called out and frantically worked to free the body.

He was joined by two other men, and together they unearthed the body of Two-Toes. He was dead also, his face nearly obliterated from the blast. This time James' weak stomach got the better of him, and running to the farthest end of the work site, he vomited until his sides ached.

"James?" Ben put a hand to James' shoulder. "Are you all right."

Wearily, James got to his feet. He felt green, and his mind refused to let go of the image of Two-Toes' faceless head. "This can't be real," he murmured, lifting his eyes to take in the all-too-real scene before him.

Light was fading from the sky, and as if noting it for the first time, Latrobe called for lanterns to be fixed in order to aid the workers.

Shaking from his head to his toes, James started back, but Latrobe put his hand on his arm. "Why don't you wait a moment."

James shook his head. "I'm all right."

But even as he spoke the words, James wondered at the truth of the matter. Images of Phineas Davis and the train accident that had claimed his life flashed through James' mind. Railroading was a dangerous business—of that there was no disputing—but this matter seemed purely senseless. A foolish argument had given birth to this incident. James wondered about Two-Toes and whether he had a wife and family. Phineas had left a wife and two very small children, and although the accident was nearly seven years behind him, James shuddered as though it were only yesterday. Absentmindedly, he rubbed his leg as if feeling the injury all over again.

"Are you certain that you aren't hurt?" Latrobe asked him, eyeing the leg suspiciously.

James forced the thoughts from his mind. "I'm certain."

"Here's a live one!" The cry rallied the men to work faster. If one man had survived, there might well be others.

James instantly left Latrobe's side and, with new resolve, resumed his place beside the other workers. So long as there was even one man missing, James pledged to himself that he would remain.

Within twenty minutes the others were accounted for. Three men were dead and three were seriously injured. James had never felt more tired or dirty, but more than this, he felt the discouragement and grief of the men around him. Gathering up his courage and his wits, James called the workers to a meeting at the far end of the work site. He wanted to remove them from the reminder of death and destruction; he wanted to encourage them and help them to look toward the next step. But what was that step?

Anxiously, James glanced around for Ben Latrobe, but unable to find him, he called out to the men instead.

"If I might have your attention for a moment." He shifted nervously as the men gathered round. Some, sporting makeshift bandages to patch up injuries they'd sustained in the explosion, looked up at James in painful anticipation. Others, coated in grime and sweat from their rescue efforts, stared blankly, as if still in shock and disbelief at what had happened.

James dropped his gaze to the ground. What could he say to these men that could in any way compensate them for what had happened? How could he bolster their spirits when discouragement threatened to destroy his own?

"You must understand," James began, "that what happened today need never have happened." He lifted his face to look upon them once more. "Either we work as a team following one master plan, or we follow our individual way—with obvious results." He paused, struggling for words to express what was on his heart. "I feel very responsible for what happened here today."

Murmurs of protest rose through the crowd, but James raised his hands to continue. "I failed to bring two men together. I failed to help them see this project as the effort of many, and not of one man. As their supervisor, I should have been able to convey the importance of following directions, working together, and sticking to one plan. But somewhere along the way I failed them, and you."

James felt as though the weight of the entire matter rested upon his shoulders. Responsibilities he might have shrugged off as a youth were now impossible to ignore. He had been given a job supervising the rail crew, and because of his ability to communicate and interpret Latrobe's and Knight's intricate surveys, he had become an important part of the

B&O's westward expansion. All of this seemed to pale in the wake of the accident.

"We can work together or we can work apart. One way will achieve our objective and see us to Cumberland. The other will result in this." He lifted his aching arm and pointed to the rubble behind them.

"There is a master plan. A specific design that if followed to the letter will ensure your safety and the progress of this line. And I know you want to see the progress of this line." James studied the faces of the men around him. "You are this line. The Baltimore and Ohio is not built of iron rail and crossties—it's built of flesh and bone, of sweat and blood. You are the B&O, and without you it would pass from existence into the ashes of a distant dream. Will you let it die?"

Mutterings and a rumble of supportive responses encouraged James. "We're laying a mile of track a day. We've faced impossible odds and mastered the elements. We've done what others said could not be done. We've built a railroad in the midst of depression and financial ruin. We've faced striking workers, low wages, minuscule supplies, and the disdain of landowners, and through it all we have endured. But we've only endured because from within our circle we were strong. We were one body, following a master plan. That plan must continue to be followed, or we will fall from within. Today, three men are dead and again as many are injured as an example to us."

"He is right, you know." James turned to find Ben Latrobe at his side. "As each man seeks to perform his tasks, he must constantly be aware of the responsibility he holds to his fellow workers. You are good men and your work speaks for itself. I admonish you to listen to Mr. Baldwin. Together we can build the railroad, but separately we will tear it down. Not one of you here today works alone."

The men nodded knowingly, and while no great chorus rose up to confirm his thoughts, James felt certain the men were in agreement.

"Tomorrow we'll assess the damage and see what is to be done, but for now I want you to bathe and rest up. The evening meal is nearly ready, so see to your needs and meet up in the chow tent."

The men disbursed very nearly in silence. James stared after them, wondering if he'd done the right thing.

"They're a good bunch," Ben said, as if reading James' mind. "They'll pull together."

"It's been so hard on them. These past years haven't been easy. Some of those men have been with the B&O for the entire time, while others are new and uncertain as to what's expected of them. Sometimes it's hard to make them see this as a combined effort."

"I know," Latrobe replied. "Then just when you have them doing their job, something like this happens and upsets the entire cart."

"Yes." James looked across the camp and remembered the frightening moments during the explosion. "It's a wonder more of them weren't killed."

"Life is fragile. That's why it's best to know where one is headed when it's over." Latrobe stared hard at James. "What about you, James? Do you know where you would have spent eternity if you'd been one of the dead men pulled from the rubble?"

James shook his head in a hesitant manner. He'd crossed death's path twice now, and neither time had he been ready for the possibility of his youthful existence coming to an end.

Latrobe seemed to understand his turmoil. "It gives one a great deal to consider."

"Indeed," James replied, unable to say anything more.

Thirty-Five

Victoria

*N*anny!" Victoria St. John scurried into the room with all the energy of an active five-year-old. Her animated expression nearly caused Carolina to laugh out loud. Instead, she felt compelled to admonish her young charge.

"Victoria, you are a young lady, and thus you should conduct yourself as one. Walk, don't run." My, but she sounded just like her mother had when scolding her little sisters.

"But, Nanny, you must come see. Cynthia has babies!"

Cynthia, the stray cat Victoria had adopted, had been the subject of great speculation these last few weeks. Now the time of questioning was over.

Carolina smiled. "How many?"

Victoria danced rings around Carolina, brown curls bobbing. "Cook says there are six, but I only saw four. They are gray and white, just like Cynthia. Oh, do come see!"

Carolina shook her head. "All right, but then you must wash up for supper. Your papa is due home today."

Victoria frowned at this news, and Carolina could scarcely blame the child. Whenever the rare occasion of Blake St. John's presence took place, Victoria was relegated to the nursery, where she was expected to remain until her father once again took his leave. It had been this way the entire four and a half years Carolina had been in residence. And now, having dealt for long enough with the man's moody preoccupation and obvious disinterest in his only child, Carolina was determined to speak to him.

"Will Papa see me this time?" Victoria asked. Her childish longing brought a knot to Carolina's throat.

"I do not know," Carolina said. "But I do plan to speak to him again on the matter."

"You do?"

Victoria's hopefulness made Carolina feel guilty. It wasn't that she'd never tried to encourage her employer to take a more active role in the life of his child. She had spoken to him many times of the void he left in Victoria's life. She had even admonished the man that her own father knew more of Victoria's daily routine than did he, but St. John remained unmoved.

"I plan to talk to him," Carolina finally said, taking Victoria in hand and leading her to the back porch. "But that doesn't mean it will change a thing. We must be patient with your father, Victoria. He is a good man, but he was very saddened by your mother's and brother's deaths."

Victoria nodded, knowing full well the circumstances behind her father's overextended periods of absence. At least she knew them as well as Carolina could explain them. In the years she'd been employed to care for Victoria, Carolina had struggled to make excuses for Blake St. John's lack of interest in his only child. She found it abominable that the man was seldom in residence, and that when he was home, he insisted on having nothing to do with his precious little girl.

And she was precious, Carolina thought as they bent over the basket of new kittens. How she loved this little girl! She'd come to see Victoria practically as her own child, and in many ways—the ways which truly counted—she was. It was Carolina who had watched her take her first steps and taught Victoria her first words. It was Carolina who'd sat up through long nights of croup and other assorted childhood ailments, and it was Carolina who comforted Victoria when she was scared and dried her tears when she was sad or hurt. In every way that mattered, Carolina was bonded to Victoria as a mother to a daughter.

Perhaps the hardest thing she had to deal with was Victoria's growing number of questions concerning her father and mother. In all her years in the St. John house, Carolina had been told very little concerning either one. Mrs. Graves, the plump, elderly housekeeper, certainly never saw fit to share any information with Carolina. To the best of her ability, Carolina had tried to befriend the woman, but it was almost as if Mrs. Graves saw Carolina as some sort of threat to the peace and sanctity of the home.

Carolina could still remember the way Mrs. Graves had puffed up indignantly when she had dared to broach the subject of Mrs. St. John's death.

"But I only want to explain the matter to Victoria," Carolina had explained.

"The child need not know about such morbid matters. Her mother is gone and that's enough to understand."

"But she's asking me questions for which I have no answers."

"Then that's a sign of ill-breeding. You should take a firmer hand with the child and admonish her to speak only when spoken to."

"That's ridiculous," Carolina had countered. "Children have a right to know of their own parentage."

"Bah! Children have no rights at all, except those given them by overindulgent nannies." With that the matter had been very firmly closed.

But now Carolina was determined to get some answers. Four and a half years was a long time to walk about in the dark, and unless Blake St. John wanted to risk their amicable relationship, Carolina felt he owed her at least a brief explanation.

"Now, you wash your hands and face, and I will set our table for supper."

"Are you going to stay with me?" Victoria asked hopefully.

"Of course," Carolina replied, gently patting the child's head. "Where else did you expect me to go?"

"Won't Papa want you to eat with him?"

"I don't really know, but if he does I can join him later."

Blake St. John arrived home shortly before the evening meal. "The master bids you join him," Mrs. Graves said solemnly as she placed Victoria's supper on the small nursery table.

"I will dine with Victoria first," Carolina answered. "You may tell Mr. St. John that I will join him in a short while."

Mrs. Graves was clearly disturbed by this answer but nevertheless took her leave.

Carolina refused to hurry Victoria through the meal, and even though dinner was not included for herself, she nibbled at the things she knew Victoria would not eat.

He summons me like a servant, Carolina thought, and it gave her brief pleasure to defiantly hold her ground by putting him off.

At twenty-two, Carolina had become a confident and extremely independent woman. She had little worry about her financial status and circumstance. In her years of employment, Carolina had put aside most of her generous pay and, with her father's help, had managed to purchase stock in the Baltimore and Ohio, as well as invest in her own dreams for the Potomac and Great Falls Railroad. She'd personally felt little of the effects of the national depression. Blake St. John was outrageously wealthy. This she'd learned from Mrs. Dover, who over the years had encouraged Carolina to simply call her Cook. Cook seemed open to bits of gossip now and then, but even she, fearing for her job, refused to ever discuss the former Mrs. St. John. The master of the house had made it quite clear that the matter was never to be addressed.

Preparing Victoria for bed, Carolina let go of her frustrations and instead concentrated on listening to the child's prayers. This had been a topic of much controversy in the St. John household, for Carolina insisted on being allowed to give the child a Christian upbringing, while Blake held little regard for such matters. Carolina won out, only because of the frequent absence of Victoria's father. She yielded to his wishes, however, whenever he saw fit to reside in Baltimore, but her days of placating the morose man were rapidly coming to an end. How dare he impose his grief upon this child! She was but a babe and deserved a father's love; instead she received his condemnation and anger.

Seeing Victoria's eyelids droop in sleepiness, Carolina kissed her on the forehead and made her way to the St. John dining room. The house, her home for all intents and purposes, was always silent. She likened it to a tomb, and at times felt as though she'd been buried alive. Even Victoria was a quiet child for the most part. Her games and playtime were spent in quiet whispers and hushed conversations. In truth, the announcement of Cynthia's kittens was by far the most excitement the St. John house had seen in months.

Squaring her shoulders, Carolina paused before the hallway mirror. She touched a hand to her nicely coifed hair, thankful that Miriam had taught her the tricks of dressing it out herself. She'd chosen not to bring a maid, and while at times she'd almost relented and sent to Oakbridge for assistance, Carolina was content to care for herself.

Now, studying her reflection, Carolina wondered what Blake St. John would have to say to her. Theirs was a strange relationship. On one hand it seemed very intimate. She'd observed him grieving over his son's grave many years earlier. That had been her first encounter with the elusive Mr. St. John. And while they'd exchanged no words at that meeting, something had passed between them that kept his image on her mind. The sorrow in his eyes had been so intense, the pain so raw and fresh, that Carolina felt as though she'd actually touched the inner being of his soul. Then, of course, there had been his rescue of her from Hampton Cabot during the charity ball at the Gadsby Hotel. He'd been softer then, yet the haunted shadows remained in his dark eyes. He was unlike anyone she'd ever known before.

Licking her lips, Carolina noted her own brown eyes and the fear that seemed to edge her expression. How could she still fear a man whose child she'd cared for since infancy?

But she did fear him.

Only now, rather than his hollow-eyed stares and stern expressions she feared the power he held over her. He alone could say whether or not she remained in the household. He alone held the right to separate her from Victoria. She'd painted herself into a dangerous corner, and now, more than ever, Carolina was well aware of her circumstance. She was hopelessly devoted to Victoria. She loved the child as though she were her own daughter, and in turn, Victoria loved her as any child would a mother. In many ways they had clung to each other because there was no one else to cling to. Oakbridge was a world away, and while Carolina had missives from home and brief trips back to visit, she was isolated in a way that left her completely removed from her family. Victoria had become her family.

She smoothed her high lace collar and turned to face the closed doors of the dining room. But she isn't mine, Carolina thought to herself and gently touched her hand to the door. She isn't mine and even if I risk losing her, I must somehow try to unite her with her father.

Carolina opened the door without so much as a knock. Blake St. John glanced up, his expression sternly fixed, his dark eyes smoldering as they always were.

"Good evening, Mr. St. John," she said, feeling the discomfort of his stare.

He got to his feet in polite recognition. "Miss Adams."

She stood rigidly awaiting his command, and seeing this, he seemed to relax a bit. "Won't you have a seat?"

"Thank you."

They were both seated, and Carolina was surprised to find Mrs. Graves quickly enter the room with a plate of warm food. Carolina smiled appreciation at the woman, but Mrs. Graves merely stuck her nose in the air and exited the room.

"I'd expected you earlier," St. John said, without giving her so much as a glance.

"Yes, I know. Victoria was just sitting down to her dinner, and I'd promised her that I would stay."

He seemed uninterested and this only furthered Carolina's growing irritation with the man. Surely if she were to speak to him on matters of his daughter, she would have to swallow down her fear. Blake St. John would go on indefinitely running her life if she didn't find a way to face him and stand fast.

"Mr. St. John, might I speak to you?"

He looked rather surprised by her boldness and put down his fork. "By my leave."

"Thank you." Carolina felt the palms of her hands grow moist. "As you know, your daughter is five years old." She began that way even though she wasn't truly convinced that he did realize this simple fact. "Victoria is a very intelligent young lady, and she is also very charming and affectionate."

"Your point, Miss Adams?"

Carolina threw caution to the wind. "She needs you in her life, Mr. St. John. She asks after you constantly and desires to know you better."

"Is that all?" He resumed eating as though the words had meant nothing.

Carolina stared at him for a moment. Her temper was barely held in check as she responded. "Isn't that enough? Is it not enough to know that your own child scarcely knows you? Is it not enough that Victoria longs for a father's love? Can you not see that such a thing is essential to her well-being?"

"Does she have enough to eat?"

"Yes."

"Enough clothes to keep her warm?"

"Yes."

"Have you everything else you need to school the child, medicate her when she is ill, manage her affairs when she is not?"

"Of course," Carolina answered flatly. "But that is not the point."

"I see no other point that is valid to my concern."

Carolina slammed her fork down. "Your concern should be her welfare in matters that go beyond her physical needs."

St. John stared at her in complete surprise. Carolina swallowed hard. It was the first time she'd dared to stand her ground with her employer, and the very idea of what she was embarking upon caused her to tremble. Victoria needs her father, Carolina reminded herself once again. She needs him possibly more than she even needs me. I can't be selfish and worry that St. John might dismiss me. Oh, God, she prayed, help me in this matter. Let me say the right things for Victoria's sake.

Calming her nerves, Carolina took a long sip of tea before continuing.

"I have been in your employ for over four years, and in all that time you have scarcely seen your daughter. She longs to know of her mother and brother. Why do you insist upon distancing yourself from the one person you should love above all others?"

St. John said nothing for several moments. His eyes narrowed angrily, however, and a characteristic tick in his cheek became quite noticeable. Carolina knew she'd overstepped the bounds of propriety. She could hear her heart beating in her ears, and her mouth grew horribly dry.

"Are you quite finished?" he finally asked.

Carolina looked at him as if considering what she could say to dispel his rage. "I did not mean to be so outspoken," she admitted. "It's just that you are never here to know for yourself what I see every day."

"You forget yourself, Miss Adams. You are the child's nurse, nothing more. You have no authority to speak to me on matters that do not concern you. If you find this arrangement unacceptable, perhaps you should consider leaving."

Something in his haughtiness and blatant disregard for her concerns gave Carolina the boldness to make her next move. Getting to her feet, she slapped her napkin down on the table and moved to the doors. "Perhaps you are right. Perhaps I have grown too attached and far too concerned for Victoria's well-being. Maybe I *should* go."

Before she could flee, however, Blake St. John was on his feet. "Wait!" he exclaimed, the desperation in his tone totally out of character.

Carolina was halted more out of surprise than obedience. She turned to look up at him, feeling the heat of his stare, knowing that he would say more. To her surprise, he touched her. Lightly, with hesitant hands, he touched her arm and pulled her ever so gently back to the table.

"I'm sorry," he said. "I spoke rashly. Please, sit down and let us be more civil."

Carolina was shocked. The mighty Blake St. John was apologizing? And for what? She had been the impudent one. She gazed down at where he held her arm and felt a warm blush on her cheeks.

As if noting her discomfort, Blake quickly dropped his hold and held out her chair. "Please sit."

Carolina did as he bid, more because of her inability to speak than of any desire to further their conversation.

Blake paced behind her for a moment before finally taking his own seat. "Miss Adams . . ." he began hesitantly. "Miss Adams, you must know that I respect your understanding of Victoria. Please do not consider leaving her."

Carolina looked at him with great heaviness in her heart. "But you do not understand my love of Victoria. To stay here, to live with the child and see her long for that which she can never have, is heartbreaking. Can't you understand? You come and go at leisure. You're gone for weeks, sometimes months, and then suddenly reappear as if to remind her of what she can never have. It's cruel and heartless, and I hate seeing her so treated."

For the first time, Carolina saw Blake St. John appear vulnerable. His stern expression dropped away, and he ran his hands wearily through his ebony hair. "Being heartless and cruel is what I do best, I suppose. I cannot give her what I haven't got within myself to give."

"All she wants is a father to love her," Carolina replied.

"Exactly," Blake said, getting to his feet. He paused, as if trying to decide what he should do. "I implore you to dismiss any thoughts of leaving and . . . I implore you to forget this terrible notion of making me into a father figure for Victoria. I cannot be what you want me to be." With that he was gone, leaving Carolina to stare at her uneaten plate of food and to ponder the mysteries of what she'd just experienced.

Thirty-Six

Joseph's Visit

*M*iss Adams," Mrs. Graves spoke in a reserved, almost hesitant manner, "you've a visitor."

Carolina looked up from the embroidered sampler she was teaching Victoria to sew. "A visitor? But who is it?"

"Your father, ma'am."

Carolina instantly forgot the sewing lesson. "My father? Here?" Her animated voice betrayed her extreme pleasure at this turn of events. "Come, Victoria. Let us go greet my father."

Joseph Adams waited in the front sitting room and seemed most genuinely pleased when Carolina bounded into the room and threw herself into his arms. There was no need to stand on formalities, and the warmth shared between them was not lost on Victoria.

"Me too!" the child exclaimed without reservation and wrapped herself around the man she'd seen on several prior occasions.

Joseph laughed and exchanged a look over the child's head with Carolina. She knew he understood. She'd written many times of her frustration with Blake St. John. Joseph well knew of Victoria's need for a father figure.

"My, my!" he exclaimed and lifted Victoria into the air as though she were his own daughter. "You have grown at least a foot since I saw you last."

Victoria giggled and happily embraced Joseph. "Mr. Adams, are you going to stay a long time with us?"

Joseph shook his head. "Not as long as I'd like. But while I am here, I promise we will have a great deal of fun. Would you like to go the park this afternoon? It's a lovely June day."

"Oh, please!" Victoria squealed and looked hopefully at Carolina.

"But of course," Carolina replied to her charge's unspoken question.

It was settled then, and the three of them embarked on an afternoon of pleasure. The park had been an excellent idea, for while Victoria was preoccupied with running about, Joseph and Carolina had time for a private discussion.

Carolina felt as though she'd been let go from a guarded cell. "Sometimes," she told her father, "I feel as though I'm a prisoner. Were it not for Victoria, I would never have stayed these many years."

"You love her a great deal," her father said matter-of-factly. "That much is evident. You do realize the danger of such a bond, don't you?"

Carolina nodded. "I feel it every day. At first, I guarded myself and took special care not to get too close to her. But, Papa, everyone was doing that with Victoria. Her father never came to see her, much less hold her or play with her. Mrs. Graves and Cook are poor substitutes for grandmothers, but even they afforded her only marginal attention. I believe they are afraid to love her."

"But not you." Joseph patted her hand.

"Oh, I am afraid," Carolina admitted. Victoria had joined up with several children who were attempting to fly a kite. Smiling, Carolina turned back to her father. "But how could I let my fear keep that child from being loved? Everyone needs to feel that someone cares for them. I loved Victoria the first time I laid eyes upon her. How could I pretend to feel otherwise?"

"It won't be easy to be parted from her."

"No, and I find myself praying that such a day might never come."

"But realistically speaking, you know it must. You are twenty-two years old. Have you no desire to marry and bear children of your own?"

"Of course I do, Father," Carolina answered, her gaze ever on the wandering child. "Victoria, come away from the water!" she called out sternly. A portion of the park edged up against Chesapeake Bay, and the water made an alluring attraction for children.

"So long as you are happy," Joseph finally said, breaking their sudden silence.

"I am content," Carolina replied. She linked her arm with her father's. "But what of you, Papa? Surely you didn't make the trip to Baltimore just to find out if I was happy."

He smiled. "No."

"What is it?" Carolina halted, feeling her heart in her throat. She'd not even thought to ask of home and family.

"Your mother is no better. I'm afraid my indulging her at home all of these years may well have harmed her more than helped her. You

231

know that the doctor suggested I send her away from Oakbridge?" Carolina nodded. "I've always hesitated, feeling that I was deserting her by doing such a thing, but in truth I see now where the constant reminder of what she'd lost might well have kept her hopelessly mired in insanity."

"You did what you thought best."

"Yes, I did. . . ." He paused to look out across the water as though seeking some solace there. "Now I am moving ahead to do what just might be the hardest thing I've ever done in my life."

"What is that, Papa?"

"I'm on my way to Boston to investigate an asylum for the mentally ill."

"You are going to have Mother committed?" She tried to keep any note of accusation from her voice.

"I believe I have no other choice. She tried to stab one of the slaves."

"Oh no!" Carolina exclaimed, her gloved hand quickly covering her mouth. She ignored the fact that Victoria was now preoccupied with picking park flowers. "What happened?" she asked her father in hushed tones.

"I'm really not sure. Somehow your mother wandered down to the kitchen, and the next thing we knew she was holding a knife to the throat of one of the workers. I can't have her in the house if she's going to threaten the lives of the people around her. The asylum in Boston has a great reputation. Charles Dickens himself toured the facilities earlier this year and found this particular asylum to be of the finest example."

"Charles Dickens, the writer?"

"One and the same. The man is also a faithful humanitarian. He concerns himself greatly with the affairs of mankind, particularly of social reform. I had the pleasure of meeting him at the White House a few months past. He intends to write a great deal about this country and our social circumstances."

"And he convinced you of the merit of asylums?" Carolina asked, still not believing her father's decision.

"He convinced me of the possibilities of one such institution. I admit, I am not compelled to act on his word alone. That is partially why I am here today. I am making my way to Boston to interview the doctors and workers for myself."

"I see. And what do you believe can be gained for Mother by sending her so far from home and loved ones?"

Joseph frowned. "I don't know. I do know that no one feels at ease with her screaming and torturous cries going on day and night. It's like nothing you can imagine. I thank God daily that you and the others don't have to endure such trials. Poor Virginia bears up under it like a regular nursemaid, but I see the strain taking its toll on her. I've never told you this, but she has had three miscarriages."

"Why didn't you tell me before now?"

"She didn't want me to. The most recent time was last winter when she was so exhausted that she fell down the stairs."

Carolina wondered if it were indeed exhaustion or Virginia's penchant for liquor that caused such a fall. Realizing that she'd come across as rather harsh with her father, Carolina squeezed his arm gently. "You will make the right choice, Papa. Of this I am certain."

"I just feel that for everyone's sake, including your mother's, I can't allow things to continue as they are."

They fell silent and walked closer to where Victoria was completing her bouquet. "Victoria St. John," Carolina finally admonished, "you are not to pick the flowers, and well you know it."

Victoria looked up rather guiltily and smiled with a cherublike countenance. "But they are for you, Nanny." She held up the offering and waited for further rebuke.

Carolina rolled her eyes and took the flowers in hand. "Thank you, but do not pick any more. We wouldn't want to deny everyone else the pleasure of such beauty."

Victoria nodded and once again went bounding in search of adventure. Joseph looked after her for a time, then surprised Carolina with yet another announcement.

"I scarce remembered to share our other news with you."

"What news?"

Joseph seemed to take a mental inventory of his announcements. "Well, York and Lucy are quite happy to announce that Amy and little Andy are over the measles."

Carolina was relieved to hear this good news. Andrew Adams was barely two years old and, according to Lucy, kept her running from sunup to sundown. To learn that he and Amy were suffering a bout of measles was a frightening revelation. Carolina had nursed Victoria through just such an epidemic not even a year earlier.

"That is good news. What else? Have you heard from Maine?"

"Indeed I have. He has headed west to California with a group of other adventurers. He feels quite certain God has called him to minister to the Indians, and he fearlessly intends to meet the calling."

"I do wish he would have stopped long enough to say hello. I was quite devastated that he would journey to Oakbridge, but not to Baltimore."

"His time was not his own, my dear. He was scarcely with us for more than two days. I would have sent for you had it been longer."

"I know," Carolina replied wistfully. "I can hardly remember what he looks like."

"Well, memory would not serve you there. I sent a boy away to the seminary, and they returned to me a man. You would not recognize him. He has your mother's gentle expression and a softness of spirit that I'm sure did not come from me."

Carolina laughed. "Ah, but he has the wanderlust, and that must surely be a gift from you."

Joseph laughed at the age-old reminder of his youthful dream to explore the world. "You are certainly right in that matter. And now I have saved the most astonishing news for last—it is something I felt you should hear in person, and that's why I waited until my trip here. Georgia has eloped with Major Douglas Barclay. He is twenty-two years her senior and owns a horse-breeding farm just south of Washington."

"What are you saying, Papa?" Carolina stood, totally aghast at this news. "I can't believe it!" Then shaking her head as her mind struggled with the shock of her father's words, Carolina asked, "When did she meet him?"

Joseph shook his head. "When did she meet half the men she was to run off and marry? I tell you, I'm actually relieved. Her reputation was becoming a bit tattered at the edges. When she and the Major—that's what they call him—showed up at Oakbridge to offer this announcement, I toasted them and offered the man a belated dowry."

"Did he take it?" Carolina asked, suddenly amused with the story.

"He did indeed. My immediate thought was that at least he was no fool."

Joseph's eyes twinkled with merriment, and Carolina couldn't help but laugh. "So long as she is happy." Then calling Victoria, Carolina suggested they return home. "Come have supper with us, Papa."

"What of Mr. St. John?"

Carolina shrugged. "He is seldom around, and I don't expect him this evening."

But when they returned to the St. John house, Blake was not only there, but rather agitated that Carolina and Victoria had taken themselves out without explanation. He held back his questions at the sight of Carolina's father and even extended an invitation to dine, but Carolina could see the emotion in his eyes.

"I will see to Victoria and join you both later," Carolina said and headed the child toward the stairs.

"Nonsense!" Blake declared. "Mrs. Graves, you will see the child fed and bathed. I wish Miss Adams to remain with her father and in my company."

"Very well, sir," Mrs. Graves replied, not sounding the least bit happy.

"Come along," Blake said to Joseph. "I have some very fine cigars, sir, if you are of a mind to join me."

Joseph had never had a great love for them but, in order to put his host at ease, agreed to join him for a smoke. Carolina was grateful for his gesture and sat quietly as the men discussed the politics of the day. When the conversation finally turned to the Potomac and Great Falls Railroad, Carolina eagerly jumped in.

"Father, I've wanted to speak to you about the line for some time. Mr. Baldwin sends up scant reports on his work, but I see so many errors and circumstances which appear out of sorts that I can't help but question whether or not he's giving this his utmost attention."

"Well, he is very busy these days. He has sold his interests in the bank, but in turn has picked up business by brokering for a variety of railroad companies and other properties. Ours is not his only interest."

"Perhaps you should have someone else take over the books," St. John advised.

"I would hate to offend the man. He's been a good friend for most of my life. I'll speak to him about your concerns, Carolina, but perhaps it's nothing more than too little time spent in double-checking the figures."

Carolina said nothing more. To further discuss such a personal concern in front of Blake St. John seemed out of place. And she certainly couldn't accuse her father's best friend of the things she was beginning to believe him capable of. The surveys seemed entirely wrong compared to other surveys of the area, and for the past five years ground had not even been broken on the proposed line. Their charter was only good for another five years, and Carolina seriously wondered if she would ever see a single track laid before it was necessary to go again to the Virginia legislature for permission to continue the line.

"The Baltimore and Ohio is finally making noticeable progress," said St. John. "As I understand, they intend to be to Cumberland by November of this year."

"I've heard the same, Mr. St. John," Joseph replied. "It is especially good news to Carolina, no doubt. The B&O has far and away become her favorite railroad concern."

"Only because our own is not functional," she added. "The B&O is worthy of our trust, however. I've read their profit returns for last year, and things are definitely looking more promising."

"They've a long ways to go," St. John replied. "They struggle constantly to be issued the funds promised them."

"But their profits are up and the expenses are down," Carolina firmly interjected. "Three years ago their expenses were over three hundred thousand dollars. This year they predict to have that number reduced by one hundred thousand."

"But total receipts are down," St. John added. "I read those same reports with just as avid an interest. The 1839 statements show a gross receipt of four hundred seven thousand dollars for the main line. Last year they made little more than three hundred ninety thousand. You must see the entire picture, Miss Adams, in order to have a clear view of their situation. It is true that they show a greater net profit, but again there are many things to be factored in, and only then do you have the entire matter considered."

"I'm afraid Mr. St. John is right, my dear," Joseph said, still holding the smoking cigar.

"But they have the mail contracts now and the more powerful horizontal engines," Carolina argued. "The incline planes have long been bypassed, and the traffic on the main stem is ever increasing. Surely these things all combine to benefit the line."

"Of course they do," St. John replied. "But the line remains unfinished, and until they can reach the Ohio River, they will continue to operate as less than a profitable railroad. Then, too, they've made a grievous error by not bringing the railroad across the Potomac at Hancock, Maryland. If they had planned ahead and reasonably connected the railroad to the town, they would also have connected with the National Road and be bringing in far more freight than they are now."

"Why is it that they didn't plan for that in the first place?" Joseph suddenly asked. "It only seems logical that the railroad should make itself readily available to passengers and freight."

St. John shrugged his shoulders. "Why is it that any man fails to see what should be done before it is too late? Hindsight is always the better vision, no?"

Carolina studied St. John for a moment and wondered if there was more meaning to his words than merely talk of the railroad. She opened her mouth to question the situation further, but just then Mrs. Graves arrived to announce supper.

"I must say, Mr. Adams," St. John commented as they made their way to the dining room, "your little railroad intrigues me. Might you be looking for another investor?"

Carolina turned so quickly in her surprise at this statement that she stepped on her gown and would have stumbled headlong onto the floor but for Blake St. John's rapid action. Finding herself in the arms of her employer was most unnerving. She looked up into his dark eyes and found a hint of emotion she'd never seen before. If she hadn't known better, she would have almost thought it to be embarrassment.

As he steadied her, Blake gave her a questioning gaze. "Are you quite all right?"

"Yes, thank you. I was merely surprised by your interest in our railroad. Do you truly mean to invest in it?"

St. John pursed his lips ever so slightly and rubbed his smooth chin. "I might very well mean to do just that. Good investments are hard to ignore."

Thirty-Seven

Deceptions and Discoveries

I see little reason to continue investing in a railroad that for all purposes is nonexistent," a bearded man told Leland Baldwin. Standing in Leland's small study, a group of several investors in Joseph Adams' Potomac and Great Falls Railroad nodded in agreement.

"Gentlemen, I assure you all possible plans are being laid to meet the establishment of this line. You must understand that the depression has weakened the entire structure of the investment. However"—he raised his hand as if to fend off any further concerns—"the depression is passing rapidly away, and the financial strength of this country is returning to its former glory. I foresee little difficulty in substantiating physical evidence of your investment within the next six months."

"Six months?" the man questioned. "But that would put us near to Christmas. It's bad enough we've given over funds for these past five years, but to see little in the way of benefit—"

"Now, now," Leland interrupted, "you know full well the reputation of Joseph Adams, and of myself," he added proudly, hooking thumbs into his waistcoat pockets. "We are men of our word, and our actions prove nothing else. You will have your railroad and the connection you so desire from Falls Church to the city. But you must be patient. Come see me next week, and we can better discuss the matter then."

Reluctantly the men assembled themselves together and moved en masse to the front door of the Baldwin home.

Leland dismissed them cordially and paused to wipe perspiration from his forehead as he closed the door. The heat of the day was most unbearable, but it was made even more so by the interrogation of his investors. Making his way back to the study, he'd scarcely removed his coat and taken a seat behind his desk before the butler appeared to announce the arrival of Joseph Adams.

"Show him in, by all means," Leland replied and stood to once again retrieve his coat.

Joseph Adams entered the study appearing thinner and older than Leland had last remembered him. "Good to see you, Adams," Leland said, his arm midway in the sleeve of his coat.

"Good to be here," Joseph answered, then motioned to the coat. "By my leave, don't bother with that. I'll only be here for a few moments."

Leland happily tossed the coat aside and offered Joseph a seat. "Would you care for something cool to drink?"

"No, thank you." Joseph took a seat and leaned back wearily. "As I said, I won't be here long. I only arrived by train this afternoon and am making my way home after a three-week absence."

"Do tell. And what kept you away from home?"

"I went to Boston, Leland," Joseph replied. All pretense at formality faded as he leaned forward. "I want to confide in you, and I need your utmost confidence."

"But of course, Joseph. What is it?" Leland was greatly intrigued and took his seat quickly.

"I'm afraid the time has come for me to see Mrs. Adams cared for in a more appropriate manner. She has been quite unwell since the deaths of Penny and Maryland." Leland nodded as if fully understanding. "I have just returned from Boston, where I visited a very fine hospital in the south area of the city. The conditions are most acceptable, and the doctors and nurses very attentive. They believe it possible to help Mrs. Adams, although they cannot tell quite so well until they meet with her and evaluate her."

"I am sorry, Joseph. I had no idea things were as bad as all this. That you should feel compelled to remove . . . well, that is to say . . . that circumstances should prevent you from allowing . . ." He fell silent, unable to think of an appropriate way to express the situation.

Joseph seemed fully accepting of his frustration. "My good friend, it is with humble heart and deepest appreciation that I come to you. My son-in-law and daughter have no doubt amply cared for Oakbridge, but I am afraid I must impose upon your good will for a time longer and ask that you continue to assume the responsibility for our railroad endeavors."

Leland let out his breath in a noticeable sigh. "But of course, Joseph. You needn't ask."

"I will tell you this much. Carolina is happy to continue her consideration of the bookwork. She has taken a most thorough interest in the situation and has a great many questions to pose. I suggested she post her concerns to you in a letter."

"Of course. I'd be happy to explain any of these matters to her. She is, after all, a young woman, and no doubt the workings of legislative edicts and bills of lading can be confusing."

Joseph's tired smile did nothing to reassure Leland. He had known that Carolina Adams would be given the P&GF accounts to consider, but he'd never believed questions would result. Perhaps he had been careless.

"But surely," Leland said, hoping desperately to change the subject, "you haven't come here on the sole purpose of this matter."

"No, actually I haven't. I will be taking Mrs. Adams to Boston within a fortnight, and I was rather hoping you might allow me to be so bold as to impose our company upon you for a night."

Leland breathed a second sigh of relief. "But of course, Joseph. My home is always open to you."

"I'm afraid there is more to explain." Joseph's sad eyes intently searched Leland's face. "You see, my wife is not herself. She is given to spells of extreme distress. I cannot be more clear than to say"—he paused, obviously uncomfortable with the subject—"she wails and laments the passing of her children. She—"

Leland held up his hand. "Joseph, say no more. Mrs. Baldwin has long admonished me to escort her to her sister's home in Richmond. She, too, has been a bit under the weather and feels a respite there would see her completely healed. If you would give me the time of your travels, I will arrange to take her on to Richmond, and you may have our home to yourselves."

"I can't ask that much of you," Joseph protested.

"Nonsense. You have asked for nothing more than shelter and privacy. I will afford you both."

"I can't thank you enough."

A knock sounded on the door, and once again the butler interrupted Leland's day. "Sir, the young master has returned."

"James? Here?"

Leland and Joseph both got to their feet as James Baldwin strode into the room.

"Father," he said, bowing formally. Then, spying Joseph, James paled noticeably and bowed again. "Mr. Adams."

———

James had not intended to meet up with Joseph Adams. It had been five years since he'd had cause to face this man, and now, even with so many years between meetings, he was unnerved. This man must surely hold him malice and ill will, and with good reason. James felt the un-

240

comfortable warmth of the day add to the discomfort of his sudden embarrassment. Without thought he unbuttoned his coat.

"James, I must say this is a surprise."

"I know, Father, and I'm sorry that I didn't write ahead to let you know of my arrival."

They all sat once again, but James couldn't shake the uneasiness he felt. All at once, the feelings he'd fought so hard to bury resurfaced without warning. Seeing Joseph was akin to seeing Carolina, and the very thought warmed his blood in a way that offered him nothing but distress.

"I . . . ah . . ." he stammered. "I came in . . . that is to say . . . I arrived on the train."

"Why, how very strange. Mr. Adams, too, was on the afternoon train."

"You were in Baltimore, sir?"

Joseph nodded. "Yes, actually returning from Boston and business. But I paused there long enough to visit with Carolina."

He had spoken her name. That unthinkable, wonderful name. Visions of the woman who'd haunted him through the years came to mind and flooded his aching heart. Why could he not be done with her?

"Ah, I understand she was to have married your commission merchant. I pray she is well."

Joseph looked rather strangely at James before shaking his head. "No, she did not marry Mr. Cabot, although there was a time many years ago when he did pay her court. Mr. Cabot has, in fact, been married these past years to Virginia. I thought you might have heard."

James felt a tightness constrict his chest. His breath seemed stifled, and a gnawing twinge grew in the pit of his stomach. "No, I'd not heard. I . . . well . . . you mentioned visiting with Carolina in Baltimore, and I presumed—"

"No, no. Carolina is living in Baltimore as nanny to the daughter of Blake St. John."

"Nanny?"

Joseph laughed and James couldn't help but see him relax a bit. "You, more than anyone, should know the unconventionality of my Carolina. Four years ago she ventured to answer this man's need for a nanny, and she has remained there ever since. I believe she's completely given her heart."

James' initial relief was replaced with painful resolve. "To Mr. St. John?"

Joseph again laughed. "No, that man seems quite incapable of anyone's interest. No, Carolina has completely given her heart to young Victoria St. John. And I must say, there is no child more deserving. She is a sweet, amiable little one, and I have greatly enjoyed her visits."

"I can't say that I understand that girl of yours," Leland interjected. "To have passed aside the comforts of home, not to mention her chance at marriage, for the position of governess seems most unreasonable."

Joseph sobered. "I dare say she's not passed up the opportunity of those things. Her home is always among us if she desires to return, and as for marriage, well, that girl of mine, as you put it, has blossomed into a handsome woman. I doubt she'll have any trouble causing men of courting interest to forget her twenty-two years."

James smiled and the action was not lost on his father or Joseph. "See there," Joseph said, eyeing him carefully. "I believe Mr. Baldwin would agree with me."

James felt a sudden revelation that perhaps Joseph had always known his feelings for Carolina. Meeting the man's gaze, James knew without a doubt that his suspicions were true. He found a million unspeakable questions come to mind, then to his surprise, Joseph smiled broadly and gave him a little nod as if to approve of James' unspoken interest.

Could it be? James wondered. Could it be possible that after so faithlessly jilting one daughter, the man would actually approve of him seeking court with another of his children? James began to tremble. Carolina was unmarried and living in Baltimore. Baltimore, of all places! Why, James called Baltimore home more than any other city. How could it be that she'd remained so close in proximity to him and yet so distant?

He scarcely heard the words of conversation that passed between his father and Joseph Adams, and it was only moments before Mr. Adams was bidding them both good-bye and heading for the door.

"I understand from your father that you have remained in the employment of the B&O these past five years."

James startled, suddenly realizing that the words were directed to him. "Yes. I've worked west on the main stem and find myself at various points along the line."

"Well, the next time you are in Baltimore, perhaps you will renew your acquaintance with Carolina. I can't help but believe she would find that most enjoyable."

James met Joseph's eyes and saw nothing but forgiveness and acceptance in his gaze. "I would find that very enjoyable myself, sir."

"Good," Joseph replied as if he'd settled a long overdue account.

James watched him leave, still stunned at the sudden change in his world. Long ago, he'd given up hope that Carolina could ever mean anything more to him than a memory from the past. Now her own father was initiating the renewal of their relationship. Could it truly be possible that she would receive him after all these years?

Thirty-Eight

Unlocking the Past

A week after her father returned to Oakbridge, Carolina experienced a new development in her relationship with Mrs. Graves. During her entire course of living in the St. John house, the housekeeper had refused any friendly gesture or act of kindness toward Carolina. But then a twisted ankle resulted in a friendship that Carolina could not have foretold.

Having missed a step off the back porch, Mrs. Graves was relegated to bed for two weeks with a painfully swollen ankle. Carolina took the opportunity to pamper the older woman and to once again try to penetrate the harsh facade of rigid propriety.

One humid June evening, after seeing Victoria to bed and closing up the silent house for the night, Carolina journeyed to Mrs. Graves' room, bringing with her tea and several of Cook's sugar cookies.

"I thought perhaps you would like a bedtime snack," Carolina said, coming into the room without the slightest reservation. "Although in this heat, tea might not seem to be the most acceptable drink."

Mrs. Graves, propped in bed with her Bible, warily noted the nanny and seemed to give up a sigh of resolve. "You've been most kind, Miss Adams."

"Not at all," Carolina replied, setting the tray on the nightstand. "I'm doing my Christian duty and caring for a friend, just as you might have done for me."

"I've not been much of a friend to you. Why are you so kind to me?"

Carolina smiled and poured a steaming cup of tea. "I was a stranger to you and this house. You had seen the comings and goings of many workers who could not abide the temperament of Mr. St. John. Why should I have presented any more stability and comfort to you than

243

had the others? However, I would have thought that after a year or so I would have proved my merit."

"You did." The older woman looked away, and Carolina thought her eyes revealed shame. "I can't abide the way I've treated you, Miss Adams."

"Please call me Carolina. We are to be friends, are we not?"

Mrs. Graves smiled. "I would like that." She took the tea and the offered cookie and motioned to Carolina to join her. "Please stay. I have a feeling we should talk."

"I would say it is long overdue."

That conversation was only the first of many, and Carolina finally came to know acceptance in the eyes of the temperamental housekeeper. One afternoon, with Mrs. Graves carefully arranged for a restful period in the stylish backyard gardens, Carolina joined her to watch over Victoria at play.

"She's growing up so fast. I'm afraid I'll simply have to let her dress hems down again."

"You've done beautifully by the child," Mrs. Graves said, surprising Carolina with the praise. "Her own mother would have scarcely done a better job."

Carolina paused, teacup midway to her lips. "Can't you tell me about her?"

Mrs. Graves shook her head. "'Tis been a long time since I've even allowed myself to remember her." She looked away to where Victoria sat playing with the kittens. "She looks nothing like her mother. She favors her father's dark, brooding looks and even his temperament. Suzanna, that is, Mrs. St. John, was a happy, boisterous young woman. She brought life into this house, and when she died, the life again left it."

"How did she die?" Carolina dared ask the question and held her breath.

Mrs. Graves looked at her as if trying to decide if it was the right thing to tell the long unspoken story. "Physically, she drowned, but she was dead long before that dreadful day. You see, it was late in May of thirty-six when Suzanna and her little son, Charles, went to the park for an outing. Mr. St. John was a happy man then. He was totally devoted to his wife and son. Theirs, Carolina, was a love match. I've never seen a man so lost in his love of a woman as was Mr. St. John for my Suzanna."

"Your Suzanna?"

"I knew her from the time she was a small child. I served her mother as a chambermaid. I was given over to Suzanna when she married, but we always shared a deep abiding love. I was more mother to the child than her own mother was. In many ways, just like you are to young Victoria." Mrs. Graves sipped her tea and considered the matter for a moment. "I suppose, to my shame, that is why I found it so hard to accept you." She gave Carolina an apologetic smile at this admission.

"So, you see," the housekeeper continued, "I knew great happiness in this house, just as I've known great sorrow. Suzanna and their son Charles were all that Mr. St. John could desire in a wife and child."

"What happened?"

"Suzanna was preoccupied with friends that day. She was lost in conversation and plans for a future trip abroad when the young master fell into the harbor and drowned."

"How terrible!" Carolina felt sickened as she remembered times Victoria had wandered too close to the water at Harbor Park.

"Yes, indeed it was. Mr. St. John changed after that day," Mrs. Graves said, her eyes imploring Carolina to understand. "He was not always so harsh and hardened, but that day he lost his heart and his soul."

"It must have been Charles' grave over which I found Mr. St. John mourning," Carolina remembered.

"What's that?" Mrs. Graves clearly did not follow Carolina's words.

"I first met Mr. St. John, or should I say, I first saw him when I accompanied a friend to a concert at the church where Charles and his mother are buried. I intruded, unintentionally, upon his grieving. I felt horrible for the pain I seemed to have caused him that night."

"He was inconsolable, and even the fact that Suzanna found herself already with child again did nothing to ease his misery. He began to drink and stay away long hours from home, and poor Suzanna . . ." The old woman took a long drink of her tea as if to bolster her nerves. "She never recovered from the loss of his love. She bore Victoria in February the following year, feeling very badly that she could not replace the son she blamed herself for taking from his father. Mr. St. John came home quite drunk, and even though Suzanna was scarcely five days in her birthing bed, he raged at her with all manner of vile accusation."

"How sad," Carolina whispered, all the while watching the childish antics of Victoria, who could have no possible understanding of why her parents had rejected her.

"Mr. St. John told her that she'd killed his boy and that he could never forgive her for that, and furthermore"—Mrs. Graves paused to wipe tears from her eyes—"he wanted nothing to do with Victoria. I tried to comfort Suzanna as best I could, but she was devastated. She bid me take Victoria and give her a bath, and while I did that, Suzanna slipped from the house and . . ." The words trailed off in quivering tones of deep sorrow. "She threw herself into the harbor. She drowned herself in the same place where she'd let her son slip away."

Carolina was stunned. In all her years at the St. John house, she had never even suspected such a horrendous story lay buried in its history.

"What did he do?" was all she could think to ask.

"Once he sobered up and remembered what he'd done, he went to apologize. Of course, she was gone, and I had been quite beside myself all night with a crying baby and a worried heart. He went out in search of her, but it wasn't long before he returned. Her body had been found. Then the battle of her burial began."

"Why should there have been a battle?"

"Because it was commonly felt that she committed suicide, even though the master tried to convince folks otherwise. He didn't want her memory tainted, and she could not be buried on sacred church ground having taken her own life. St. John was livid. He denounced the church and the actions of pious, self-righteous people who would believe such a hideous thing of his young wife—all the while knowing, of course, that they were right about her suicide. Finally the clergy relented and allowed him to bury Suzanna beside her son, but Mr. St. John never forgave the church and its people for shunning him and his wife in their most grievous hour of need."

"I'm not sure I blame him. Surely the people could have understood her heartbreak. And, too, perhaps it had been an accident after all. Perhaps she had only longed to go to that place where last she had seen Charles alive. Maybe once there, she slipped."

Mrs. Graves gave Carolina a look of appreciable kindness. "You are a gentle soul, Miss Carolina. Victoria is fortunate to have you with her."

"Mr. St. John has never accepted her, has he?"

"Never, and I don't suppose he will. He locked away all memory of her birth and that dreadful night when he closed off her mother's room. That's the one at the end of the hall that always remains locked."

"Yes, I had presumed that."

"He lets no one in there, save himself, and he has yet to admit to his moments spent there. He slips in during the night when he thinks we are all asleep. But I have heard him crying there and longed to comfort him. He simply will never forgive God."

"More likely," Carolina said, sighing heavily, "he will never forgive himself, either."

Thirty-Nine

Sacrifices

*M*ight I have a word with you, Miss Adams?" Blake St. John inquired, coming into the family sitting room.

Carolina gazed up from the sewing she held and smiled. "Of course." St. John had surprised them all by appearing in time for the Fourth of July celebrations, but instead of joining them on picnics and outings to see parades, he'd chosen instead to keep to himself. This was the first time he'd even bothered to acknowledge his presence to Carolina beyond one or two brief encounters in passing.

Blake sat opposite Carolina and crossed his legs as though intending to stay awhile. Carolina, seeing the look of determination in his expression, put aside her sewing and folded her hands in her lap.

"I have come to some conclusions," Blake began. "It hasn't been easy, considering the matters before me, but I have chosen a path that I feel content with and hope you will endeavor to understand and to accept my choices."

"I'm certain my acceptance has never been overly important to you," she replied coolly.

"That is not entirely true." Blake paused as though struggling heavily with what he was about to say. "You see, I've come to greatly respect you, Miss Adams. You have offered my daughter the proper upbringing to which she was entitled. You, being a lady of refinement and knowing the proprieties of society, have instilled in Victoria the necessary elements of breeding."

Carolina frowned. Knowing that she should hold her tongue, she barely bit back a snide reply. How would he know what she had brought to the life of his daughter? He scarcely acknowledged the child's existence.

"I know what you are thinking," he said, fixing a dark, impassioned gaze upon her. "You needn't play games with me, and I give you leave to speak freely with me because the matter I intend to speak to you about is of utmost importance to both of us."

"I'm sure I don't understand." Carolina tried to imagine what he would say next. Blake St. John never failed to amaze her, and this moment was no exception.

"I desire to go west. I have recently acquired the book *Astoria*. Are you familiar with it?"

"Washington Irving," she declared with a nod. "Yes, I've read it. He speaks of westward adventure and the formation of trading posts and of Astoria, in the Oregon Territories."

"Yes," St. John agreed. "I have found this to my liking and believe I will explore the possibilities for myself."

Carolina felt her heart give a leap. "What of Victoria?"

"Well, that does present a problem, and it is precisely why I would speak to you now."

"I don't understand. Surely you don't propose to drag us along with you to the West? A child would never survive the—"

"Never!" Blake interrupted. "Even I would never propose such a thing. You must try to understand, Miss Adams. I know you cannot forgive me for my actions—I neither expect or deserve that. But surely you can see how difficult my prolonged presence in this house is . . . for me and for . . . everyone. Thus, I cannot stay here another day. Nor can I bear yet another moment of her presence."

Anger raged inside Carolina. How dare he speak of his child in such a manner! She opened her mouth to reply, but he held up his hand to quiet her.

"Please." His voice was desperate. "Please hear me out."

"Very well." She tried to settle her mind and still the angry retorts that hung on her lips.

"I know I have unfairly dealt with you regarding the matter of Victoria, but suffice it to say, her mother's death and passing is relived daily when I lay eyes upon that child. You cannot be so cruel as to hold against me that which I can scarcely admit to myself." He got up and paced the floor behind the chair, pausing only long enough to stare out the front window into the darkened city street outside.

"I want to go west, but I do not desire to take Victoria with me. I implore you to understand that it is actually my wish to never lay eyes on the child again." He turned abruptly, startling Carolina with the intensity of his stare. "That is where you come in."

"I'm sure I don't understand."

"I desire you to remain here. To live on as Victoria's sole caregiver.

I will, of course, set up a bank account from which you will never want. You may draw upon it freely and furnish the place as you desire. You will be given a free hand with all of my accounts and may proceed with Victoria's upbringing as you see fit, whether you desire to send her away to finishing school or to see her married early to some suitable young man. You may then close the house and take the proceeds from the bank, leaving Victoria whatever you choose."

Carolina felt her eyes widen and her mouth grow slack. The stunning declaration was more than she could fathom. "Do you actually mean to give your child to me?"

"You are the only mother she has ever known," he reasoned. "She has great affection for you, and I know by your own admission that you in turn care for her as if she were your own."

"That much is true, but it hardly offers reasoning to your proposal. How could you consider leaving her for the unknown West? How could you go through life never knowing what became of her?"

"Understand me, Miss Adams." He gripped the back of a nearby chair and continued pleading. "I cannot give the child what she has need of. I cannot live with her any longer, and it is my intention to leave Baltimore for all time."

"Would you see her orphaned?"

"Would you?" Blake asked her bluntly. "For you are truly mother to the child. If you will not agree to the terms of my proposal, then Victoria will have no one."

"That is hardly fair," Carolina declared, getting to her feet.

"Perhaps not, but it is the way I see it, and those are my terms. I leave it up to you, Miss Adams, but with or without your approval, it is my plan to make for the West before the summer is out."

———

Carolina felt a deep burden upon her in the days that followed Blake's declaration. How could she desert the child she'd come to think of as her own? On the other hand, how could she remain in the St. John house with Blake gone, probably forever? There would never be a moment's peace, and Carolina would literally find her life frozen in time. Gone would be any chance to seek expanding her education or of marrying and having a family of her own. And, too, no doubt her respectability would suffer if she should decide to stay on. People might see her as St. John's "kept woman." It was already a questionable arrangement, but were legal papers to be drawn up with a bank account at her disposal, tongues would wag and with good reason. No, her reputation was already hanging by a thread. To pursue an even more open state of dependency upon the elusive Mr. St. John would leave her in questionable public standing. Surely Blake could see that such a choice would condemn her to a life of solitude.

Yet was it really solitude? After all, she would have Victoria and there would be no possibility of dismissal. But what if Blake found his heart suddenly mended by the change in location and remarried? Carolina's heart felt torn at the very thought of Blake appearing one day to present a new wife and mother for Victoria. It would be wonderful for him, she thought, but how very hard it would be to let go of Victoria and give her over to another woman.

She'd had no opportunity to speak to Blake about her fears, nor was she certain she would feel comfortable enough to address her thoughts with him. Nevertheless, when the evening finally did arrive and Blake forced the issue of her answer, Carolina voiced her concerns, even the most delicate ones.

"What is to stop you from disappearing for a number of years only to reappear and lay claim once again to your home and daughter? And you would be well within your rights to do so," Carolina reasoned. "But where would that leave me? You are asking me to give up my life and my future plans without any compensation or assurance that I will not be the one left out in the cold when all is said and done."

Blake started to speak, but Carolina would not let him steer her away from her determination to bare her soul. "No! Hear me out. For if I do not say what is on my heart, I will forever be condemned to live with the knowledge that I left this matter undone." He sat back in his chair and waited. "You must understand, Mr. St. John, Victoria has become very important to me. Of course you know that I love her; of that there can be no question. She is a dear little girl and I adore her. But what is to become of our relationship should you one day reappear with a new Mrs. St. John? The child I have come to love and to whom I have devoted my entire life would suddenly be taken from me."

Blake scowled and his countenance darkened in a foreboding manner. "There will never be another Mrs. St. John. My heart and soul went into the grave with my wife and child. How could you be so cruel as to suggest the possibility of another Mrs. St. John?"

"Be realistic, Mr. St. John," Carolina said, feeling quite bold. "You are a young man of handsome appearance and quality breeding. You are wealthy, and that in and of itself is enough to attract many a woman. Perhaps removing yourself from the place of your sorrow will allow your heart to mend and seek another. After all, it's not been that long since the death of your wife."

Blake looked at her as if trying to weigh the validity of her statement. "My looks and breeding, my money and position, are immaterial. I have no desire to ever take another wife. I will never love another soul on this earth and that includes my daughter."

"You are heartless!" she declared, hands on hips.

"Yes, and I've tried for lo these many years to tell you just that. I am heartless and without feeling. My emotions and feelings are dead, just as my wife and son are dead. They will not be reborn from the grave, and neither will my ability to feel and care for another."

He stood without warning and crossed the room to where Carolina stood. Leaning very close to her face, he spoke slowly, with deliberate caution. "It is solely in your hands, Miss Adams. Either you will remain with Victoria, or you will dismiss yourself from her presence. You accuse me of being unable to see Victoria's needs, but I see them quite clearly. You are the one she needs, not me. I have made the ultimate sacrifice by seeing that to remove myself from her life and securing your position with her is in keeping with her very best interests. Perhaps now, if you love her as you swear, you should be prepared to sacrifice as well."

He left her to stare after him and contemplate his words. Carolina felt as though she might burst into tears any moment. The man was impossible! Partly for his lack of feeling and partly for his pinpointing the truth of the situation in such a way that Carolina was held totally responsible for the outcome.

But instead of crying, Carolina fell to her knees in the middle of the family sitting room and prayed. First, she prayed for guidance and direction. Second, she prayed for Victoria and the future that the child would have. And finally, she prayed for Blake St. John that his eyes might be opened to the truth of God's love and his heart healed from the past injustices and pains.

Forty

Paying the Piper

*L*eland Baldwin basked in the glory of the moment. Philadelphia had received him quite heartily, along with his brother Samuel Baldwin. And a proposal for the development of a western Pennsylvania railroad had been met with great enthusiasm. He offered the moon, the stars, and the sun, and in turn his investors gave over a great fortune. Everyone was eager to put the depression behind them and find new means in which to make money. And most men were enthusiastic to connect with the West and promote the solidarity of a nation.

Counting his pledges and actual cash investments, Leland was dumfounded to realize an initial outlay of over one hundred thousand dollars.

"This will see me set with the Potomac and Great Falls investors," he told Samuel.

His brother, every bit as rotund as Leland, shifted nervously in the carriage and motioned to the cashbox Leland refused to secure. "Lock it all up now and let us put it where thieves won't be inclined to ease our burden."

"I hardly worry about thieves," Leland answered, locking the box. "I have a great deal more to concern myself with. If I don't show some kind of physical evidence that the P&GF is well on its way to development, I may have a riot among its investors. Those men refuse to be put off much longer, and while I was able to show a hefty loss in the initial onset of the depression, the years that have followed have been trials in creative bookkeeping."

"Indeed, but how will you justify to the Pennsylvania investors that their line lies idle?"

"Simple enough. There is the time element involved with securing the charters and land surveys. These things take time, and with that

252

time, I can well be on my way to making the P&GF a profitable line. Don't you see, Samuel? We have but to rob one piper to pay the other. All the time we keep the music playing by simply adjusting the purse strings."

"Sooner or later it must all come to a conclusion."

"Yes, but by that time I hope to see a tidy profit, and in turn I can repay some of what I am, shall we say, borrowing against." Leland smiled at his own inventive genius. "Either way, I do not have to bow and scrape to make ends meet, and I am still held in esteem as a beneficial businessman. Men will flock to me as they learn of the profitability of the P&GF, and just imagine how pleased Joseph Adams will be."

"From the sounds of it, you'd better be more inclined to please Carolina Adams. Is it true that her father actually lets the little chit make decisions about the business dealings of the railroad?"

"Absolutely. He's allowed her an education that has made her wiser than I would ever have imagined a woman could be. She posted a letter to me pointing out the inaccuracies in my accounting, suggesting that I might want to forward her the receipts and investment ledgers in order that she herself could scour them for mistakes."

"Such nerve!" Samuel snorted and popped open a snuffbox. He procured a pinch for himself, then offered it to Leland.

"No, no. I've no desire for it just yet. I have a great deal of thinking to do, and I do that best unhindered by pleasure."

"As you wish, brother." Samuel replaced the box in his pocket and waved his handkerchief back and forth as if to ease himself of the heat. "These humid days are far from a favorite of mine. I do hope you haven't planned any further excursion. I have a desire for a bath and change of clothes before we dine."

The carriage pulled up in front of the hotel, and Leland nodded his agreement. "A bath does sound like just the thing to cap off this day."

He handed the cashbox and his walking stick to his brother, then allowed two footmen to assist him from the carriage. Samuel followed behind and handed both back without ceremony. Passing into the lobby, Leland was surprised to find not one, but three messages awaiting him. All were from Washington, and all bore ill tidings.

Glancing through the brief messages, he turned despairing eyes upon Samuel. "I must make for home. Edith is quite ill."

"At this hour?" Samuel asked, looking around to note the time on the grandfather clock that graced the entryway.

"I'm afraid I've little choice. She fell unconscious several days ago, and by the looks of this last message posted July seventh, she has not awakened. I fear she may well succumb to her illness this time."

"Has she suffered these episodes before?"

"Indeed. The doctor says she has a weak heart. He bleeds her constantly to take the pressure off, but it hasn't seemed to help much. Now the doctor has informed me that after her last bleeding she fell into a deep sleep and has not yet recovered. He fears her general state of health may be such as to make recovery impossible."

"I am sorry, Leland. Do you wish for me to accompany you?"

Leland could tell very well from the look on his brother's face that he had no desire to follow him through the night to Washington.

"No, remain here and see to any straggling investors. I will arrange to take the train. Have my things sent to me."

Leland made his way from the hotel and hailed a hack. He was reluctant to leave Philadelphia, while at the same time anxious to be back where he could not only look in upon Edith, but lay out a plan of action regarding the P&GF. Finally, he had the capital with which to create a sense of activity and accomplishment, and the feeling left him exhilarated in spite of Edith's illness.

Edith. He thought of her while passing through the evening twilight on his way to the station. He would miss her when she was gone, but in some ways he would also find great relief. His worst fear was that she might find out how he had destroyed her family fortune and swindled their friends. He didn't care that some folks found him ruthless and insensitive, nor did he concern himself that others felt he could be rather underhanded in some of his business dealings. Rumors certainly couldn't hurt him in that aspect, especially not when he would eventually show the world his worth by producing a fine example of a railroad in the form of Joseph Adams' Potomac and Great Falls line. No, what kept him struggling to meet the constant demands and deadlines that besieged him was his desire to keep Edith safely ignorant of the circumstance in which he worked.

She had never learned of their peril during his banking years. And if she had noticed small family heirlooms missing, she had never once raised a concern about such matters. Edith was simpleminded enough that she suited his purposes perfectly. She was highly regarded in Washington, and because her family had been well received, she had secured for them a respectable position within an elite social circle of wealthy peers.

He smiled when he thought of her. He did love her, and she had given him a son to carry on the family name. God only knew what the boy was up to these days. He certainly wasn't meeting any criteria Leland had set out for him, nor did he care to inform his father of his whereabouts. From time to time he saw fit to notify his mother of his well-being and his work upon the Baltimore and Ohio, and often his letters were posted from Harper's Ferry or Baltimore. But beyond his brief visits to check in on Edith, James was seldom in residence. Of course, Leland knew he had only himself to blame. He'd made it clear that James was no longer welcome in their home, yet little by little he had relented his stand for Edith's sake.

But James didn't seem to mind being sent from the house, and that was perhaps even more disturbing to Leland. James appeared content to stay away for long periods of time and to offer up little explanation for his absences.

Leland tried not to allow the matter to eat at him, but it was highly difficult to try to explain James' actions to his circle of business friends. A son was a reflection of the father, and to admit to James' unorthodox relationship was to admit to his own failure. It was better by far to make up what he could not confirm. To those around him, he was nothing but the proudest of fathers to a son who held a futuristic view of the world and the machines that would drive it forward through the century.

But to James, who knew full well his father's disappointment, Leland would remain fixedly disapproving and openly hostile. He tolerated his son for Edith's sake, but beyond that he had little use for James, and from what Leland could gather, the feeling was mutual.

"Let him make his own bed," Leland murmured to himself. "His failures will catch up with him soon enough, and then he will come crawling back to me for instruction." But even as he said it, Leland doubted his own words. James, he knew, would probably lie dead in a ditch before admitting that he needed his father's help in any matter.

Forty-One

Proposals and Promises

Carolina knew no peace as she awaited the arrival of Blake St. John. He had sent word to her in the nursery that they should meet at seven o'clock in his study, and thus far, nearly twenty minutes after the hour, Carolina was still awaiting his appearance.

She fretted over what he would tell her. Worse still, she worried that he would demand her agreement to remain with Victoria or, upon her refusal, order her to pack her things and be gone. She had prayed for guidance and sought verse after verse from the Scriptures, but an answer eluded her in such a way that she had no feeling of certainty in either choice.

Carolina sighed and looked around the sparsely furnished room. Blake did his business in this room, yet there was very little of anything personal about the man to declare his ownership. On the walls hung portraits of long dead ancestors, and on the shelf were books related to business and law. Carolina saw nothing that offered even the slightest glimpse into the heart and soul of Blake St. John. But then, hadn't he told her that his heart and soul were buried in the graves of his wife and son?

"Sorry to have kept you waiting," Blake announced without warning. The door slammed shut with such a report that Carolina jumped noticeably in her seat. "Again, I'm sorry," Blake offered.

He was dressed impeccably in his favored choice of dark navy frock coat and silk-print vest. His sleek, snugly fitted riding pants betrayed his whereabouts for the time he'd kept Carolina waiting.

"That is quite all right. Victoria is busy with Mrs. Graves."

Blake nodded, then as if seeing her for the first time, sat down behind his desk and studied her without a word. Carolina grew quite nervous under his scrutiny, but she tried to refrain from fidgeting. Instead, she grasped the lightweight muslin of her dress and fought to steady her nerves. Why didn't he speak? Why didn't he demand his answer and let her be done with this nightmarish ordeal?

But she had no answer. She hadn't decided what she would say if he insisted she choose one way or the other. God knew she'd tried to realize what was best, but every time she looked into Victoria's trusting face, she couldn't imagine saying good-bye. Unwadding the material of her skirt and smoothing away the wrinkles, she dared to look up. Meeting his dark eyes, she was surprised at the emotion she read in his expression.

"I have something to say to you, and while we have not been able to reach an amicable decision thus far, it is my hope that perhaps this proposal will meet with your agreement."

"I see," Carolina said, feeling relieved that he had decided to come up with yet another way to resolve the situation.

"I ask only that you hear me out before making up your mind or deciding against it. Will you give me your word on it? Will you hear me through?"

Carolina narrowed her eyes and tried to imagine what St. John would say next. To demand such a promise from her no doubt signaled some manner of unacceptability in what he would suggest. Hesitantly, she nodded. "All right. I'll hear you out."

"Very good." He leaned forward and folded his hands together. "I have given thought to everything you said regarding my suggestion and proposal. It is true that I had given little regard to your future; however, that is no longer the case. I realize that to take on the responsibility of Victoria will most likely relegate you to a position of less-desirable marriage material, although a gentleman would have but to look at you in order to find merit in taking you as a mate."

Carolina felt her cheeks grow hot, and she quickly lowered her face to avoid Blake's notice.

"Furthermore," he continued without hesitation, "I realize that to take my money and perform the duties that would suggest matrimonial obligation would lessen your reputation in the eyes of the public. Do not believe that I am unfamiliar with the gossip of this town. Those good folk who would call themselves Christian are most unforgiving and judgmental. I have little doubt that they would see you as less than the soiled doves who frequent the harbor walk should you set yourself up under my roof in such a personal way. Therefore, I am prepared to make a most unusual proposal."

Carolina looked up and found him quite intent on her reaction.

"I am not of the mind to ever marry again," he went on. "As I told you, I will never love another. However, I note that you, too, are without any particular ties to one gentleman or another. Is my assumption true?"

"Yes," Carolina admitted, wondering where he was going with this line of conversation. A nagging fear began to build within her, and the suggestion of what she was thinking was too unbelievable to imagine.

"Then given these facts, I am suggesting that we marry for the sake of Victoria."

He waited, as if expecting some violent reaction, but remarkably Carolina felt a strange peace. Not so much with the idea of marrying a man she could never love and who would certainly never love her, but rather it was a relief that he concerned himself with her welfare above his own.

"It would, of course, be a marriage in name only. To be quite blunt and perhaps completely out of keeping with acceptable conversation, I must honestly say that it would never be my intention to share your bed, nor to father additional children."

Carolina felt her breath quicken and her heart race. Just the suggestion of such things was far more than she'd ever related in conversation with a man.

"I would give you my name, my fortune, and my daughter. You in turn would give me a stable home for the child and oversee my affairs, thus freeing me to leave the state. You would have my entire fortune at your disposal to do with as you saw fit. My lawyer would handle the actual paper workings of my affairs, however he would be left with instructions to yield to any decision you might make. You would be Mrs. Blake St. John, and you would be mother to Victoria."

Carolina was stunned beyond words. There was no need to worry about responding in haste to his suggestion; she could scarcely breathe, much less voice a protest.

"I would then be able to leave before the summer is out and make my way first to New York, where I have other matters to settle. It would be my plan to winter in Chicago and hook up with a team going west to Oregon in the spring. I would give you my solemn vow to never again return to Baltimore, nor seek to make any claim upon my rights as your husband."

"What if the West didn't agree with you?" Carolina asked, suddenly finding her voice.

"I promise you, I would not return to Baltimore. Perhaps I would venture to Europe or maybe farther yet, but I would not impose myself in your life, of that I assure you."

"But what of the vows made? What of the pledges to God to take care of each other, to cherish, and to love? You are suggesting that I promise before the God I esteem and worship that I will say one thing and do an entirely different thing?"

Blake eased back in his chair and ran a hand through his ebony hair. "It matters not to whom you make the pledge. I see no reason to set this thing up in church. I do not esteem God, as you put it, and I certainly have little regard for the church. A quiet ceremony here, in the parlor, would be far more to my liking. There is little need to make the rhetorical pledges when we both know that such matters do not concern our arrangements."

Carolina shook her head. "I do not believe I could marry under those circumstances. I just don't know how I could promise my life to a man I had no intention of being wife to."

Blake pounded his hands down on the desk and swore softly. "You stand on ceremony and religious nonsense when the life of a child is at stake?"

"Why condemn me, when you have little regard for that child?"

"At least I am honest about it."

"How dare you?" Carolina jumped to her feet and leaned menacingly across the desk. She felt a rage inside her that would not be ignored. "You know full well that I love Victoria. You dangle her before my nose like some kind of human carrot and expect me to yield to your idea of justice and resolution." Her voice was unnaturally calm as she met Blake's angry eyes. "Like a coward you run from life and love and throw your only living offspring into the path of oncoming destruction with nothing more than the simple explanation that at least you are honest. Well, good for you and your honesty, Blake St. John. A more selfish creature I have never had the misfortune to meet."

"Calm yourself, Miss Adams. You may rage at me all you like, and it will not change my offer. I will not be moved from my decision to leave."

"And if I say no to this preposterous proposal?" She was breathing hard and pulled herself back from the desk, as if hoping the distance would dispel her misery.

"Then I will take Victoria and deposit her in the care of the state orphanage."

Carolina gasped. "You wouldn't. Even you can't be that cruel."

Blake stood up. "You underestimate me if you think not." He walked to the door of the study and opened it slowly. "I believe I have said all that I care to on the matter. This is my final offer, and I will need your answer by the end of this week." He turned to go, then glanced back at her with a cold and calculated look. "I promise you one thing, Miss Adams, this is no idle threat. I mean to be about my business within two weeks' time."

Forty-Two

Reconciliation

$\mathcal{O}$n the final day given Carolina to make her choice, two letters arrived by post. One was from her father and the other was from Lucy. Taking herself to her room, Carolina opened her father's letter first.

1842, July 20

Dearest Daughter,

I have seen your mother safely to Boston, and she seemed content that the nurses were so congenial to her condition. One woman, Nurse Ribley, offered your mother a baby doll, and she took to it with great comfort. The doctor suggests no contact with her for at least three months, and while it will be difficult to heed his advice, I am convinced that nothing else can be done to benefit her.

Virginia believes the timing to be a godsend, as she announced that she will deliver a child at the end of September. This, of course, is very stunning news, given the fact that she shows no sign of this condition and yet it is already July. I assume she kept it to herself because of her three previous miscarriages. Hampton seems pleased with the prospect of an heir. He works from sunup to sundown, and often I don't see him for days as he masterminds one innovation or another. He is too heavy-handed with the slaves, and I've often admonished him to ease up, but he is quite capable of turning a profit for us. And given the way Oakbridge has flourished when many around us have failed, I must give the man credit.

Carolina scoffed at this idea. Hampton Cabot was a man who sought to benefit himself and no one else. She would never trust him.

She read on and learned that Georgia was quite happily settled and, for the first time in a long time, seemed to have found the perfect place for herself. There had been a brief missive from Maine. It seemed he had spent time in the ever-growing settlement of Dubuque, on the Mississippi River.

He told of the incredible beauty of the land and the impressive expanse of the Mississippi, while also relaying that lead mining was the main attraction to the progressive nature of this particular community.

"Of course," her father wrote, "the letter was dated in June, only weeks after he'd departed from Oakbridge. He must have made good time indeed in reaching the Mississippi in that short time."

The letter concluded by asking about her general state of health and the conditions in which she was enduring the summer. If only you knew, Papa, she thought and folded the letter to replace it in the envelope. She suddenly longed for a lengthy chat with him and wondered what he might say regarding the matter of Blake St. John's proposal.

Lucy's letter offered the highlights of their steamy summer in Philadelphia. Lucy, however, was glad to be back in her home city. Her father's health was failing, and it seemed that the doctors believed him to have some sort of liver disorder. Lucy related that his skin had turned positively yellow, and she feared he might not live through the summer. Since VanBuren left office, York and his family had settled in Philadelphia, and he had been working as a congressional aide to his father-in-law. With the man now ill, York had assumed many of his father-in-law's duties and found that people respected his ability to serve in government. Lucy fully expected him to run for her father's office during the next election, and with Henry Alexander's support, she had little doubt he would be elected to Congress. Carolina smiled at this thought, knowing very well that nothing would please her brother more. The letter continued with a surprising addition that, while Amy and Andy were doing well, Lucy believed it very possible that she was again with child. She promised to confirm this in future letters and signed it with great affection.

Tucking the letters into a desk drawer, Carolina took pen in hand and thought to write her father about her circumstance. She hesitated, however, and stared at the blank piece of paper for some time. Her family was doing well, and this brought her great joy, but it also made her realize how unnecessary her presence was in their lives.

Oakbridge ran smoothly without her, and while she might not approve of Hampton's manner, she certainly believed her father capable of keeping him under control. Virginia would bear a new heir and certainly had no need of Carolina. In fact, Carolina had little doubt but what Virginia would take special delight in pointing out that Carolina was an old maid with no hope for a future beyond playing auntie or nanny to someone else's children. That was something Carolina could never abide.

Maine was securely away doing the work of God, a noble cause to be sure and one that Carolina actually envied. At least he was out in the world living life as he saw fit. He knew what he was called to do, and he had not turned his back on that calling.

Mother and Georgia were both safely settled, and even her father sounded far happier than she'd known him to be in months. There was no need for her to hurry home to Oakbridge. No one waited there for her return. No one pleaded with her to come back.

She sighed and replaced the pen in the inkwell and walked to the window. Down below, the bustle of the Baltimore street only served as a reminder that the entire world continued on around her, with very little consideration as to where she fit in or what she might do.

Blake St. John was offering her a vast fortune. Not just money. Hardly that. He was offering her the freedom of a married woman whose husband had given her complete control of her life. He was offering her a child whom she loved as her own. There was no telling what the future might hold for her if she agreed to marry the man. She could certainly buy more railroad stock. That thought made her smile. She could venture to Europe and see the world that so often had held her spellbound in books. Yes, she could travel with Victoria, teaching her as they went along their way. She could speak French adequately enough that they might even take up residence in Paris for a time. The possibilities began to stagger her mind.

"Marriages were arranged all the time in the Bible," she murmured. "Is it any different only because I myself make the arrangements?"

She thought of Victoria and knew without any further consideration that she could never allow the child to go to an orphanage. So long as there was breath in her body, she would fight by whatever means it took to save the child from that fate. And, in her heart of hearts, she knew that if her only means to save Victoria was marriage to Blake St. John, she would marry him.

Stunned, she stepped back from the window and nodded. "Yes," she whispered. It was that simple. Blake would have his freedom, and he had already demonstrated his disregard for Victoria. It would matter little to him whether she went to an orphanage or grew up in Carolina's tender care.

"But it must matter; otherwise he would not have proposed such a marriage to me." She smiled. He did care about Victoria, if only a little. He cared enough to humble himself and join with a woman he would never love, all in order to meet Carolina's demands of security and well-being.

It was the first time she had realized that Blake's proposal had come solely out of his concerns for her reputation and future happiness. Now who was being selfish? she thought and felt a bit of shame for her earlier misgivings.

You only fear that if you marry Blake St. John, you will forever lose any chance of marriage to James Baldwin, she chided herself. But James Baldwin clearly doesn't even know I exist. He has all but forgotten me by now, and the evidence is in his lack of communication. He could find me if he wanted to. He knows that Papa would tell him of my whereabouts. He surely knows that his own father is in touch with me via the monthly statements regarding the Potomac and Great Falls Railroad.

If James Baldwin loved me as I love him, Carolina thought with a heavy heart, he would long ago have sought me out and declared such a thing. Hugging her arms to her body, Carolina felt an unseasonable chill. It was said that time could heal all wounds and that the heart would forget its sorrow, but five years had done little to dull the ache or fill the void left by James.

Her mind went back in time to Granny's words of knowing the truth within yourself. "The truth is, I love one man who will never love me, and I will marry another who feels exactly the same way." She tried not to feel morose. It was still her choice, she reminded herself. She could walk away and forget Victoria. She could close her mind and heart to the entire matter, and no one would ever blame her if she did just that. But deep inside, the one truth she was sure of was that she would forever condemn herself if she walked away from Victoria.

"I am resolved to be happy," she whispered, choking back tears. "I will marry Blake St. John and take Victoria as my own daughter, and I will be happy, even if it means I might never know the love of any man."

She went to the desk once again and picked up her pen. She would write her father immediately and request that he come to Baltimore to stand with her as witness to her marriage. Carefully, she worded her message, then blotted the ink and hurriedly placed the letter into an envelope and sealed it before she could change her mind.

Next, she changed into a very becoming gown of mauve silk and mulberry lace. The color suited her and the style made her look very mature with its tight-fitted bodice and high collar. Next, she dressed her hair, parting it carefully in the middle to sweep both sides back into a fashionable bun. She wrapped a mulberry-colored ribbon around her head several times, artfully weaving it into her hair. The final touch of her toilette was to spray on a hint of lavender scent and attach an emerald broach to her bodice.

Standing back to take in her appearance, Carolina smiled stiffly. Whether Blake St. John appreciated her efforts or not, she felt worthy to accept his proposal and to take charge of his household.

Hearing the arrival of his coach, Carolina steadied her nerves and gave him enough time to settle into his office before making her way downstairs. With letter in hand, Carolina walked down the long narrow hallway, pausing at the top of the staircase to whisper a prayer.

"Father, I know there is much I cannot know about the future, but I am asking for Your guidance in this matter now, just as I've asked for it this entire week. It seems that often we must step out in faith, trusting You to be true to the Word You have given. I am afraid, but I trust You to lead me forward. I will agree to become Blake's wife, but if this is not Your will, then I rely upon You to put the matter to rest and resolve the situation in another way."

Gingerly she put forth first one foot and then the other. She walked slowly, almost ceremonially, down the stairs. Mrs. Graves appeared as she reached the bottom step and, with one look at Carolina, seemed to know what she was about to do.

"Are you certain, dear?" she asked, taking hold of Carolina's arm.

Carolina had confided the entire matter with the housekeeper, and now she read the utmost of concern in Mrs. Graves' eyes. Nodding, Carolina handed her the letter. "It must be for the sake of the child." Then she smiled gently. "Who am I fooling? It must be this way for my sake as well, for without Victoria I would surely die of a broken heart."

"You will have me as well," Mrs. Graves offered with a tenderness that warmed Carolina's heart.

"I will depend upon that."

Mrs. Graves took the letter and departed, leaving Carolina to approach the door of Blake's study alone. Pausing for only a moment, Carolina entered the room without knocking.

He gazed up as if to silently inquire as to the cause of this intrusion. His gaze traveled the length of her body from head to toe and back again to meet her eyes. He knew. She felt certain by the confident way in which he rose to greet her. The slightest bow was given, and even though words were unnecessary, he insisted on confirmation.

"You have come to give me your decision?"

Carolina nodded. "Yes. I will marry you."

"On my terms?"

"On your terms," she replied softly.

He smiled, then reached into his desk to pull out a portfolio of papers. "A wedding gift," he said, sliding the parcel across the desk.

Carolina picked up the packet and pulled out the contents. Her breathing quickened as she carefully considered what she held. "But these are stock subscriptions to the Baltimore and Ohio Railroad."

"Yes. A great many shares."

"You did this for me?" She felt a sudden surge of unexplainable emotion. He had listened to her desires and taken note of her dreams, even though he seemed a heartless, inconsiderate employer.

"You have given me my freedom," he said simply. "I hope this might give you yours."

Forty-Three

Independence Day

The July twenty-fourth marriage of Blake St. John to Carolina Adams took scarcely more than ten minutes. At the conclusion, Blake calmly walked from the room, and Carolina turned to embrace her new daughter.

Victoria smothered her face in kisses and clung so tightly to Carolina that it was easy to forget Blake's disinterest.

"Now you are my mama and not my nanny!" Victoria declared.

"Yes, but I've always felt I was that," Carolina replied. "Are you happy, Miss Victoria?"

The little girl nodded enthusiastically and slid down from Carolina's embrace. "Now we get to eat cake! Cook said it was the finest cake she's ever made."

"Then by all means, we must enjoy her efforts," Joseph Adams assured. Victoria took herself off to arrange the matter, while Joseph turned to Carolina. "Are you quite all right?"

"Yes." Her reply lacked a certain confidence that she knew was expected of her. "Thank you so much for being here."

"I can't say that I wholeheartedly approve of this match." Joseph took hold of her hand. "I know why you've made this sacrifice, but I had hoped for a different outcome."

"Such as?"

"A marriage of true love would have started things out nicely."

"Ah yes." She looked up at him and smiled. "True love."

"I don't pretend to understand everything that has happened, but I do trust your judgment in this matter. I know you have done this thing for Victoria, and that is to be admired."

"Don't give me overdue praise, Papa. I did this selfishly for myself. I can't imagine life without her, and I chose this path with my own needs in mind as well as hers. Besides, there seemed little reason to concern myself with

265

remaining unmarried. There were hardly any suitors beating down my door to seek an audience with me. Besides, perhaps this way I can continue to involve myself with the railroad. Mr. St. John gifted me with a good many stock subscriptions in the B&O. Perhaps I will one day own enough of these to be a major shareholder. Then even a board member. Imagine it, Papa." She smiled reassuringly and felt relieved when a twinkle sparkled in her father's eyes once again.

"Knowing you, it could very well happen."

―――――

Her wedding day would be long remembered, and so too the empty bed she went to that night. Nothing had changed except her signature on a piece of paper and her pledge to remain faithful to a man she might never see again.

Carolina doubted seriously that she'd had more than two hours of sleep before the first light of morning touched the horizon. She now faced living with the consequences of her actions. The possibilities that arose in her mind were frightening at worst and exhilarating at best.

Joseph had taken the evening train back to Washington, feeling it a strange imposition to remain in the house with the newly married couple. Then, too, he told Carolina several slaves had gone missing, and he feared Hampton's retaliation against them once they were found.

Carolina had understood and silently wished she could bundle Victoria up and make for Oakbridge alongside her father. But to do so would only bring public humiliation upon the St. John household, for what bride left her husband on their wedding night? So she stayed for the sake of the family image.

Family. Her family.

She was no longer Carolina Adams, rebellious young woman longing for a university education and a place on the railroad board. She was Carolina St. John. Wealthy wife and mother. A woman with instant social responsibilities in a city that would never stand idly by and allow her any extended privacy.

No, once word got around the city of her marriage, there would be the ladies of the church to answer to, not to mention her neighbors. Throwing back the covers, Carolina tried to push all thoughts of the interrogations to come from her mind. She wondered instead what it would be like to have breakfast with her husband. Would he speak to her differently now that they were man and wife? Would he see that he had made a mistake and declare they should seek an immediate annulment?

Dressing in a simple morning gown, Carolina went downstairs, where Mrs. Graves met her with a sealed envelope.

"He left this," she said and handed over the letter.

"He left it? You mean Mr. St. John is gone?"

The housekeeper nodded. "He left quite early this morning."

"But I've been awake most of the night and I heard nothing." She took the letter and opened it. The words were simple and to the point. She had maintained her part of the agreement, and he was now seeing to his. He asked her to understand and to explain the situation to the household staff in whatever manner she desired. He concluded by saying that he was taking his manservant with him and that his lawyer would arrive later that morning to go over the affairs of his estate with her. There was absolutely no mention of Victoria.

"Well, it holds no great surprise," she murmured, folding the paper.

"Has he gone for good, then?" Mrs. Graves inquired cautiously.

"Yes, I suppose he has." She still found it hard to believe.

"Cook will be relieved," Mrs. Graves said, daring the slightest smile. "The master positively set her teeth on edge."

Carolina smiled and nodded. "He did mine as well."

This broke down any concern by Mrs. Graves that Carolina was going to assume some position of formality. "So, what is to be our first order of business, Mrs. St. John?"

"The first order of business would be that you not call me by that name. We are friends, you and I. I would have it no other way."

"Of course we are friends, but now that you are married, society will deem it inappropriate for me to call you by your first name. I don't mind, and you have never taken to calling me by anything other than Mrs. Graves."

"I suppose you are right, but what if we agreed to formalities in public and resolved to remain less rigid in private? I might even be given to use your first name, if I knew what it was."

The older woman smiled. "Isadora. My name is Isadora."

"Funny how in all these years I didn't know that," Carolina mused. They walked together to the dining room, where Carolina noted a single place setting had been positioned for her breakfast. "The second order of business," she said, turning to the housekeeper, "is that my daughter will share my meals from now on. Unless, of course, there is some formal gathering that makes such a matter uncomfortable."

Mrs. Graves smiled and nodded. "I'll see to it immediately."

And so the first morning passed amicably with a delighted Victoria joining Carolina for breakfast in the main dining room rather than the nursery.

"I have a mommy now just like Abbey and Jeremy," she said, referring to her only friends, the children next door.

"That is right," Carolina assured her, "and we will be quite happy."

"Will Papa be happy, too?" Victoria suddenly asked.

Carolina put down her fork. "I don't know. I hope so. You do understand that he makes no plans to ever return to us?"

Victoria solemnly nodded. "I remember what you told me."

Carolina's heart went out to the child. "You remember then, too, that you are not to blame yourself for such affairs. Your father is not like most men, and I will not pretend to make excuses for him. I cannot abide that he would go away and leave you, and I will not tell you that most men act this way. Therefore, you must not believe for even a second that his actions have anything at all to do with you."

Victoria nodded. "I will remember what you said, Mama."

Carolina smiled and felt a tight warmth in her chest. In spite of all her earlier misgivings, Victoria set her heart to peace with that one simple word.

"Carolina," Mrs. Graves said, appearing rather fitful. "Mr. St. John's lawyer, Mr. Swann, is here to see you. I chided him for making such an early appearance and put him in the front sitting room."

Carolina laughed and got to her feet. "I don't suppose this shall take all that long. The man will obviously be quite taken aback by this new arrangement and probably intends to continue handling all of our affairs. Once I tell him that I expect to have an educated part in the matter, he will probably leave in a huff."

"May I come, too?" Victoria questioned eagerly.

Carolina shook her head. "No, not this time. You've plenty of years to learn the various matters of business. The nicest part is that I will never deny you the right to educate yourself and be a part of such things." Victoria smiled as though she fully understood the implications of Carolina's words. "Now, finish your breakfast and then go wash up."

Carolina made her way to the front room. "Good morning," she said, sweeping into the room as though early morning meetings were quite normal.

"I am Mr. Thomas Swann," said the lawyer, standing and offering her a deep, respectful bow.

Curtsying, Carolina motioned him to retake his seat. "I am Mrs. St. John."

He sat and immediately reached for a valise. "I apologize for the early hour, but Mr. St. John was quite adamant about my coming early. I have here the entire matter of Mr. St. John's estate. There are many papers for which I need your signature."

"I see, and what might these be?" she asked, truly ignorant of the matter.

"First of all there is the matter of the deed to this house." He procured the papers in question and handed them over to Carolina. "You will see that I need your signature here and here," he said, pointing out the appropriate lines.

"This house is to be put over into my name? What of Mr. St. John?"

"He relinquished all ownership. In essence this house is a gift to you." Swann sat back and looked at her strangely. "I know all about this arrangement. Mr. St. John came to me some months ago and asked how such a circumstance should be handled, and we began immediately to set the matter into motion."

"He came to you months ago?" Carolina asked in a tone of disbelief.

"Indeed."

"I don't understand. This matter has only come to my attention within the last few weeks."

"Apparently Mr. St. John had it on his mind for a much longer time. He made it clear earlier this summer that he intended to go west before the summer was out. He wanted to have his affairs in order and the issue of his daughter resolved."

Carolina was dumfounded. Blake St. John had actually planned for this day months in advance. What she thought had been his spontaneous reaction to her refusal had, in fact, been an option he'd considered all along. In that moment, she felt completely manipulated and horribly used.

I'd deliberated in misery over this, she thought, and he already had it mapped out. What arrogance!

Swann, apparently unaware of her feelings, continued with business. "He tells me that you will want to take an open hand with the business matters and that I should advise you on a weekly basis of the standings of your investments and dealings. I shall be happy to come here each and every Friday afternoon and do just that. Will that meet with your approval?"

Still stunned in the realization of St. John's actions, Carolina stared at him dumbly. Here was yet another surprise. This man had fully accepted the fact that she would be in charge of the estate. Feeling such surprise that he would address her in such a respectful and accepting manner, Carolina nodded. "It would be quite agreeable."

Mr. Swann ran through a variety of other issues before rising to leave. He departed, having received her signature on the deed to the house as well as a dozen other papers pertaining to the St. John holdings. Carolina was stunned to learn that she now owned properties in New York and Massachusetts, as well as Baltimore, and was the sole owner of several bank accounts and investments totaling into the millions.

Stunned, Carolina could only sink to the safety of a nearby chair after seeing Mr. Swann out.

"Are you quite all right?" Mrs. Graves asked, coming in with a look of worry.

"Isadora," Carolina said, using the name for the first time, "you will not believe what I have just witnessed."

"Was he vicious and cruel?" the woman asked, seeming to take instant offense for whatever wrong might have been done her young mistress.

"No, on the contrary. Apparently our Mr. St. John made his wishes abundantly clear. Wishes, in fact, that he's been making plans on for several months. Mr. Swann informed me that Mr. St. John had arranged this entire matter some months back, and he continued our meeting by treating me not only with respect, but without the least condescension. It is one of the first times I've not been treated as a mindless creature by a man who did not know me personally." Then laughing she added, "For that matter, it was one of the nicest meetings I've ever found myself a part of."

"Well, it's a good thing," Mrs. Graves responded with a hint of a smile playing upon her lips. "The poor man would never have known what hit him had you been given cause to take him to task."

Carolina smiled and for the first time realized what real freedom she had suddenly acquired. She would answer to literally no one. She was no longer her father's responsibility, nor was she the concern of the man she'd married. For all intents and purposes, Carolina St. John was answerable only to God. Then, as if to dispel this sudden feeling of smug control, Victoria bounded into the room and threw herself into Carolina's lap.

"Are we going to the park today?" she asked wistfully.

Carolina laughed, then sharing a coy smile between the child and housekeeper, she shook her head. "No, I believe we shall do something even better."

"Better than the park?" Victoria questioned. "What is it?"

"Shopping. We shall go shopping and buy up a whole closet of dresses for you and a new doll and a set of new reading books so that we might further you along on your lessons."

Mrs. Graves smiled. "That sounds much better than going to the park, Miss Victoria."

"And we shall take Mrs. Graves with us," Carolina added. "She has need of a great many new things, as do I, and afterward we shall dine at one of the restaurants where they serve iced creams."

Victoria's eyes grew wide, as did Mrs. Graves'. "Is this a special day?" Victoria asked in awe.

"Indeed it is," Carolina replied. "It's our own private day of independence, and I mean for us to have a memorable time of it."

Forty-Four

Coming Together

*M*ustering up his courage, James stood outside the St. John house and knocked. The heat of August was heavy upon him, but not nearly so heavy as the anxiety he felt in awaiting the appearance of Carolina Adams.

He'd thought out many times just exactly how this meeting might go. His appearance would of course be a shock, but after the initial effects wore off, he hoped that Carolina might allow him a chance to explain himself. Explain the feelings that had grown in his heart ever since the night of her sixteenth birthday—feelings that had caused him to forget his promises and his father's wishes and reject marriage to a woman he didn't love.

"Yes?" an elderly woman said, staring at James as though he might well be an uninvited peddler.

"I am James Baldwin," he answered, procuring a calling card. "I'd like to speak with Miss Carolina Adams."

The old woman took his card and ushered him into the foyer. "Wait here while I let her know."

James stood faithfully, hat in hand, while the woman took herself down a short, narrow hallway. He heard her whispering, then the scuffing sound of a chair being pushed across the floor, and finally the stunning vision of Carolina appearing in the hallway.

She was radiant and far more beautiful than he'd remembered—and he remembered a great deal. This was a grown-up Carolina, stately and elegant in her afternoon dress of green watered silk. Her hair, swept up in ringlets of chocolate brown, beckoned his touch, but the shocked look of disbelief in her dark eyes quickly took away any thought of boldness. He suddenly felt very shy and very inadequate to the task at hand.

"James," she barely whispered the name. She came to stand within three feet of him before she stopped and shook her head. "I can't believe you are here."

James smiled weakly. "Me either. It took long enough to get my courage up."

Carolina looked at him in disbelief. "Your courage for what?"

James fidgeted with the rim of his hat and cast his gaze to the floor. "I've long wanted to speak to you on several matters of extreme importance." The speech was long rehearsed, only now his throat was suddenly dry and his words no longer sounded quite so smart.

"Well, why don't you come in," she said, glancing backward to where Mrs. Graves stood silently as if to guard her mistress. "Mrs. Graves, would you be so kind as to have Cook furnish us with tea?"

The housekeeper nodded before turning a corner at the end of the hallway and disappearing.

Carolina opened the sliding doors to the left of the foyer and motioned James to follow. "We can talk in here."

She swept ahead of him, and James felt as though he'd fallen into the deepest of dreams. She bore herself in such regal fashion that James felt quite overwhelmed. Why had he come? This whole thing might well make fools out of both of them.

Carolina took a seat and waited for James to once again take up the conversation. He studied her for a moment, unable to find the right words. He tried to envision the lovely creature he'd last seen so long ago at the Gadsby Hotel. She had looked perfectly grown-up then, or so he had thought. However, it was easy to see that she had been still a girl then compared to the *woman* she now truly was.

"I know this is a surprise," he said softly. Watching her carefully for any signs of distress or discomfort, he continued. "I learned from your father that you were living here in Baltimore. I, too, live in Baltimore when I am not tramping west with the B&O."

"I see," she replied, but the look on her face betrayed her utter confusion with his appearance.

"Carolina . . ." He paused, then made himself continue. "May I call you by your given name?"

Carolina smiled and her eyes lit up in such a way that James instantly felt his heart in his throat. "Of course, James. We are old friends."

The words sounded strained, but James took advantage of their truth. "That we are, and that is partly why I am here today. You see, there are things that I feel should have been said a long time ago. Things that have rewritten the course of my life, and now, well, I feel a reckoning time has come."

"Is this about Virginia?" Carolina asked.

"When I broke our engagement—" James began but was stopped by Carolina's stunned gasp.

"You?" Carolina breathed. "But I thought Virginia dismissed you. Although it makes sense now why she always blamed me for the breakup by encouraging your love of the railroad."

"She had no right to blame you," James protested.

"I realized that and told her so. Your love of the railroad was something that would have resurfaced sooner or later. My encouragement might have brought it about sooner than expected, but better that than to see my sister married several years and then have it come back to life."

"I must tell you," James said, "that I broke the engagement because I could not marry a woman I did not love. You see, there were other things."

Carolina eyed him suspiciously. "Other things? Such as?"

James bit at his lower lip and drew a heavy breath. "It isn't easy for me, and seeing you like this so . . . well . . . so grown up and . . ." he stammered, unable to go on.

"And?"

"And I have to explain what really has happened and—"

"Mama!" Victoria St. John called as she came bursting into the room. She paused for a moment to smile shyly at James before bounding into Carolina's arms.

James felt his breath catch. "Mama?" he asked, seeing the tender scene before him as an intrusion upon his own feelings.

Carolina nodded. "You mentioned having spoken with my father; I assumed that you knew."

"I knew that you were acting as nanny to the daughter of Blake St. John."

Carolina smiled and stroked Victoria's head. "I married Mr. St. John last month and became mother to Victoria."

James felt as though his entire world had come apart. He likened it to falling from the train the day it had derailed and killed Phineas Davis. He was falling and falling, and the slow motion in which the painful event seemed to play itself out was no different than the setting before him now. He couldn't let her know how devastated he was by this news. He had to pretend that the suddenness of it was all that had caused his silence.

"What a surprise," he said, forcing himself to concentrate.

"Yes, for all of us," Carolina murmured and turned to her daughter. "Victoria, this is Mr. James Baldwin. He is the man I told you once tutored me in my studies."

Victoria smiled at James and scooted off Carolina's lap in order to curtsy. "I am pleased to meet you, sir."

James stood rather awkwardly and bowed. "Your servant, Mistress Victoria."

"Victoria, please go on upstairs and busy yourself with your reading. I must speak with Mr. Baldwin for a time."

The little girl was obviously disappointed, but her respect for Carolina won out, and after offering her mother a quick peck on the cheek and another curtsy to James, she hurried off through the double doors and up the stairs.

"I am sorry for the interruption, but we have the house very much to ourselves, and Victoria tends to believe it her right to concern herself with all matters of life."

"I seem to remember that same attitude in yet another young woman," James said softly.

With a smile that broke through the years, Carolina nodded. "Guilty as charged. Now you were saying that you wished to explain something."

James shook his head. "It really isn't all that important. I simply wanted to find you and see how you were faring. It was shameless of me to have waited this long. I am surprised that the university has not figured in to your new life."

"No, but that desire no longer drives me as it once did. Lucy Alexander, now Lucy Adams and happily married to my brother York, once told me that the most important lessons in life could be had for free and without benefit of a classroom. She helped me to realize that the limitations set out by the people of this world needn't be a reason for a full-scale war. There are other ways to undermine the strategy of the enemy and win the battle."

"Must there be an enemy?"

"Of course not, but in the case of women being educated, I believe there are a great many enemies afoot. But seriously, hearing such things is not why you came today. It's been a long time, James."

"Yes." He felt his throat tighten again. He was too late. His pride and his lack of self-esteem had caused him to wait too long, and now Carolina, his Carolina, was married to another man.

Mrs. Graves arrived with a serving cart laden with treats and two silver pots containing both tea and coffee. "Thank you, Mrs. Graves. I'll serve."

Mrs. Graves eyed James for a moment before bobbing a slight curtsy and departing. Carolina was already pouring coffee for him when he looked back at her.

"Thank you." He seemed unable to say anything more.

"So, have you been with the B&O all this time?" Carolina asked, pouring her tea.

"Yes. I've worked along the main stem from Harper's Ferry west."

"And do you still anticipate opening to Cumberland this year?"

James felt relieved at having the conversation turn to the railroad. "Yes. If all goes well the line is planned to open in November."

"How wonderful!" she declared with the same spark of enthusiasm he had remembered from her childhood. "I am positively thrilled and can hardly wait to take a ride upon the rails."

"You have business in Cumberland?" he asked without thinking.

"Good grief, no," she laughed. "But I do have business with the B&O. Mr. St. John gifted me with a wedding present of B&O Railroad stock subscriptions, and I intend to continue purchasing more in the future."

"Your husband gave you railroad stocks for a wedding gift?"

"Yes, well, you might say that ours is a most unconventional marriage," she said, and for a moment James thought she sounded sad.

"Where is Mr. St. John? I thought I might at least meet him."

"No, you won't meet him," she replied flatly without further explanation. "Now tell me more about the westward line. Has there been great difficulty of late? I've hardly had time to read up on the news."

"We're making good progress. There's always personnel troubles and things like the weather, supply shortages, and theft, but for the most part we are doing well."

"I am glad. Perhaps we shall yet see the thing built to the Ohio in our lifetime."

He smiled. "Of that there is no doubt."

"Unlike the P&GF," she said, taking a long sip of tea. "I fear that our railroad may never be realized."

"The P&GF? You mean that you are still working to see that line built?"

"Hasn't your father mentioned it?" Carolina asked quite seriously.

"We scarcely talk, but no, he's not mentioned it to me."

"I thought as much." Now a fiery intensity grew in her eyes. "James, I would like to speak quite frankly with you about the Potomac and Great Falls Railroad."

"By my leave," he replied, intrigued with her air of hostility.

Carolina replaced her cup and looked at him as though sizing up an opponent. "I believe there are more problems with the line than anyone realizes, with exception to your father."

"What are you saying?"

"I'm saying that I believe your father has poorly managed this matter, and I intend to get to the bottom of it."

She got to her feet and walked slowly about the room, apparently waiting for James to respond to her accusation. James could hardly keep his thoughts on what she was saying, thinking only of her beauty as he watched her walk slowly back toward him. His heart began to pound ever harder. "I'm still uncertain . . . ah . . . as to what you . . . ah . . ." he stammered.

"I'm simply stating the facts of the account. Your father sends me reports of the status of our line and financial statements regarding investors, supply shipments, and subscription sales. There are many errors, both glaring and subtle, and I believe that in five years we could surely have seen a portion of the line built, if not indeed all of it put together."

"But these have been extremely lean years," James countered, regaining his composure. "Even the B&O, or maybe I should say, especially the B&O, has suffered because of the depression. Investors can refuse to come through, and the money is not always a certain thing."

"Yes, but my father, if you remember, is the main investor in this proposal. He may have limited large sums, but he never pulled his funding altogether." She finally took her seat and, twisting her hands together, appeared to struggle for what she might say next. "I'm not trying to cause a scene between us, James, but I believe your father is not dealing honestly with the investors."

"You are calling him some kind of a cheat?" James heard his voice edge with irritation.

"I am merely saying that things are simply not adding up. I want a better look at the ledgers and the financial reports, but so far he has put me off with one excuse after another. Of late, it has simply been impossible to get ahold of him, and my letters go unanswered."

"Perhaps because my father finds your interference to be objectionable," James retorted before he could stop himself. He knew his anger was less about Carolina's accusations than it was about the way she seemed so unmoved by his presence, while he, on the other hand, was falling apart inside.

Getting to his feet rather abruptly, he took hold of the sudden animosity and thrust it between them like a shield. "I can't believe you would call my father a liar and a swindler, and yet that is surely what you must be suggesting."

Carolina stood as well and faced him squarely. "If there is no other explanation for the miscalculations I find, then let that stand as a possibility. Your father need only answer for himself."

"My father's word should be enough." James shoved his hat on his head and bowed. "I believe we have nothing further to say to each other." With that he let himself out and hurried down the street, angry with Carolina, yet half wishing that she might call him back. Which of course, she didn't.

Irritated beyond reason, James found himself walking in circles before finally deciding to seek the company of Annabelle Bryce. Perhaps Annabelle could suggest how best to rid himself of the heartache that threatened to smother his very breath.

Forty-Five

Seeking the Truth

$\mathscr{I}$s there a possibility that her concerns are valid?" Annabelle Bryce asked James.

He scowled at her, knowing full well that she'd stand firm and not take offense. "I cannot even imagine such a thing. My father has always prided himself on being a man of integrity."

"But you yourself told me that he had wanted your help in making a good marriage," Annabelle said softly and joined James on the settee. "What if things went terribly wrong after that failed and your father had to use the investment money to keep himself solvent?"

"Then it would really be my fault," James replied.

"And that is what frightens you more than the truth of whether or not he has cheated your friends, is it not?"

"I don't know. It's just that—" James buried his head in his hands. "She is married, Annabelle. She has married that St. John man and is now a mother to his child. When I think of her in his arms instead of mine—"

"Poor James," she whispered and put a comforting arm around his shoulder. "If only you had acted sooner."

James threw off her attempts at solace and got to his feet. "I have ruined my life many times over. I followed by own course of study at college. I rejected my father's designs for a career, and I left my family to figure for themselves how they would survive the depression." He shook his head as Annabelle opened her mouth to speak. "No. Do not offer me any words of comfort, for there are none. I left one woman because of love for another, and yet I let that love founder. Five years, Annabelle. Five years and I sat back and held my thoughts to myself and said nothing, and now I am paying the price for my silence."

"James, you must think this through, and you must find the truth of what is happening with your father. You wouldn't want him to be disgraced before his peers, and if Carolina's suspicions are true, it is only a matter of time before she makes such things public. She will protect her own father first, and rightfully so."

"I know. I know. Just as I should have protected mine."

Annabelle sat back and looked very thoughtful for a moment. "You should have told her how you felt."

"For what purpose?" he asked in disbelief. "Further humiliation?"

"No," she replied softly. "I simply believe that the truth of things should have started there. You could have made clear the mistakes of the past, and you could have explained your feelings for her without making a fool of yourself or of her. From what you've told me, I don't believe for one minute that she is without feelings for you."

"It doesn't matter now. My pride kept me away too long, and now she is lost to me forever."

"It would seem so . . . lost at least as a wife . . . but her friendship meant something to you also, did it not?"

"The last thing I want is the friendship of another woman," he replied bitterly. Then, relenting, he added softly, "Yes . . . it did."

"Then you should tell her everything. Go back to her and explain the past. Set the record straight and then promise her that you will seek out the truth on the railroad issue."

"She'll think me a complete fool."

"Does it matter? You will know the truth, and the truth within you is far more relevant than the misconceptions of those around you. With the truth firmly established within your own heart and soul, God will set the rest of the world at peace for you. The Bible itself states that when a man is trying to please God, He makes even his worst enemies to be at peace with him." She paused to smile in a rather sad, sweet way. "And, James, in your case, *you* are your worst enemy."

He calmed and smiled at this. "You are right, but I wonder how it is that you know me so well."

"Because I see myself in you. You must make peace with yourself and with God, otherwise you will never know the truth of any matter."

James studied her for a moment. She had remained a good friend through his years of suffering. She had known the real reason behind his turmoil, and yet she'd not rejected his company for it. In spite of all his misgivings, his ramblings and runnings, Annabelle Bryce had been a rather soothing constant in his life.

"I have to think about all of this," he said, reaching for his coat. "May I come back tomorrow?"

"I am afraid not," she said, getting to her feet. "I leave in the morning."

"Leave?"

"I am an actress, remember? I'm headed for Chicago."

"Chicago? Why in the world would you trek across the wilds to Chicago?"

She laughed. "Because the money is good and the acting easy. It's been so long since they've seen much in the way of entertainment that they'll believe me to be a gift from God."

James reached out to take hold of her hands. "You are a gift from God," he said quite seriously. "I honestly do not know what I would have done without you. I sometimes wish—"

She hushed him with a finger to his lips. "No, don't speak it. Wishing has its merits, but in this case it would be quite moot."

He nodded, kissed her finger, then stepped back and bowed. "I shall miss you. Will you return soon?"

"I have no way of knowing." She walked with him to the door. "I will better know my way once I've seen what is before me."

"As will I."

With that, James stepped into the fading light of the August day. The yearning within him was as strong as when he'd first come to Annabelle. His heart still ached and felt as though it would never again beat without a reminder of what might have been. He started for home, but just then a steam whistle blasted from somewhere in the early evening, and James felt a strong need to go to the rail yard.

Perhaps that is the only place I truly belong, he thought, and stuffing his hands in his pockets, he quickened his step.

Forty-Six

Salvation

Do you think the new baby will like my present?" Victoria asked, clutching the brown-paper-wrapped parcel to her body.

Carolina smiled. "Of course he will." Word had come that Virginia had been delivered of a son on the twenty-first day of September, and nothing would do by Victoria but that they should go shopping for the new child. "Master Nathaniel Cabot will be completely won over by such a perfect rattle."

Victoria beamed proudly. "And you will tell Mrs. Cabot that I picked it out myself?"

Carolina knew it would never matter to Virginia that the child had painstakingly sought the gift, but she assured her little daughter that the information would be relayed.

When they arrived home, Carolina allowed the footman to help her down, then directed him to carry in the purchases. "Cook will be expecting that basket of seafood," she told him. "See that it gets to her right away." The man nodded and immediately went to the task. "Come along, Victoria. We will see about something to eat."

She had barely reached the door when Mrs. Graves pulled it open and offered up the words, "You have a visitor."

Carolina felt her heart lurch. Could it be James again? She'd never been the same since his visit. Each night she had restlessly tossed and turned in her huge empty bed, realizing she had made a very serious trade in marrying Blake St. John in order to keep Victoria in her life.

"Who is it?" she asked cautiously.

"Mr. Swann."

She breathed an audible sigh of relief, but Isadora thought it to be irritation. "I can send him away if you like."

"No, that won't be necessary. However, if you would see about something for Victoria to eat."

"Look at this, Mrs. Graves." The child was already tearing away the brown paper of her purchase. "I found a rattle for Mrs. Cabot's new baby."

Mrs. Graves smiled and acknowledged the piece while Carolina pulled off her gloves and hat. "You go along now with Mrs. Graves while I speak with Mr. Swann."

She waited until they were well down the hall before sliding open the sitting room doors. "Mr. Swann, I had no idea you might pay us a visit today."

The man instantly jumped to his feet and bowed. "I apologize for this intrusion, but it could not be helped."

Carolina noted his grim expression and waved him back to the seat. "By all means then, pray continue." She sat opposite him and waited for his news.

"This will come as some shock, but there is no other way to say it but to come right out with it."

"I see," she said, even though her mind was racing with the possibilities of what "it" might be.

"No, I'm afraid you don't." Swann shifted uncomfortably. "I was posted a letter this morning sent two days ago by Mr. Ramsey, your husband's man."

"Yes?"

"It seems that Mr. St. John has ... well, he's been ... ah ..." He paused as if trying to think of the word, then suddenly he spilled it out without warning—"Killed."

"What!" Carolina exclaimed, her hand quickly going to her heart. "What in the world are you saying?"

"It seems there was a carriage accident in New York City. Another man was injured, as was Ramsey, but Mr. St. John sustained enough injury to bring about his instantaneous death."

Carolina was stunned. Suddenly, after only two months of marriage, she was a widow. Her thoughts went to Victoria, who was now truly orphaned.

No, Carolina thought. She has me and she will always know that I love her. She is no orphan. She is my daughter.

"I know this is hard for you to take in, but I needed to make arrangements for the body, and it seemed only appropriate that you be the one to decide those things," Swann continued.

Carolina looked at him, feeling nothing but concern for her child. "Mr. Swann, you are one of the few people to know the truth behind my marriage to Blake St. John. I have little doubt that you, more so than me, should make such arrangements. I barely knew the man for all the years I spent in his house."

Mr. Swann smiled sympathetically. "I do understand. I suppose the best thing would be to arrange a plot beside his wife."

"Yes, I do believe that would be best. He disdained the church, but surely in death he would expect a Christian burial."

"Whether or not he would, the living survivors who cared for him probably would."

"Yes, I agree. Oh, how is Mr. Ramsey? Were his injuries bad?"

"A broken leg and some cuts and such. He cannot travel to accompany the body and has in fact informed me that he will stay on in New York. He felt there was little reason for him to return to Baltimore."

"I suppose I can understand that. Pay his expenses and give him a tidy sum to set him on his way," Carolina told Swann.

"I will see to it yet today, and I will forward enough in the way of funding to allow him to ship Mr. St. John home."

"Yes, that would be quite appropriate."

Carolina felt rather strange in speaking of such matters with Mr. Swann. Only last week they had pored over investment information and plotted strategies for increasing the St. John fortune. Now Blake was dead, and his dream of going west would never be realized.

"What business did Mr. St. John have in New York City?" she asked, suddenly realizing she had no idea why he delayed in pushing west.

"Railroad business. He had a good friend in New York who had encouraged him to get in on a new railroad venture. Mr. St. John thought perhaps to set himself up with another line and see it through from coast to coast. He was very excited about the prospects of a transcontinental railroad."

"Mr. St. John said that?" She was amazed, for Blake had rarely told her anything of his personal interests.

"He did indeed." Swann smiled. "I think you had much to do with that. Railroads were only a minor concern of his until you showed up."

"Did you disapprove of his new fascination?"

"Not at all. I have always seen the merit of rapid transportation. Locomotives will write the pages of our future."

"I quite agree." She considered Blake's business once again. "What railroad had he concerned himself with in New York?"

"The Erie. I believe they are calling it the New York and Erie Railroad. The intention is to have a railroad that runs from the New York City harbor to Lake Erie. This would allow the southern portion of the state to enjoy the same freedoms and benefits that the northern portion enjoys with the Erie Canal."

"How very interesting. And Mr. St. John was on business with this matter?"

"Yes. He had tickets, however, to take the canal west, and from there was scheduled to meet up with several gentlemen who were going to the Oregon Territory with one of the fur trading companies."

"It's so sad he will never realize his dream," Carolina said softly. She looked down at her hands, which she'd been twisting rather nervously. Blake was dead. It was no easy matter to imagine how she would explain his passing to Victoria.

"I will trust you to make whatever appropriate arrangements you deem necessary," she said, gazing up at Mr. Swann. "I will speak to the minister and have him prepare a eulogy that avoids the religious rhetoric Mr. St. John so hated."

Swann got to his feet. "I will do as you bid and hope you know that should any need arise, I am at your service."

Carolina nodded and rose. "I thank you, Mr. Swann."

After he had gone, Carolina went to the dining room and found that Victoria had already finished her lunch and was up in the nursery preparing for their reading lesson.

"Isadora, if you would, we need to discuss something," Carolina said, coming down the hall toward the kitchen.

Mrs. Graves, who was just coming from having removed Victoria's dishes, seemed to note the concern in Carolina's voice. She followed Carolina into the kitchen without a word of questioning.

"Cook, we need to talk."

Mrs. Dover turned, a bulk of dough between her pudgy fingers. "Of course."

"Please, both of you sit down." Carolina motioned to the small kitchen table. The two older women eyed each other as if to question the knowledge of the other, but nevertheless did as they were requested.

"Mr. Swann brings us bad tidings. Or maybe I should better say, sad tidings. Mr. St. John has been killed in a carriage accident."

"No!" exclaimed Mrs. Graves.

"Lord preserve us," said Cook.

"I've instructed Mr. Swann to arrange for the body to be brought home for the funeral. I will speak to the minister and see to it that the funeral might be done in a way fitting Mr. St. John's tastes and desires."

"When did it happen?" Mrs. Graves asked.

"I'm not sure. I believe sometime last week. Mr. Ramsey was injured badly enough to lay him up for a while. It is his desire to remain in New York City, and thus I have instructed Mr. Swann to see to his keep while he recovers."

"Mr. St. John dead," Cook muttered. "It just don't seem possible."

"No, I suppose it doesn't seem possible to me, either," Carolina replied. "I suppose it won't seem real until I see the body for myself. Now, if you'll excuse me," she said, getting to her feet, "I must go to Victoria and tell her."

"Poor little tyke. 'Tis a good Lord that saw fit to put you and Mr. St. John together before taking away her papa," Cook declared.

"Yes, I thought of that, too," mused Carolina. "Victoria will surely be more dependent on us than ever before, for even though she scarcely knew her father, she at least counted on his existence."

Carolina made her way upstairs and entered the nursery, completely uncertain of what she should say. Would Victoria be able to understand that her father's death was a permanent thing? So often Blake had come and gone in the life of his child that Carolina seriously wondered if Victoria would simply see this as yet another of his absences.

"Mama, I can read this whole page without any help," Victoria said upon seeing Carolina.

"That is wonderful news," Carolina replied. "But right now I have some sad news, and I want you to come sit with me a moment."

Victoria dropped the book and hurried to Carolina's side. "Is the baby sick?"

Carolina looked at her in confusion for a moment. "What baby?"

"Mrs. Cabot's baby."

Carolina sighed. "No, sweet. The baby is just fine." She led Victoria to a settee where they often cuddled for stories. Sitting down, she pulled Victoria onto her lap and hugged her close. "I'm afraid your papa is the one who is . . . well . . ." She stammered for words. "Your father has died, Victoria."

The child's dark eyes seemed to narrow as though she were taking in the information and forming it into an understandable manner. "Did he go very far away?"

Carolina nodded. "Yes, and he can never come back to us. Except," she paused, realizing that the funeral might well confuse the child, "his body will come back, and we will put it in a beautiful box and bury him in the ground."

"But the ground is dark and smelly," Victoria replied.

"Yes, but your papa's body will not know this. You see, people have souls inside their bodies, and it is this soul that makes them who they are. That soul leaves the body when a person dies, so the body we put in the ground is much like our clothes. We take off our clothes and put them away, but it doesn't change who we are simply because we've removed them, now does it?"

"No." Victoria hugged Carolina and remained silent.

"I want you to understand that I will always be your mama, even though your papa has died. You mustn't be afraid that I will leave, too, because I will always be here for you." Carolina felt bad that she couldn't assure the child of such a thing truthfully. It was always possible that she, too, could die tomorrow. "People can die at any time, Victoria," Carolina said, raising the child's face to meet her loving gaze. "But God looks out for us, and if we love Him and accept His Son Jesus as our Savior, our souls will never die."

Victoria seemed to understand, but Carolina couldn't be sure. She wanted for the child to say something, and when Victoria spoke, she was surprised at her request.

"Can we go into Mother's room now?" Victoria had never called Suzanna St. John anything but Mother.

Carolina nodded. "If you would like."

"I want to see what's in there," Victoria said, scooting down from Carolina's lap. "I want to see why Papa locked it up."

Carolina had to admit that her own curiosity about the place had been piqued at times. "Let's get the keys from my dressing table."

Victoria remained silent as they retrieved the keys and unlocked the door to Suzanna's room. She walked in quietly, almost reverently, Carolina thought, and peered at the room as though trying to find some link to the past.

Over the fireplace, a large oil painting by Samuel Morse portrayed a blond-headed woman and small boy. The woman looked quite cheerful, and the boy on her lap was darkly handsome like Victoria and Blake St. John.

"Is that my mother and brother?" Victoria asked.

"Yes," Carolina whispered. "I'd imagine so."

"She doesn't look like me," Victoria stated, not seeming overly concerned.

"No, but you and your brother share your father's dark features."

"Are they in heaven?" Victoria suddenly asked.

"I believe so. Your mother loved God very much. Mrs. Graves told me that much."

"What about Papa?"

It was the question Carolina had hoped Victoria wouldn't ask. Should she lie to the child, giving her the idea that everyone went to heaven? When she was older, she would of course learn the truth of the matter. Was it kinder and gentler for one so young to believe that God took in all people, as Victoria took in all strays?

Swallowing hard, Carolina prayed for guidance, and as she opened her mouth to speak, she thought of the verse that declared that the truth would set you free. Surely truth and freedom were what they both needed.

"I don't know, Victoria," Carolina finally answered. "A person must repent of their sins, remember?"

"That means stop doing them and be really sorry for what you've done, right?"

"That's right." Carolina led her to the dusty canopied bed and sat down on the edge. "A person must be genuinely sorry and desire to be better. But that's not exactly how they are saved, you see. God loved us so much that He sent us Jesus."

"Jesus is God's Son," Victoria interjected.

"That's right. Jesus came to help us better understand God and to give us everlasting life. When we accept Jesus as our savior, we are making a choice to forget about having our own way. We turn away from evil and bad things. We ask for forgiveness and we believe by faith that God will save us from our sins. Do you understand?"

"Yes," Victoria answered very solemnly. "And you don't know if Papa was sorry."

Carolina was amazed at the understanding of one so young. "That's right. I do not know if your papa had asked Jesus to save him. But I do know that your mother did and that your brother was too little to know right from wrong."

"So God forgave him anyway?" Victoria asked, seeming quite intent on the answer.

"I believe God forgives all of the little children. There comes a time, however, when children learn the truth of right and wrong. They learn about sin and salvation, and then I believe God expects them to make a choice. A choice for the wrong things of life, or for His way."

"I want to go His way," Victoria suddenly said. "When I die, I want to go to see God and my mother and brother. Maybe even Papa."

Carolina felt a swell of pride in realizing that she was leading this child to salvation. How like God to take a moment of seeming devastation and replace the misery with joy.

Carolina slipped from the bed and knelt down. "Come kneel here," she instructed Victoria. "We will pray together and tell God how much you love Him and how you want to be His child."

"Can I still be your child, too? Even when I'm God's child?"

Carolina smiled and felt warm tears slip from her eyes. "Especially then, Victoria. Especially then."

Forty-Seven

Coming to Terms

*J*ames hurried on his way to the Pratt Street Station and was almost regretful for having not taken a cab when the rain began to pour in earnest. Under his arm he carried a satchel for his father. Uncle Samuel had been most adamant upon locating him, saying that since he must journey back to Washington anyway, he could surely deliver these papers to his father.

James was far more concerned, however, with the reason he was eager to return to the capital. His mother had fallen gravely ill last August, and his father was just now seeing fit to tell him of the matter. Ducking under the awning of a nearby tavern, James looked around to see if there might be a hack he could hire. His agitation grew, realizing that no sane person would venture out into the sudden downpour. He pulled out his pocket watch and grimaced. He'd have to hurry along on his own. There were barely fifteen minutes before the Washington train was scheduled to pull out.

Could his life possibly grow any more despairing? His father had noted quite impersonally in his letter that "Mrs. Baldwin, succumbing to her usual complaint, has taken to her bed. The doctor remains gravely concerned that she has not yet recovered."

That was it. The entire message was nothing more than a bulletin of affairs. No emotional plea for James to return home. No suggestion that her last days could be made better by knowing that her son had come to be at her side.

He will never forgive me, James thought, making his way ever closer to the station. Stepping from the curb, he found himself in ankle-deep water and growled angrily as he pressed forward.

And perhaps I do not deserve his forgiveness, James chided himself. The now wet satchel suddenly slipped under his arm, and he fought to

287

grasp it more firmly, but to no avail. It fell into the mud and water and spilled its contents out into the street.

"Could I possibly be any more clumsy?" James muttered and bent to retrieve the papers. "Father will hang me for this as surely as he would like to hang me for all of my other offenses."

He gathered the rain-drenched papers and tried to shake off the excess water, but the steadily pouring rain defeated his purpose before he even got started.

"Oh bother!" he exclaimed and stuffed the wet pages back into the satchel. "I'll dry them on the way to Washington."

Barely making the last call for the train, James pushed his way through the gentlemen's car and found a seat where he could lay out his things. He was soaked to the bone and felt a chill take him, though the day was mildly warm.

Pulling a damp handkerchief from his pocket, he used this to wipe the better portion of water from the satchel before opening it to do the same for its contents. Muttering to himself, James scarcely noticed what he held in his hands until he saw the smudged imprint of PO-TOMAC AND GREAT FALLS RAILROAD.

These were railroad stock certificates, he realized and felt a surge of concern that he had somehow cost his father yet another monumental charge. But why did Uncle Samuel have the certificates?

James flipped through the soggy pages. There were hundreds of certificates within the satchel, but not all of them bore the P&GF name. Some were for other railroads, obscure lines James had never heard of. He thought little of it at first. His father was, after all, brokering the creation of several railroads for a variety of investors. But behind these were other papers, deeds to lands in the western territories. It didn't make sense.

Carefully, he blotted the wet pages and waved them back and forth in order to dry them. In a little over two hours he would be faced with making an excuse for why valuable railroad stocks and land deeds were ruined, and he didn't relish the idea of giving up without a fight.

Checking inside the satchel for any remaining certificates, James found a folded piece of paper and opened it. It was a letter from his uncle to his father, and the words on the page made his blood run cold.

Leland,
 I believe you will find these of authentic quality. I've gone over them in detail and find no flaw to prove them as other than the real article.
        Ever your brother,
        Samuel

James reread the brief missive. Of course they were authentic certificates. Why shouldn't they be? His father was, after all, vice-president on the board of the P&GF. He had created the design of the stock
certificates, and he alone had been responsible for their issue.

He folded the paper and his mind dredged up the concerns of
Carolina Adams. No, Carolina St. John, he reminded himself. She had
been concerned that something was amiss. What was it she had said?
For the love of all that was right, James couldn't bring to mind her
exact words.

He shoved the still-damp papers back into the satchel but placed
the note from his uncle into his vest pocket. Something was wrong,
and now he realized how astute Carolina must have been to see this
from nothing more than letters and reports given her by his father.

"Carolina."

Even breathing her name was painful. It reminded him of his own
foolishness. It reminded him of the woman he loved. The woman he
would always love. How could he have left her in Baltimore on such
bad terms? Better that he would have swallowed his pride and at least
apologized, even if he couldn't bring himself to do as Annabelle suggested and declare his feelings.

She was married, he reminded himself, and to make open declarations of love to a married woman was akin to dishonoring her with an
adulterous affair. He could never ruin her reputation by making indiscreet declarations. After all, who knew what servant might overhear
him and in turn share this knowledge with others?

He sighed. He'd done his best to learn more of Blake St. John, but
everyone who would speak to him of the man always said the same
thing. He keeps to himself. He is long absent from Baltimore on various
businesses that have made him enormously wealthy.

Long absent, he thought. Was that truly what Carolina wanted? A
husband who was never around to hinder her in her studies and interests? Perhaps she had married St. John in order to have enough
wealth to force her hand upon the world. But no, he reasoned with a
shake of his head, Carolina was not like that.

He sighed long and heavy, wishing with all of his heart that he
might be able to turn back the hands of time. He was filled with regrets
so consuming, his only thought was of how he might avoid feeling
anything for anyone ever again.

Then, as if to offer a painful reminder of the present, the satchel fell
from the seat to the floor when the train passed over a particularly
twisted portion of line. Reaching down, he picked up the satchel and
held it against his damp coat. How could he ever learn the truth of this

situation without further alienating his father? And how could he bring up such a matter when his mother lay gravely ill?

The miles rattled by with his traveling car companions sharing hearty laughter, sordid stories, and of course, the ever present spitting of tobacco. But they might well have been completely absent from the car. James scarcely heard or saw them, for his mind was overwhelmed with his father's business dealings, while his heart was consumed with one dark-eyed young woman who resided in the house of Blake St. John. Coming to terms with either matter would take a great deal more patience and faith than he knew himself capable of.

He let his head drop into his hands. Not since those days following Phineas's death had he felt so helpless. So utterly defeated. He vaguely smelled the odor of whiskey as a group of men in the back of the car were pouring drinks. James well knew he'd find no answers there, but for a brief moment he was tempted to find at least escape. Then he lifted his head and, for an odd reason, was not at all surprised by what—or whom—he saw.

"James, is that you?" Ben Latrobe was entering the car.

"Hello, Ben," James said in an incredibly casual tone.

"Are you all right?" Latrobe slipped into the seat next to James.

"So, what brings you out on the evening train?" James felt instinctively it was more than coincidence that Ben had appeared when he did, yet still James was reluctant to bare his heart.

"I've a meeting with investors in the morning. And you?"

"My mother is ill."

"I am so sorry, James. It must be bad for you to take on so."

James nodded. "But not more than I could bear—if it were only that." He looked at Ben with wasted eyes, then shrugged. "What am I saying? How do I know what I can bear? No . . . I don't feel as if I have the strength to bear anything . . . anymore."

"Go on, James. Maybe it will help for you to talk about it."

"You believe in fate, don't you, Ben?"

"I believe God's direction in all things."

"Yes, that's what I mean. Well, I think God directed you to be here right now. But even knowing that, it isn't easy . . ."

"No, of course not. When is life ever truly easy?"

"You would know that as well as anyone, wouldn't you, Ben?"

"I had a son die in his infancy, after watching him suffer for two months. Then, not long after that, I saw my work literally crumble before my eyes."

"I heard it mentioned that you were also quite ill for a time."

"I suffered excruciating headaches and heart flutters. I sought all manner of medicines and treatments. I finally found some medicine that helped, but only one thing helped the awful sense of failure that had probably caused the headaches in the first place."

"Your faith, right?"

Ben smiled. "Yes . . ."

"Tell me about it, Ben."

For the next hour the two men talked—as they had talked many times before, but also in a far different way, for this time James actually listened with his heart, not just his mind and his good intentions. He really heard and understood how a man's strength was so completely paltry next to God's weakness. He saw how foolish it was to carry burdens alone—how impossible! He saw how the true measure of a man was not in some frivolous outward show of strength, but rather in having the ability to admit one's need, then take steps to seek the One who would meet that need.

"Ben," James finally said, "I have reached a place in my life where I just can't make it alone. I am so very tired of being alone. And I know what I must confront in Washington. I *can't* do it alone."

"And you need not, James."

"Would God truly stand with me—after all these years I have so ignored Him?"

"You know the answer to that, don't you, James?"

"Yes . . . but it seems almost too easy."

"The easiest—and the hardest—thing you will ever do is to let God take up your burdens. I suppose it is especially difficult for men."

"That must be why He has had to bring me to a place where I cannot bear taking another step alone."

"But that is truly how you feel?"

"Oh yes, Ben!"

"Then why don't you pray right now for God to intercede in your life?"

"Here. . . ? On the train?" Then James grinned. What better place? How very natural it would feel talking to God with the sound of the chugging locomotive in his ears and the feel of the vibration of metal wheels against the track beneath him.

Forty-Eight

Father and Son

The Baldwin house was silent as James entered from a light drizzle and deposited his wet hat and coat on a nearby chair. Ollie, the new housekeeper, took up the wet articles and informed James that his father was not yet home. James felt a small amount of relief. It was almost a reprieve. If only he could avoid ever having to deal with his suspicions.

The satchel, which James had come to despise these last few hours, felt oddly lighter, yet he still gripped it with slightly trembling hands. He felt confident in what he must do, but still fearful and nervous. He remembered what Annabelle had once told him about taking one step at a time. That's what he must do now. Trusting God was still very new to him, and he supposed even God would understand his moments of wavering. At least Ben had said that would be so.

He tossed the satchel aside, taking the opportunity to see his mother before dealing with his father. Climbing the stairs, James felt a sense of foreboding. Up until now, he'd allowed other thoughts to consume his worries regarding his mother's illness. Now he had to face facts. His mother was very ill—maybe even dying. Suddenly railroad swindles and such seemed most unimportant.

He opened the door after knocking very lightly and found a stranger sitting beside his mother's bed.

The woman looked up and asked, "And who might you be?"

"I'm James Baldwin," he said, his gaze leaving the woman's scrutiny to behold his mother's pale face. "I'm her son."

"Ah yes. They told me you'd be making an appearance."

James grimaced. She said the words as though he were some sort of circus novelty. "And you are?"

"I'm Mrs. Schultz. Your father hired me to sit with Mrs. Baldwin."

"I see." James moved forward and took the empty chair at his mother's bedside. "How is she?"

The gray-haired woman frowned. "I'm afraid she's very weak."

"Is she awake? I mean, has she regained consciousness?"

"From time to time. Mostly she sleeps. The doctor declared it the best thing for her."

James took his mother's hand and lifted it to his lips. Placing a tender kiss on her cold fingers, he held on to her, reluctant to let go.

"Is everything being done?" James questioned.

"Everything humanly possible. The rest is up to God."

The door opened and Ollie entered. "Master James, Master Baldwin has returned and is waiting for you in the study."

James nodded and tenderly kissed his mother's hand once more before leaving her side. He glanced back at the door, feeling guilty for having ever left her—wishing he could stay at her side. But he would return as soon as he spoke to his father—that is, if the man didn't force him from the house.

He walked slowly back downstairs, wondering if he possessed the strength to deal with his father. Had he been the cause of their demise? And if so, how could he right the wrongs of his past?

Spotting the rain-soaked satchel, James took it up and drew a deep breath. He stepped up to the door of his father's study and, without thinking, opened the door before knocking.

"Hello, Father."

"What in the world has gotten into you, boy? You know better than to enter this room without knocking."

It was just like old times. No friendly greeting, just a reprimand. James had hoped for more, and the disappointment stirred his old defensive responses.

"Why is that, Father?" James tossed the satchel across the desk. "Because someone might see you with these?" Leland paled, and James suddenly knew the truth of the matter.

"Why?" James asked. "That's all I want to know."

"I haven't any idea what you mean," Leland said, scrambling to remove the satchel before it dampened everything under it. "You rudely burst into my office, making insinuating noises, then demand me to answer to you." Leland carefully placed the satchel on the floor beside him and coughed loudly in order to draw his breath.

"You needn't play this game with me anymore, Father." Wearily James took a seat in the leather chair opposite his father's desk. "I know those certificates are less than authentic. What I want to know is why?"

Leland stood indignantly, bringing both fists down on the desk.

"Boy, I sent for you because your mother may well be dying. While she wastes away upstairs you would stand here and interrogate me for imagined wrongs."

"I've just come from my mother's bed. I know she is ill. She has been ill, according to your brief explanation, for some time." James could not keep the bitterness from invading his voice. "You might at least have seen fit to contact me sooner. You might have given me that much."

"I sent for you when I felt there was nothing left to be done." Leland seemed to relax, and James knew it was because he thought he'd successfully diverted the conversation. "Your actions indicated to me that you cared no more than that."

"That is not fair, Father. You know why I have stayed away. I never wished to hurt Mother."

"But that was the result."

"For which I am deeply ashamed. And I only pray I can make that right with Mother. But what about you, Father? Can you right your wrongs so easily?"

"You make no sense, James." Leland sat down hard and pulled out a handkerchief to dab around his mouth. His gaze darted about the room before settling on the papers in front of him. "These are ruined," he said angrily. "A whole morning's work that I shall have to rewrite."

"The stock certificates and deeds are ruined as well," James offered softly.

"What!" Leland struggled to retrieve the satchel and opened it with great concern. "What happened to these?"

"They fell into a puddle of water. The satchel opened and the contents spilled out, which is why I discovered something is amiss."

Leland shook his head. "I merely had Samuel draw up the certificates. He knows a good printer—"

"Stop it!" James leaned forward, pulling his uncle's note from his vest pocket. "This letter clarifies things quite nicely."

"You have no right to read letters that were not intended for you."

"And you have no right to swindle the community of its hard-earned money. I want you to tell me exactly what you have done, and then we will figure out a way to undo it."

Leland stared hard at James for several minutes. James could hear the irritating tick of the clock match his own heartbeat. He'd never thought out how he would come to get the truth from his father, but he'd certainly not planned to be so aggressive and angry. He didn't think that after what happened on the train with Ben he ought to get angry, yet he wondered if there could have been any other way. It seemed as if something demanded the truth and would settle for nothing less.

There it was again. The truth. The truth seemed so relevant to every walk of his life that James could scarcely distance himself from it for more than a few moments. Annabelle spoke of truth and of making peace with himself. Ben Latrobe had spoken of the importance of following truth and keeping to the master plan. Carolina had desired the truth, but he had been unable to give it to her, because she would then have seen inside his heart. But he now believed he could at last face the truth, because he knew he would not have to do it alone.

"The truth, Father. I think after all that we've been through these last few years, I deserve your honesty, just as you deserve mine. If it makes you feel better, I'll go first." James shifted and settled back into the chair.

"I couldn't marry Virginia Adams because while tutoring at Oakbridge I fell in love with Carolina Adams. I knew it would be a great disgrace to leave one sister for the other, and so I gave Virginia her freedom and, with it, proposed that she save face by breaking the engagement herself. I'm sorry I ruined your plans for prosperity and family security, but that is the truth of the matter."

"Bah! The truth of the matter is that you were a selfish young whelp, and you saw your way as being superior to any other plan."

"Yes, that is true as well," James said, surprising his father. He could see by Leland's expression that he expected further explanation. "I was immature and very selfish. I desired my own way. I wanted my own career, one that suited me and did not follow the designs of another. I wanted my own choice of whom I would wed, not a woman selected for me from a list arranged by my mother. I even wanted my own future. Not one created by you or Mother or even Joseph Adams. I wanted my own life, and yes, that was rather selfish in light of your circumstance."

"My circumstance?"

"Something has obviously gone terribly wrong in your life, and because of it you have found yourself in less than honorable dealings. I want to know exactly what is going on and how we might correct the situation."

Leland laughed and shook his head. "You are still naive and immature."

"Perhaps, but I am growing up very quickly. You see, I'm devoted to a woman who is married to another. But because of that devotion, I will not see her family name dragged down through the swampy Washington mud. Now will you tell me what those certificates are all about? If you don't, I'm taking the matter to Joseph Adams." James wasn't totally sure if he'd really do such a thing or not, but it seemed enough to throw the possibility out as a threat.

Leland's expression fell and his shoulders slumped. He took a deep breath and shook his head. "It isn't an easy matter with a simple explanation."

"I'll wait as long as it takes to hear the truth from you. No matter how complicated, the truth is all I desire in this."

"Yes," Leland replied, nodding. "Yes, I know it is." He looked at his son as though realizing that with this moment, his world would completely change.

"A long time ago when funds began to run short, I asked Samuel for suggestions on how we might engage in other business. The bank was suffering because people were swindling me with false bank drafts and loans that folks had no intention of ever repaying. Samuel suggested we produce our own bank drafts to compensate, and it seemed reasonable."

"Reasonable?" James questioned. "It was illegal."

"Yes, but you must see that back in thirty-two the system was already running amuck. It's the reason Jackson opened the private banks in the first place."

"You mean to tell me that your illegal activities in counterfeiting began ten years ago?"

Leland shrugged. "Somewhere around that time. Anyway, James, you can't imagine the situation because you were still away at school. Funds were short and that is the simple matter of things."

"But what of Mother's fortune?"

"Yes, well, that was a matter of our high standard of living and my inability to manage a plantation. It was the main reason we sold the place and moved to this house."

James suddenly realized that none of this was his fault. He'd blamed himself, thinking his father had fallen into ruin because of his decision not to marry Virginia Adams. Now he could see that his father had clearly been on a downward descent for more years than he'd even imagined.

"We can make this thing work," Leland offered, taking James' silence for acceptance.

"The only way we can make this work is to return the money you've swindled. May I assume the other railroad stock represent nonexistent lines, too? Aren't they simply paper railroads?"

"But it needn't concern you," his father argued. "The railroads may one day truly exist. It's only a matter of time and investor regard. You don't understand how these things work, James. Take the land deeds, for instance. People—hearty, eager people—buy these deeds for dirt-cheap prices and head west. They might never find the courage to go west without a deed in their hands. Once they reach the wilds of un-civilized territories, many of them will begin to build and may never know another moment of discontent. Others may be found to have false deeds, but because they are already there, they will have to re-main. Few would ever have the funds to return and blame me for their misfortune. Besides, I don't handle the matter myself. There is another who acts as a front, and I pay him well enough that he'll never open his mouth to speak against me."

"You cannot continue this way, Father."

"I can't continue any other way, James. You don't understand what this depression did to the country and to this family. You live in your carefully constructed world of railroads and unrequited love. You know nothing of what it means to maintain a standing in society and care for a wife who expects to hold her head up high among her peers and wear the very latest fashions from Paris. You know nothing of the re-sponsibility of keeping servants, a house, carriages, and a business. So don't tell me what is to be done."

James sadly shook his head. "Then I suppose everything Carolina suspects is true."

"What do you mean?" Leland growled the question.

"I went to see Carolina in Baltimore. She suggested that there might be problems with the P&GF. She found discrepancies and a variety of things that didn't make sense. She'd been trying to get a hold of you in order to gain a better understanding, but apparently you were never available."

"I've been busy," Leland offered lamely.

"Obviously," James countered. "A little too busy."

"Don't take that tone with me, boy. I've tolerated just about as much from you as I intend to take. You've only been asked here because of your mother."

"Yes, I am aware of that. Please humor me, however, and answer one simple question. Has it ever been your plan to see the P&GF to completion?"

Leland laughed. "Why should anyone want to bother with that line? Whose brilliant idea was it to run a railroad from Falls Church to Washington, anyway? Nonsense and bother. That's all it is. There isn't enough commerce to make the line self-supportive, and without that, even the families benefited by running crops to the city will end up spending more money in upkeep than in benefits received. Sooner or later they'll realize I'm doing them all a favor."

"By stealing their money?"

"Get out!" Leland declared, getting to his feet. "I won't stand for you speaking to me that way."

"I'm sorry, Father. I want to work this out. Is there nothing we can do—not only to make things right with the railroad but"—James paused and looked at his father with great longing—"also between us?"

"You can forget this conversation and forget what you found in that satchel."

"I can't do that."

"Then I want nothing more to do with you."

James rose slowly. "I will go, then, *for now*, but first I will see my mother again. Then, I will go to Oakbridge and speak to Joseph Adams."

"If you so much as mention this—"

"You'll do what?" James implored. "What more can you take from me that you haven't already taken? You robbed me of my youth by pushing me into education and industry. You robbed me of the woman I would have married by insisting I wed another. You robbed me of my mother's company, and you robbed me of a father because you refused to waste your precious time being one."

Leland appeared shaken by this and, to James' surprise, put a hand to his chest and sat down in obvious discomfort. "Don't go to Adams." The words came in between gasping breaths. "P-please!"

"Are you all right, Father?"

"I'm . . . fine. I have trouble from time to time. It's nothing." He leaned back in the chair still clutching at his chest. "You can't do this to me. You can't tell Joseph, or I may well be taken away to prison. Would that be your price?"

James wearily sighed and ran a hand through his hair. "I can't leave things as they are. I have to think this through. I want to help you make this up—set things right. Perhaps there is a way to do so and still save face. But we must do something, for if Carolina suspects, surely others suspect as well."

"I don't see how that slip of a girl could figure out things so complicated and clearly outside her realm of understanding."

James smiled and walked to the door. "I do. She had a very thorough teacher."

Forty-Nine

Rough Places Plain

For Carolina, the funeral of Blake St. John was a monumental moment in her life. She was a widow now, and yet she'd never truly been wife to any man. Having buried Blake in the cemetery plot beside his beloved Suzanna and son, Charles, Carolina felt that she had come full circle in her adventurous young life. There was still Victoria to consider, but that was something she did with a great sense of pride. Victoria would be raised as her child and never would Carolina allow for anyone to consider her otherwise.

Carolina worried about Victoria and wondered if the death of her often absent father would be hard on the child. So far she'd said very little, and even when they'd stood together at his burial, Victoria seemed far more interested in the decorative gravestones than in her father.

Carolina could hardly blame the child for her lack of feeling where Blake was concerned. He'd made it clear that he didn't care about her, at least not in the sense that she needed him to care. It was still unimaginable to Carolina that anyone could be so heartless and indifferent to a child of their own making.

With the funeral already a week behind them, the daily routine seemed hardly disrupted. Carolina and Victoria had just enjoyed a brisk fall morning at the park and now stood in the front entryway taking off their wraps. The post had arrived in their absence, and Carolina was happy to find a letter from her father. Sending Victoria to play in the nursery, Carolina settled down to a cup of tea and broke the seal on the envelope.

1842, October 1

Dearest Daughter,

I received your letter today and was sorry to hear of Mr. St. John's passing. I was even more sorry to be absent from you at such a time. How very strange this life we live, and how very unusual for you in this circumstance. Have you thought yet of what you will do now? Please know that you are always welcome at Oakbridge. You and Victoria would certainly give me much pleasure.

Your mother is quite well at this writing. I have had a most positive report from her doctor. She no longer weeps all night and is quite functional at mealtime. I look to this with a hopeful heart.

Virginia, Hampton, and baby Nate are ever unchanged.

The news is that Georgia has announced she is with child. The doctor believes the child will be born sometime in May.

York and Lucy are bringing the children for a visit and may well be here by the time you receive this letter. Perhaps that will entice you to come ahead for a visit.

> *I remain ever your loving father,*
> *Joseph*

Carolina folded the letter and gave long thought to her father's suggestion of a visit. It was exactly what she desired. The peace and serenity of her childhood home blocked out all other fears, both real and imagined. She was saddened by Blake's death, not because she'd lost a great love, but because one so young should die so embittered and lost. But perhaps more than this, Carolina was still devastated by the argument and harsh words she'd shared with James.

She scarcely allowed herself to think about him, for when his image flooded her thoughts, she was almost compelled to seek him out. She longed to run to him now, tell him that she was free, and declare her love. But, of course, she couldn't very well do that. James was angry at her betrayal. To imagine that she had suggested to him that his father was dealing in an underhanded manner would surely keep him from ever having any positive feeling for her.

Tapping the letter against the desk, Carolina made her decision. She would return with Victoria to Oakbridge. Not permanently, of course, but rather for a short stay. Perhaps a month or two away from the rush and fuss of Baltimore would do them both good. In the quiet of the Virginia countryside perhaps they could plot and plan together for their future.

Carolina smiled. She knew Victoria would love this suggestion. She adored Grandfather Joseph, which was what he insisted she call him upon Carolina's marriage to Blake. Grandfather Joseph was the father image that Victoria so needed in her life. He was gentle and loving and never failed to hold her close whenever she threw herself into his arms. Carolina felt tears come to her eyes. He had always been a loving father, and she remembered fondly the feeling of security and happiness she had known growing up. Joseph Adams had been a very busy man, but he'd always taken time out to be a faithful father to his children. No wonder Victoria loved him so. No wonder I love him so, Carolina thought.

Later, sharing her idea with Victoria, Carolina was met with immediate approval.

"Can we go now? Today?" Victoria had asked in her animated way.

Carolina laughed. "No, not today. We have only buried your father last week. It might appear inappropriate."

"But Papa wouldn't care," Victoria argued, and Carolina knew she was right. He wouldn't care. Even if he'd still lived, he would hardly consider their absence from Baltimore a problem.

"You are right, Victoria. Your father would probably want us to go." She considered the matter for a moment. "We will go on Thursday. That is only two days away. We will take the train to Washington, and from there we will hire a carriage or send a messenger to Oakbridge and have someone come to the city for us."

Victoria clapped her hands and danced around. "How long will we stay? Can we stay for Christmas and my birthday?"

"Perhaps Christmas, but we would certainly return before your birthday. After all, what would Cook and Mrs. Graves do without us all that time?"

"They could come with us," Victoria said, suddenly giving the matter sober thought. "But maybe they'd like to go see their grandfathers."

Carolina smiled. "I'm not sure they have grandfathers who are still living, but perhaps a respite away from their responsibilities would be to their liking. We shall approach them immediately."

And so it was decided that the house would be closed for a short time. Carolina was uncertain as to how long she and Victoria would actually stay at Oakbridge, and so Mrs. Graves gave her the address of her sister. Carolina promised to post her a letter noting the time and date of their expected return to Baltimore, with Mrs. Graves in turn promising to return in plenty of time to open the house and air it out.

Carolina's last order of business was to contact Mr. Swann. For this she took the carriage to his office and surprised him by arriving completely unannounced.

"Mrs. St. John, I must say this is a surprise," Swann said, coming from behind his desk to bow.

Carolina curtsied and allowed him to lead her to a chair. "I have come on particularly pressing business that I wanted to discuss in person."

"Pray tell me what is on your mind," he replied, retaking his seat at the desk.

"There are several matters," Carolina began. "First of all, I'd like accounts set up for Mrs. Dover and Mrs. Graves on the chance that anything should happen to me. I would suggest the sum of five thousand dollars each, to be paid out upon my death." Mr. Swann nodded and made notes on a sheet of paper. "I will also want to set up an annuity for them upon their retirement from my service. I don't want these women lacking for their necessities in old age."

Swann again nodded. "Did you have an amount in mind?" he questioned.

"Not exactly. I have no idea, to tell you the truth, of their circumstance outside of my home. I will leave it up to you to consider their living and give me a figure."

"Very well. Is there anything else?"

"Yes," Carolina replied. "I want to set up a trust for Victoria. With no other living relative and both of her real parents dead, I want to assure both her and myself that should I die before she is of age, she will have all that she needs to survive. My brother and sister-in-law York and Lucy Adams, currently of Philadelphia, would be my choice for raising Victoria, but until I acquire their assurance that such a thing would meet with their approval, we will leave that unmentioned in the trust."

Mr. Swann nodded and put pen to paper once again. "Is there anything else?"

"Yes. We are leaving tomorrow for my father's plantation. I'm uncertain as to how long we will be gone, but should you need to reach me, simply post a letter to my attention, in care of Joseph Adams, Oakbridge Plantation, Falls Church, Virginia."

"Is there anything else I can do for you, Mrs. St. John?" Swann asked.

"No, not at this time." Carolina got to her feet, and Swann quickly rose to assist her. "I will inform you of our return to Baltimore."

He escorted her out to the carriage and, after handing her up, surprised her by saying, "Mrs. St. John, you are an admirable woman. I know very few people who would give so faithfully to those around them. You are truly good."

"It is what I feel God would have me do, Mr. Swann. It doesn't come from my goodness, it comes from His," she answered.

"To be certain," Swann replied and stepped back to give her a sweeping bow. "Godspeed."

Carolina returned home to find that the railroad tickets had arrived and that Mrs. Graves had everything completely packed and ready for the trip. After a lively supper answering Victoria's many questions, Carolina tucked her daughter into bed and together they prayed.

Carolina picked up the lamp and started for the door, but Victoria had yet another series of questions in mind. Sleepily she asked, "Why do you love the railroad so much?"

Smiling, Carolina put the lamp on the desk and came to sit beside the child. "I don't know that I have a simple answer," she said softly. Taking Victoria's hands in her own, Carolina thought back to her first experience with a locomotive.

"When I was fifteen, the railroad came to Washington City. My parents took me to see the first locomotive to come to the city, and I was amazed at the noise and the smell and the size of such a monster.

"A man offered me a ride and helped me onto the platform behind the engine before I could object. Not that I would have," she said with a grin. "I rode only a few yards, but it was such bliss, and I felt the wonder of it all flood my soul. I knew this machine had the power to take a person on wonderful adventures and to fulfill dreams I had yet even to think of. I sensed that this machine, above all others, would play an important part not only in the future of America but in my future as well. And, because of that, I wanted to be a part of it."

Victoria yawned and patted her mother's hand. "And we shall ride on the locomotive tomorrow," she said, her eyes drooping in sleep.

Carolina leaned down to kiss her forehead. "You sleep now. Tomorrow we shall venture to Oakbridge, and we can talk more about the railroad then, if you like."

Closing the door quietly behind her, Carolina leaned back and sighed. It was as if all the problems and complications of her life had suddenly been worked through. Her father would say that the rough places had been made smooth, and that if one would only trust God, that would be the outcome every time.

Looking at all that surrounded her life, Carolina was amazed at how intricately God had made those rough places plain. She was no longer in a marriage of convenience, a marriage she had been quite uncertain about participating in. Yet Victoria, the reason for such a marriage, remained safely in her care and would forever stay that way. It was as if a door had opened onto a new chapter of life. A very promising chapter.

Fifty

Knowing Peace

$\mathcal{L}$ooking out the window of the Baltimore-bound locomotive, James Baldwin gave his mind over to the seriousness of his father's deception. He was headed north with only one thing on his mind. Carolina. He had to speak to her and apologize for his anger, and then somehow he had to swallow his pride and admit that she had been right all along.

In only two weeks' time, the Baltimore and Ohio would reach completion to Cumberland, and he was scheduled to be on the westbound celebration train. But celebrating was hardly what he felt up to. All he could think of was that his father had caused much grief and harm to hundreds of people, but perhaps more despairing, his father was responsible for delaying the dream Joseph and Carolina had shared for the P&GF. It was that betrayal that injured him more than any other.

He had to remind himself once again that God now shared his burdens, and that somehow things would work out to a good conclusion.

The scenery moved by at a steady pace, passing the point of his accident just north of Washington. James could see no scars upon the landscape to mark the occasion, but deep inside there were still scars upon his heart. His body, too, bore jagged white reminders of injuries sustained. He wondered what Phineas would think of the railroad had he lived. It was certain he would be pleased at reaching Cumberland. He would no doubt ride proudly on the engine or on the tender, where he could get a perfect feel of the line and the engine.

James couldn't help but smile and remember a very young and excited Carolina Adams sharing the tale of her first locomotive ride. Thinking of it now, James pulled two white kid gloves from his pocket and spread them out on his lap. They were Carolina's gloves. They were the gloves she had stained while taking her first railroad excursion.

Tracing the faded black smudges, James thought of how Carolina had shared with him that these gloves represented her dreams. She would sleep with the gloves sometimes and think of what the future might offer her and how she might play a part with the railroad.

They were very small reminders, James thought, impressed with how tiny her hands must have been to fit such gloves. He doubted her hands were much larger now, even if seven years had passed since that day.

He rolled the gloves back together and stuffed them in his pocket. He would return them to her today and explain how they had disappeared years ago. He thought of the day he'd taken them from her room. Carolina had been steeped in sorrow. Margaret Adams had put an end to her daughter's tutoring sessions as James was to become Virginia's husband. She had deemed it unacceptable for the sessions to continue and had assigned Carolina duty in housekeeping and more mundane feminine responsibilities. Carolina had felt betrayed by this, and by the announcement that James would marry Virginia.

This thought came unbidden to his mind, but he was certain of its genuineness. He hadn't believed it possible then, but over the years James had come to realize that Carolina had given him more than her esteem as student to tutor. She had come to care for him, of this he was certain. It made more sense to believe this, especially now looking back in time, than to believe her too young to be capable of such feelings. Annabelle had helped him to realize this, yet Annabelle could do nothing to keep him from regretting such a realization.

How could I have been so blind? he thought. If only I'd known that she cared. I would never have accepted Virginia's proposal that we marry, but instead, I would have held out, insisting that the tradition of oldest daughter marrying first be done away with. Then I would have married Carolina, instead of leaving her to fend for herself and marry that St. John character.

The car lurched, and a spittoon fell over and rolled down the aisle. It did nothing to halt James' memories. Thinking of Carolina and Annabelle, James again reflected on his father's actions and how he might make peace with the Adamses. Annabelle had said that when a man was trying to please God, He would make even his worst enemies to be at peace with him. She'd also pointed out that James was often his own worst enemy.

And he had almost forgotten that he did not have to face Carolina, or even his father's investors, alone. The thought comforted him. He finally understood what Ben, Annabelle, and even Carolina so long ago had been talking about. God was a friend he could have at his side no matter what.

God, he prayed silently, I don't know Your ways as I should. I've listened to the words of my friends, however, and they have brought to me an understanding of Your love and sacrifice, and while I am still uncertain and my faith still weak, I do want to know the peace You offer. I want to be at peace with myself and those around me, and I want to correct this matter that my father has so recklessly created.

Thickly forested landscape passed by the window as James took a deep breath and immediately felt a sensation of stillness. It was as though the wrinkles of his life were being smoothed out, things set in order. His soul was at rest for perhaps the first time in his life, and James knew what it was to place his future in God's hands.

———

After seeing to railroad business, James hired a hack to take him to the St. John house near Federal Hill. He felt a new confidence that gave him courage to do what he had to do. Carolina might be out of reach romantically, but he was determined to present himself as a faithful friend, an acquaintance she might trust and believe in when times of trouble came upon her. He didn't know if he could ever do as Annabelle suggested and declare his love to her, but he would pledge his undying devotion to their friendship and pray that she would not throw it back in his face.

The cab stopped in front of the imposing brick house, and James stepped down with a lightness of heart that surprised even him. There was still a good portion of anxiety, even anticipation, at the thought of seeing her again, but he squared his shoulders and made his way through the wrought-iron gate and up the front walk. Today, he would set things right with Carolina. What happened from that point would rest in God's capable hands.

Sounding the knocker, James waited until the stern-faced Mrs. Graves answered the door. The woman appeared as though she was ready to step out for the day, and James offered her a brief greeting and handed her his card.

"Might I speak with Mrs. St. John?"

Mrs. Graves shook her head. "Mrs. St. John and Miss St. John have closed the house for a short time and will be unavailable."

"When will they be returning?" he asked, unable to hide his disappointment.

"Can't say. Mrs. St. John was uncertain."

"Might I inquire as to where they have gone?"

Mrs. Graves frowned. "No, you may not. I am hardly at liberty to discuss such things. Now if you'll excuse me, I have a stage to connect with."

She closed the door in his face, leaving James both stunned and dismayed. He turned back to the street and began to walk toward the Pratt Street Station. There was no sense in remaining in Baltimore if Carolina was gone. Perhaps Joseph Adams might know his daughter's whereabouts, but that would require returning to Washington and making a journey to Oakbridge.

He had not been to Oakbridge since that fateful day when Virginia had found him embracing Carolina. It had been an innocent embrace. Maryland had just been buried, and Carolina was crying tears of sorrow in his arms. But try as he might, James remembered all too well that on his part, the embrace had meant much more than comfort. That embrace had made up his mind that his feelings for Carolina were real. Much too real, in fact, to continue with marriage to her sister.

Yet could he really return to Oakbridge now? It would certainly mean a confrontation with Joseph that James was not certain he was ready for.

"Where are you, Carolina?" he murmured against the noises of the city. "Where are you?"

Fifty-One

Two Hearts Unite

$\mathscr{H}$urry, Mama," Victoria said, pulling at Carolina's gloved hand. The train had only a moment before it stopped at the Washington Station. "I want to see Grandfather."

Carolina laughed and allowed the porter to lift Victoria from the passenger car, while she struggled to make a ladylike departure on her own. Catching her foot in the hem of her navy wool traveling outfit, Carolina lost her balance and would have fallen but for the sturdy hand of a passing stranger.

"Allow me to assist you," came a very familiar voice.

Carolina steadied herself on the ground and looked up into the eyes of James Baldwin. "Mr. Baldwin," she breathed, hardly daring to believe he was really there.

"Carolina," he whispered as his face lit up with recognition and what appeared to be pure joy.

Carolina wanted nothing more than to lose herself in his eyes, but Victoria was quickly pulling on the sleeve of her caped jacket.

"Hurry, Mama."

"Victoria, mind your manners," Carolina said rather sternly. She turned from James to see Victoria's joyous countenance fall. Softening, Carolina added, "I'm just as excited as you are." She winked at the child and was rewarded with a giggle.

"You remember Mr. Baldwin, don't you?" she asked Victoria.

"Yes," came the suddenly shy voice, "I remember." The little girl stepped away from Carolina and curtsied deeply. "Good afternoon, Mr. Baldwin."

"Good afternoon, Miss St. John." He bowed and gave her a smile. "I must say," he continued, "this is quite an unexpected pleasure."

"Were you traveling on this same locomotive?" Carolina asked, noting that his very stylish Chesterfield coat was wrinkled.

"Yes, in fact, I've come from a very unproductive trip to Baltimore."

"Unproductive?"

"Indeed. I went there this morning with the sole purpose of seeing you, but, of course, you were already out and about Baltimore preparing for your trip to Washington. Or so I assume."

"We were just now on the ladies' car." Carolina seemed to think about his words for a moment. Thoughtfully, amid the rush of debarking passengers she asked, "Why did you come to see me?"

"To apologize," James said without hesitation. He glanced around. "What say we collect your baggage. Do you have someone arriving to drive you to Oakbridge?"

"No," Carolina said, her heart racing within her. He was so handsome and self-confident, and there was something in the way in which he looked at her that left Carolina weak in the knees. He seemed older, but also stronger, more vital.

"Then please allow me to drive you both to Oakbridge. We can discuss business on the way."

Business, thought Carolina, disappointed. He wants to discuss business. She smiled quickly so as to cover any disappointment that might show. "I would hate to put you to such trouble, Mr. Baldwin."

"No trouble at all."

"Did you already plan to go to Oakbridge?"

"I do now," he replied with a rather mysterious smile.

He collected their bags while Carolina and Victoria waited inside the depot. Victoria couldn't contain herself and danced around the room taking in all the people. Carolina was certain that she thought Grandfather might magically appear at any moment, even though he had no idea they would be arriving today.

Carolina straightened her skirt and retied the ribbons of her bonnet in a nervous fashion. In her mind she thought of her regret in having never declared her feelings to James. Such things were simply not proper, she knew, but in her heart she was certain that propriety went right out the window in such matters.

She watched him, intrigued by the grown-up man she'd scarcely dared herself to see when he'd visited her in Baltimore. He was by far and away more muscular than when he had tutored her. Working on the rail line had no doubt accomplished this feat. He appeared, if possible, taller than she'd remembered and certainly more striking. His dark hair had been carefully cut to a fashionable length, but it was windblown from the trip. His face was clean-shaven, which made him appear quite youthful, but his eyes, so blue and intense, took away any doubt of his maturity.

"Here we are," he announced, a baggageman quietly following behind with their things. "I've managed to secure a brougham and driver, and so if there are no further objections, we shall journey to Oakbridge."

Carolina nodded. "By all means, and thank you very much."

James helped Victoria and Carolina up into the enclosed and very private brougham before hoisting himself up the step and taking a seat opposite the ladies. He tapped on the roof, and the driver heeded his signal by moving them out into the late-day traffic.

Carolina wondered if he would speak of his business, or if Victoria's presence might cause him to remain silent. More annoying than trying to second-guess James, however, was the bevy of thoughts that ran unchecked in her own mind. Should she tell him of Blake's death and of her own freedom? Should she tell him of her feelings in the past and how regretful she was of the time they'd lost? Surely it would be foolishness to bring up such things. James might well be engaged to another woman by this time. Or worse, he might be married. She wondered how she might inquire of this without appearing too forward.

Victoria teetered on the edge of her seat in order to peer out the window and take in the Washington sights. She'd only made this trip on three earlier occasions, and it had been well over a year since the last one. Carolina decided not to chide her for her conduct. She was only a baby, after all, and there would be plenty of time for growing up and accepting adult edicts. She thought of Maryland, who drove their mother to near-panic by running up and down the grand staircase at Oakbridge. Margaret had feared that Mary would one day die from a broken neck after taking a tumble down those stairs. No one had expected yellow fever to steal the child away on a peaceful summer's night. Carolina touched Victoria's dark curls, as if in touching them she could bring back a pleasant memory of her sister.

"I mentioned apologizing," James said, suddenly opening the conversation. "I meant that. I was harsh and narrow-minded when last we spoke. I hope you will forgive me."

Carolina lowered her face. "It is I who should apologize. I was unthinkably rude to suggest the things I did. You had every right to get angry."

"No, I didn't." James' voice compelled her to look up. His eyes locked on her face and refused to look away. "You were very right in your concerns."

Carolina felt her breath quicken. "I was?"

"Yes. The problems you suspected . . ." He paused and glanced at Victoria as if trying to decide how much to say. "The problems with the P&GF were valid."

"They were?" She could scarcely believe he was saying these things. To admit them was to incriminate his own father.

"Unfortunately they were. However, I intend to find a way to straighten out the entire mess. That was the other reason I had wanted to see you in Baltimore. I realize now is hardly the time or place, but rest assured, I intend to arrange a meeting with you and your father to discuss the matter. I doubt seriously my father will attend, but nevertheless, we will endeavor to set the record straight."

"I'm stunned. I . . . well, that is . . . I appreciate your honesty, James." She relaxed against the plush leather upholstery.

"I owed you that much," James replied. "And much more."

Victoria grew bored as they passed from city to country. With a yawn, she leaned back against Carolina. "How much farther before we get there?"

"Quite a few miles, and the roads are a bit mucky, it appears," Carolina answered.

"Yes, we've had several rather heavy rains, but it seems dry enough. It will only slow us a bit," James said, smiling at the young child. "You are a very pretty girl, Miss St. John, and may I say that your coat and bonnet are quite fetching."

Victoria beamed under such praise. "My mama picked them out for me. She said green suited me."

"And indeed it does," responded James.

Carolina looked down at the new coat and bonnet and laughed. "Most colors suit Victoria, but she outgrows them nearly as fast as I can hand over the coin to pay for them. She's already grown two inches this last year."

"Well, you shall be a very handsome woman," James said with genuine affection, "just like your mama."

Carolina felt her cheeks grow hot and pretended to fuss with Victoria's bonnet. "Why don't you rest against me while we travel, Victoria. Perhaps a nap will pass the time more quickly."

"I don't want a nap," Victoria pouted, even while struggling to hide another yawn. But it wasn't long before her eyelids grew heavy and the rhythmic rocking of the carriage lulled her to sleep.

James watched them for a time before speaking. "I hope you know I meant that compliment."

Carolina looked at him and saw the sincerity in his expression. "Thank you," she whispered.

"And I really am quite sorry for my anger during our last meeting."

"I, too, apologize," Carolina said, seeming to surprise James. "I suppose I just wanted to hurt you."

"Hurt me? But why?" He was genuinely intrigued.

Carolina swallowed hard. "I suppose revenge. I wanted to get back at you for hurting me." At his puzzled expression she held up her hand to ward off his question. "I know it was childish, but it hurt me very much when you went away without a word."

"I tried to tell you that I was leaving. I even went in search of you, but my father was demanding that we leave—"

"What are you talking about?" Carolina asked.

"The day I left Oakbridge. I truly tried to find you and explain my feelings to you."

Carolina smiled. "I was speaking of when you left Washington and my sister."

"Oh."

The silence hung painfully between them. Finally Carolina summoned up her courage and whispered, "Why did you leave?" He met her gaze with such intensity that Carolina felt her cheeks grow warm.

"Because I was in love with the wrong sister," he said simply.

Carolina felt her heart pound harder in anticipation of her most secret thoughts becoming spoken declarations. James had loved her. He'd just said it. She felt woozy and weak inside. Surely for the first time she had a hope beyond the despair that had followed her from the night of her coming-out party. He loved her six years ago. But was it too late now? Was there someone else?

As if reading her thoughts, James chuckled bitterly. "Oh, what a mess. If only I'd been honest and forthright. If only I'd been truthful with you then, it might be my ring and not St. John's that graces your finger."

Carolina felt her eyes grow wide. He didn't know! He didn't know that she was a widow—that St. John was dead. Barely able to breathe, she knew words were impossible. Instead, she pulled off her left glove and held up the ringless hand.

He looked at her for a moment as if trying to decide what it all meant. His expression was such that Carolina's next words came out in a mere whisper. "St. John is dead. Ours was only a marriage of convenience for the sake of this precious child. I never loved him, nor did he love me. That's why I will not wear widow's weeds."

James shook his head. "It can't be. I cannot believe it."

Carolina, feeling rather shy, bit at her lower lip before answering. "It's true enough. It's just me and Victoria now. She has no one else."

"I won't pretend to be unhappy by this news," James replied. "Is it too late for us to make amends for the past? Is it too late to start over and make a new life . . . together?" he asked, looking at her with such passion that Carolina thought her heart might burst.

"My father would say it's never too late to make things right."

James searched her face. "But could you love me? After all that's happened. Could you forget . . . forgive?"

"I fell in love with you . . . without meaning to," Carolina said, her voice trembling. "I knew you were intended for Virginia, and it made me feel so guilty. I felt scandalous, if not downright sinful, in losing my heart to my sister's intended, but Granny always said you couldn't choose who your heart picked to love. And my heart picked you then." She smiled and squared her shoulders for confidence before looking back at him. "It picks you now."

James' face seemed to light up with a glow of triumph. "Then before I ask you properly to be my wife, I must tell you everything, lest there be any secrets between us."

Fifty-Two

The Gloves

*C*arolina listened intently as the miles passed by. James poured out his heart and explained all that his father had done. She was angry, she had to admit, but her anger wasn't directed at James. Nor, she assured him, did it change her feelings for him.

"I'm afraid," he said, still finding it impossible to believe they were having this conversation, "that if we do not act quickly, your father's good name will be ruined along with my father's. Of course, I'd like to keep my own father from a hangman's noose if it is at all possible."

Carolina looked at him with sympathetic understanding. "I wouldn't want that, either. As much as I resent your father risking my father's capital and our dream, I don't want that."

"There is something else you should know." James suddenly felt an urgency to share his newfound salvation with Carolina. "I've only recently reconciled myself to God. Some very dear friends helped me to see the error of my way and to find the truth in Christ. I must say, until that moment, the truth had never been of much concern to me. Getting by, easing my way in life—those were the important things. But now I see things differently. I see the value in seeking God's will over my own and of following His plan for my life. I won't promise to be perfect at this, but I am trying."

Carolina surprised him by grinning. "You aren't the only one who is trying, Mr. Baldwin. I reconciled my life to God after Mary died, but let me tell you it has been sorely tested ever since. I've made many mistakes in trying to learn about trusting God, and like you, I'm only coming to understand what truth is all about."

"Then it would seem everything is settled between us. I've shared all matters with you that pertain to my secretive past." He smiled and reached out gingerly to take hold of her hand. "I only wish I'd known sooner. I only wish it would have been me with you in Baltimore. I envy St. John."

"Don't," she said flatly. "The man was incapable of love. He felt only anger and bitterness over the deaths of his wife and son. He'd have nothing to do with Victoria and disappeared from the house shortly after we married. I only agreed to such a thing because he threatened this baby." Carolina used her free hand to gently stroke Victoria's head.

James felt a surge of elation. "You mean, you and St. John weren't . . . that is to say . . . he never . . ."

Carolina shook her head quite seriously. "Never, and now I suppose all of my secrets are out as well. I make a most unusual widow, wouldn't you agree?" She allowed a rather coy smile to accompany her words.

James laughed boisterously, and Victoria stirred and moved away from Carolina to snuggle against the upholstered corner of the carriage.

Seeing that he'd nearly awakened the child, James quieted and asked, "So is all forgiven?"

"Forgiven and forgotten," Carolina replied. "But before you ask your question, I have one to ask you. If we marry, can you love Victoria as your own? Will you be a father to a child who has never known a father's love?"

James felt his heart swell with pride. Love that child? Without a doubt he could love her, if for no other reason than that Carolina cherished her as her own. "I would be proud to be her father, just as I would be proud to be your husband." He slipped across and squeezed into the free space beside Carolina. Pulling her into his arms, he sighed. It seemed forever that he'd longed to hold her like this. Her sigh against his ear indicated her own sense of contentment.

"Marry me, Carolina. Marry me and make me the happiest man alive."

"Will you let me continue to study? Will you teach me about the railroad and all manner of masculine things?" she asked teasingly.

James pulled back only a bit and leered a grin. "There are a great many masculine things I intend to teach you about."

Carolina blushed crimson and lowered her face. "I'd rather have no other teacher."

James lifted her face gently and lowered his lips to hers. "So long as I live, there will be no other teacher save your loving husband."

He kissed her long and lovingly, feeling her melt against him, stirring his heart and soul to passion. He pulled back breathlessly, almost frightened at what he felt for her. The intensity of his longing was more than he'd expected.

Feeling moisture form on his brow, he reached into his pocket for his handkerchief, but his hand touched Carolina's gloves instead. Remembering them now, he pulled them out and held them up. "I have no ring to place on your finger, at least not yet. But these belonged to you long ago, and I took them in hopes of finding a young, sorrowful girl who wandered in the orchard ready to bid farewell to her dreams. I intended to hold them up as a banner, as a symbol of the hope beyond her sorrow." He smiled and took up her left hand in order to place one of the gloves upon it. Slowly, methodically, he eased her fingers into the stiff glove, kissing each finger before hooking the button at the wrist.

When he looked up again, there were tears streaming down her face. "I was taken away from you before I could explain," he whispered, "but I'll not be taken away now. These gloves represent both our past and our future. Will you marry me, Carolina?"

Nodding, she whispered, "Yes, James. I'll gladly be your wife."

Fifty-Three

New Beginnings

*C*arolina and James married at Oakbridge on the twenty-ninth day of October. Both had agreed that wasting any further time was in keeping with nothing but silly traditions and observations. Both knew, as well as Joseph, that Carolina's marriage to Blake St. John had been a sham, and even Victoria was delighted at the prospect of having a new father.

The wedding was quite simple. Georgia and the Major arrived barely half an hour before the ceremony. Virginia, miserable that Carolina was marrying James, stood scowling with her husband while Lucy acted as matron of honor and York stood as best man. Virginia had made it quite clear that Carolina was jeopardizing the family name by marrying so soon after becoming a widow, but no one paid her any heed.

Carolina felt a sense of relief and accomplishment that her wedding should take place in the home she'd always known and loved. This was the place where she'd fallen in love with James; it seemed only fitting that she should seal her life together with his in this same house. She felt blessed to have her family gathered round her, and felt an honest sorrow that James' parents could not be present for their celebration. Leland had refused to attend, whether because of his embarrassment at James knowing the truth of his deception, or his concern at leaving Edith in her illness. Edith's health weighed heavily on James' mind, and Carolina knew it was his deepest regret regarding their wedding day.

Her own regret came in the absence of her mother. Lightly fingering the satin of her mother's wedding gown, Carolina felt her eyes well with tears.

"Are you ready, my dear?" Joseph asked in a joyous tone. Seeing her tears, his expression grew quite serious. "What is it?"

"Mother." The simple word said it all.

Joseph nodded. "You look very much like her just now. I was taken back in time for a moment." He touched her wet cheek. "She is here with you in spirit. Her mind may be confused by the sorrow of her loss, but her heart is unchanged in her love for you. Remember that."

Carolina nodded and attempted a smile. "I will, Papa. I promise."

"Now come. This is to be a happy day," he said, taking hold of her arm and leading her to the doorway.

When they reached the parlor, she looked up to find James awaiting her, and this time the smile came more easily. "It is a happy day," she murmured. "The very happiest day of my life."

———

"But I don't understand why you have to rush off," Georgia declared from the refreshment table.

"I've already told everyone else," Carolina said, radiant in her new status as Mrs. James Baldwin. "James and I are taking places on the B&O's celebration trip to Cumberland. It's our own informal honeymoon. We will hurry back to Baltimore and leave Victoria with Mrs. Graves, my housekeeper, then on the third of November, we'll journey west and see exactly what they've managed to accomplish with the railroad."

"How dull," Georgia said, rolling her eyes. "The Major took me to Paris for our honeymoon."

"I offered her the moon," James laughed, "but if there isn't a railroad to be had on it, Carolina wants nothing to do with it."

"I'm surprised to learn that you'd have time for such folly," Virginia said rather bitterly. "You never seemed to have time for such things when we were planning a wedding."

A hush fell on the room as all stunned faces turned in disbelief to Virginia. It was impossible to imagine even Virginia being so indiscreet.

"I think that's enough, Virginia," Hampton said, taking an obviously tight grip on her upper arm. "This is a day of celebration, and we wouldn't want to dampen spirits by bringing up old memories." He leveled a glare at Carolina, which told her he hadn't made this announcement out of any sympathy for her cause. She rather believed it was more his own embarrassment that caused Hampton to put Virginia firmly in her place.

"Well, I for one shall miss you dearly," Joseph said, raising a glass of punch to the happy couple. "To you and to James, I wish only the very best. It seems a long overdue happiness." Everyone but Virginia raised their glass and drank to the couple.

"What about me, Grandfather?" Victoria asked, pulling on his coat.

"Yes, what about you?" Joseph said with a wink. He raised his glass again. "To my granddaughter Victoria, may you grow healthy and strong and keep your heart ever belonging to the Lord."

She beamed him a smile and giggled. "Mama says that always loving God is the only way to be happy."

"Your mama is a wise woman," Joseph replied, catching Carolina's pleased expression. "You know," he added suddenly, "I believe it would be quite a treat for us if Victoria were to stay on here while you and James take your wedding trip."

"Oh, could I, Mama?" Victoria questioned excitedly.

"I suppose we should ask your new papa. After all, he is in charge of our family now."

James laughed. "As much as any man is ever in charge of a houseful of progressively minded women."

Everyone enjoyed his jest, while Victoria came to take hold of James' hand. Seeing the intensity of her expression, Carolina held her breath, wondering how James would respond to his new daughter.

"Papa?"

Without hesitation, James handed his glass to Carolina and knelt down to receive the child. He smiled. "That word sounds very nice to me."

Victoria's dark eyes widened. "You like being a papa?"

"I like very much being *your* papa."

"Why?" Victoria asked, and the room grew completely silent.

"Because I love you," he replied, knowing the child's hunger for a father's love.

"I love you, too." Victoria said, wrapping her arms around James' neck and burying her face against him.

Carolina felt tears anew come to her eyes, and when she met her own father's expression, she thought she finally understood the love and pride he felt in his children. He had given her the best of love and life, and now he happily gave over that task to another. Not because he no longer wanted the position, and not because he begrudgingly recognized her cause to sacrifice for another. No, this time Carolina knew that he understood in full. He was giving his daughter in marriage to the love of her life, and that in and of itself was a most cherished moment in his life.

Her thoughts were broken as James stood up, still holding Victoria. "So would you truly like to stay here with Grandfather Adams?"

Victoria pulled back and nodded, her brown-black ringlets bobbing.

James smiled and with the slightest glance at Carolina gave his approval. "Very well then. We shall leave you to your grandfather's care."

Victoria clapped her hands as James returned her to the oak wood floor. She scurried to where Joseph stood and took hold of his hand. "Here I am, Grandfather. My papa says I may stay."

November 3, 1842, found the Baltimore Pratt Street Station alive with activity. It seemed as though the entire city had turned out to be a part of the celebration.

They were opening the line to Cumberland, Maryland. It had been a long time in coming and was the pinnacle, to date, of Louis McLane's career with the Baltimore and Ohio Railroad. The 7:00 A.M. departing train would hold nearly forty passengers, all dignitaries and guests of the B&O. Newspapermen sketched pictures of the belching engine and cars as they awaited the signal to start them on their journey. Several of the newspaper reporters would journey with them to Cumberland and record the actual thoughts of folks who would see their first locomotive. It was hard for even these seasoned veterans to believe that in a little under ten hours, they would arrive some one hundred seventy-eight miles from their point of departure. The atmosphere was one of sheer exhilaration and speculation.

Making their way on board with the others, Carolina gripped James' arm very tightly, almost afraid that if she let go she would suddenly find that it had all been nothing more than a dream.

A blast of the steam whistle sent a thrill through her and caused her to tremble noticeably.

"Frightened?" James asked in disbelief.

"Never!" Carolina declared, meeting his gaze. "I'm too excited."

Taking their seats, he grinned. "Me too. It's been a long time in coming, and I have to admit there were times when I thought it would all fall apart. But we kept sight of the dream and brought it into existence."

"I felt the same way about us," she murmured softly as the train whistle sounded two more times and the band began to play loudly from the platform outside her window.

The locomotive strained to pull that first bit of weight, then slowly, like a billows pumping life into a fire, the wheels groaned and turned and pulled them forward. Inch by inch, yard by yard, they passed the station and headed west over the Carrollton Viaduct.

At last it seemed to Carolina that she was not only touching her dream but actually being welcomed to participate and share in such things. How very like God, she thought, for surely it was He who gave her the dream in the first place. And without a doubt it was He who gave her a hope beyond. Looking away from the window and into the face of her husband, Carolina offered silent thanks for her blessings.

"I love you," she whispered.

James pulled her close, defying social proprieties. "And I love you, Mrs. Baldwin. Forever and always, I will love only you."